NEW TOWN. OLD SECRETS. UNEXPECTED LOVE.
NO MATTER
What
"I'LL BURN IT ALL TO FIND YOU."

Jenny, Sarah, Anita & Holly

Thank you for the love, laughs, and research ideas.

Your wellbeing and mental health mean a great deal to me. It's precious, and we need to look after it. I want nothing more than for you to enjoy this book with all the ups, downs, and shit that goes on in between these pages, so please take a look at the triggers and warning below:

Violence, sexual/explicit content,

PTSD/mental health, trauma, touches on kidnapping,

Hero complex, fire.

If you are good with all of the above, read on and enjoy.

Acknowledgements

There are so many people I want to thank for being part of this journey. So many of you have been by my side, enjoying the ride of highs and lows with me.

Jenny, thanks for the strong coffees and reading aloud 'I Dreamt Of You' (the smutty bits) to whoever will listen, at the pub, cricket club and James work place. I love you forever for this.

Anita, you are what you are, never change, your dirty mind is equal to mine. I could write a book just from our chats. (I wont, but I could). Thank for everything.

Holly you have been the best, you're the first person to read them, thank you for all your advice, help and support. The side notes still make me laugh, if I can read them.

Aaron, my silent supporter, best friend, and husband, you are with me through it all, the late nights, the stress, the tears of sadness and the tears of joy. The endless snacks you know make me happy. You are the one person I will always want by next to me, even if you are asleep.

Ruth, I'm so freaking glad I met you. My #bookwife, when I need advice you give it to me, honestly and thoughtfully. I just wish you lived closer. It's like I have know you a life time and it's been less than twelve months. Book talks with you are life. Thank you for everything.

Nikki, Ashley, Laura, Cortney, and Hannah, my awesome Beta readers. I could not have asked for a better team to Beta read for me, you have helped me make this book what it is now, your advice was so valuable to me, it made me realise I was holding back in areas I should not have been. You have all helped me to be a better writer. Thank you.

Sarah Baker, editor, proof reader and all time spice queen. You have made this whole experience like a dream. Your words and notes on my manuscript, encourage me to go further, be bolder and just let rip on what the story needs. The little hearts you leave along the way make my day. There are not enough thank yous' in the world to convey how I feel.

My boys, George and Harry, you are way to young to read my books. but I hope you will some day. I want you to know that you are both the best things in my life, you make me so happy, your smiles and cuddles melt me. Everything I do is for you.

Save the best till last. To my readers and supporters, what can I say, what I have would not be possible without you all. I can't thank you enough for everything you have done and keep doing for me. I write these for you.

Bekki xx

A little note from me...

From time to time, life will throw a huge ass boulder in your path. It can stop you, throw you off course or lead you on a new journey. The more we can accept the changes around us and embrace them, the easier life will become. With acceptance comes new and exciting possibilities you may never have noticed before. Embrace the change and live a life full of love, joy, excitement, and reflection.

– Bekki Vowles xx

*Our greatest glory is not in never falling, but in
rising every times we fall.
~ Confucius*

Contents

Chapter One

Utterly Sick

My pile of post looks so overwhelming, the last thing I want to do after a full day of back-to-back meetings with clients is open it. All I want to do is go home, put my feet up, and forget about this case and all the cruel and evil things the Summers' Organisation submitted innocent people to. I let out a sigh and pick up the first envelope, which has a sticky note attached.

I'm sorry, Jess.

Shaking my head, assuming she's opened something personal by mistake, I slide the contents out of the envelope onto my desk, instantly seeing a picture of someone who resembles my husband fucking someone else. Actually, there are several pictures of this person with different women in all sorts of positions. *Fuck.* These women say hello to me every day. They're my neighbours.

My arms fold around my stomach, a small gasp leaving my lips. I can't quite register what I'm seeing, but at the same time, I know who it is.

My husband.

Flicking through the rest of the images, I notice a typed note on a torn bit of paper.

Attached is a sonogram, where you can make out the shape of the innocent baby in the black and white image.

I'm shaking.

I've never wanted to hurt anyone in my life, well not intentionally anyway, but at this point I don't know what I'm capable of doing. Well, I do. I just don't want to use it on my worthless piece of shit husband, although he deserves everything he gets after this. It's taking all my self-control to keep myself in check.

I also want to be sick.

I can't move; like time stands still while I absorb what's happening. I just sit here, not really believing what I'm seeing.

He's stabbed me in the back. Not just once, but several times. That trust, the faith you have in someone, in the one you chose to spend your life with, the one you intend to grow old with. It's been smashed into tiny fragments and I'm not sure I will ever be able to find it again.

Not only has he been unfaithful to me, his wife, but he's got another woman pregnant. Is that how little respect he has for me? I can't resent or be angry at a baby. It was only a few years ago we talked about having children. I said I wasn't ready; I wanted other things first. He said he understood and we would wait.

Am I not enough?

I've thrown past boyfriends out of my flat before now, poured drinks over their heads for lesser things than this. I won't stand for it, I never have. No-one treats me like this. With all these feelings bubbling in my chest, I grab my keys and bags and march home. Well, I drive. I'll be surprised if I don't get a speeding ticket.

In my car, I can't stop the images floating around in my mind as I try to figure out when he would have been able to do all this. *His weekend away with friends. Night's out with the boys, staying over at a friend's house.* I never thought anything of it.

If I don't kill him, my brothers will. They've never liked him, just tolerated him for my benefit. I guess they won't have to now.

My tires screech to a stop on our drive. Getting out of the car, I slam the door and walk into our beautiful terraced townhouse. I'm holding back the fight I have inside me. My anger, shame, and disgust want to spill out, give him everything he deserves, but I won't let him have the satisfaction of seeing me crumble.

I find him inside, looking like the ideal husband. Loose-fitting jeans, pulled tight at the waist by his belt, a dark red V neck jumper layered over a white tee, stretched across his broad chest. His hair perfectly styled with a little too much product.

As he stirs the creamy white garlic and mushroom sauce, he's cooking me... well, reheating with a glass of red wine ready and waiting for me, like he always does when he hears my car pull up.

I take the glass from his outstretched hand with my shaking one, hoping he doesn't notice. I drain it and he refills it for me, smirking. He probably assumes I've had a bad day.

What a wanker.

As he places the bottle down in front of him, I hand him the large brown envelope I was gripping in my hand this entire time.

I'm seething inside, trying to keep my rage contained. For now anyway. I'm not sure how much longer I can lock up what feels like it's about to detonate.

"What's this?" I'm searching his face and demeanour for a sign of guilt or fear. But there's nothing.

"Open it and see." my voice is harsh, but quiet. "I'm sure you'll find it a surprise. I most certainly did. That's for sure." Sarcasm drips from each word.

Frowning slightly, he carefully opens the envelope. I watch the colour drain from his face, but he masks it quickly. "What is this?" He stares at the first image.

"What do you think this is, Andy?"

"Looks like two people fucking." there's a notable shake to his voice.

"Looks like *you* fucking someone else, Andy."

"That's not me," he hisses, his entire body shifting uncomfortably from side to side.

"Are you saying I'm mistaken? That it's not you in those pictures? The man I've been with for nine years. Are you saying I wouldn't recognise you? You," I shout. "Butt fucking naked, balls deep in some other woman."

His jaw tenses. "Yes, you have it wrong, Charlie. Why would I risk what we have? All of this?" His hand runs down his face in frustration.

"I have no idea, Andy, but you did, and you have. Don't lie to my face. I can see the evidence as clear as day. It's right there in your hand."

"Charlie, this isn't what it looks like." Fucking hell, he can't be serious. Does he think I'm stupid?

"You have got to be kidding me. Really, please do enlighten me. Did you trip and accidentally fall out of all your clothes and your dick land in another woman?" Pausing for breath, I add, "Multiple other women?"

"Fuck." He knows there's no way to talk his way out of this.

"Or were you just playing lucky dip with the neighbour's vaginas?" I add. "How stupid do you think I am?"

"Shit, Charlie."

That's all he says. In a second, the shock at being caught is gone, and he's back to... indifference? He knows he's been caught red-handed. There's no going back now.

His reaction, or lack of it, hurts. How can he not care?

"How long?" I'm asking, but I'm not sure I want to know. My heart is breaking, and there's nothing I or anyone can do about it.

"Umm... two years... give or take," he tells me like he's sharing that we're having curry for dinner.

"Shitting hell!" Pain rears through me, jarring my heart. There's been no change in our sex life... I mean, it's never been out of this world, but we get the job done.

Should it be like getting the job done?

"Are there any more I should know about, or is this the full dossier of women you've been fucking behind my back?" I don't want to know, but the words are falling out like vomit now. I can't help it. Anger does this to me.

I know my answer before he even says a word. I've always had the ability to tell when someone is lying. I don't know how I missed the one I'm facing now. All his tells are right there. He touches his chin and ever so slightly cocks his head to the side.

"There have been a few more... but they don't mean anything to me."

It's like a slap to the face, waking me up after all these years. "Is that supposed to make me feel better? You have slept with women behind my back, one of them pregnant with your baby, and they mean nothing to you? That makes it worse, you fucking prick. How could you?" I'm still rooted in the same spot. If I move, I think I'll kill him. I won't be able to stop myself.

"Don't raise your voice," he barks back, throwing the photos to the counter. "This is your fault. If you had paid me more attention, worked less hours, we would have been able to have a family when I wanted one."

How can he blame me for this? What happened to it being a joint decision? I mean, *I* would have to have the baby, not him... it would have been our decision to have a child, not just his. It's my goddamn body. I would have to change so much of the life I love. The life I have worked so fucking hard for, just to please him? No fucking way.

"How dare you." Screaming in his face, from across the kitchen island, my whole body begins to shake, as utter fury takes over. "How fucking dare you blame this on me." The laugh I air is masked with an undeniable edge of sarcasm. I can't take this. I'm so angry, I can barely breathe through the tightness in my chest. My hands fist at my sides, my knuckles white with the force. I want to punch his smug face. I want to really hurt him like he's hurt me. No, worse.

"You cannot be serious. I did this for us." I gesture towards our newly renovated home.

I worked so hard to get us here, and he's throwing it back in my face. "Everything *we* have, *I* worked my arse off and bought for us. The holidays, the house, the cars, your lifestyle, everything you do, I pay for. And you go and do this..." I break down, forcing the words out, trying to conceal the wobble in my voice from all the unstable emotions whirling through me. I feel utterly sick to my stomach knowing what he has done.

While I was working to give us a great start and a pretty fucking awesome lifestyle, he was doing that with them. No wonder he never wanted to get a full-time job. Living off of me and doing exactly as he pleased was just what he wanted.

"Would you have ever told me if I hadn't found out?" Then it hits me in the chest all over again... all these women.

I thought I knew him.

"I guess I would have had to at some point," Andy says, shrugging his shoulders like it's no big deal. He's so relaxed, I just don't get it. I've outed him. Does our life together mean nothing to him?

How could I have let this happen? *It's not your fault, Charlie...* at work, I'm strong, tough. I won't take any shit from anyone. I have to be as a criminal prosecution solicitor. I can tell when people are keeping something from me. It's what makes me good at what I do. I guess that's in question now too.

"What the actual fuck... you would have ignored this whole situation for as long as you possibly could, wouldn't you?"

He rolls his eyes like I'm being dramatic. His whole state oozes arrogance. A sense of self-importance I have never seen before. The way he's leaning against the counter, one hand casually tucked away in his trouser pocket while the other now holds a glass of wine like nothing is his fault. How have I not seen this before, this ugly, lying, cheating side of him?

I'm done. I don't want to hear or look at him again. Reaching over, I pour myself another glass of wine and take a step towards him.

"Get the fuck out of my house." The words come out calm, but he looks at me, taken aback. "Get the fuck out of my house now," I repeat.

"Whatever Charlie. Call me when you want to talk about it." The nerve of this man. I watch as he grabs the keys to the car—the car I bought him—and leaves, slamming the door behind him.

It's only then I allow myself to crumble.

Chapter Two

Stay

Eight Months later

Standing in my office, the shelving system I have that held all the law books, awards, and certificates, now sits empty; a vivid representation of what my life looks like right now. Taping another box shut, I add it to the pile that will go into storage for when I move.

Running my fingers over the smooth mixed tones of the dark walnut desk I've sat at for the last few years, it feels surreal. I never thought I would give up something I worked so hard for. It's never been in me to quit anything, but now I'm here, packing it all away.

"Last day then?" Simon asks like it's a question. He's been trying to get me to change my mind about leaving as he wanted me on this case more than anything, but I can't stand the looks that people give me anymore.

After Jess found and read what was inside that envelope, everyone seems to give me those looks, pitying me for what happened. I even had the odd comment that he had every right to do what he did. As a woman, _I_ should have treated him better.

Misogynistic pigs, the fucking lot of them. It's been difficult, but I lack the energy to care anymore.

Andy tried to make the divorce difficult for me, saying his infidelity was all my fault. Luckily for me, Simon's a great boss, who has a fantastic divorce solicitor on staff. She dealt with it all, got me what was mine, and handed him his arse in court, leaving him with the small amount he put into the house. I think he really believed that he would come out better than he did. I almost laughed in his face. Anyway, he's now living with his new girlfriend and baby girl.

I'm not that heartless. I do actually hope he can be a good dad and role model for her. That baby girl needs to be the good thing to come out of this, even if it still hurts to think about what he did, and how she came into the world.

"Yes, Simon, for the last time it's my last day, and you know it." I say as I place a picture of my brothers into the box of personal things. It's the only box coming with me; the rest will be delivered by the movers in a few days' time.

"I'll keep trying, Charlotte. I want you to stay. You have one of the best research heads I have ever seen." He means well; we make a good team.

Simon walks into the room fully and shuts the door behind him.

"I just wanted to say something." Placing his hands on the back of one of the leather chairs that sit in front of my desk, he leans forwards. "Will you keep researching for me? We need you on this, Charlotte. Something's not right here and I need to know I have someone in my corner." This conversation feels like I am fighting a losing battle. There's a shimmer of hope in his eyes—*hope's a dangerous thing*—I hate it. I can't give in. Not now.

"I'm in your corner, Simon, but I can't work here anymore. Everyone knows what happened between me and Andy. Fuck, a few even saw the photos. I need a fresh start. I've given you almost eight months to get used to the idea while I settled my divorce. I've stayed longer than I should have. I need something different."

"I understand, but you have been on this case from the start. Don't you want to see it through?" I groan as he knows that's the one thing I'm frustrated with.

We should have gone to trial already, but our first witness retracted her statement and has not been seen since. It's the only reason I have stayed as long as I have. I wanted to see this case go to court. I wanted this finished.

"Simon, don't." Sighing, I look at him properly. He looks tired. Rounding my desk, I come to stand next to him. When he turns to face me, I know he wants to tell me something. Placing my hand on his sleeve in encouragement, he spills what has obviously been on the tip of his tongue since he walked in.

"Our second witness disappeared last night. We are back to square one, again." Dipping his head, he leans down but brings himself back up a little straighter.

"Shit, that's..." I can't even finish what I'm going to say.

"Yep, I'm beginning to think we have a mole, Charlotte. The way they seem to be one step ahead of us... goddamn it."

"That can't be right. You just need a good night's sleep, a few less wines and to get stuck back in." I'm brushing over the seriousness of what's happened; the last witness is presumed dead. It's been almost a year since she went missing.

"You are using my own words against me, Charlotte. That's what I said to you about that arsehole ex-husband of yours, and you never took my advice then."

I smirk, trying to lighten the mood. I know he thinks it's ridiculous to give up everything I have here, but if I'm honest, I don't have anything other than Simon and Annie, my work bestie, here in London anymore.

My brothers moved down south years ago, starting up their own business with their best friend, and my parents work part-time and travel the rest of the time. Truly living their best life.

"I kind of took your advice. I got stuck back in but never gave up the wine," I say, nudging his arm. The thickness of the situation dissolves a little, even if just for a few moments.

He laughs and pushes himself off the chair. He's not a big guy; a little shorter than me, my dad's age, greying hair, with a small middle-aged belly from too many nights eating and drinking the finest food he can find.

"Why would we give up the wine?" we both say together, chuckling. There's a double knock at the door and we put our professional faces back on.

"Come in," I say. Josh, one of our associate solicitors, walks in carrying a huge stack of files and a small smile planted across his lips.

"Who are they for?" I ask as he dumps them on my desk.

"You. You need to sign them before you leave today. Standard NDAs and handovers from your cases." He winks at me. He's great, but he can be a little creepy at times.

"Thanks, but don't wink at me again. It's weird." He laughs, not taking any notice of me. Glancing over at Simon, I find him watching Josh with a look of suspicion.

"Well, after today, I won't see you again," Josh mutters, his smile faltering a little before he masks it. Simon shakes his head, pointing at the door for Josh to leave. Pausing at the door, Josh adds, "Don't worry, Simon, you have me now." Simon grunts as Josh closes the door firmly behind him.

"Charlotte, please reconsider?"

There's something I'm not understanding, but I don't want to know. I need an out, and this is it. As of tonight, I'm no longer Charlotte James-Hudson, criminal prosecution solicitor, at Holland and Brooke. I'm Charlotte Hudson, florist. And I can't wait.

"Simon, please, I need this. You know I do." My voice comes out strong; what I feel underneath is anything but. "I'll be in touch. You know you can call me anytime. You are more than just my boss. You're a friend, Simon."

He replies with a nod before he leaves and I don't see him again for the rest of the day.

I take a moment to think about the place I'm moving to. It's a beautiful place just by the coast. A small town is just what I need, and it's close to my best friend, Millie. She needs me more than ever right now.

My house is sold and I've been down to check out the property I've bought—a beautiful shop with an apartment above. I will be doing it all up.

Luckily, the shop needs more work than the apartment, so I can move straight in. I've not told Millie about Andy's cheating or the divorce yet. Actually, I've not told anyone other than Simon and Annie, my work bestie. Oh, and the entire office building I'm leaving behind.

I don't want the questions that will come with it all. My brothers are still on tour. I'll tell them first, but I don't know when they will be back. My parents, well, they live in their little bubble and I don't want them fussing over me. There is no one else. Not anymore. I'm starting this next chapter of my life all on my own.

Chapter Three

Everything

Owen

I already knew everything there was to know about *her* before she walked in through The Manor's main entrance. Well, the basic things you can find out about a person without looking too deep into their history. I'm supposed to be protecting Millie, her best friend, but she has all of my attention.

Smart doesn't even cover the level of education she has. The cases she has covered and won in her career are astounding. There is nothing sexier than a smart woman. Okay, maybe I dug a little deeper than planned. The picture I have of her from the background check we did, just doesn't do her justice.

She surprises me, she's different. Not what I expected.

I watch her walk in knowing who she is, but I've not been able to take my eyes off her. I'm tracking her every movement from across the room, like I need to commit it to memory. The way she walks with determination and a light bounce like she has too much energy. The way her arse moves and her hands glide along the sides of her jeans every time they pass her thighs with each step.

She's gratifying.

Inwardly groaning, I have to adjust my trousers because of the effect she's having on me. I'm literally growing uncomfortable.

Clearing my throat, I try to focus back on the job I'm here to do. It's difficult as she's the only thing I see.

That picture I have of her saved on my computer is a world away from the woman I am looking at now. I knew she was hot, but this woman, this devastatingly smart, faultless, gorgeous woman, has me hook, line, and sinker.

The visceral reaction I've had since the moment I laid eyes on her is intense. The rush of heat radiating over my chest from just seeing her... it's insane. I don't know what this feeling is. It's more than lust. I long to get to know her, really get to know her.

Charlie.

She has changed so much from that picture, and yet hardly at all, but the small things matter. Her slightly wavy hair is loose, grazing her shoulders. It's almost white-blonde now, like she's been in the sun. I want to see how it feels, gripped between my fingers. Her slender figure is still slim, but the curves seem a little more refined.

I'm itching to touch her. To feel her smooth skin against mine. She's fit, not just sexy fit, but fit fit. Like she works out a lot. Her jeans hug her backside and its peachy curve has my eyes following her as she walks into the restaurant alongside the woman I know to be her friend, Millie. Charlie's easily three inches taller than her. She's easily five foot seven. Standing, she would come up to my chin. The perfect height to breathe her in and discover her scent while holding her tightly in my arms.

Walking into The Manors' restaurant behind them, I move discreetly and sit at the table just off to the side of them.

Leaning over, as she pulls her seat in to sit at the table, I get a glimpse of her creamy soft skin, just above the neckline of the bright green top she's wearing. My eyes fall to her breasts. *Fuck...* what I would give to be able to hold them in my hands and taste those creamy peaks on my lips.

Fuck. I have no idea who this person is that has taken over my fucking body. This is not me. The strength of my reaction to her, the pull I have to be next to her. Don't get me wrong, I like what I'm feeling. I'm just not used to it.

"Why am I always the one that people see first?" Leon laughs into my earpiece, snapping me back to reality and the job I'm supposed to be doing. Leon's my business partner and best friend. Well, one of my best friends. He's the brains behind our security business, Cerberus. Also, our firearms expert. Shit, that man likes weapons. He may even sleep with one under his pillow. He's been by my side for over fourteen years while we served together in the Army, and when we walked out.

He's one of the best, good to his core, and will put a smile back on your face, even if you don't realise you need it.

I have no idea what they have been talking about, I can only guess that Millie, the woman we are here to protect from her abusive ex, has just told Charlie about the security team she has watching out for her or any signs of her ex messing with the new life she now has with Jack. He's the one who hired us to protect Millie, Jack's our best client and friend. Charlie's just noticed Leon. It's not hard. He's built like a bear and is just as mean when he wants to be.

"Earth to Owen. I'll give you a hundred quid if you make the blonde jump." He means Charlie. "She'll never spot you. It's like you disappear in a room full of people. Your very own superpower. I love watching the magic happen." Leon laughs to himself as he waves at Charlie from over at the bar, shaking his head at the same time. It's a standing joke about my so-called superpower. I may be tall, but if I don't want to be seen, I won't be. Taking my phone from my jacket pocket, I sit back.

Our job started out looking out for Jack, Millie's boyfriend. We've been his security team for years. But things soon became complicated. A few weeks after him and Millie started seeing each other officially, it became clear that someone was out to get Millie, and in turn, took a dislike to Jack.

Millie's ex, Glen, is a real piece of shit and he was the reason for an arson attack on Jack's club in Ibiza a few weeks ago, and we have been on high alert ever since. If he is willing to burn a club full of people down, then we can only imagine the lengths he will go to in order to get back at Millie for leaving him.

Luckily, no-one was hurt. Everyone was evacuated just in time, thanks to the systems we recommended. They were lucky.

That's why we—myself, Leon, and our team—are here. They can't find the ex. The police think he is hiding out in Spain somewhere. I have a few of my guys looking into it for me. In our line of work, protecting people, it's a case of what you know and who you know. It helps get the job done. And done well. I won't let it be anything less, not where people are involved.

"Deal," I mutter as quietly as I can into the mic hidden in my collar. Contemplating what I'm going to say, I shift in my chair, sliding my phone into my jacket pocket. Charlie's been looking around for the second member of Millie's security team. For me. After Millie jokes she'll never be able to find us, well, me. But like Leon said, my superpower, I can't be seen unless I want to be.

Standing slowly from my chair, I'm silent. I don't attract attention from anyone around me. Charlie doesn't even glance my way as I stretch to my full six-foot-four height. Moving toward their table, I round the back of Charlie's chair. Millie's eyes clock me for a nanosecond before she returns her gaze to Charlie, the slight smile on her face, trying to hide her amusement as I step closer to Charlie.

Sliding my fingers across the soft, creamy skin of Charlie's bare shoulders, as I stand behind her, her warm skin gets my heart racing. She freezes for a moment as I lean down, sweeping her silky hair away from her shoulder, the feel of her under my fingertips stealing what I was about to say from my lips. Placing my mouth just below her ear, feeling her pulse rise beneath my thumb resting on her neck, I whisper, "I know everything about you, Charlie. Andrew was stupid to treat you the way he did or let you go, but thank him from me because you'll be screaming my name for the rest of your life." Her heart rate quickens under my fingers as she takes in a sharp breath, but before she can reply, I pull away to walk to where Leon is waiting at the bar.

Where the fuck did that come from?

Leon clamps his huge hand on my shoulder as I sit on the bar stool next to him, knocking me slightly off balance. Looking over at them together, I heard Millie tell her who I am as soon as my back was turned, laughing at her friend's reaction. Charlie's not even looked in my direction.

"I owe you some money," he says, his eyes wide with amusement. "With what you just said to that poor woman, I'm sure as shit you scared the fuck out of her, but on a whole new level, my friend."

"Shit, you heard?" I hang my head at the realisation I had forgotten about my mic and earpiece.

"Oh, I heard everything. I'm a little shocked, but happy for you, man. You might want to introduce yourself first, though. You know, like a normal person." He's laughing at me now. "You also get to watch her party tonight. They've just planned a night out, and you missed the entire conversation while you were lost in your own little world, thinking dirty thoughts." I rest my elbows on the bar and dip my head into my hands for a moment.

"I... Damn it, I need to get my shit together." Sitting up again, I look at Leon and the shit-eating grin plastered on his face and laugh with him. He knows me too well. I can't and won't hide anything from him, but that's a conversation for after our shift. Apparently, it's going to be a long one.

Leon is finding this whole situation far too funny; it makes me want to punch him in the face. I love the guy, but I want him to stop laughing at me. *Bastard.*

We have eyes and ears on Millie in the club they've ended up in after they left the bar. Sitting across the room again from her and Charlie is like being in my own personal hell. Especially since Charlie's outfit is blowing my mind.

Everything is on show, or might as well be, in a short black leather skirt with a vibrant pink top that shows her perfect breasts and lean back.

I don't want to be hearing any information about her second-hand through my earpiece like I am now. I want to hear it all from her. From those fucking lips, she's painted bright red tonight.

Currently, Millie is trying to get Charlie to go over and talk with some random fucking dude just by the bar. My blood is boiling at the thought of her going home with someone else.

What I want to do is go over there and take her home with me. Caveman style. I know it's wrong to think like that, but right now I don't give a fuck.

I want her.

Shit. I have to contain these feelings. My knuckles are turning white from the pressure I'm exerting on my water bottle as I try to repress these ungentlemanly thoughts.

I want to. I really fucking want to, but I won't. My mum taught me better than that. She doesn't even know me yet. I want to get to know every inch of her; know what makes her tick, what will make her smile, laugh, and even what makes her lose her shit. I want it all.

I've not been like this with anyone, ever. My heart is racing.

I marched my ass into the army as soon as I turned eighteen and never looked back. There was never time for something serious. I never wanted it, but with her, I feel this pull. I'm drawn to her. Watching her dance like no one was watching, the way she moved her hips, it's a surprise I can stand up with the hard on I have going on in my jeans right now. She's got my attention in more ways than one.

They only left the dance floor when Charlie took off her shoes, Millie dragging her to sit down at the tables surrounding the dance floor.

Leon and I secured the place before they arrived. We even have the B team on night watch for when we deliver Millie home tonight.

I can't help but scowl when Charlie and Millie walk over to the bar. Charlie's eyes flick towards me for a moment. She knows who I am now. Glancing at Leon who's just moved seats to see over the bar while they order more drinks, then Millie slides Charlie up towards the dick-head, she pointed out a few minutes ago, leaving them to talk. Millie moves off to the side, watching Charlie with a smile on her face.

His hand comes around to her back to the low-cut top, touching her bare skin. My heart rate spikes. I know I have no right to go over there and remove his hand, break his fingers, and throw him out, yet that's all I want to do.

Focusing my attention on Millie, where it should be, she heads towards the toilets. I note the time out of habit from years in the military.

A few minutes later, when she still isn't back, I signal to Leon that we need to check on her.

Making our way over, I push on the bathroom door, but it doesn't budge. It's locked. My already spiked heart rate kicks up a notch, but this time for a completely different reason. I put all thoughts of Charlie and that fucking dick-head out of my head. I have a job to do.

Breaking down the main door to the toilets, we find Millie looking dazed, leaning against the wall, trying to support herself. "Shit, Millie... What's happened? Are you hurt?" Running to her side, I look her over for any sign of injury.

I guide her to the small seating area. "Millie, what happened?" Kneeling in front of her, I look up to see Leon checking the stalls.

"I don't know. I think I had too much to drink. I must have passed out when I got in here, sorry... I... don't know, how long?" She seems a little confused.

"Shit, Jack's going to kill us. I don't think you drank that much. You were here for almost fifteen minutes." Looking to Leon for conformation, he nods.

"Three glasses of red, four cocktails and some water in between."

Lifting her head, her eyes are slightly glazed, her hands shaky in mine, unsteady even if she is sitting down—clear signs her drink has been spiked. *Fuck... How?* We had eyes on the bar all night. I don't know how it could have happened.

Pressing my fingers to the pulse on her wrist. It's racing. Looking over to Leon, his forehead is wrinkled in question as well. *I must have missed something. How could I have?*

"What did you just do?" Millie asks, her words slurred, voice shaky.

"I checked your eyes for any sign of dilation, your breathing's accelerated, and you're shaking and unsteady" my voice is calm, I don't want her to panic "I'll ring Jack and tell him what happened." Millie freezes.

"You think I was drugged?" Her eyes go wide. "Don't tell him... please. I wasn't drugged, it's my own fault, for mixing drinks. Plus, I've been a little stressed. Just take me home." She's pleading with me. "Jack's away tonight and I don't want to worry him any more than I need to. He has so much on his plate already, I don't want to add to the stress he already has on his shoulders after everything I've caused." *Fuck,* I hate she blames her situation on herself and not her ex.

"I have to tell Jack, Millie, he's my boss, and it's my job to make sure you are safe. And right now... I'm not sure you are," I admit.

"Please, please Owen, I don't want him to worry, this is all my own fault. He doesn't need to know. There was no way I was drugged... I mean, I got the drink from the bar myself. No one could have got to them. If they had, you or Leon would have seen." She's right, we would have. I just can't explain how this happened. Maybe she's right.

Turning, I look to Leon, holding a silent conversation, and shaking his head.

"Your call," he says.

"Okay, but if he even asks you if anything happened tonight, you tell him the truth. I'll get shit for it. I hate keeping secrets, especially ones like this. Even more so because it's Jack. Are you sure you're okay?" The worry in my chest tightens further.

"Apart from feeling a little foolish and a tad nauseous, I'm fine. Let's go and grab Charlie, and go home." Millie stands up with my help. I can't help the small smile that appears at the sound of Charlie's name.

I make the decision to take her home against my better judgment, but I know it's best for Millie. I understand her reasons for not telling Jack, even so, it still makes me uncomfortable. I've never held back in any of my reports, and Jack's a good friend as well as a client.

Leon starts to head outside with Millie to his car, and I head over to where Charlie is still being groped by that dickhead, blissfully unaware that her best friend has been drugged and struggling in the bathroom.

It's my fucking absolute pleasure to pull her away.

I whisper in her ear, "We're leaving," while I remove the guy's hand from her lower back with a vice-like grip that has him shaking his hand after I release it. Leaning into him, just to be sure he gets the message, I grit out through clenched teeth, "Touch her again, and you'll find your balls detached and floating in the sea." He backs up and turns around, walking away quickly.

Turning back to Charlie, she looks pissed. "What was that for? We were just talking?" She eyes me with suspicion, before realising who I am.

"We need to leave. Millie's not well." Her face changes instantly, eyes darting from me to try and find Millie.

"What happened? Is she okay?" She looks beautiful as she pushes past me. I don't care as long as she is not in another man's arms.

Chapter Four

Delicious Shivers

Charlie

"Millie, what do you want to do?" I ask when we step through the door of her small cottage. Owen and Leon dropped us off after they assured us that the night security team would be watching the house tonight.

"I want to sleep this off. You don't have to stay, Charlie. I'll be fine."

"I'm not leaving you alone after that, not while Jack's away."

"Fine, but you'll have to sleep on the sofa if that's okay?"

"Perfect." I know she's scared. Who wouldn't be when your ex is trying to ruin your new life?

Millie heads upstairs and grabs me some pjs. Coming back down with some sheets and a blanket to make up the sofa, she protests when I take them off her and do it myself. After a long hug, we say goodnight; she heads off to bed, not saying another word. I listen for a while, making sure she's okay. Then, when I think she's asleep, I pop my head into her bedroom to check on her.

I've been on Millie's sofa fidgeting for about an hour, trying to get to sleep, I can't do it. It just won't happen. The events of tonight keep replaying in my mind. Millie was fine one moment, then a few minutes later, I was told by *him*, one of Millie's security team, that we were leaving the club because Millie wasn't well. On the way home, she told me what she thinks happened. I'm not so sure it was the drink.

By the time I got outside, Leon, the bigger one of the two that were with her today, the one that looks like a big teddy bear, had her in the waiting car. The man I now know is Owen, slid in beside me, watching Millie, and me, his thigh pressed against mine. His appraising gaze making me hot all the way back to Millie's cottage.

The thought of Owen, his eyes watching me all night. That's the turmoil that's been tormenting me since he whispered in my ear at the restaurant this afternoon that I would be screaming his name for the rest of my life. I liked it; I liked that he watched me in the bar and the club. How is it I only met him today? It feels like I know him already when we've hardly spoken.

I'm restless. Every time I close my eyes, I feel his warm breath on my neck, his lips just below my ear as he whispered those words to me, while I ate lunch and the delicious shivers that followed. It's ridiculous.

When his fingers grazed my shoulder, shitting hell. It was like fire across my skin. I can still feel them now. Like a scorch mark left behind from a blaze burning the imprint of him on my skin.

How can he make my body come alive like that? I've never felt anything like it. I was so turned on and I didn't even know what he looked like, but that voice was deep, rumbling, and *oh my life,* I wanted him. Owen.

I should have been outraged. It should have creeped me out, but my mind and body had other ideas. I almost came on the spot and I had to squeeze my thighs together to try and get some relief from the undeniable tension building in me.

Just from a few seconds of contact? How is that possible?

I think back to this afternoon. When I left Millie after our lunch and got my first good look at him. I could feel his eyes on me as I made my way back to my room in the hotel, The Manor, where Millie works and I'm supposed to be sleeping.

He was hot, not my normal type. He seemed a bit geeky, sexy geeky with his dark messy hair, but also *so* manly, and… well, my mind went to what those fingers could do to me, his hands on me, trailing lower… I need to breathe before I get carried away again.

He's already lit a flame inside me. I mean, *what the fuck?* I've been fucked over on an ultimate scale by my ex. I don't need or want to be that person again. Letting myself be vulnerable with someone else after what Andy so cruelly did to me. It's a ridiculous thought, but what if I let my guard down and we become something, there is nothing stopping it all from happening again. The hurt, the pain. No. I'm not ready for anything like that. Even talking to the guy at the bar tonight, I knew nothing would happen between us.

When I saw him again tonight at the bar, all I could think of was how I touched myself to the feel of his fingers on my skin, my cheeks flushed at the memory of his name leaving my lips as I came apart just thinking about him. I tried to ignore him, forget about him. Focus on something else.

I tried, but I just can't seem to do it.

Get your shit together, Charlie, I berate myself. *You have stuff to do, and your business to set up. Get that man out of your head.*

But I can't get him out of my head. Maybe I need a quick fix. Using my hand didn't do the job, it only made the desire I feel for him stronger. Maybe if I can use my purple vibrator when it arrives with all my moving things, I'll be able to get this lust I have for him gone, get him out of my system.

Turning over as my overtired body still fidgets, I grab my phone to check the time and see it's already after two in the morning. Just as I place my phone back down, a message comes through.

Unknown: *I can't stop thinking about you ~ O*

Owen? If it is you, that makes two of us. Wait, how did he get my number? Sitting up, I wonder if I should text him back or make him wait. I'm sure there is some sort of rule about replying straight away, or is that for guys? Ugh... who cares?

Me: *Who is this? And how did you get my number?*

The dots appear, telling me he's typing back.

Unknown: *You know who this is and I have ways of finding things when I want them...*

And I want you.

That's direct, and I like it. My body lights up from that message, so imagine what he could do if we got together. It's obviously been way too long since I had an orgasm from a real-life person. All I can think of is... well, another happy ending for me. You can't have too many orgasms in a day, right? In a totally non-relationship way, just as friends with benefits. Or just benefits, as we are not friends. *Acquaintances with benefits?*

Unknown: *I'm outside.*

Me: *And?*

Unknown: *I want to see you.*

Me: *How do I know you're not a serial killer?*

Mostly? Wow… that is hot. Okay, so I may have read too many dark romance books lately, because that turns me on way more than it should, and scares me a little at the same time. Or is that excitement?

I can't have this hot, strange, beautifully geeky, rumpled, just got out of bed, sexy, possibly glasses-wearing, kind of man, thinking I like the idea of danger turning me on, not that he would know this unless he can read my mind.

It's like my fingers wrote okay without my brain registering what they were doing. I place my phone down on the floor and stand up, taking a quick peek at the shorts and a vest top Millie lent me, as my stuff is at the hotel. She's a lot shorter than I am, so it's like a crop top, flashing my belly button and my ass is hanging out of them.

I flip on the small lamp beside the sofa and take a quick look in the mirror that hangs above the huge fireplace on the opposite wall. My make up is gone. I look okay. A little flushed and my hair is messy from all the tossing and turning, so I run my fingers through it, trying to tame it before taking a few deep breaths for courage before I walk barefoot towards the door.

Opening the door as quietly as I can, I peek out, and there he is, leaning against the frame of the small porch, waiting. I can't help it. My eyes wander over him, taking in every delicious inch. His still messy, dark hair that falls slightly over his forehead is cut close at the sides. It would be cute if it wasn't so sexy. His black shirt is undone a few buttons from the top, just showing a hint of tanned olive chest.

His muscular, lean physique makes him look like he's built like a swimmer with broad shoulders and a slim waist, disappearing into his faded black ripped jeans.

One muscular leg is crossed over the other, his boots undone. His elbow is against the wall while he runs his hand through that messy hair.

My insides do a little dance, telling me it's ready for whatever he is willing to give me. *Anything*. So, when he steps forward, I lean into him. "This is ridiculous," I whisper, more to myself than him.

"I know, but it feels so fucking right." His quiet tone reaches my ears. I press my hand to his chest. The feel of his hard, sculpted muscles under the softness of his shirt is warm and inviting.

"It does." I breathe out the words as a small gasp escapes me as heat runs through my fingers, spreading up my arm, igniting everything in its wake. Looking up at him from below my lashes, I'm met with his intense gaze. There is a silent agreement between us, an understanding that this needs to happen.

The next thing I know, I'm being lifted off the floor. His hands are under my arse pulling me up as his mouth lands on mine, his soft lips nip at my lower lip, feverish, tasting me with longing and impatience as his mouth takes mine, demanding more.

While he moves us back into the cottage. I'm pressed against him, my bare legs wrapped around his waist. I feel him everywhere; the roughness of his jeans, his hard cock ready for me; gasping through the kisses he's submitting me to. I love it. The thrill, the excitement. I want more. It's not enough.

He closes the door quietly behind us, while holding me close and kissing me. What we're doing, the caress of his mouth on mine, isn't kissing. That word doesn't do justice to what's happening right now, his moans, entice me to hold on tighter, he devours me, his tongue desperate to find mine, soft and searching, there is no description suitable for how his mouth is enticing electricity to rip through my body.

Fuck, he tastes good, so freaking good. It's intoxicating. Like mint, coffee, and warmth. I need it; I need him.

His teeth nip at my lips, sending a delicious bolt of lightning to my most sensitive parts. I'm craving him, pulling him closer. My hands tug on his already messy hair, trying to bring his mouth to me. His hand clamps on my arse, holding me to him, his rough fingers digging in, making me grind against him. Fuck, I love it. I want to lose myself in him. I want to give him control of my body. "Fuck," he curses when I reach between us and find the button of his jeans, popping it open, before reaching for his zip.

"Just for the record. I don't want serious, not now," I pant. I have to say it out loud before whatever this is happens. Not in all my years with Andy did it feel like this. This is a whole new experience of sensations and I want it so badly.

"As long as I get to have you, that's fine. We'll work on it." *We'll work on it?* I don't have time to contemplate what that could mean as he reaches under my too-small top, his thumb brushing the side of my breast, my back arching to meet his touch, my nipples hardening at the shivers he's eliciting from my body. Oh my god, he's good.

His head drops to my shoulder as he trails kisses down the side of my neck, tilting my head for him to get better access. My pulse quickens, his lips quirk up like he can feel it.

"This is fast, but..."

"I don't care," I tell him, reluctantly shifting my body. I manoeuvre myself so I can get the zip down on his jeans. The heels of my feet digging into his side for leverage. My fingers slide inside his underwear and get the first feel of him. He's huge; long, hard, and thick. My breath catches. As I wrap my hand around his length, hissing as I start to move my wrist, stroking his huge length. We move into the living room. Crashing onto the sofa, Owen falls towards me, his hands landing on either side of my head. His face is so close to mine. I can see the full range of colour in his eyes.

"Perfect," he mumbles into my ear, lifting my top to expose my breasts. Owen bows his head and takes my pebbled, sensitive nipple in his mouth, teasing it with his tongue. My back arches and I almost explode. As his mouth teases my breasts, he presses himself into me, his cock against my aching pussy.

Hard and hot.

I shove his jeans and boxers down the best I can.

"I'm clean..." I say between breaths and being devoured by him. "I got tested after Andy—"

He cuts me off. "Don't say his name when I'm about to fuck you. Only mine. Say it."

Holy fuck. "Owen," I say on an exhale, never in my life have so few words, made me weak and wanting.

"Charlie." His heated breath is on my neck. "I'm clean too. I don't want anything between us. I want to feel all of you when I fuck you." His words do things to me. I want them all over me, everywhere. His hand comes between us and he makes quick work of my short shorts, almost ripping them off. His hand slides up my thigh, my breath catches in my throat as he hovers his thick fingers over my entrance. Tempting me, I edge closer, needing the contact. His breath ragged on my skin.

"You're ready for me." The deep gravel he emits is all I need to hear.

I'm ready, really ready. I don't want to wait. Lifting my hips to meet his hand. His fingers slide over my clit, my breath catches as more sparks fly over my body. I feel like I'm on fire, hot, blazing flames engulf me the more he touches my skin.

"Please, I need more." I can't help myself; this is intense. Biting my lip to keep myself quiet, I'll do all I can not to scream. I writhe under him. His lips take my nipple and I start to climb higher.

"Owen, please." I know I'm begging, but I really couldn't give a flying fuck right now. I need him. I need to feel him.

"Anything you want, Angel." My back arches as he circles my clit. My legs start to spasm, my heart pound, and I lose all thoughts as tingling sensations overtake my body when he presses his fingers harder against my aching clit. I come hard and fast. I don't have time to come down from my high when I feel him place himself at my entrance, gasping, I'm so wet, as he slides his length against me. I'm ready for him. All the air leaves me and the air around me ceases to exist. I'm breathless as he thrusts into me. A slight sting ebbs away as fast as it came.

He stills, his gaze connecting with mine, giving me time to adjust to his size. "Fuck, you're so tight, you good?" I can't form words, so I nod, holding him tighter. He's in so deep I feel full, connected in a way I never expected. A hungry ache inside. He doesn't pull out. He presses deeper, whimpering, moving my hips to accept as much of him as I can. Pulling out slowly, he eases back in. It's torture. He pulls out again, this time slamming into me. Crying out, he brings his lips to mine, swallowing down the moans, keeping me quiet.

He keeps going, pistoning into me with such force my body trembles. His lips trace down my neck, where he sucks, licks and nips at my tender skin. A deep groan comes from his throat. It lights me up like a star at night, whimpering as his thrusts come fast, pinning me to the sofa. Kissing me roughly to silence me, but I'm not sure that's enough to stop me. I hold on like my life is in his hands. My hands in his hair, around his back, his bare tight arse. I want it all.

"Charlie, fuck…" he states, panting like he's claiming my name for himself, resting his forehead on mine. His thrusts become frantic, edging us both closer to bliss. He takes me harder, reaching the spot inside me that's already sensitive, his length growing harder, filling me. I take what he's giving; every thrust, every grasp, every kiss, all of it. He consumes me. I feel him everywhere. It's… magnificent. His teeth nip at my lip while his hand wanders and presses my already over-stimulated clit. I'm building again. This man. Who the fuck is he?

"I need you to come again, Charlie. Let me see you. Don't close your eyes. Watch me fuck you." I open my eyes, doing what he asks without question.

He fucks into me over and over again, one hand holding him up, while the other grips the back of my neck. I lose it and my whole body tightens with the anticipation of what's to come, clenching around him, convulsing when his thrusts hit the bundle of nerves that send me over the highest edge I've ever flown from. Coming like I've never had an orgasm before. Feeling his length swell inside me as the waves of my own pleasure overtake me again. He comes with me. In me. I feel him; his hot release.

"Angel," he groans, still moving inside me, overwhelming me with sensation, prolonging my pleasure. Holding me in place with his hips, his finger glides against my cheek, gracing my lips with my own name, his eyes fixing on mine. "Charlie," repeating the words on a whisper, "Charlie." Emotion thick in his voice, kissing me deeply, tenderly.

"I'm sorry," he says into my neck as he thrusts one last time. My back arches, accepting him, my stomach tingling with after-waves of my high, placing my shaky hand on his chest, his heartbeat wild just like mine. I don't want to move. This feels too good, scary good. I couldn't if I tried. His weight on me feels divine. Our bodies pressed together so deliciously. Our ragged breathing the only sound in the silent room.

"What for?" I ask, running my hands down his back.

"I took you without asking if you were on anything... I'm sorry, I just..."

"I'm on the pill. We're okay." He lets out a sigh and stays right there in between my legs. I'm not sure I want him to move just yet.

"Hmm." He shifts and moves away from me, standing, before putting himself back into his boxers and jeans. I watch every move as I lie there, naked as the day I was born. I don't even remember my top being removed. I stand on shaky legs, the slight soreness between my thighs feels so good, even the wetness of his cum leaking from me makes me shiver. Stumbling slightly when I move, I have to pause for a moment to gain some composure. I hear a low laugh behind me. No doubt he's proud that he's made me feel like this, grinning like an idiot back at him. Shaking my head, I move to the small downstairs toilet, grabbing my shorts and top on the way. I've never been embarrassed about my body. I've worked hard for it.

When I come back out a few minutes later, he's at the door, fully dressed. I'm taken aback for a moment, a flash of disappointment he's ready to leave so soon. Then I remember that this is what I wanted; he's respecting my wishes.

His eyes roam over me, full of heat as they land on mine... Shit, he's already hard again, the visible outline just as prominent as it was before when we stepped into the living room. If I had to guess, if I gave him the go-ahead, he'd have me against the wall, for a repeat of what we just did in seconds flat. Taking a steading breath, I squeeze my thighs together and step forward.

"Well, Owen, it was nice to meet you." I smile, placing my hand on the door behind him. When I pull it open, he slides his hand over mine and pulls me towards him.

"There is no way we're done yet. Not after that." He moves his hand down to my hip and holds me close. "I'll see you tomorrow, Charlie."

Chapter Five

Skills

Owen

I've been doing security since the day we stepped out of the Army almost eight years ago. It's not that dissimilar. We protect people, only this time, we get paid very highly to do something we love. It's on our terms. We pick our clients, we even have a waiting list for those who want our more specialised services.

We needed an out after what happened to our unit on our last tour. Myself and Leon took Cole and Ethen with us when we quit the forces. They were all that was left of my A-team when we were in Afghanistan. They're my A-team here too. There was no way I could leave them behind. *Not after that.*

Others have joined us over the years and we have bases all over the UK and abroad now, including a special unit we co-work with when shit gets bad.

The day we handed in our uniforms, I knew we needed to stick together. That shit, the dark stuff, the stuff you try not to focus on, it can creep up on you and knock you on your arse quicker than a sniper's bullet. I should know, I was that sniper.

We stick together, that's our rule. If you work for us, you're all in. Brothers in every sense of the word.

We had it all lined up, ready to just walk into. The office/warehouse, the contacts, all the gear we would need to work private security. Myself and Leon worked hard to get it all together. We used all the resources we had to get the contracts ready and signed for when we needed them.

When we told Ethan what we wanted to do, he gave us the financial backing we needed; he comes from a very wealthy family. Told us to get what we needed, and he'd join us. His words were, if we were going to do this, then we needed to do it right. What surprised us the most was his grumpy arse had the contract drawn up to say the company was split equally between the four of us. We've never looked back.

Jack was one of our first clients. We met a few times over the years. When we were on R&R after a tour, it was always in one of his hotels. We hit it off, would let him know when we would be about, and he would set us up with everything we needed. Still does.

When we offered him our services, he jumped at the chance, saying it was just the right time as his business was expanding considerably, and he could use people he trusted. He's had us on a retainer ever since. We are an integral part of his security team, for him and all the businesses he has around the world. We vet, employ, and maintain all the services he needs.

Our history made the decision so much harder yesterday when I told Millie I wouldn't tell Jack about what happened in the bar. It went against everything I am, and have built this business to be. It's already tormenting me. Like I'm being pulled in two directions.

Leon's pissed off. Right now, he's giving me shit down the phone while I sit in my truck. I deserve it.

"You are one lucky son of a bitch," he shouts at me, through my truck's speakers. "Where is your head? You don't do this shit. We tell the truth, and you just lied to our best customer. Not only that, he's our friend, O. You know what he'll do when he finds out?!" This is obviously a one-sided conversation. My hands manoeuvring the steering wheel as I pull away from the shop.

He's been going on for the last few minutes like this. If he was in front of me and not yelling down the phone, I would no doubt have had to go in the ring with him to fight it out. I hate it when he does that shit because he would win. The man is a beast.

"I know. He'll fucking murder me. I've read Millie's history and the things Jack has told us about her ex. I just couldn't do that to her. I know I've fucked up. I'll sort it out," I tell him, dragging my hand down my face as he continues to yell at me.

"Lucky motherfucker, that's what you are. I have a feeling this shit is just getting started." We had confirmation earlier today that the Spanish police have confirmed they have Millie's ex in custody. "Something is off. Both of us know it." He's right. My gut is telling me something's not right and I really don't like it when that happens.

"I can't shake the feeling either. I'll wait to see if our guy comes back with an image we can match up with. I need eyes on before I believe it's him." Jack insisted we step down the security for the annual ball he's organising for his employees. He's so relieved that this whole thing with Millie's ex is over. We insisted on putting a B-team in place instead. I'm not comfortable with it, but those are the orders, and as of this afternoon, we are officially invited to be part of it.

"I'll ask again, Owen. Where is your head right now?" Leon repeats, "Or who is it focused on might be the better question." I hate that he knows me so well. I can't hide anything from him or the others. They say men don't talk about personal stuff with each other, but we know that keeping thoughts and feelings back can end up getting you killed.

"Fine, it's on her. Charlie. I mean, you know me, and you know me well. I don't get like this. It's..."

"Freaking you the fuck out?" That's an understatement. I've always been focused on my work. Women have come and gone, sure. But no-one has ever held space in my thoughts like Charlie is doing right now and has been since the moment she walked into The Manor. Maybe even before that.

"Yep." It's all I have to say on the matter.

"You slept with her, didn't you? Fuck's sake, man," he mutters, letting out a gruff sound of frustration. "You were working last night, and you slept with her?" I have no idea how he does it. He's always been able to read me and the others like an open book.

I don't say anything. If I do, I'm not sure what will come out. After overhearing most of her conversation yesterday with Millie, I knew Charlie was picking up the keys to the shop and apartment today. That's why she was supposed to stay at the hotel last night. I have my ways to find where she is. She's not hard to find. I've just picked up some food and drinks for me and Charlie and I'm driving over to her shop now. She doesn't know I'm on my way, but I know she's there. I may have tracked her car on the system we use.

"I'm going to take that silence as a yes. That's twice in less than twenty-four hours that you've gone against your own code. The code you made us all sign a contract to, and swear by. Sort your shit out." I turn and head down the back street so I can park in the small delivery bay at the back of the shop, which used to be a hardware store. I've seen many changes in this small town since we located here after we left the army; most of them good.

"I'm heading to sort it out now." I'm unable to hide the grin on my face and am happy Leon can't see it. I hang up. I'll deal with him tomorrow. As of now, I have a free night I didn't know was coming, now we have the B-team on Millie and Jack. I know how I plan on spending it. In between the thighs of a woman I can't get out of my head.

After what we did last night, my dick has been thinking about her nonstop too. Every move, every moan. As soon as she opened that door last night, the way her fingers spread over my chest, the instant heat. Fuck, I knew she wanted it just as much as I did. When she looked at me, those ice-blue, almost violet eyes had me.

My cock twitches at the memory, at the anticipation of what tonight could bring. I'm hoping for rounds two, three and four. She told me she doesn't want a relationship. I'm okay with that and will respect it as much as I can, but there are many things I'm willing to give up, and Charlie is not one of them. I won't let what we have be a one-night stand. She deserves more than that after what her ex-husband did to her. I want more. I just don't know what that looks like for us yet. But fuck me, it was the best sex of my life, with a woman who ignites every part of me.

Grabbing the food and beers from the front seat of my truck, I climb out, shutting the door behind me. The back door to the shop is just ahead. Walking towards it, I push... *Unlocked.* Shaking my head, I'm frustrated because anyone could just walk in. Proving my point, I walk right in. I'll need to have a word with her about it. Maybe install a latch. A bell, or even a camera, or a combination of the three would work best. I've got a few back at the office. I'll link it up to our system so she doesn't have to pay for anything. I'll fit them for her next time I have a few free hours.

Protective much?

I already know the layout of the shop. I couldn't help myself. This shop is big and the apartment upstairs has the same footprint. It's a big space, other than the flower shop she planned to open, it makes me wonder what she has planned for the extra space.

Placing the food and drinks in the kitchen, I hear her voice float through from one of the smaller rooms back here. I follow the sound, leaning against the doorframe, watching as she talks to herself, sticking the colour swatches to the wall while tossing the ones she's not so fond of to the floor.

She's wearing a matching set of dark pink leggings and a sports bra, showing off just how toned she is. The contrast against her pale skin is striking.

Charlie's deep in thought and she's not noticed me yet. I can't take my eyes off her; the way those leggings hug her arse, and the gap of bare skin between her top and trousers. Those places I would willingly trail my tongue over. I swallow, knowing how good she feels in my hands. Having those legs wrapped around me. She might as well be naked for all that she's wearing. I fucking love it and hate it at the same time.

Thoughts of peeling them all off slowly and savouring every touch race through my mind. Each delicious part of her creamy skin, to taste her on my tongue, swallowing down every bit of her I could.

Stepping forward, I move in and catch one of the cards she doesn't like before it hits the floor.

"I liked that one," I say, making her jump as she whips her head around. Her fist is clenched like she's ready to strike, only lowering it when she sees it's me. I'm close enough to smell the cherry flavour that's imprinted on my mind, millimetres away from touching her smooth skin. Her hand reaches her chest, fingers splayed, like she's trying to soothe her racing heart.

"Owen, you..." Her cheeks flush a pale pink as she takes a slow breath through her peach-coloured lips.

"Made you jump?"

She nods, turning her attention back to the wall littered with colourful cards. Placing the card in my hand on the floor with the others, I stay close to her, my body thrumming at our proximity.

"Why are you here? And how did you get in?" she asks, a hit of indifference in her voice. The pulse in her slender neck races. Maybe it's because of the memory of what we did last night. Maybe it's the thought of my mouth on hers. My hand itches to move closer so I can feel the rhythm below my fingers. I like that this is what I do to her.

"I brought us dinner. Figured you'd been here most of the day."

She turns around, her chest grazing mine. "We," she gestures between the two of us, "are not seeing each other. You don't have to bring me dinner. Last night was a one-time thing... a great one-time thing." Tapping her finger on my lips, she sighs. "It won't be happening again."

I really like that she believes that. It's a lie, but I like that she's trying to convince herself. Capturing her delicate finger between my lips, I suck, teasing the tip with my tongue. She pulls it out with a pop, and my cock immediately stands to attention.

"What I want is you. Relationship or not, I want you." It's the truth. Running my finger down her exposed side, the reaction I'm causing is as clear as day, goosebumps exploding in my wake.

Swallowing like she's trying to gain some semblance of composure, Charlie turns away from me. "If you must know, I've not been here all day. I've had a day in the spa up at The Manor, relaxing and enjoying myself after a tough couple of months." My hand reaches her hip, pulling her back to me, her arse against my crotch. Fuck, she feels good. She sighs but doesn't move away. Watching as she tries to make her breaths slow and even, her fingers fidgeting with the cards she's holding. I won't give up, not now I've had her.

"You hungry?" I say into her ear, nipping the soft flesh, then tentatively licking away the sting I know I caused. She shakes her head and lets out a breath. When she relaxes into me, I know she's lost the battle with herself. My hand snakes its way up the front of her sports bra, brushing the exposed skin of her stomach on the way up. My fingers lightly tease her nipples through the thin material. She shivers as I hold her firmly against my chest, my other arm wrapping around her waist.

"Just sex, that's all?" Her hands brace on the wall in front of her, while her hips stay pressed against me, teasing me, when she does the smallest of wiggles. I'm ready to explode from the slightest bit of friction.

"This is not just sex, but for now it's anything you need it to be." I'm direct, but I mean it.

"Just sex. It's all I need right now."

"Right now?" I question, only half-joking.

"Yes, right now, Owen, shit."

"Keep your hands on the wall. Don't move." She does as she's told, while I unzip her sports bra, letting her breasts free. I cup them as she moans, arching into my touch. My dick's already hard from the sound, begging to be set free of its jean-clad confines.

"I don't understand… how you do this to me? But I want it," she says, slightly shaking her head with each word.

Moving my hands slowly down her beautiful body, I feel everything as I go. The soft, supple skin of the breasts, the smooth plains of the flat stomach, and as I dip my hand down the front of her leggings and into her knickers, the small silky patch of hair between her sweet thighs. Her breath catches and her head falls back. "Fucking hell," I mumble into her ear. She's wet, so wet… easing my hand back out, a small whimper of what sounds like frustration escapes her lips.

"Patience," I tell her as I peel down her leggings, taking down her knickers with them. Dropping to my knees as I help her step out of them.

The view from down here is beautiful. She is glistening and I've barely touched her. This is all for me.

I undo my jeans. Taking myself out, I groan at the relief and fist my cock for a moment while I watch her in this position: legs slightly parted, her palms still planted on the wall. She glances back over her shoulder, her eyes widening when she sees how hard I am. She knows she does this to me. Fuck, it just makes me harder.

My fingers find her entrance as I stand behind her, pressing my front to her back. Her breath quickens as I sink a finger deep inside her tight, slick warmth I could feel forever. She pushes back against my hand as if she needs more. I add another finger, curling them to find the spot I know will make her come.

"Fuck… Owen… I need more, now," desperation ebbing from every word.

I love that she knows what she wants and is willing to tell me.

"I going to take my time with you, Charlie." Moving my hand from her abdomen to find her clit, she bucks into me. It's so hot the way her hips move, so I give her more. Adding pressure where she needs it.

"Yes... Fuck." Her walls clench around my fingers and she groans as I pull away from her clit, planting a kiss on her neck as I pinch and tug at her sensitive nipple. I can't stop the smile that's tugging on my lips, I'm going to try as hard as I can to persuade this woman to be an 'us'. I want so much more than she's willing give right now. I can only dream about a life with Charlie in it at this point. Wrapped in my arms, making the best fucking sounds I've ever heard come from another person's lips.

I've not moved my fingers inside her yet. They're still curled at just the right place, letting the anticipation build. I pump them in and out. From this position, I can't see everything, but I can feel it; her heat on me, how wet she is, her body writhing under my touch.

I can't get enough.

I want to watch her come, taking her hard and fast against the wall. My fingers come back to her clit, circling while the ones inside her move slowly in and out.

"Yes," she cries as I slide my cock through her folds, coating myself in her arousal. Her forehead presses to the wall as I feel her quiver around my fingers, her climax close. Her hips buck, trying to take what she needs.

"Take it, Charlie. I want to watch you come undone, then I'll fuck you just like you need me to." My words ignite her heat, her sweet juices coating my dick as she grinds herself harder against me. Working her hips against my hand and my dick, adding to the pressure she needs. My fingers circle her clit again and again, all while my other hand pumps into her. I watch as her skin flushes deeper, her breath coming in shallow pants, like she can't get enough air in her lungs. I double my efforts and watch as she falls over the edge; her body, going tense, her walls convulse around my fingers. I don't let up, working her through it.

"Owen... Ahh... Fuck..." Her head whips back as she almost collapses in my arms.

My name on her lips is something else. Her hands are still braced on the wall and I wrap my arm around her waist, nudging her thighs wider with my knee. Positioning myself at her entrance, I go slowly, pushing inside her. Gasping at the intrusion when I plant myself in deep, feeling her stretch around me. "Charlie." Staying there for a moment while I savour every second of this incredible feeling of her wrapped around my cock. Her fingers try to grasp the wall. It's agonising, but worth every fucking second.

Coming out slowly at first, then slamming into her, fucking her hard. Her head dips as she takes everything I'm giving her.

She arches her back to get more. My hands come to her hips, bending her further over, going deeper with every thrust. Fuck, how can this be better than last night? But somehow, it is...

"Angel..." I slam into her while taking her nipple and twisting it in between my fingers.

"Owen... Again." I do it again. Then I feel it. She comes again, this time bigger and better than the last, spasming around my dick, choking it. I can't hold on. I thrust in one final time before I explode, coming with her and spilling my load deep inside her.

"Angel," I whisper into the back of her neck as we both fall to the floor, still inside her as she sits on my lap, her body draped back against mine.

I can't help touching her. My hands wander over her body, sweet, sweaty, and satisfied.

"I've been thinking about that all day," I admit.

"I'd like to say different, but I can't," she admits, smiling.

"Um... did you say you bought dinner?" she asks.

"I did. Pizza." She wiggles her hips. I'm still half hard, almost ready to go again, but she eases off me, stands, picks up her clothes, watching her every move as she heads for the door.

Standing, I make my way into the kitchen, adjusting my clothes as I go. Picking up the now-cold pizza and beer and heading back to what I'm assuming will be her office, and placing them on her desk. When she walks back in a few minutes later, her face is flushed, a beautiful pink tint creeping up her cheekbones and her hair has that just fucked look about it. I decide there and then that I like that look. Flushed and fucked.

"I didn't know what you liked, so I brought a margarita and a pepperoni. Can't go wrong with either." Opening a beer, I hand her one.

"Good choice. I like both," she says, opening the box and grabbing a slice of the pepperoni.

"When do you move upstairs?" she shoots me a look. Her brows pinched together in confusion.

"Before I answer any questions, you need to answer some of mine first. If we are going to do this 'friends with benefits' thing, I need to know a few things." "I'll answer anything you want, but some things I'm not allowed to tell you." I know she has an inquisitive mind. You have to be when you're an ex-prosecution solicitor; I can only imagine the things she wants to ask me. I need to be at least a little cautious with my answers.

"Umm, okay, how did you get my number?" she asks, tilting her head to one side.

"That's easy. The same place I got your address, the shop details, floor plans, and some other stuff. I... searched for you on the system I have. It gave me all the basic information I needed to know about you." I choose my words carefully. I can't tell her too much about the system I use, which could tell me a hell of a lot more, including money, purchases, every moment ever electronically recorded from her life, and more. But I won't. I want to hear it from her sexy as fuck mouth first.

"And I know nothing about you, other than your job and what you look like half naked."

"Well, we can rectify the latter... just say the word and I'll show you what I look like fully naked." I watch as her eyes sweep over me, but she shakes her head. Moving further away from me.

"It should creep me out that you know stuff about me, but I'm weirdly okay with it... and I don't know why. What else do you know about me?" She nods, letting me know it's my turn to speak.

"Okay... I looked you up as soon as Millie got in touch with you. I needed to check you out, make sure you were not a threat to Millie and Jack." She raises her eyebrows at this, but I carry on. "I know what you used to do. I know you quit your job recently. I also know you were married for six years. Your divorce finalised just over two weeks ago, and that prick cheated on you." She visibly flinches at my words. "Sorry, that was insensitive of me," I say, holding my hands up as a way of apology. She nods, but waves for me to carry on.

"I know you have trained over the last few months to become a florist, and have bought this shop and the apartment above to live in. I know you own that Porsche 911 that's sitting outside outright. You're twenty-nine. I know when your birthday is... and that's it."

Letting out a breath, she looks like she's taking it all in before she says, "I think we need to play a game of twenty questions. I'm asking, you're answering."

"Go ahead," I reply. I'm not hiding anything from her.

"One...What's your full name? I've had sex with you twice and still don't know if Owen is a nickname or a given name."

"Owen Archie Stone." Her eyebrows raise slightly, a small smile curving her lips, letting me know she likes what she hears.

"Two... how old are you?"

"Thirty-two. My birthday is the twenty-second of April." I smile.

"I don't need to know your birthday, three...who do you work for?"

"Myself, it's my business, Cerberus." She lets out a laugh.

"You named your business after the gatekeeper of the underworld, the Three Headed Hound of Hades." I shrug. She knows her Greek mythology. Taking another drink, she looks at me for a second before saying, "You intrigue me, Owen Archie Stone. Now pass me some more pizza." I can see it in her eyes. I'll win her over.

I hand her another slice. "Four... Where do you live?" She's perching on the edge of the desk now, the flushed and fucked look disappearing before my eyes.

"I have a house on the seafront."

"There's more to that. Tell me."

"Fine, I have a few houses up and down the country. I like to develop them in my spare time."

"Full of surprises. Five... what else do you like doing in your spare time?" This time my eyes wander over her, and she blushes again.

"You, for the last two days, but otherwise I like to work with my hands. I like to work wood, carpentry." I watch as she slowly swallows.

"You are good with your hands; I'll give you that," she teases.

"Anytime you want them, Angel, just say the word, and they are all yours." I tug her from the desk and back her up against the wall. I cage her in, my hands on either side of her head when my mouth lands on hers. Fuck, she tastes good. She sighs and pushes me away. Standing back, I smirk.

"Ask me number six..." I wrap my hand around the nape of her neck and let my mouth devour her before dragging my tongue lightly over her flushed skin. Her hands fist my shirt, pulling me closer. "Ask away Angel."

"Six..." Whimpering as I lick the curve of her neck. "Where are you from?"

"Up north." she moves her head to one side, allowing me better access.

"Seven... where's your accent gone?" My lips hover over hers, her breath hot against me.

"Too many years in the army, never went back home." I kiss her, my lips on hers, my tongue seeking entrance. I want to claim her as mine.

This woman is going to ruin me.

Chapter Six

Moving In

Charlie

It's official. I move in today, and I get to take the first load of deliveries for the shop. Not flowers, but display equipment I'll need for when the renovations are finished. Walking around what will be the shop area, I'm trying to decide what to do first. I've got so much I need to do with the layout before I can even open Magnolias.

The builders start the renovations on Monday. There will be some demolition of walls, the existing counters, and shelving to happen first, and I want to be part of it all. Sledgehammer, here I come. It'll be good to get my aggression out. I've already agreed with Grady, my contactor, that I can do some of it. *Supervised.*

Pinning the plans to the walls ready for Monday, I step back and take a look around. My vision for the shop is bright and colourful. I want it to stand out; vivid pinks, greens, purples, oranges—a whole array of beautiful colours, just like the contents of my wardrobe. Wearing bright colours can really lift your mood and that's what I want. I want my customers to feel welcome and uplifted when they walk in.

Looking over to the colour swatches on the opposite wall, I need to decide on what I want for the office and the apartment so I can get the order in before they start decorating upstairs next week. But I just can't focus. I can't keep my mind out of the gutter. Off Owen. We never got to the end of my twenty questions. Owen had other ideas with rounds two, three, and four with so much kinky fuckery in between, and a hell of a lot of orgasms. It's no wonder I'm in a daze and unable to put anything into action. That was before we got to eat the rest of the cold pizza and drink the warm beer. I'd never been so hungry.

Or horny.

Just standing here, I can feel where he's been. Remembering what we did, I ache in every muscle, some I never even knew existed. Even with going to the gym as much as I do. Each throb reminds me how he used his mouth and that magic fucking tongue of his to make me come so hard I saw stars. Right there on the edge of the shop counter. Then I remember all over again just how he fucked me up against the wall I'm looking at right now, my legs wrapped around him so tight, I can feel the ache there too. The office, the kitchen, the shop, you think it would have satisfied the itch, but I just want more... of him, more of what we did, more of, shit, *no.* He made the need I have for him worse, not better.

I give up, sinking to the floor, crossing my legs, and leaning back against the cold wall, staring at the large windows that should face the street but are currently covered up. I give myself a few minutes to calm down and get focused.

The movers should be here in about fifteen minutes to drop off my belongings from the house. Then I need to crack on. Get this done. Closing my eyes for the briefest second, this was not how it was meant to go. No men, that's what I said to myself on the way down here. Hold off until I'm settled in.

That didn't last long, not even one day, and I slept with someone I don't even know and have been continuing to sleep with him. It's been two days, two freaking days, so much for my no-men rule. My shoulders drop at the thought of my lack of self-control.

My phone buzzes in my pocket. I fish it out to see Annie's smiling face, my work bestie and paralegal from my old firm. Swiping the button, I answer the video call. "Good morning. Are you at work already?" I ask, as she holds the phone back so I can see the office and her outfit, She looking amazing as always.

"Yep. Got an early meeting with Simon. I just wanted to check in and see how the move went?" Groaning, I forget she's not seen it in real life. She'll laugh when she sees the mess I have to deal with.

"I'll turn the phone around and show you the shop. It needs so much work doing to it, but the contractor said he should be done in four weeks, so more like six." I laugh and she chuckles with me.

I turn the camera. "I didn't realise just how big it was," she says with a gasp. "I bet you have so many plans for it, shit it's a mess!" she adds, eyes wide. "I want workshops, events, a section for local business to display their work, so many things," I tell her excitedly. "I just need to remember to pace myself. This is not London, and things may work a little differently here."

"I still can't believe you did it. You left me here to deal with all this, and Simon's moody face."

"Give him some slack. He's so stressed out with that case." She just raises her eyebrows. She's not as sympathetic as I am. "I'd like to say I'm sorry, but I'm not."

"I could use a good sleep. Maybe I'll come and visit soon. Once you're all up and running."

"You don't fancy helping me? Getting your hands dirty?"

"Not a fucking chance. I don't get my hands dirty for anyone. Do you know how much these nails cost to maintain?" She waves her highly manicured nails into view, then I show her my less than perfect ones, making her tut. "How the mighty have fallen," she chuckles, "it's only been two days. Right, got to go. Speak soon." Hanging up, sighing, my head falls back onto the wall. I'm going miss our daily chats. My mind goes back to Owen as soon as I look around me again.

Closing my eyes, smiling to myself as I think about the hours we spent tangled together. It's never been like that for me. I had to kick him out at three this morning. I needed my rest, and I knew he would have just gone for round five had he stayed. The man is insatiable. Even that blows my mind. Sex *four times.* I mean... Fuck. Literally. The smile that pulls on my lips says it all.

I enjoyed every second of it. Even kicking him out was satisfying. The kiss he left me with was beyond torturous. I had to fight the urge to haul him back through the door for a repeat performance. He knew it too. That's the most unbelievable thing. He walked out of here, knowing exactly what he was doing to me. Judging by the tent in his jeans as he left, it wasn't just me who was affected by the kiss.

It's been a good couple of days all round. Millie called yesterday to tell me her good news. They got him. Fucking Glen. He was in Spain and the police have him. The sense of relief I feel is overwhelming. I bet it's nothing compared to how she and Jack are feeling today.

She also said she was ready to let her hair down at the ball on Saturday. I'm so excited for her and comforted to know that she'll be safe now. With Glen behind bars and in another country, it's a good feeling. One I want to celebrate with her. Millie can finally build the life she wants and so desperately deserves.

My eyes fly open like a bolt of lightning has struck my thoughts. *Shit...* tomorrow. The ball's tomorrow. I still need to get a dress. I may be able to wear that couture dress I found in a little boutique shop in the back streets of London. It's stunning. I just hope I can find it when my things get delivered. I don't have time to go shopping today.

I let myself go back to thinking about how well everything is going. I have a fuck buddy, a new shop, and an apartment I can't wait to get settled in.

I can't see the walls in my apartment for all the boxes and furniture in the way. The movers have been and gone. I'm sitting on the sofa upstairs when my phone buzzes with a message.

Millie: I feel terrible not being able to help you out today. I hope it's going ok.

Me: It's going great. Don't worry about me. You have far too many things to get sorted for the ball. How's it going?

Her position as purchasing manager at The Manor seems to have developed into events manager, helping Jack set up the ball with his best friend and business partner Dan.

Millie: There's still so much to do, but I've given everyone a list and that alone makes me happy.

Me: *laughing emoji.* I forgot how much you love a list.

Millie: Lists are life *serious emoji.*

Me: *laughing emoji.* Do I need to bring anything for dinner tonight? I can't wait to catch up with you and Jack.

Millie: No, just your beautiful self.

Me: Okay x

I turn my attention to the contents of my life filling the space around me. The last time I moved I had so much help. My brothers, Christian and Corban, helped Andy move us into the three-story house. While myself, Mum and Dad unpacked all the basics and set us up for our first night together in our new home.

There's a thickness in my throat when I think about how long it's been since I've seen my brothers. I miss them. They got assigned to some special unit in the Army. Untouchable, they called themselves and unreachable for anyone around them.

I open Instagram. I know I shouldn't, but I look at Andy's profile, seeing the pictures of the new baby. She's cute—looks just like him. I can't help the pang of jealousy. That could have been us.

I think deep down I wasn't ready because I didn't actually want kids with him. I still like to torture myself about it all anyway. The what ifs, the could haves and whys. *Would we have broken up anyway at some point?* I mean, even if he hadn't cheated *multiple times* with *multiple* women and then got one of them pregnant. I don't know. Maybe? It still hurts. I don't love him anymore that's for sure, but the pain is still there. Along with my fragile heart and determined mind. My trust in men has been obliterated.

Back to the task in hand, pushing myself off the sofa that's still wrapped in industrial cling film. *I'll take that off later.* Making my way back downstairs, there are a few boxes left that need to be taken upstairs and that one huge snug chair. The movers buried it under some boxes and now I have to move it up by myself. *I can do it. Right?*

I've already taken the cushions up, so it's just the chair itself. But after moving the boxes up and down the stairs helping the movers, for the last god knows how long I feel like I can't lift my arms anymore. It's curved so maybe I can roll it up? Maybe I can wait till Monday and ask one of the builders to do it. Nah, why ask a man when you can do it yourself?

I'm about to push it towards the stairs when my phone rings and it takes me a few seconds to realise it's upstairs.

"Fuck-sake," I curse while I sprint up the steps with heavy limbs. Grabbing it off the sofa where I left it, I answer it without looking.

"Hello," I say, slightly out of breath.

"Is everything alright, Charlotte?" Now there are only three people who call me by my full name: my mum and dad and my old boss, Simon Brooke.

"Simon, what do I owe the pleasure of your call? I'm sorry, it's moving day. I had to search for my phone."

He chuckles. "I want to ask you a question?" As always, he's just business.

"Fire away," I say, settling down on the sofa that's facing the wrong way in my living room.

"I'd like you to continue working with us. For me." I thought he would have given up by now.

"Simon, we've been through this," I tell him, a little frustrated he keeps asking.

"You were always good at seeing what others couldn't, finding the missing pieces to the puzzle. I need someone on my side, Charlotte," he says, and I can hear him tapping his pen, probably against his huge antique oak desk. Something he only does when he's under a lot of stress.

"Thank you, but I'm going to have to say no. As much as I would like to help you, I just don't have the time right now. What else has happened, Simon?" Leaning forward slightly, my stomach in knots. The last case I worked on, I had to hand back to Simon to take over when I handed in my resignation a month ago. I don't want to get sucked back into that world.

"I can't tell you, not unless you decide to work for me again. Just say you'll think about it... please?" he sounds even more anxious and worn out than usual.

"I'll think about it, I promise. Is everything okay?" my concern rises when his voice wavers.

"In all seriousness, Charlotte, I don't know anymore." He hangs up before I can say another word and the knot in my stomach gets a little tighter because Simon's never done that before. *Shit.*

I'll call him back in a few days. See if I can get to the bottom of this.

"Who was that?"

I scream as I look up to find Owen standing in my kitchen. Leaning against the countertop like he has always been there. "Fuck me," I mumble.

"With pleasure," Owen replies, raising his eyebrows at me, before looking through a box in front of him.

"Ha, funny. How do you do that? With the sheer size of you, how do you sneak up on people like that?" Standing, I walk to the kitchen, moving the box away from him. It has a few bedroom items in I'm not willing for him to see.

"I've already seen what's in there. You can be sure we'll be using those at some point." That sets my lady parts on fire, right there. I back away slightly because if I don't, I will jump him. I want to shower first before I do anything else. Again? Was yesterday not enough? My body reacts to him just standing there. Lean, muscled, dark, sexy... my body inwardly shivers with the thought.

"Stealth is my superpower." he reaches for the box again, but takes it to the bedroom, placing it on my bed. That's one thing I've managed to get sorted today, so it's ready for me to collapse into later.

"Comparing yourself to a superhero is a little big-headed, isn't it?" leaning down, I shift a couple more boxes, and when I turn around, I crash into his chest. Hard, sculpted, warm, solid, unbreakable.

Planting my hands on him, his hands go to my hips and he pulls me closer. So much for trying to maintain my distance. My body tries to defy me, wanting to get as close as possible.

"Who was that on the phone? It sounded serious?" he asks again, but I'm not willing to answer.

"Nothing you need to know about," I say, still trying to escape him as his hands sneak down to my arse and it does all the amazing zingy things to me.

Taking a deep breath, I manage to catch myself before I get lost in him. Again. "No, I need to get stuff done before I can even think about doing that again," I tell him, looking over him, like the hot, sinful, tempting god of a man he is. "And I'm not sure I can. My lady parts can only take so much. They may need a rest." My lady parts, however, seem to have other ideas. I need to take control of the urge to lift his t-shirt and lick him.

Pointing down to the offending and treacherous area, I look into those emerald green eyes of his and watch the frown form on his face. Then a look crosses his face. I'm not sure what it is; a glint in his eyes.

"I can help on every count. No sex, but I will make you feel better. What stuff do you need to do? Other than me." smirking at me, I can't help but laugh. He's got such an easy charm about him. Cheeky, but so caveman at the same time. I want to be disgusted at myself for how much I like that side, but I just can't. I like what I like... and right now, caveman is apparently doing it for me on *every* level.

"I need that big chair downstairs moving up here, I need to find my dress for the ball tomorrow and I need to get showered before I head to Millie's."

"Consider it all done," he states before heading downstairs without a backwards glance.

I start hunting for my dress. Three boxes and a lot of mess scattered around my new apartment later, I spot a sea of blue and gold. Bingo. Taking it from the box, I hang it up, ready to take into the bathroom later so the steam when I shower can ease out the creases.

"Who's taking you to the ball?" Owen appears again. The frown on his perfect, menacing face is set firm as he looks over the dress.

"No one. Millie only invited me the other day. I don't know anyone apart from her, Jack, Em, and Dan, and I suppose you now. That reminds me. We need to finish those twenty questions," I add, trying to sort the carnage around me.

"I'll take you." It's not a question. I'm stunned for a moment. I don't want to date anyone. I don't want a relationship. What we have already is good, more than good, *amazing actually*. The sex, that's what I mean, that's all it is. Amazing sex.

"This," I say, pointing between us, "is just sex. If you take me to the ball, it means more. I'm not ready for more. I don't want or need more." Although, the way my body reacts to him, I'm not sure I want to get rid of that soon either.

"No strings attached, promise." Arching a single dark brown eyebrow, those eyes focus on me. *Shitting hell, I'm in trouble.*

"Umm... I'll think about it. Did you need a hand with the chair?

"Already done. We just need to take that shower."

We?

"What? How? How did you do it? You know what, I don't care, but thank you... wait..." I pause when I notice a look in his deep green eyes. Maybe it's mischief. Need. I don't care what the look is, it sets me on fire.

"We... are not taking a shower together. I'm hot, sweaty, and dirty. Not happening, Owen. I'm showering on my own." He stalks towards me. Oh my god, I want to tackle him to the floor and take whatever he is willing to give me, even in my current state. The worst part is, I know it will be good. I need to find a better word to describe what happens between us, because *good* does not do it justice. It feels...

Intense?

Heated?

Powerful?

Right?

"Yes, we are. I said I would make you feel better and the best way to do that is to... let me make you feel *good*." Emphasising the word *good*, his tongue traces his lower lip as he reaches for me. "Plus, I like you hot, sweaty, and dirty. It's one of my favourite combinations so far." I step back, but my legs hit the bed and I have no option but to stay where I am, trapped.

"How could you possibly make me feel *good*?" I tease, slipping off my trainers and stepping up on the bed, so my chest is directly in his face. I grab the hem of my top, lifting it over my head, and tossing it down beside my feet.

"I'll soothe every ache you have in that shower." His voice is playful and low. Reaching round to my back, he unhooks my bra and slides it down my arms. His fingers graze my sides, while he runs the tip of his nose down the centre of my chest, my body erupting with shivers so divine I have to hold back a moan.

"Umm..." It's a low rumble that makes me squeeze my thighs together. He smiles, as he hooks his thumbs in each side of my joggers, slipping them off along with my knickers. And just like that, I'm naked in front of Owen Archie Stone, again, while he is fully dressed. I need to rectify this situation.

"This is not fair. Strip and I may see about the shower thing." I can't help but laugh a little as he strips in what feels like seconds, leaving him stark naked in front of me. For a man I've slept with multiple times, I've never seen him naked. Last night it was too dark to take in the fine details of his body, but right now, in the brightly lit room of my new apartment, I can see *everything*.

My tongue slips out to lick my lips in appreciation, pulling my bottom lip in between my teeth, in the hope this will stop me from whimpering like a puppy ready to lick... well, anything right now.

Lean, muscular, and magnificent.

What really takes my breath away is his tattoo. I'm not sure how I could have missed it. It is huge and dark, with shades of greys and blacks. The design is exquisite; fire and flames all wrapped in a design style I have never seen before, like a mix of tribal and intricate life-like drawings. It's beautiful and breathtaking just like him.

Reaching my hand out to trace it, I start at his shoulder, outlining where the flames run down his arm, my breath catching when I trail my fingers over his tight pecks flickering around his side and back, down to below his boxer line, where they would disappear if he were wearing any, but right now he's not and my fingers keep going towards where the intricate mix of flames and triable design end and his impressive manhood stands proud.

I need to breathe.

"You like?" he questions, but I can't reply. It's phenomenal. He's phenomenal. With this and his cheeky, manly, demanding, caveman ways combined, I... how can I combat what is happening in between my legs... between us?

Freaking impossible

I try to clear my throat, but it comes out as a whimper. I look up to find Owen's hooded eyes, a deeper shade of emerald, searching for what, I'm not sure.

"Take me to the shower," I say on an exhale. He takes my hand, lacing our fingers together before leading the way.

I'm glad the apartment was refurbished before I bought it. It's light, bright and spacious. The bathroom is no different, with a walk-in shower and separate bath.

Owen turns the shower on and pulls me in, making me gasp as the cold water hits my overheated body.

Stepping under the water with me, he lifts my chin with his fingers and kisses me. His kiss is tender, deep, and sensual, his fingers tugging at my wet hair, exciting a gasp from my lips.

"Let me clean you up," he says breathlessly against my lips when he eventually breaks our kiss. He turns me so my back faces him as he squeezes the cherry-scented shower gel directly onto my body, working it up into a bubbly lather with his hands.

I've never showered with anyone like this before and I'm wet in more ways than one as he cleans every inch of me with tenderness and warmth. When his hand dips between my thighs, the low rumble in his chest tells me he likes what he's found.

"You feel good, Angel," he says into my ear, before he spins me around, pressing my back to the cold shower tiles. "It's all you," I tell him. He lowers himself to his knees, water droplets hitting his back, like they are trying to put out the flames that cover his body, but with no success.

Spreading my legs, he lifts one over his shoulder, followed by the other. My hands grip his hair. I'm already on edge, and he's not done anything yet.

Balanced between the wall and his shoulders, his face is between my thighs and his hands hold my arse in place, his mouth and tongue already lapping up the effect he has on me.

"Oh, my god." He possesses me like he's ravenous and can't get enough. I know I'm swollen down there from what we did yesterday, but I don't care and he doesn't seem to either.

With each lick, suck, and swirl of his tongue, I have to grip harder, my head falling back onto the tiles as the crazy feelings he's stirring up inside me sweep over me. Pleasure surges through me, wrapping around my core, tightening until it's all I can focus on and I come. No, I explode. When I slowly float down from my high, he's still enjoying every second of what he has just so expertly bestowed on me. Looking up at me with so much heat in his eyes, I know I need to repay the favour if we are not having sex tonight. He needs to enjoy this too.

Owen slowly lowers my legs that feel like jelly, but holds on to me when I wobble. He captures my mouth with his in almost the same way he did with my core. It's hard, bruising, and soul-capturing. My arms wrap around his neck, gliding over his broad, toned shoulders. Desperate to return the favour, I slide down against the tiled wall until his engorged dick is aimed right at my face.

"Angel, you don't have to... fuck—" That's all he gets out as I take him in my mouth.

Chapter Seven

Face-to-Face

Owen

The way she went down on me in the shower just about blew my mind. Watching her sweet lips wrap around my shaft and have her swallow down every drop when I came was breathtaking.

Beautiful.

She thinks I didn't see it in her eyes when she was staring at me, tracing my tattoo like she owned me. She's not willing to admit it yet, but something's changed. It's something I'll work on if I can set some work things straight. I said I'd take her to the ball, and after our shower together, she agreed. Just so we could have some more kinky fuckery. Her words, not mine. They bring a smile to my face, just like she does every time I think about her.

I'm back at my desk. It's more like a studio apartment than an office. It's well past office hours. Everyone has either left or is out doing what they are paid to do. Apart from Leon. He's in the office next door. He tore me a new one after I disappeared on him again today. Even though our current case has been downgraded, we still have a shit-tonne of paperwork and documents to go through. I need to catch up. I've been more than a little distracted.

My gut's telling me something is off with Millie's ex. I get the feeling something isn't right. I just need to prove it. The reports indicate the Spanish police have him in custody, but I'm still waiting for face-to-face confirmation. Elliot, from our northern branch, flew out the other day. He's trying to gain access for us, but the police are being stubborn even though we have the right paperwork.

I need confirmation it's actually him. I need eyes on him. I never close a job until I have seen them in the flesh, behind bars, dead, or somewhere in between. Then I know that whoever I'm looking after is safe.

I can't concentrate. The stuff with Jack and Millie is fucking with my head. Even though the job is almost done, I just need to tell him about what happened when Millie was drugged. I'll do it tomorrow. Leon's still pissed with me about it and it's toying with me. When I'm not a hundred per cent the team feels it too and that's the last thing I want. We're family, and I over-stepped.

I know when I tell Jack I withheld information about Millie, he'll want to kill me. We may lose any future work with him and his companies because of my stupid decisions.

It'll be a huge loss for us, but it won't send us under. Even if I remove myself from the job lists for a while, the boys will be secure even with my fuck up. I have to tell him the truth. It's keeping me awake at night. Between the pull I feel for Charlie, this job, and things with Jack, I feel like I need to step back. My actions have and will affect those around me. One in particular. *Charlie,* I should never have asked her to the ball. Not when I knew I needed to tell Jack. But when I saw that dress, imagined her in it, the realisation that someone else could be taking her, some other fucker could have his hands on her, it hit me hard. I couldn't let that happen.

Maybe tomorrow will bring a new, better perspective and I won't have to do what I don't want to do—let her down. Not now, when I can see the change in her eyes.

Chapter Eight
Renouncing Men

Charlie

Applying my final layer of nude lipstick, I take one last look in the mirror. My backless dress looks so good and I know it's going to drive Owen crazy when he sees it.

I feel like a schoolgirl getting ready for prom. The anticipation, waiting for my date to arrive. Although I did make it clear, this was not a date. He's just taking me. An escort. I chuckle at my own joke. An escort indeed. If he put those skills out in the world, he'll be booked solid for years to come. An uncomfortable feeling settles in my chest at the thought of him with someone else. Rubbing it away with my freshly painted nails, I move into the living room to wait. He should be here in a few minutes. Just as I'm about to place my phone in my tiny gold bag, it buzzes with a message from the man himself.

The OG: *Charlie, I won't make it tonight – O*

I'm confused. There's nothing more, no explanation. I'm way more disappointed that he won't get to see me in this amazing dress. Maybe I'll send him a photo and show him what he'll be missing out on.

When I don't get a response, I let out a sigh, as disappointment rears its ugly head. I put my phone in my bag. It must be work-related, I understand if he has to leave unexpectedly. I'm not an idiot. I'd never stop him from doing something that needs to be done. I'd expect the same in return if I needed to do something urgently.

Grabbing my keys from the side, I get in my car and drive the short distance to The Manor Hotel, where I plan to leave it for the night.

I can't wait to see Millie all dressed up. I love that she invited me as soon as she knew I was here to stay. Millie wanted us to have some fun, the three of us together. I don't know Em that well yet, but I'm sure after yesterday when I offered to step in and help with her wedding flowers after her florist cancelled on her, we'll become good friends. Even with the disappointment sitting in my chest from Owen backing out, I'm really looking forward to tonight.

Walking up the lantern-lit steps, the place looks absolutely breathtaking. There's a theme for the event, and this one is most definitely jungle. Fitting for some of the music-themed nights they put on at Jack's club in Ibiza. And Millie's gone all out with helping Jack and Dan plan the event. This is *amazing*. There are plants everywhere. It's delicately lit, allowing a seductive yet vibrant atmosphere. The music's playing already, and as I step inside, I spot Jack and Dan at the entrance to the ballroom, giving out goody bags to anyone who enters.

I'm not going in yet. I told Millie I'd wait at the bar for her. Jack nods when he spots me making my way over to the main bar area, while Dan gives me an excited wave.

Walking through the huge archway, my heart stutters, then drops.

He lied.

Blinking rapidly, because I really don't understand what I'm seeing. Owen's sitting in an armchair in the bar's lounge area, suited up, drink in hand, talking with Leon like he belongs there.

He *fucking* lied.

His phone's sitting on the table in front of him. He ignored me and my message. And came anyway.

I'm so fucking angry. That's one thing I will never take from any man again: lies.

My stomach sinks as my anger rises. Balling my fists at my sides, I stand at the entrance, watching in disbelief.

Then it hits me, smack bang in the face, realising what this is, what he did. Was it all just a plot to get me into bed? Don't get me wrong, I'm all for it, but... why tell me different? Why behave like you wanted more? He kept saying he wanted more. I can't take my eyes off him, unsure of everything.

He stands and turns, his eyes catch mine, a slight frown creasing his brow. *Did he think I wouldn't come on my own?* Shaking my head and holding my hand out to stop him as he starts walking towards me. I don't want to hear it. He stops. He knows he's fucked up. Regret written all over his face.

I don't want to admit how naïve I've been. I should never have let things happen with Owen, or at least see past what should have remained just sex. That's what I told myself. But when I said yes to him bringing me here, I don't know. Maybe it's some fairytale shit that deep down has me wondering if I could at least have a relationship again. To trust again. I should have known better.

Foolish hope.

And once again I crash and burn...

I don't care, well I do, but after tonight I won't. I'm going to allow myself one night to feel sorry for myself, then tomorrow is a new day. One without Owen. Fucking. Archie. Stone.

I make my way to the bar and order the first of many drinks. I still want an explanation. I just want a few minutes to get myself together. I deserve that, right?

Leon must have stopped him from coming after me, or I think he did because he's not next to me trying to explain what happened tonight.

Drunk, that's what I want to be right now. I want to forget; I want to sink into oblivion. It's the only thing I think of, so I don't lose my shit in front of the whole goddamn ball. *Foolish.* That's how I feel.

I'm not much of a drinker. In my old job there was never time. Even over client with clients, it was only one glass. Then after Andy did what he did and fucked up life as I knew it, I've drunk a little more, but never to excess.

Okay, there have been a few times in between, where I've drunk so I can numb, so I don't tear shit to pieces or ruin something I shouldn't.

Three drinks in, I'm still alone in a room full of people when I hear a familiar voice. "Something wrong, Charlie?" Millie appears next to me, looking like a million dollars in the sexiest emerald green gown I have ever seen. Em is by her side looking equally as stunning in a pale yellow dress that looks like it was made just for her. Brushing her hair behind her ear, she looks away, like she wants to leave us to it. I can't blame her really. The mood I'm in, I'm not going to be good company.

Even after all these years, Millie knows me well. She's been through so much and I wasn't there to help her. My heart sinks every time I think about it. I should have been there for her. In my inability to see what was really going on, I stepped away when Glen said she wanted nothing more to do with me. I should have fought harder to keep her in my life. I regret so much when it comes to Millie. And it's all my own fault. She looks so beautiful tonight, stunning, and happy, even after everything she's been through with that fucking ex of hers.

"Nope, nothing, just need to renounce men for a while," I tell her, putting my glass back down on the perfectly polished dark wooden bar. "They're all dickheads." I pick up another full glass of gin. It burns my throat when I swallow. They both stare at me before Em excuses herself. Millie stays while I order another double gin with a few shots of tequila to chase it down.

"What's happened? I didn't think you'd seen or heard from Andy in ages. What did he do?" She leans back against the bar, looking around her, but I can't look around. If I do, I'll start throwing things in *his* direction, hoping to hit him where it hurts.

"It's not Andy," I mutter, noticing the slight slur in my voice. "Although he's been showing off the baby on Instagram like we were nothing, and that just adds to my stupidity." I lift the shot glass to my lips and down it. *So good.* The buzz hums under my skin.

"If it's not Andy, then who has you renouncing men?" She's facing the crowd, in the opposite direction to me, her back leaning on the bar. Glancing at Millie, I watch as her eyes fall to Owen. I know they do. She shifts, looking back over her shoulder at me with unanswered questions in her eyes.

"It doesn't matter. I'm going to have a few drinks and enjoy myself." I don't really want to spoil her fun. She's worked so hard on this ball. Even with her shitty ex trying to sabotage her life, she does things to her best. I love that about her.

"Charlie, I think there's more to this. Please tell me," Millie pleads. I let out a sigh and knock back another shot. I can feel it numbing me from the inside, which is just what I need.

"If it has anything to do with the tall, dark-haired beauty of a man who seems to have eyes on you constantly?"

"Nope. It's my own stupidity, Millie. I need to get a life." I shrug.

"You and me both." She laughs, and side hugs me as she orders a glass of fizz for herself.

"You have started the best life here for yourself, Millie, all on your terms. And Jack, you have him hooked. He's one of the best. I can tell just by the way he looks at you. It's beautiful to see the two of you together. What you two have, it's what we're all looking and hoping for." The blush that runs across her cheeks says it all. "I'm proud of you, Millie." She nudges me, smiling like she knows what I'm saying is the truth.

I'm not sure I have that hope anymore. I'm tired of trying.

"Right, don't let my sorry ass drag you down. Go and see if you can find that dream man of yours. I'll be around, doing what I do best." Although I don't know what that is anymore. It used to be my old job, but since those photographs were dropped on my desk, I couldn't just sit there anymore, knowing that the people I worked with, the people I spent most of my time with, knew all about what happened. I couldn't do it.

"We will talk about this, Charlie," she warns. "You're not getting out of this conversation. We're getting together next week. I want updates on everything." She points her finger at me, before raising her eyebrows towards Owen.

"You can't hide from me, Charlie. I know you," she says.

"I know you do," I laugh.

Watching her walk away, I know I'll have to talk to her eventually. I just need to get shitfaced first. Forget this evening, the last few days with Owen, and start again. Maybe it's third time lucky. *Hope?* It's a flicker, which I stub out before I let myself think any further.

"Two more shots please," I ask the hot barman. His eyes drift over me, staying focused on my boobs for a flicker of a second before he smiles and grabs the bottle, pouring me liquid gold. Well, tequila.

"On the house," he declares before winking at me. I smile back because who doesn't like a bit of attention after a shitty evening?

"Haven't you had enough?" I shiver, his voice affecting me in ways that should be illegal. It's Owen and my brain turns to mush for a split second, remembering how he did all the things so well. Then my anger flares. He does not get to tell me what to do. I've known him for four days.

Just four days? Is that all? I feel like I've known him forever.

"What did you just say?" I don't even turn around, knocking back both shots before the urge to throw them in his face overwhelms me.

"You heard what I said. No more, Charlie. It's no good for you." I can feel him behind me. He's not touching me, but I feel him. Warm, addictive. My body wants to betray me. It wants to be in his hands, wrapped around him, letting him do it all. Kinky fuckery, not kinky fuckery, anything in between. My body would happily accept it. I would happily accept it. But today my anger wins. Right at this moment, I'm glad my dress is sexy as fuck. I want to shove what he could have had in his face. I know it's not the mature thing to think, but where has being mature got me so far? Cheated on, repeatedly, divorced, moving across the country, starting again. And then this... fuck being mature.

Taking a deep breath, I nod to the barman and he pours me another, his eyes shifting warily between me and Owen.

"What I do tonight is none of your business. You made your choice, Owen." He has some nerve, trying to tell me what to do. The second I spin around, I know he's right and I've had too much, in too short a space of time. My brain takes a second to catch up with the move and I sway a little and his hands are on me. They burn... so hot. I can't take it.

"Don't," I whisper, sucking in a shallow breath.

"Charlie, please let me explain," he spits out, but I shove his hand from my waist and step to the side. I need space from him.

"I don't like liars, Owen."

"Charlie, I didn't lie. I just—" He tries to reach for me again, but I hold my hand up to stop him mid-sentence. I thought I was ready for an explanation. Turns out I'm not. I can't be around him.

"Too late, I'm done." I walk away as fast as I can. It's a good job there are two bars in this place.

I find a hideaway; a small lounge just off to the side of the main event, sinking right into a huge sofa.

I'm drunk, drunker than I've been in a long time. I can't feel my lips. Stupid feelings. Stupid me. No. Stupid men. Stupid heart. *Stupid hope...* I'll just sleep here. I'm not sure I can stand anyway, or use my thumbs to use my phone and get an Uber. I have no coordination, that's why I sat down in the first place. Now I can't stand up.

I lean my dizzy head against the arm of the sofa and let my eyes drift closed, ready to let sleep take over. There's a lot of noise going on right now, music, people laughing and talking. I let it take over, washing over me like a warm blanket of noise.

"Shit." It's a faint sound. I like it. I don't open my eyes, I can't open them. Whoever that is can just leave me alone. I must be drunker than I thought because I feel like I'm floating. Warm and safe, that's what I feel now. I know I'm dreaming because I hear that voice again. This time it's closer, almost like a whisper in my ear.

"Charlie, I'm putting you in my room for the night. Sleep it off. We'll talk in the morning."

"Umm." Sleep, fresh start, third time lucky...

My phone won't stop ringing, the sound of a million messages coming through at the same time. I don't want to move. I'm not hungover, maybe still a little drunk. I don't want to move because it means facing things. I just want to ignore it all, the mess, the lies, the flicker of hope I had, my own stupidity... Owen. I want to go back to starting again, again.

I'm not even sure where I am. I know I'm in a bed, still in my dress, albeit a little less put together than I was at the start of the evening. It's also not my bed. I also have no idea what time it is. It's not quite dark out, but that means nothing in the middle of the summer.

Eyeing the nightstand next to me, I recognise the style of the room, the neutral tone with pale greens and hints of black. I'm at The Manor. I have no idea how I got here or whose room it is. Lifting my phone from the nightstand, I unplug it, rolling over onto my side, a small note crunches, sticking to my cheek. Extracting it from my face, in its now wrinkled state, I read it.

I would never lie to you, Angel.
Sleep it off, we'll talk tomorrow.
O xx

I suppose that solves the mystery of whose room this is, who brought me here, and whose bed I'm in. He's still looking out for me.

Looking at my phone, I have fifteen missed calls from Owen, as well as messages from Em, Dan, and more messages from Owen. They all say the same thing.

Millie's been shot.

And I slept through it all.

Chapter Nine

Unknown

Charlie

I can't catch my breath, I don't know what to do. I'm shaking almost uncontrollably. There's a pain in my chest I can't get rid of. The harder I try to soothe it with the palm of my hand, the worse it seems to get.

Standing in the middle of the room, I'm looking around for something that will help me. I can't think straight. Millie's been shot, *fucking shot*. I know nothing else. No details, nothing. Tears stream down my face as my phone that's still in my hand starts to ring. My eyes are too blurry to focus on who it is, so I swipe to answer.

"Finally, Angel. Where are you?" I can't answer as a sob escapes my throat. "Shit, I'm sending someone to pick you up. Are you still at the hotel?"

"Yes," I manage. It's weak and lifeless.

"Be outside in ten minutes. Cole's on his way to you."

"H… how…" I break down, fumbling to get myself together. I need my shoes.

"I'll explain everything when you get there. Millie's in surgery."

Finding my small bag on the table where my phone was, I walk to the door, my phone still pressed to my ear.

"I'm just leaving the police station. I'll meet you there," he says, his tone rushed.

"Owen..."

"Everything's going to be okay, Angel," he tries to promise, but even I can hear the slight hesitation in his voice.

Leaving Owen's room, I make my way downstairs. I don't know what I expected, but this was not it. It's chaos, people everywhere, scattered, mingling with the police, giving statements. What was warm, buzzing and fun has now become a crime scene, one my best friend was the centre of.

Millie was shot.

I can't get my head around it. These things don't happen. I mean, you hear about it happening. You just never think it will happen to anyone you actually know.

Walking through the reception area, I'm approached by a police officer, asking if I am willing to make a statement. I shake my head. There's nothing to tell right now.

"Here's my card, if I could just take some details from you?"

"She's my best friend. I need to get to the hospital." My voice is a gravelly whisper.

"Sure, miss..." It takes me a moment to register what he's asking. He wants to know my name.

"Charlie... Charlotte Hudson. I own Magnolias" I don't know why I say it, it's not even a shop yet.

"Magnolias?"

Now I have to explain. "The old hardware store on the hill."

Nodding, he notes it down. I give him my number, then move around him. Stepping outside, I see more disarray as police officers set up tents, talk over radios, and get what they need. *It must have happened out here.* I see the crime scene team kneeling by a car, a pool of blood drying on the floor. I'm standing, staring, when I feel a hand on my elbow. My eyes are drawn up to see Cole standing next to me, ready to take me to Millie.

The ride to the hospital is silent, well I think it is. I'm so lost in my worry for Millie, I can't think past the pain she must be in. I have no idea how long it takes us to get there. I don't even know if Cole spoke to me.

I don't even wait for the car to pull to a stop before I'm swinging the door open and jumping out. I hear a loud low curse as I do. I just don't stop, running into the hospital.

I see him immediately, Owen walking towards me, his worrying gaze lands on mine. His pace picks up, running to me, and I stumble into his open arms. He engulfs me, holding me while I cry into his chest, his hand stroking my hair tenderly. I feel safe.

"Angel, let's go somewhere a little more private." Agreeing with a small nod of my head, he guides me to an empty waiting room. He tenses slightly as the door bangs behind us. Sitting down, he rests me in his lap, holding me tighter, allowing me the time I need to get myself together.

"I need you to listen, Angel," he mummers into my hair, placing a soft kiss on my temple as I lift my head to meet his tired eyes. "I'm going to tell you everything. I just don't want to do it all in front of Jack and the others. They've been through enough."

"Oh god, yes, okay." I grip his shirt in my hand, anchoring myself to him.

"Millie's in surgery. She's been there for a few hours now. Glen," he starts, and I shudder at the name.

"Wait... I thought he was..." I ask confused, "he was in Spain?"

"The police got it wrong. It wasn't him." Anger laces his words as he holds me just a little tighter, his jaw tense.

"Fucking hell." It's all so surreal.

"He grabbed Em outside, made her send Millie a message saying it was her life or Millie's. She..." he pauses sucking in a breath, "Millie should have come to us. We were standing right in front of her when she left the ballroom. Fuck." It's killing him. His whole body is tense, shaking slightly as he says, "Instead, she went to change places with Em and decided to do it on her own without our help." He's not blaming her, he's blaming himself. I just watch and listen, still unable to really believe what's happened.

"By the time I got there, Millie was swapping places with Em. Dan tried to grab her. I had to hold him back," he looks up to the ceiling, "then, the fucker stabbed her..."

"Holy shit, Owen?" I let out a pained cry. Glen stabbed her. My heart's breaking for her, for everything she's been through.

"After that, he pulled a... a gun out on her, shot once at the ceiling." He flinches at the memory. "Jack came rushing out. It took everything I had to hold him back. I had to choose. I couldn't let them both be hurt, I knew Leon was coming around the front of the building to get behind him, and then he was walking away with her." He's sucking in breaths like he can't remember how to breathe. "Locked the glass entrance door behind him and threw her down the steps." My hand flies to my mouth. I feel sick. I want to comfort him, but I can't, I'm too stuck in my own shock and grief to move. Instead, I grip his shirt harder, hoping at least that he can feel that I'm with him "Within a minute we had the door unlocked, but we had to watch as he repeatedly beat her and held the gun on her." My hand presses to my stomach. How can anyone even possess such evil thoughts? My heart's broken for her.

"I..." I don't know what to say. I just sob harder for my best friend.

"As soon as we broke down the door, Jack and I ran out. I watched Leon take him out, pushed Millie to the side, I went to help Leon. A fight broke out. I watched the gun fall, the two of us trying to get Glen under control as he kept reaching for the gun, edging closer. He was feral, lost it. That's when the gun went off. He shot her. The bastard shot her." He freezes, his breathing laboured. Placing my hand on his chest, I tap over his heart.

"Owen, it's okay." He looks lost for a moment.

"It's far from okay, Charlie. I watched your best friend get shot. I watched as Jack caught her as she fell, the look on his face as she collapsed." Shaking his head, he clears his throat. "Anyway," his tone neutral, impassive almost, "that bastard is now behind bars. We have enough charges against him that he won't be seeing the light of day for a very fucking long time." He's cold, he won't look at me. I don't know what to do, so I just hold him, like he's held me through this. We sit for a while before he says anything else.

"Before we go and see the others, I wanted to explain what happened earlier between us." I raise my head from where it's been resting on his chest, looking at his beautiful forest-green eyes.

"You don't need to. It's not the right time, not now."

"Now is exactly the right time. I never lied to you, Charlie. I wanted to clear the air between myself and Jack. I knew he'd lose his shit with me when he found out I'd lied to him, and I didn't want you to see or be part of that. I tried to speak with him, but time ran away with me. I sent you that message because I thought..." His shoulders sag. "I don't know. I don't want you to see my mistakes. I'd planned on leaving after I spoke with Jack, then Leon sat me down..." His eyes meet mine. "Then you walked in. I didn't know what to do." Taking my hand with his he says, "I still needed to speak with Jack, but you were pissed I was there when I said I wouldn't be." Raising my hand to his lips, he kisses the tips of my fingers. "I tried to stay away from you. I just can't," he says in defeat.

"I don't want you to stay away from me." He feels too good to let go.

"I'm sorry. I never wanted to hurt you, I've never," he lets out a tired breath, "wanted to be *more* with someone."

"Owen, I may have overreacted," I admit. "When I saw you, I should have given you a chance to explain. That's on me, not you. Plus, we don't need to be anything more than what we are right now." He looks up, a small hopeful grin playing on his lips.

"So..."

"We can take it day by day. I've been burned, Owen, but what we have feels too good to pass up."

"I'm not happy your ex hurt you, Charlie, but I am grateful it brought you to me."

"Okay," I mumble. I don't really know what to say to that.

"Fuck, Charlie, I'm so sorry." The pain I feel with his words makes him easy to forgive, not that there was anything to forgive. Miscommunication's shit.

"I'll make it up to you," he says as his lips lightly brush over mine as we relax into a kiss that could take me away from everything going on around us. Deep, sensual, tender. So light, I could stay like this forever. Owen pulls away a few minutes later, setting me on my healed feet. His thumb traces away the tears that have stained my cheeks.

"We need to find the others, and I need to fill Jack in on what happened at the police station."

"Okay, lead the way." Leon joins us as we make our way up. I'm not classed as family, but the nursing staff don't question me when we get to the waiting room. I guess when you're as rich as Jack, you have some pull over who you let in.

Seeing Jack sitting there, his tux jacket discarded, his hair falling down his face, pulls at my heartstrings. I don't have to ask how he's feeling. He's distraught. It's written all over his face.

"What's the news?" I ask calmly, the wobble in my voice betraying me.

"No news yet," Jack replies. "She's still in surgery." he dips his head into his hands.

"She's stronger than she looks, Jack," I add, my hand giving a reassuring squeeze to his shoulder. Sitting with Dan and Em, on the opposite side of the waiting room, she tells me about the baby, and that they are all okay. I never knew she was pregnant. I guess Millie did.

Sitting back, I close my eyes and listen to Owen tell Jack about Glen's arrest, and all the finer details he told me before we came up here.

"We managed to give him a good kicking before the police arrived," Leon adds, a pleased smile on his face. Owen comes to my side a while later, wrapping me in his arms where I fall asleep on his chest, to his steady heartbeat, until a doctor walks in, stirring us all.

"Are you Miss Monroe's family?" she asks softly, holding the door slightly open, walking in when Jack confirms.

"Yes, how is she? Is she okay? Can I..." his words are rushed. We all wait for the doctor to answer.

"Miss Monroe's surgery went well. She is and will be okay, if not sore and in some pain for a little while. She's sleeping off the anaesthetic right now, and needs her rest," she adds.

"Can we see her?" Jack stands. He's not really asking. I think he'd go in anyway, no matter what they told him. I'm so glad she has someone like Jack now. Someone who really cares for her.

"I can't let you all in," she says. "Just one for tonight, and I shouldn't even be doing that, but given the circumstances, one of you can go in." we all look at Jack, nodding in encouragement for him to go.

The relief I feel overwhelms me. Owen pulls me close again, settling back into the chairs where we stay most of the night.

Chapter Ten

Unconventional

Charlie

She scared the shit out of all of us. After her emergency surgery, she was unconscious for almost six days. She's doing well, still recovering from the bullet wound to her abdomen, and will be for a while. She's even better knowing that her ex is behind bars, and will be for a long time.

Things changed pretty quickly between myself and Owen the night Millie was shot. He was everything I needed and more at the hospital. He told me about the conversation with Jack, why he said he couldn't make it, that he'd tried to get Jack alone before the ball, but it never happened. That's when he messaged me. He didn't want me any more involved than I already was. He said if it wasn't for Leon, Jack would have punched him. He didn't want me to see that. Owen understands that he should have been honest with me about it all. He was easy to forgive. There's also something he's not telling me. I have no idea what it is. I just know he's keeping something from me. He's a little more reserved when I ask him about work, especially about Millie and the case against her ex. I'm sure he'll tell me when he's ready.

I'm used to noise in the week. I've been rudely awoken every morning since the builders started on Monday. I gave them a key to let themselves in. Biggest mistake I ever made. I now have no warning before they arrive. And it's just noise. For at least eight hours of my day.

Owen's had to stop me going downstairs on a number of occasions in my underwear, to tell them to shut up. I don't like being woken up. I'm not a morning person. It takes me at least two coffees to realise what planet I'm on.

Today's Saturday, there should be no noise, there should be silence. Only silence.

"What's that noise?" I groan, feeling the bed for Owen, but I come up empty-handed. *What the hell?* My Saturday is going from bad to worse. Since last weekend we've not left each other's beds. He stays here mostly because the hours he works are utterly mental.

Sitting up, listening carefully, I can't hear anyone talking, just the sound of a drill being used. And the chime of a bell? Slipping my feet into my flip flops, I make my way through the kitchen, descending the stairs in just my bright pink knickers and one of Owen's shirts.

Searching around the shop for the offending noise, I find Owen, crouched down, looking ready to eat. He's dressed in dark jeans and a tight black t-shirt—his signature look.

"Owen, what are you doing making noise on a weekend?" I ask, surprised by what I'm seeing. He stops what he's doing and his eyes drift over to me. He laughs before groaning when he notices I've not buttoned up the shirt.

Kicking the front door to the shop he was drilling closed, he steps closer, tugging me into his chest in one quick movement. Ignoring his now roaming hands, I want to know why he has disturbed my sleep.

"Answer my question. Why do I hear noise?" I ask, pouting like a teenager.

"I'm fitting your new entry bell for the shop. You're always working upstairs or in one of the back rooms. You have no idea who's coming and going. At least this way you'll know when someone comes in and you can pop your beautiful head out and see who it is." He kisses my nose and I have no idea how to respond to that.

"Wow, I don't know what to say. You may have a slight hero complex," I tease softly.

"You don't have to say anything. I've also replaced the lock on the back door, so people have to buzz to get in."

"Oh, well, er, thanks." I like that he cares. We're not official, we've not told anyone about us. It's unconventional what we have. It's what we both want. It suits us. We do our own thing, then we come together and blow each other's minds.

There are the occasional moments when we act like an actual couple, like having lunch together... and dinner... and breakfast every day. *Huh, I guess we're more like a normal couple than I thought.*

"You're welcome. Now about this outfit you keep coming downstairs in." Taking a quick look down, I smile. The shirt smells of him. Clutching it, he lifts it just enough to get his hand on my arse.

"What about it?" My body reacts to his touch with a shiver that goes straight to my core.

"It looks better on you than it does me. I have a distinct feeling it's also why the builders keep coming early. Builders don't come in early. Ever." He's as serious as Owen gets, his tone laced with a hint of jealousy.

"Oh, well, if it gets them working a little *harder* in the day for me, I'm okay with it." Spinning out of his grasp, I make my way back upstairs, Owen following close behind. Flicking on the coffee machine when we make it to the kitchen, Owen grabs two cups from the cupboard and hands them to me.

It's a very domestic scene, one I'm not sure about, it feels too comfortable, but it feels right to have him here with me. Watching as the machine lights up, I grab the cream and sugar, while Owen places our cups under the machine, the smell of coffee filling the room.

"I know this is not how you planned your Saturday morning to go, but I have a job I need to be on today, and I wanted to fit the bell before I left." It's sweet. I like this side of Owen; the side that wants to take care of me. "I was planning on coming back to bed to wake up very slowly before I left," he adds, brushing the hair from my shoulder, his lips pressing to the pulse point on my neck.

"I guess you missed out this morning, then." I fucking love tormenting him. It sparks the fire in his eyes, turning them a deeper green. I reach for the coffee capsules beside him and his hand wraps around my wrist, bringing my hand to his hot mouth where he sucks on the tip of my fingers.

"You think I'm going to miss out?" I know what's coming, the anticipation that's building in my lower belly sparks to life.

"Yes, I do." We both know he's not going to be missing out. This is the best sort of foreplay. This side of Owen is my favourite. He's a god in bed, demanding my body to bend to his will. I fucking love it. I'll submit to him. *Any fucking day of the week.* I love the power play. Teasing him only makes him worse. It brings out the possessiveness I crave from him.

Getting bolder with my words, I say, "I think you'll have to wait." His eyes turn darker, a playful smirk turning up the corner of his lips a fraction, suggesting otherwise. We stand in silence for a few moments, our gazes locked as the anticipation builds like a heavy weight in the room.

His tone is so low, I barely catch it. "I hope you're ready, Angel." The thrill that sweeps through me makes my nipples harden until they're painful.

"I'm ready...but I have places to be today too. I need to get myself ready to visit Millie." He freezes for the briefest of moments and covers it quickly.

"Visiting starts in an hour and I don't want to miss my time with her." Before I can move away, he captures my mouth with his in a kiss so dominating it sends me weak at the knees.

"You will pay for that, Angel. I'm going to be hard all day. Just wait until I slide into bed later. I'll have you on your knees, fucking you so hard you'll be begging me to make you come." Holy fucking hell, this man. He's creeping in, burning down walls one at a time.

I don't have any words. I just let out a breath while his smirk widens to a full-blown smile.

Fucker.

"Looking forward to it, OG." He looks puzzled. I've not told him what I have saved him as in my phone.

"What does OG mean?"

"That's a secret I may keep for just a little while longer," I tease, as he taps my arse before picking up his coffee.

"Right," he says, frowning. "I'm sure I'll be able to get it out of you later."

Laughing, I have no doubt he will get an orgasm out of me later. I add, "I'm sure you will." I move to get dressed.

"Hey, you," I say as quietly as I can. Millie was asleep when I got here.

"I told Jack to head home and rest." Rolling her eyes, she nods towards the window leading to the hall. Jack's like a guard dog that never leaves.

"He's still outside, isn't he?" I ask.

She sighs. "Yep."

"You caught yourself one of the best there, Millie. I don't think you could have designed a better man for yourself."

"I know. I have to tell you something." Sitting in the seat beside her, I place some chocolate cake on her table. Watching her eyes light up, she takes it and gets stuck in. If it wasn't for the chef at The Manor, I'm not sure she would never eat an actual meal. She could live off coffee and chocolate cake if you let her.

"What did you need to tell me?"

Putting down the fork and swallowing the huge bite she took, she pauses for a moment before she shouts, "I'm engaged!"

"Oh my god, Millie, that's so fucking amazing," I cry, jumping from the chair. I want to hug her so hard and I almost do, but then remember she's in a hospital bed and sit back down. Instead, I take her hand and kiss it.

"I know. Look." She shows me the ring.

"Shitting hell, that's huge," I say as I pull it towards me to take a closer look. It's stunning.

"I know. Isn't it beautiful?" Her cheeks turn a deep shade of red.

"It's perfect Millie." Tears well in my eyes when we look at each other.

"Take a wild guess how he proposed?"

"Oh shit, was it bad?"

"No, it was perfect. Just very Jack style of doing things."

"Go on, tell me."

"I woke up with it on my finger."

"What?" I ask, confused.

"When I came round, it was already on my finger. He put it on me while I was unconscious. He said he wanted to know how it looked, but then he fell asleep and forgot about it. It was only when I said he had some explaining to do and showed him that he remembered doing it. I told him to ask me, and he did." Happiness is written all over her face.

"I can't tell you how happy this makes me, Millie. I promise I will be there for you through anything from this moment forward."

"Is that your proposal?"

"Fuck off." I laugh.

"Two proposals in one week. I'm a lucky woman. I'm going to have to turn you down though." She giggles and winces. "You see, I've met this man, six five, blue eyes, blond, and I think he really loves me for who I am."

"If I have to give you up for anyone, I guess it could be Jack." Jack opens the door, coming straight to Millie's side when he notices she's crying, wiping the tears away with his fingers.

"Why are you crying?" His concern for her is cute.

"I just told Charlie we're getting married."

"And it made you cry?" he questions. His face is priceless, eyebrows almost reaching his man bun, but I can see the small smile he's giving her.

"Happy crying. I had to turn down my other proposal today though." Fuck me, Jack's face turns to thunder and I have to bite the inside of my cheek to stop myself from laughing.

"Who?" It's one word. He's restraining himself. "Was it one of the doctors? A nurse?"

We both burst out laughing. We only tell him what she's talking about after a few minutes when he starts asking who he needs to fire.

It's good to be here with Millie. I know I've made the right decision to move down here. It's going to be good.

Chapter Eleven
Not Enough

Owen

It's been fourteen days since I fucked up and told Jack what happened to Millie at the bar. Right before he made his big speech at the summer ball. Not great timing on my part, but he heard me and Leon talking about everything that had happened. It's safe to say he lost his shit and took me outside.

How he kept his cool, I have no idea. If it was the other way around, and it was Charlie, I wouldn't have held back, friend or not. Which makes him a better man than me. Leon had to step in and calm him down after he pinned me against the wall. I would have let him hit me. I deserve everything coming to me from Jack. _It's all my fault._

He proceeded to tell me he'd deal with me later. I knew I'd lost us a contract, our best client, and maybe a friend. My head has been pounding with all the what if's and should haves about their safety.

Jack's not spoken to me since the night of the ball. I know it's because Millie's still in hospital, but I can't help but think that's it for our friendship. I'm in knots, going round in circles constantly. I should have had more staff on,

I should have refused to let Jack step the security down, I should have been quicker in my response. I didn't do enough before or during the ball. It's that simple.

My actions put everyone at risk, a whole hotel full of people, people I care about.

What if Charlie had been with Millie?

Leon's been trying to talk to me, get me to see sense, trying and failing. I can't look him in the eyes. It's all my fault. The more I think about it, the harder I hit the keys on my laptop, shuffle the paperwork, the statements, the images, and the police reports, as if it will give me some sort of redemption from the mistakes I've made.

My desk and office are a mess, just like my head. My brothers trust me to do my job well and do it right. I did neither of those things that night.

I should have flown to Spain myself; I should have followed my gut instinct. I knew something was off about the whole situation. My gut has never been wrong. I've always acted on it, but not this time. *Why?* All the signs were right fucking there. I should have kept the security up even after Jack insisted we step it down. I should have put more guys on the B team that night. I should have been part of the security, not a goddamn fucking guest. *Fuck.* Four guys, we only had four guys on the B team. The risk should have been minimal. Guess what? I was wrong about that too.

A lot can happen in one evening.

I'm questioning everything I did.

I'm questioning everything I do.

Fourteen days ago, shit went down that I should have been able to prevent. Millie got shot on my watch. Thank fuck she's okay. No thanks to me. Jack's not spoken to me and he's put Dan in charge while he takes care of Millie. I don't blame him. I don't want to talk to me either. Even the mention of her name brings it all back...

Bang—my ears ring with the sudden noise. The gun crashes to the ground, my eyes raise, and see Jack running towards Millie. Time slows down, my chest caves. I can't breathe. I caused this. *He's scared, confused. Millie's white as a sheet, holding her stomach. Jack's anguished cry as he calls her name.*

I caused this pain. *She doesn't respond, nothing. I'm falling, wrestling that bastard to the ground. So much blood.* I can't see straight. I can't get the air I need. *The sight of her being shot, the way she went down, Jack's face as he watched the woman he loves almost die.* Blinking rapidly, I try to get myself out of this fog I've stepped into. Clutching my chest through my shirt, I'm at my desk, not in the hotel. Millie will be okay. *If it wasn't for you, it would never have happened.* I didn't do my job. I didn't protect them.

I made the right decision to keep away from Charlie, my angel. When she called me a liar, all I wanted to do was tell her everything, and after I spoke to Jack, I searched for her, only to find her passed out on a sofa. Wrapping her in my arms felt right, taking her to my room, inhaling her scent. I knew I couldn't keep away. She's becoming my everything.

Even more, when she came running into the hospital looking for Millie, she looked broken. The fear in her eyes and her tear-stained cheeks broke me. She needed someone. There was no way in hell I was going to let anyone else comfort her.

I took a scared Charlie into my arms and held her so fucking tight. I didn't let go all night. She fell asleep there, in the hospital waiting room, while we waited for news on Millie. The pure sadness and helplessness she showed me are things I never want to see on her beautiful face or in her eyes again. I wanted to be that someone. That someone who held her, made her feel safe... but I didn't. I didn't do my job. I put Millie in danger. I put that fear, sadness, and helplessness in my angel's eyes.

That's the big question that keeps looming over my head: if I can't keep a client safe... how can I possibly keep someone I'm starting to care about safe?

I'm questioning everything—my actions, my responsibilities, my choices, my everything. My mind is split. I'm at war with myself.

The day of the ball, when I messaged Charlie, I was determined to keep her at arm's length, take a step back. After that day, I changed my mind. I can't keep away from her. I've been with her every night since. I wake up next to her each morning, with her sweet cherry scent filling my lungs. Something she said would never happen. Things have changed between us. If only she knew what I was thinking. Planning. Every night I'm wrapped up in her, I can't help but think what if...

I need to take a step back. I need to get my head right.

If I can stay away, step back, then she'll be better off without me. She'll be safe. The others on my team will keep her safe when I can't.

Leon knows something is off. The looks he's giving me are questions I don't want to answer. He'll try and fix it like he always does. He'll have the answers, the steps I need to take. Ones I've taken before. I'm just not sure I can do them this time.

What happened at The Manor was only a glimmer of what happened on our last tour. But that's enough. People died then and people nearly died again because of me.

I got out last time; I got us all out. I was better; they are better for it. But this, what if I can't... I'm not ready to lose what she is becoming to me, but I know the best way I can keep her safe, protect her even, is to step away. I know she'll hate me for it, but I'd rather that than watch her get hurt in any other way.

"Mate, what are you doing?" Jerking my head up, I didn't hear Leon come in. I've been so lost in my thoughts. He sits his gigantic frame in the chair in front of my desk. His eyes raking over the mess.

"It's past midnight, O, and you're still here, again. What are you doing?" he repeats, leaning forward, resting his elbows on his knees, his hands dangling free between his legs and his eyes intent on me.

"Going over all the information we have, I need—"

He cuts me off. "You don't need to do shit, O." I can tell he's trying to keep his voice even for me. "You did everything right. You know you did. We did." he corrects himself, and points between us.

"I could have done more, Leon. Going through this, I can see what I should have done." I say, looking at all the paperwork I've printed off tormenting me.

"It's not on you. There was no way we could have ever known that her ex had a look-a-like. That shit is crazy, and you know it." Do I? Looking down at my desk, I close my eyes and see it all. Remembering Jack's face when he saw Millie. Holding her while she bled out. The noise of the sirens surrounding us.

It's all on me. I'm the problem. He's trying to talk me down from the spiral I'm in to get me back to something that resembles normal. Unfortunately for Leon, my guard is up.

"No, I should have done so much more. I should have—"

"Don't start with that. You know better than to think like that, especially when you know you can't change what happened in the past. We learn and adapt," he yells this time. Standing up behind my desk, I start pacing, my hand running through my hair. I need to gain control back. I feel like I'm losing it.

"Fuck learning and adapting. It's on me," I shout, jabbing my finger hard into my chest. My frustration and anger coming out. "I know it is. I won't let anyone else take responsibility for what I should have done, Leon. Not again." I don't raise my voice often, but this whole situation is pissing me off. The constant questions, the looks. I can't take it.

"Okay, okay, sit your arse down. I'm not here to argue with you... I can see it's getting to you. We were both there when Millie was shot. It could have been either one of us that got shot. That dude was crazy as fuck. He lost it when I pushed Millie away from him. Owen. You know when someone's cornered with no escape, they will fight like their life is the only thing left. They fight to survive. He fought for what he desperately wanted to do. In his fucked up mind, killing Millie was the only thing left in his life that mattered. That's what he did." He takes a deep breath, his eyes honed on mine. I know what's coming.

Flinching as visions play on in my mind. *I can't get hold of the gun. It slips through my fingers onto the floor below us, myself and Leon, failing to get him under control. His arm reaches out and takes the gun, firing it towards Millie. It's too late. I can't stop it. Bang.* I flinch. *Leon's fist connects with Glen's face and he goes down.*

Scrunching my eyes shut, I open them to see Leon focused on me. Did he see me flinch? I need to leave before he reads anymore into what's happening with me.

"We need to deal with it, Owen. We need to talk about what happened. One on one." He's looking me over. I think he sees it. My struggle, my torment, but I can't be sure. "I've booked a meeting with Jack and Dan for a few weeks' time. We need to settle this, see where things are heading. Jack's happy to meet, but he wants Millie in a better place first."

I stay standing but close my laptop and grab my hoodie from the hook by the door. I don't want to talk about this. Not now. It only makes me feel worse. I'm angry at everything right now. I'd do anything for my brothers. I'm just not sure I can face this, face Jack just yet. I need more time. Closing my eyes, I take a breath in.

"I'm out. I need to get back to Charlie." Even the mention of her name has me relaxing just enough to be able to move forward, but it's edged with something I can't and don't want to think about.

Leon follows me, his heavy steps matching my ghost-like ones.

"So, it's serious between the two of you?" This is what he's good at, making people feel good. "I've never seen you with anyone before, not like this." his normal self, just like that, bringing the conversation back to a safe place. Little does he know that it's the ignition point for me. My angel. It starts and ends with her. Everything, good, bad, no matter which way I turn, she's in my head. I'm responsible for what happened to Millie, and if I couldn't stop her from getting shot, how can I protect Charlie? If the time came, would I even be able to save her? What if I can't save her? She's better off without me.

"It is what it is," I say without looking at him as we walk towards the lift.

"Don't give me that shit. I know you. You really like her." I know what he's doing. He wants me to tell him about the one thing that matters, but it won't work. I still can't help the ghost of a smile that crosses my lips.

"I do like her, more than I care to admit right now, but..." I almost tell him what I'm not ready to admit to myself.

"I'm happy for you, man. It's about time." He claps me on the back as the lift doors close behind us.

On the drive to Charlie's, I sit and think of everything I need to get in order for what I need to do.

Chapter Twelve

Wood

Owen

Blowing off the last fragments of dust from my workbench, I feel the grain of the wood beneath my fingers. It feels good. Smooth and warm from the heat of my hands working the tools, getting the design just right. There's something I love about working with my hands. I've always loved it. I don't think when I work on a project; I like that it can take me away from the invading thoughts, especially lately. I need the peace it brings me.

I've not seen Charlie all weekend.

Fuck, I hope she likes it. It's taken me weeks to complete. In between everything I have going on, I've been working on this, as a little surprise for her. After three failed attempts to craft the delicate magnolia flower from oak, I finished it today.

Looking up, I catch a glimpse of Cole's green truck when he pulls up to the side of the house. What's he doing here? Turning round, I knock my drill off the workbench. The noise it makes causes me to flinch and stumble backwards. My breath gets stuck in my throat, choking me for a split second before I realise it was just the drill. Steadying myself on the wooden surface, I take some calming breaths. This is getting out of hand.

Taking the newly carved sign for Charlie, I place it under a towel to keep it from prying eyes. I want hers to be the first to see it. I still need to apply the oil and attach it to wall fixing I've had made for her. It will be as unique as she is when it's finished.

I wanted to give her something special. The way she's handled all the work that's been done in the shop, as well as starting a new business on her own is inspiring. Charlie's already got orders for when she opens in a weeks' time. I know she's excited about the opening event she's been planning with Millie.

Sliding the sign back against the wall, Cole's frame comes into view, walking into the attached garage I've converted into my workshop.

Frowning at him, I start to clear away the shavings and tools.

"Thought I'd check in," he says, looking around.

"Not you too?" This is getting stupid. I don't need to be checked on like a child. Leon's been on my case. No matter how many times I tell him I'm fine, he still asks the question.

It's what good friends do.

"What do you mean? I've been away on a job for the last week. I've not seen you, man."

"Right, sorry." Fuck, I've not even noticed he's not been around. Now I feel like shit.

"I had today planned out: the open road, my bike, and a pub lunch."

"What changed?" I ask, sweeping up the last few bits into the bin.

"My bike had other ideas. It's in the shop being repaired." He looks miserable at the thought.

"You not doing it yourself?"

"Nah, I've got my mate doing it. He owed me a favour." Fixing bikes for Cole is like me working with wood. He loves it.

"I thought I'd come to pester your ass instead. What you been making?"

"Nothing much, just working on my carving technique. It's not gone well," I say, pointing to the pile of broken wood in the corner that will now be used in the fire pit.

"Better than I could do. Do you remember when you tried to teach me?" I do vividly.

"Never again. You ruined almost all of my tools. You're lucky you're allowed to set foot in here." Yet give him a bike and he can fix it, no matter how intricate the work is.

"What were you trying to carve? It looks complicated. A flower?"

"Yeah, I thought I would to start easy. Apparently, it's not as easy as it looks." Looking me over, he's sussing me out.

"You did it though, didn't you? You did it, and you don't want to show anyone." Moving to stand in front of the covered sign, Cole catches what I'm doing and laughs.

"Let me see. I bet it looks badass." Cole's the youngest of us all. He was only on his second tour when our unit was ambushed on our last mission in Afghanistan. There was no way I was going to leave him behind.

"No way. You'll see it soon enough," I say. Taking the hint, he moves to lean against the bench.

"How's things with Charlie? Leon said it was serious."

"Fuck, that dick's the biggest gossip." we all know it. I had no hope of ever keeping us a secret. It'll just make it harder.

"If you're up for it, I thought we could head out to the pub. Mike's got a new mega club sandwich I want to try."

"What the hell is a mega club sandwich?"

"Three layers of sourdough bread, avocado, bacon, tomatoes, cheese, salad, and chips on the side." He licks his lips like he can taste it already.

"Fuck, that sounds good, but you can take the Avocado out. I'll have extra bacon."

"Deal. Let's go."

"Edward, it's good to see you." I shake his hand as we sit at my desk, a little more relaxed than we normally would be for a business meeting, but I've known Edward for some time. We work in security and our paths cross from time to time.

"You too. How are things?" Ed asks. We have so many NDAs between us, we need to keep it simple.

"Good, busy, but good," I reply. I have no idea why he's here today. This is unlike him. He even made an appointment, but gave no details as to what it's about. "Everything okay?" I add, prompting him a little.

"Not sure. I may need your help." His brows drawn together as he leans forwards.

"May? What's happened?" I'm confused. Usually it's a we do or don't have a job, never a maybe.

"The guy I'm working for, he's recently taken on a new business partner."

"Let me bring in Leon, so I don't have to relay this info later." Picking up the phone on my desk, I dial the number for Leon. "Can you come into my office? Edward's here," I say when he picks up.

"On my way."

A few minutes later, Leon walks in, sitting across from Edward, on the other side of my desk.

"Carry on, Ed. What's been happening?" I nod as Leon gets comfy.

"That's the confusing thing, I don't know. I just feel like I'm going to need you soon."

"Why? Are you stepping away from the family?" Ed's been head of security for the same family for a long time. He and his team cover it all. Family, house, events, away, everything.

"No, I couldn't. She's like a daughter to me."

"Okay? Sorry, Ed, I'm not getting it." Me and Leon share a look. This is out of character for him. He's usually on point with what he knows.

"I know. I'd like to keep you on retainer. This new partner of my boss, he's had some ideas I'm not happy about. Nothing set in stone, but I'd like a back up plan in place just in case."

"And you want us to be your back up plan? What about your team?" Stress shows on his face and he hangs his head slightly, giving it a slight shake as he says, "It can't be my team. I'll need an external team for this."

"Okay," I say again.

"Look, I know it's not much to go on, and I'll tell you more if and when things change. If I have you on retainer, how quick can you get cover for someone when it's needed?"

"We can have a full schedule worked out in a few weeks once we know what we're dealing with," Leon says. I only nod in agreement, still confused as fuck.

"I can work with that. Thanks Guys."

"I'm confused, Ed. What happening?" Leon adds. I'm glad it's not just me.

"All I know is that this new guy has other ideas about the security we have in place, and for whatever reason, my boss is listening. I can't let her out in this world without some sort of protection, and I know Cerberus are the best."

"Then you have us on retainer whenever you need us."

"Agreed," Leon says.

"Thanks. Look, I need to get going. Send me over any paperwork I need to fill out. I'll get it back to you in a few days."

"Done. You can count on us, Ed." he's up and out the door before we can say a proper goodbye.

"What do you think of that?" Leon looks as baffled as I do.

"No idea. We just need to make sure you can be free when he needs you."

"Yeah, you mean us, not me personally." he laughs.

"Sure, maybe put Cole on it. He's been doing loads of aways jobs. He might like the change to a few local jobs when they turn up."

"Done, done and done."

The light's fading when I walk into Charlie's, the night sky growing darker. I fucking love watching her; she's graceful in everything she does. Even standing on a dining chair reaching to hang a picture on the wall behind the table.

Her long slender figure's striking. My eyebrow arches when she lifts onto one leg, extending further onto her toes to reach a little further, pressing the frame to the wall.

My tongue darts out to lick my lips when the shirt she's wearing rides up her creamy thighs, revealing her perfect peach of an arse in a thong. My cock is instantly screaming at me to be released.

Not saying a word until she steps down, I walk a little closer. "Hey, Angel"

"Hey yourself, OG," she says, with a small gasp. I think she may be getting used to me just turning up.

"Fancy telling me what that means yet?" she smirks, shaking her head. I can think of a few ways to get the information out of her.

"It's what I have you saved as in my phone as," she says, moving to the opposite side of the table, trying to set some distance. I think she knows what's coming.

"I know," I tell her, placing my hands on the table, my eyes focused on her.

"You do? Do you know it's something you do very well?" I'm getting a better idea of what it could be just from the way she's crossed her legs, squeezing her smooth thighs together.

"And what do I do very well, Angel?" I tease, following her around the table. My dick loving the chase.

"Many things, Owen. Many, many things, but this one is specifically in relation to me." She smiles, standing behind the chair that's now separating us, the room crackling with tension.

"Hm, is it something between the two of us? Something only I'm going to give you?"

"Fuck, you know, don't you?" she's breathing heavily, a sure sign she's as turned on as I am.

"No, but I'm guessing it has something to do with the way you're pressing your thighs together right now." Spinning the chair to face her, I stand in front of it.

"Maybe?" she says, as I sit down and pull her between my thighs. Slowly unbuttoning the shirt she's covered herself up with.

"The way your breathing has escalated, just at the thought." Undoing the last button, I pull it apart to see her. Fuck, she's stunning, she's everything.

"Maybe." She's almost panting now, I place my lips on her stomach, pulling her closer, my hands on her bare arse. The need to dominate her is overwhelming. It's even better that I know she'll let me. Licking my way up, she gasps when I take her nipple between my teeth and pull.

"How you're already wet for me?" I add, moving slowly over to the other nipple, drawing it into my mouth, circling it with the flat of my tongue.

"Maybe..." she whimpers

"Soaked, there's no maybe about it. I know you are. I know how I make you feel. I know that I'm the only one going to give it to you." Tracing my fingers lower over her abdomen, she moans, tilting her head back.

"You are..." she breathes out, as I stroke my fingers over her silk thong, feeling just how wet she is for me.

"I am what, Charlie?"

"You're the only one giving them to me." Her words rushed as I press a little firmer into her clit.

"What's the OG, Charlie?"

"Orgasm Giver." Her words are quiet, but fuck if it doesn't make me proud that she calls me that.

"Fuck, yes. Only me, Angel" My finger traces the wet line of her centre.

"Only you, Owen." I remove my hand and she moans in protest.

"On your knees, Angel." She does, no questions asked. I love that this strong woman wants to submit to me.

"Take off my jeans." I instruct, watching her hand slide over my thighs, as she works her way towards my belt, her fingers grazing over my dick on the way. Undoing my belt, then my jeans, shifting slightly when she pulls them over my boxers, she leans forward, placing her hot lips on my cock.

Hissing out a breath, my voice rough. "Do that again, and I won't last long enough to give you what you need, Angel." My jeans come off, and she sits back on her heels.

"Now my boxers, slowly," I demand. It's killing me. I want to fuck her, but seeing her like this sets me on fire.

"That's it, good girl." It's the first time I've called her it, and the reaction she gives me is pure perfection. She shivers, closing her eyes and taking the praise I'm giving her. She peels off my black boxers slowly, her eyes fixed on my erection. It's almost painful holding back, but I want to savour this.

"Stand up." She gracefully stands. "Strip." Dropping the shirt to the floor, she hooks her thumbs inside the thong and glides it down her toned legs.

"You see this, Angel?" I ask, taking my cock in my hand. "This is what you do to me, every goddamn second of the day. You're all I think about." She is naked in front of me. Her beautiful body on full display just for me. "Turn around, Angel." she does, looking back over her shoulder at me. Fucking hell, she's... breaking me.

"Spread your legs." With my cock in one hand stroking myself, I glide my fingers through her soaking wet folds. She whimpers and I watch as her legs tremble.

"Straddle me." She's perfect, doing as I ask without hesitation. She hovers over me, my hand reaching between her open legs. She's soaking already. Her back to my chest, her breasts a vision as look down her beautiful body. My hand reaches for her perfectly slender neck, holding her to me. Her head tilting backwards allows me more access as my fingers dance on her throat. My heart is racing just as much as hers. Positioning myself at her entrance, my hand on her hip, I bring her down hard against me, filling her in one perfect, smooth action.

"Owen…" She groans my name out, my fingers tightening just a fraction around her neck, feeling her breath hitch just a little more, giving her time to adjust to the intrusion. Her legs spread wide over mine, she has no control, her toes grazing the floor. I push up, making her groan again, her back arching as her head rests on my shoulder. Tracing my hand over her stomach, moving down her tender skin, I feel us connected. Pressing her clit, I thrust again, her walls tightening around me like a vice.

"Fucking… fuck!"

Charlie reaches down, supporting herself with one hand on my thighs. Her other hand reaches for my balls, squeezing them, sending white-hot heat up my spine.

"Angel, fuck yes," I yell. It's taking everything to keep control and fuck her like she needs me to. Thrusting up into her harder, she shouts my name, so I do it again and again, my hand at her neck, holding her to me.

"Detonate, Angel. Come all over me." Tilting her head, I kiss her hard. It's messy and everything I want it to be. "Good girl," I whisper into her mouth.

She grips me with her fingers, her pussy tightening as her orgasm takes over. I watch as she loses herself, taking me with her. My vision blurs, my hands holding her hips tightly to me. Pounding into her, a primal instinct takes over, fucking her harder, filling her with everything I have.

Charlie leans back against me, breathless. Gripping her chin with my hand, I turn her head, devouring her mouth with mine. She tastes just like sweets and warmth. Slipping out of her, my warm cum leaks out between us. Using my fingers, I spread it around her already slick folds. Fuck. I'm almost ready to go again. When we part her lips are swollen, my favourite look on her. Flushed and fucked. Lifting her carefully on shaky legs, I move us to the bedroom, where I watch her fall asleep.

I won't let myself stay the night. I leave before she wakes.

Chapter Thirteen

In My Bed

Charlie

Six weeks have changed so many things in my life. Well, maybe not many but one. And it's a huge one. Odd really, how I can feel so strongly for someone I know is backing away from me. Someone who I hardly know yet, but feel like I have known forever. He's ingrained in my every cell. I know that makes no sense whatsoever, but I can't help it. I have feelings for him, that tall, god-like man with the fire tattoos. My mistake? I let myself see what could be. I dared to peek into the future, to see us, myself and Owen as an us.

Us.

Walking back to the flower shop, he's all I think about. My footsteps remind me how I hear him at night. How I hear him in the morning. The shiver that coats my skin from the light breeze of the summer afternoon gives me flashbacks to his touch.

The ding of the door, when I enter, has the builders saying, 'hi' as I walk past them to the kitchen to make them all a drink. I've seen the changes in Owen since Millie's shooting. He's isolating himself, withdrawing. It's changed him, triggered him in some way.

Stirring the three strong teas, with extra sugar, I can't help the surge of hatred I feel towards Millie's ex, Glen. I would kill him myself if I ever had the chance. I'd beat him black and blue for what he's done to Millie. I was so selfish that night. I could have helped. I could have been there when she got that message from Em, the night of the ball, that it was her life or Millie's. My best friend chose her own life. She knew Em was pregnant and willingly walked into Glen's gun-holding hands, and where was I? Throwing a self-pity party. I know deep down there was no way I could have predicted what would happen, or even if I could have actually helped, but given the chance, I would have done anything to prevent Millie from getting shot. Even putting myself in the line of fire.

In the end, Owen was there when Millie needed him, and when I needed him in the aftermath. Forgiving him for lying to me, that was easy. That's when it changed for me, my feelings. I'm not sure it was for the better, but my heart took over my head. Now my head is trying to have a serious talk to my heart—it's not working, no matter how much I try. Hanging my head while the tea stews. I wasn't even there and I can see how difficult it must have been to be part of it all. Owen had to hold Jack back, while Millie was helpless at gunpoint. A tough choice to make. I can't imagine how you would come to process that.

Owen's been on a roller coaster of emotions since then, none of which he talks about, but I can see them playing out in his eyes and his actions. Conflicting emotions, torn between wanting to give me more, and something else, something darker, something he's trying to hide and keep me safe from.

When we're together, he can't get enough of me, just like I can't get enough of him. The way he is with me, physically we are good, explosive even. Mentally, however, the heaviness that encompasses him when we speak. Like he wants to know everything, about me, my day, my interactions, my life, but doesn't process the answers, or never stays long enough to talk.

Placing the mugs on the counter, I make my way back upstairs as the builders shout their thanks. Owen confuses me. A few weeks back we spent every moment we could together, breakfast at mine, he'd bring me lunch, we'd sit on the unfinished floor and eat, chat and laugh. Sneak in a quickie before he went back to work. He'd help me with the shop refurbishment, bring his tools around at the weekend and build something unexpected, like the sign that now hangs over the shop front. I cried it was so beautiful. It's in pride of place. It really took my breath away, just like he does in those moments.

But then the lunches stopped. He would be gone before I woke, and the weekends became mine, with no sight of him. Not in the waking hours, anyway. The nights are still ours when he climbs into bed with me. I've not asked how he gets in; I've not given him a key. I'm just glad he chooses my bed every night. There's just something not right. *I know it,* and that has my mind reeling. I feel it in my chest, in the pit of my stomach, and in every breath I take. I can feel him pulling away like he's torn. Sitting at the table in my finished apartment, no boxes in sight, I pull out my laptop, checking on the case I left behind to see if there is any news. Simon's asked a few times since I moved in if I would consider working for him again. The answer is still no. It doesn't stop me from checking in though.

Climbing into bed hours later, I drift, knowing Owen will be here when he's ready.

I feel the bed dip when he climbs in beside me, his arms sneak around me, his warm breath on my skin. I feel his hard length pressed into my back as he holds me close. My chest tightens, just that little bit more. I should have been stronger, but I think it's too late now.

"Angel, I want to give you something," he whispers across my back. I try to roll over to face him, but his hands hold me in place at my hips. "Stay there."

His hands slide around my neck and I feel something cold against my skin. My hand moves up to feel what he just placed there. A necklace. He places a soft kiss on the side of my neck, where I know he likes to feel my racing pulse and right now it's beating hard. I feel the smile on his lips before he flips me over, his body pressing against mine.

"This," he says, softly tracing the line of my new necklace with his fingers, "I want you to wear it all the time, no matter what." He places a kiss where the small silver pendant sits. I can feel the engravings, but I can't see them in the dimly lit room.

With only the light of the full moon lighting my bedroom, it's easy to see what he feels right now. His eyes soft and tender, caring, wanting, his frown set in place. In his body language, loving almost? Tracing the chain of the necklace, letting me know it's important to him. Maybe I got it wrong about him backing away. A bubble of hope appears in my chest. I want to take all his worries away. But the way he said it, *no matter what,* I want to ask him what that means. I want to say something, but I can't. I'm scared what the answer would be. The words won't come out.

I'm protecting myself from the hurt I think is coming by not asking. Ignorance is bliss, right? I don't want to know. It's better I don't. I won't be able to handle the truth. Because I'm not falling anymore, I've fallen with a loud and messy bang. My hands come up to my chest, to where the necklace now sits across my heart.

"Thank you. I will... Always." when I move to get up, I want to take a look at what he has bought me, but he yanks me back down. Landing back beside him, he cups my face in his hands and places a soft kiss to my lips.

"Promise me... Angel, please, no matter what." his voice is thick with emotion. His words scare me. He's mentally pulling further away from me. I feel the shift in what's happening. It's deep, just like his eyes right now. Telling me his unspoken words of need and desperation, of what will happen next, all messed up with sadness and lust. It's a heady mixture, one I would never regret looking into if I could do it forever.

I have a feeling after tonight things will be different, very different.

My heart sinks a little. I hope to whoever is listening that I have it wrong.

"No matter what," I whisper back into his lips before they crash down on mine. Bruising them with everything he has and everything I want to give in return. My heart can't take it. It feels so full, but so lost at the same time, I don't know how but I shove it all down, somewhere deep to deal with another day. It's going to ruin me.

We move together; he lets me take control, something he never does. I push him down and straddle him, his hands grip my hips tight, guiding me as I slide onto him in one move. A soft moan escapes my lips, his eyes never leaving mine, filling me so completely. This is different. I know it is. This means more.

What have I done? I let him sneak his way in. If this is it, I'll take it.

All of it.

Everything.

Anything he is willing to give me. Because right now, in this very second, connected to him, I'd rather have this than nothing.

His hands trace my body, rolling my hips against his. He sinks deeper, his touch leaving flames across my skin. Like he wants to remember everything, every detail. I savour every touch of his warm callused hands, rough but so tender on my skin. His eyes bore into mine, and it takes everything not to break down and tell him how I feel, because I know it won't make a difference, not now. I won't cry.

I'd wait for him. My lost soul.

"Angel." His hand moves up from my hips, gliding his fingers up until he rests them over my heart, pausing for a few seconds before bringing them to my back, as he sits up, face to face with me. Still holding my gaze, he places a soft kiss on my parted lips. Resting his forehead on mine, he starts to move with me. Driving deeper, finding the spot that makes me crazy.

"Take what you need, let me watch…" And I do. I chase the feeling of him so deep inside me, the feelings I have and can't share with my words, I show him. With every touch, caress, and kiss. I drown in him. Engulfed by the flames that are Owen.

I'm not sure any other man will live up to how he stretches me, how he makes me feel. How Owen Archie Stone makes me feel everything. After everything I've been through, I never thought it was possible. I take it all. When I'm close, he thrusts up and his words echo in my mind.

"You're mine, Angel. Say I'm yours…" I can't speak as the most intense orgasm takes over me. "I'm yours," I manage to say when he slams into me one more time, and he comes with me, sending me higher. My head drops back and Owen places his hand on my heart again, as his thumb circles my clit. I hear it, but I don't think it's me, something that resembles a sob, as I let go.

I'm his.

I don't remember much after that. I must have fallen asleep. I woke up to the sun rising; golden yellows with hits of reds. A new day.

Owen was gone. The bed was empty, cold. This time, it felt different.

Last night is a night I will never forget. The necklace, it's so beautiful. My fingers tremble every time I touch it. The words turn in my head on repeat…

No matter what.

You're mine.

I'm yours.

Every time I touch the delicate gold chain. *No matter what.* With the most staggering gold locket I have ever seen. *You're mine.* Engraved with the most intricate design—angel wings tangled up in wisps of fire. It's sealed shut. *I'm yours.*

The memory of his eyes haunts me, even now, eight hours later. You could see the pain, lust, and desperation in them. I've tried so hard to get on with stuff today, but I just can't. The builder keeps asking me questions I have no answers to, not today. He stopped asking a while ago and left me to my thoughts.

My overwhelming thoughts.

Tonight, that's what it comes down to. I don't know what it will bring. I'm not sure what I will do if Owen doesn't climb into my bed tonight.

Shatter.

Break.

Crumble.

I've been standing here most of the day, watching the builders finish up the work. I officially open on Monday. The work is done, apart from a few last-minute things. I've got my first flower delivery tomorrow morning at the crack of dawn, and orders to get ready to send out.

The papers I have been staring at for hours in front of me shift slightly as the front door opens and the bell chimes. Looking up, I watch as Leon steps inside. I know before he says anything…

Owen's gone.

Chapter Fourteen

Pain

Charlie

I've never felt anything like this. Pain, like my chest is being ripped open and my heart is being torn into shreds. I'm sinking to the floor without realising, my stomach doing the same, my lungs constricting like a vice, making me gasp for air. I knew it would hurt, but this is unbearable.

How did I let this happen?

It's what I expected. What I knew would happen? *Isn't it?* I *knew* he was saying goodbye to me last night.

The necklace... I clutch onto it, like a lifeline connecting me to him. There are people all around me, looking at me, and then there's Leon. I can't hear them. I barely register they are there.

I let the walls around my guarded heart fall and crash. He did that; he made me believe. He made me have hope. I'm angry at him for that. He made me think I could. *Hope*, that's what makes it hurt so much more. *I had hope that we could have been something.*

The next thing I know, I'm in Leon's arms being carried upstairs to my apartment and being placed on the sofa. My fingers brush the soft fabric of the very seat I lay next to Owen on while we had our first actual conversation. One that didn't revolve around what he wanted to do to me. Easy, like we had known each other for a long time. I'm not sure how long I sit with Leon, but he breaks the silence first.

"Charlie?" I don't look at him. I'm not sure I can. I just bury my head deeper into his chest.

Why did he leave?

"I'm sorry he did this to you. I know it means nothing to you, but I know how he felt about you. This situation with Millie. Well, it's taken its toll on him. I want you to understand, this isn't anything you have done. Not even close."

I'm listening.

My voice comes out calm and even. "I never thought it was... but if it's not me, then help me understand. Because right now I... I just don't."

He lets out a grunt before he continues. "Before we left the army and built our company, something happened that devastated us all. Me, Cole, and Ethan, but especially Owen. We each have our stories from the few days of hell we went through, but Owen took what happened personally. We lost six of our closest friends and brothers in those few days. They all died, and we had to watch." There's so much grief in his eyes as he speaks. "There was nothing we could have done. We made it out when others didn't. It's his story to tell, but it's affected him ever since. What happened with Millie triggered him after what we went through."

I'm staring at Leon, confused. I'm not sure I understand why this would make him leave me. As if he can read my mind, he pulls a note from his back pocket, holding it just out of reach.

"When I arrived at the office today, I knew he'd gone. Me and the boys have already started looking for him. Cole has taken the lead on tracking him, but he's in the wind. He's gone to clear his head, get himself straight. I should have seen the signs sooner and for that, I'm sorry. I thought he was dealing with it all okay." Leon shakes his head. "He left this."

I need to sort my head out. I can't keep her safe. If I'm around, things go wrong. You won't find me, although I know you'll try. I'll be back. I just don't know when. Until then, it's all yours. Look after her for me.

~ O

He left because he thinks he needs to keep me safe and he thinks he can't. I don't know what he needs to keep me safe from. I've never felt safer when I was in his arms. But apparently, having him around, I'm not safe. Where is the logic in that? I don't need saving, I never have done. My brothers made sure of that, took me to every kind of MMA class, event, or tournament they could. And I never stopped.

Owen could have kept my feelings and heart safe, but he left and tore them to shreds. Now, I don't feel safe with him gone. How stupid is that? How could he be so... heartless with me, my feelings... everything?

Why can't men be more open with their feelings? Be honest.

He doesn't know me well, or at all, if he thinks that I can't look after myself. With everything he found out about me from his stupid 'system', I thought he would have found out this about me. It's something I have always done. I can look after myself. My brothers made sure I could when I took the career I did and they left for the army. They made sure I would be strong and resilient. I've made them proud.

Owen, he left for me. Even if I don't understand fully, I can't make it make sense, and that makes this so much worse than what Andy did. He could have just talked to me. We could have had something, but he thinks he is protecting me by leaving. I'm glad Leon told me, but the hurt and the pain is unbearable.

I need to get a grip; I need to show Leon that it's nothing. What we had, it was nothing. *I need to believe it.* It's the only way I can... I don't know, survive this. I don't think he's coming back. And if he does, it won't be for me, it will be for his business, his brothers in arms.

What's six weeks between two people? Nothing, apparently.

Although, he left for me.

Leon's told me what he could, all the things he knows. I believe he's telling me the truth. Standing abruptly, I leave Leon on the sofa, as I go to my bedroom, closing the door behind me. I change into a pair of shorts and a sports top as quickly as I can, grabbing my hoodie on the way out.

"Can you take me to the gym?" I ask. I don't trust myself to drive right now.

"Are you sure? We can talk about it if you want. I'm here for you, Charlie." I can't take the kindness in his eyes. It's too much.

"I don't know you well enough to talk to you about this shit. I just need a lift." I'm being a bitch, I know I am. "If you don't want to, I'll ask one of the builders downstairs, I'm sure they'll be more than willing to take me."

"I said I would. Let's go." he's fucking smiling. "I think we're gonna be great friends, Charlie. I can see why Owen was hooked on you." Glaring at him for a split second, I refocus. It's not his fault, and I need to make sure I remember that. He came to me, told me what he knows. Putting on my trainers, I walk to the kitchen, I fill my water bottle and head for the door.

I need this.

I need a release on the punch bag. I need my fists to connect with flesh; I need the release only fighting can give me.

I don't speak a word, putting the address in his GPS. I just look out the window, avoiding Leon's gaze.

Pulling up outside the huge grey warehouse, it's a little rough around the edges, but inside is a whole different story, with a black shutter for a door giving the only hint to what could be inside.

Opening the door and stepping out of the car, Leon's eyes lock with mine before climbing out. He types out a message on his phone as I walk in. He must like the response, smirking, his eyes brightening just a little. He heads in, taking the lead and walking ahead of me. He's sussing the place out. His eyes roam over the huge space, filled with the best boxing and gym equipment money can buy.

My brothers and Alexander did good with this place and I can't wait for them to be home so they can run it. I'd smile, but I don't want to as it only makes me miss them more.

I can feel the buzz already, the anticipation, and the relief I know will come once I've unleashed this tension.

Stepping up to the punch bag, with no warm up, I let rip. Focus, fight. My fists mash into the bag, each one bringing me closer to the release I need. Every kick lays me bare and brings it all to the surface. Knowing Leon's watching my every move just makes me go harder.

When a guy asks me to spar with him, I nod and get into the boxing ring. Leon swipes a hand over his face, watching intensely from the side.

"What are you doing?"

"I'm doing what I do best. Something Owen should have stayed to learn about me."

"Okay, um... shout if you need me."

"I won't, but I appreciate it."

I'd laugh, but it just seems to not be there right now. Securing my gloves, I stand in my corner.

This is what I love, this is what got me through so many bad times. I need this like I need air sometimes.

The guy steps forward. He's cocky. His eyes move over me, a clear smirk on his face. He's about my height and maybe weighs a little more than me. Lunging forward, he aims for my face with a right hook. In my peripheral, Leon takes an instinctive step forward. As I jab the guy in the ribs, I swipe his legs and watch him start to topple. Adding a fierce kick to his ribs, he goes over.

"Fucking hell," Leon gasps from the side. Helping the guy up, he smiles at me. We punch gloves, it's like shaking hands for boxers. I think he may like that he's found a worthy opponent in me.

We take our corners again and this time he gets a punch in on the left side of my ribs. Grabbing his arm, I flip him over, smashing him onto the mat with a loud thud, pinning him with my knees.

"I'm done," I announce an hour and a half later and I head toward the showers.

"I'll meet you by the door. I need to speak with Shelly," he adds and walks towards where she's working on reception.

Walking through the corridor, after my shower, my body now hurts along with my heart. It was enough to distract me for a little while, but it will distract me every time I move for the next few days. I'll jump back into training. I need something else if I'm going to survive this.

Slipping outside while Leon fills out forms for all the guys on his team. I make a call to Simon, telling him I'll come back and work for him on this case. Shutting off the call just as Leon walks back outside, I slip my phone back into my pocket.

Chapter Fifteen

Productive Days

Charlie

A few weeks later.

"Yes." I'm on a roll, mentally ticking another item off my list for today. I've been productive and I freaking *love* productive days. And today has been one of those rare days when you feel on top of it all. Well, work things anyway. Personal life stuff... not so much.

Last week, I went down to the local small business hub with Millie because she would not stop going on about it. Jack only let her step foot out of their new cottage if she agreed to go in a wheelchair with him by her side. It's sickeningly cute how much they love each other. She's still recovering, but determined to live.

It's an old office block that's been converted into studios that you rent for next to nothing. It's a genius idea. The percentage you pay is based on the amount you earn. Then there are extra benefits for the more you earn. *Brilliant.*

Millie and I had endless chats about the people, the crafts, the community, but most of all, the artists. All at their new cottage, while Jack stood guard, not letting her lift a finger. I finally gave in after she showed me some of the images from one artist in particular. Stunning. So many interesting creatives, from all walks of life, I could have stayed there for hours. I did, in fact, stay for hours. I want to work with them all. That's my new aim anyway.

Right now, I'm setting up for three back-to-back meetings I have with a few of the most amazing small business owners I have ever met. Ivy is the first on my list for today, followed by Aggie, then Jenson. Ivy creates dried flower art and wants to put on workshops for anyone interested. We hit it off within seconds. That was even before we bonded about being divorced and telling her about the workshop space I have created in Magnolias. We have messaged every day since and she can't wait to see the space and get advertising for her workshops. That meeting starts in twenty minutes, but I've been so rushed off my feet, I've barely had time to set up like I wanted, let alone think. That's just how I like it.

Can you procrastinate from dealing with your thoughts?
Abso-freaking-lutely you can.

Walking into the back room with my hand full of flowers, notebooks, and pens, I set about getting the large workbench set up. Popping a variety of flowers in small random jars, mugs, and glasses to give a cute feel to the space. I've put together a small gift for everyone I'm meeting today. I want them to remember the meeting when they got home, so I've organised some speciality chocolate. These are hand wrapped with a personalised note from me on each of them. Plus, a small wild flower bouquet to take home.

It might seem like overkill, but I want us to set off on the right foot if we will be working together. I want it to go well. The more people that use the space, the more revenue I'll be able to bring in, eventually giving me the freedom to do more. I even have a meeting with the bookshop down the road about doing a reading evening, where their clients can just come and read. We'll bring in extra sofas, comfy chairs, and serve snacks and drinks from Bruno's and The Brasserie. Who wouldn't love that?

Doing these beautiful things in the day kind of levels out the harrowing images and unforgettable words I have to read in the documents and files Simon sent over.

I feel like I'm living a double life. The last few weeks have been crazy. Almost surreal. The case against Mr Summers seems to be going nowhere. This organisation he has are sick and twisted. The worst of the worst, in every single imaginable way possible. Anyone who comes into contact with them seems to be unalived once their purpose has been served. I'm one of the not so lucky ones who gets to see the images of those who have been even less lucky. Simon made a joke the other day about me being an amateur sleuth. Although there is nothing amateur or funny about any of this.

We both know that.

No one at Holland and Brooke knows I'm researching for Simon and digging into everything about Mr Summers and his life. It's exhausting. There has to be something we are missing, which is why I'm now digging into the dark web.

Simon has been right in his assumptions about there being a leak in the company. Mr Summers, and whomever else is working for him, always seem to be one step ahead of us. It's downright scary what their people are doing. Even worse, how they seem to be able to get away with it.

Rainbows, sunshine, and flowers by day, kidnapping, drugs, and murder by night.

Hearing the bell go on the front door, I make my way back to the shop, brushing my hands down my apron. I may need to think about hiring someone, just to help out when I have things like this going on. I can't be in two places at once. Maybe someone part-time.

The bell was one of the many security systems that Owen put into place. The night he left, he added a video surveillance system for the front and back of the building, and all the rooms downstairs, as well as a coded entry system at the back. He also fitted sensors in every room, and a wireless monitor in my office, that all links up to my phone. Apparently, it's all backed up to his system in the office that Cerberus uses as their base. It's a massive overkill for my little flower shop, but I can see he wanted me to be safe. It's his way of making it happen while he's gone.

I spot Leon in the shop. He always looks out of place in here, towering above the displays of flowers that line the walls. Over the last few weeks, we've become sort of friends. I know he's only doing it because Owen asked him to, but I think we really get along. Huh, *I managed a whole two hours today before I thought of Owen. I supposed that's progress.*

"Can you be ready for eight tonight, Charlie?" he asks, picking up one of the bouquets, sniffing it, and putting it back down, before he scratches his nose and then sneezes.

"Why do you do it if you know you're going to sneeze?" I ask, shaking my head at him with a smile.

"No idea. I suppose it's just a natural reaction to smell 'em."

"Sure, where are we going? I need to know what to wear." The whole team seems to have taken to watching out for me. It's nice to have them around.

"The Brasserie. Mike's putting on a band tonight and they're meant to be good. Thought we could check 'em out."

"Okay. I'll meet you there. It's at the bottom of the hill. No need to escort me." I know it's pointless. Leon or Ethan will arrive just before eight to walk me to wherever I need to be. It's like I have my own security detail sometimes.

"When does Cole get back? He messaged me saying he was on babysitting duty again this week. He's not happy," I ask, smiling. It's funny how much he hates this assignment.

Leon rolls his eyes. He knows he hates watching the girl, or woman. I don't know much about her other than she is the daughter of a high-profile judge. I've heard about him in my past work life, but our paths never crossed.

"He'll get over it. He can take it up with Owen. He's the one who assigned him before he left." He pauses, realising what he's said and tilts his head in apology. It fucking hurts just hearing his name. "He should be back in time to meet us later. One of us will be here to walk you down to Mike's," he promises before he leaves me to get on with work.

I can hardly move when I walk through the door of The Brasserie, especially with Cole, Ethan, and Leon surrounding me. The man I really want by my side is missing. Not missing, just gone.

Eyes follow us when we move through the pub, looking for a table. These men attract attention wherever they go. They command respect, which they receive in spades, but they are kind and thoughtful and that's after only knowing them a few weeks. I get the feeling they would do anything for those they love.

They must love Owen.

"Guys, you really need to step this down a little. It's getting overwhelming." They all stare at me like I've said the craziest thing and laugh. "Fine, let's find a table, so I don't have to stand all night." Glancing around, I spot a group ready to leave and we head towards their table at the back of the pub. "This round is on me. What are you all having?" I ask.

"Water."

"Coke."

"J20, please," they all say at the same time as they take their seats.

"No one is drinking? Why?" They pass each other a look like they can read each other's minds and don't want to tell me anything. Then I get it. They're on duty. They're looking after me. Even with nothing threatening me, they are taking Owen's request seriously.

Shitting hell.

Standing up, I place my hand on the table, ready to give them shit. "Let's get one thing straight right now," I whisper shout, smacking the table with the palm of my hand, getting the attention of a few other tables around us. "I. Do. Not. Need. To. Be. Looked. After. Maybe if Owen took the time to get to know me better, he would have realised that for himself. This stops now." I'm angry, honoured, and embarrassed all at the same time.

"Charlie, that's not what this is. Yes, he asked us, but we want to make sure you are okay. We like you—" I cut Leon off before he can say anymore.

"Then be a friend, not my security team." Shoving off the table, I move to the bar and ask Mike to take the non-alcoholic drinks I order over to our table. I need a few minutes to get myself together.

Mike comes back a few minutes later with my wine and a packet of crisps.

"Sit, eat, and have a drink," he says from behind the bar. "How is the shop getting on? I've heard so many good things about what you are trying to do. I'm impressed. If you ever need to use The Brasserie for anything, let me know. I can supply the drinks for any event you have planned."

"I'll let you know. I could use you for the bookstore evening. That would be great."

"Let me know when. I'll book the wife a ticket. She loves anything book-related." Mike looks over towards the guys sitting at the table, then back at me, curiosity etched on his deeply tanned face.

"What's going on with them? They keep looking over at you? My wife reads those romance books, the why choose or reverse harem kind, is this one of those?" I almost spit my drink out, covering my mouth just in time to save the mess on the bar, but it dribbles down my chin. Mike hands me a napkin, smirking while I recover.

"No!" I can't help but laugh. "Your wife has great taste in books, but this is not what *that* is." I know my cheeks have turned a little pink. I don't embarrass easily, but when a man asks if you are part of a foursome, in the middle of a bar, it's going to happen.

"Lay it on me, kid, I'm all ears," he says while wiping the bar down. There are other customers waiting, plus it's not the time or the place to talk about this.

"Another time, Mike, but thank you. I needed a good laugh."

"You are very welcome," Mike says with a smirk before moving on to serve someone else.

"Charlie, can we start the night again?" Leon appears beside me, perching on the stool while two pints of ale and a whisky on the rocks are placed in front of him. Eyeing them, I realise Leon must have ordered a fresh round. They're making an effort and I appreciate the gesture.

"Okay... let me help you with those." Picking up one of their drinks in one hand and my own in the other, we move back to the table, where I'm sitting in the middle of them all. They nod in my direction one by one in a silent apology. I know they mean well, but I don't need to be reminded of what Owen left them to do.

"How was babysitting duty?" I ask Cole to clear the awkwardness from the air.

"Of all the things you could ask Cole about, you know he's just going to whinge about it," Leon says, as Cole sets off on a rant about the girl he is watching, and just how much she pisses him off. Ethan gives me a look, not saying a word, while he drinks his whisky.

"She's an entitled rich bitch, living on daddy's money. Gets anything she wants, never worked a day in her life," he huffs out, arms folded over his huge chest and crisp white shirt.

"She sounds lucky. Not everyone gets the chance to get everything they want in life," Leon chimes in, causing Cole to frown.

"If you think she's lucky and not an entitled bitch, you take the next babysitting duty. This is not what I signed up for when you and Owen started Cerberus." All eyes land on me for the briefest of seconds, trying to gauge my reaction at the mention of *his* name.

I don't react. On the outside anyway.

"My job is to hunt people down, find their ass and haul them back." The aggression in his voice has me shifting slightly in my seat. He's a little scary. If I had had a man like Cole after me, I get the feeling he would stop at nothing to get the job done.

"Do you know what she did this week?" He has the table's full attention. "She went clubbing. Not to one of the ones on her parents' approved list." Strikes me as a little controlling, I think to myself. "And not any of the ones we have vetted and know are secure. No, she went to Praise, fucking Praise. One of the worst clubs you could ever go to. It's full of dickheads, scum, deadbeats, and every known criminal within a forty-mile radius." He's gripping his drink so hard I'm wondering how long it will take for the glass to break.

"That club is notorious for being a place you go to get fucked up. Or hire someone to fuck them up for you," I add in and they look at me like I've let slip information I definitely shouldn't know.

"How do you know about Praise?" Ethan asks, his tone cold and serious, looking at me like he wants to lecture me if I don't give him the right answer.

"Please tell me, you have never been there, or plan on ever going there?" Cole adds in, Leon looks like he's ready to lock me away to keep me safe. I can't help but laugh. It's a nervous laugh, but I don't think they know that. *Do they?*

"Oh god, don't be ridiculous..." I say, thinking on my feet. I can't tell them how I know it. "It came up a few times while I was working at Holland and Brooke. A lot of shit went down in that club. I can't believe it's still open. I thought they shut it down a few years ago." This seems to settle their curiosity. *You hope* my internal voice chimes in.

"Good," Ethan almost shouts. "That place is more trouble than you need in your life. The further away you can get the better." Ethan is deadly serious right now. Although I think he might always be serious. I'm not sure he has cracked a smile yet this evening. Or since I met him. This is probably the most words he has spoken to me.

"That's almost exactly what I told Miss Byron. I had to drag her out. But not before she almost got pawed by some nasty-looking dude almost twice her age," Cole adds.

The club is the one Mr Summers owns and where he runs all of his dealings from.

"Can we join in?" a familiar voice asks from behind me. Turning around, I see Millie, shadowed by Jack.

"Oh, my god. Yes, please do. There is way too much testosterone on this table," I declare happily. Chairs are added and room is made for them both to join us. I watch as Jack helps Millie sit down, pulling his chair closer to hers.

"I didn't think he was letting you out yet?" I nod towards Jack, who scowls at me, before turning to the others.

"He can't keep me away from you, plus I've not left the cottage in weeks. As much as I love it, I needed a change of scenery. For my sanity," Millie replies, side eyeing Jack.

"It's been a week," I laugh, "but I, for one, am so glad you are here." She smiles. "So, no wheelchair today?" I add playfully. She whacks my leg.

"No," she grumbles. "It may be outside. I refused to bring it here. I don't really need it" We both chuckle, then she gets that look to say we need to talk.

"Good, now explain to me what this is?" She gestures towards everyone sitting at the table. I knew she would do this. Walking in and finding me with three huge men, ones I've only known for a few months, is not something I would normally do. I've not avoided her, but I have not been honest with her about me and Owen. *Still stings.*

"What do you mean?" I say before taking a large sip of my light and fruity red wine.

"Don't play that with me, Charlotte Hudson."

Huh, she full named me. Now I know she's serious.

"Okay, but not here. Too many ears."

She nods, then slowly stands. Jack immediately stands with her, helping her. "Thank you," she whispers. Jack cups her face and places a kiss on her lips. "We will be back in a bit. Relax, I'll be fine."

"Charlie, follow me." Millie moves across the room, Jack goes to follow, but Millie gives him a loving but aggravated look that tells him to sit back down. "If he had his way, he would carry me everywhere."

Following her, we make our way to an office through the side door at the back of the bar. I forgot she used to work here. Oh, and Jack owns the place. I guess that gives her free rein on where she can go. When I glance around, all eyes are on us. Shaking my head at them, they all look away. Sheepishly.

"Explain what this is, Charlie. I walk in to find my best friend sitting with my old security team. They look like they are on duty. What have you not told me? Are you in trouble?"

Sinking into the deep brown sofa that sits against the wall, Millie comes to sit next to me. I help her as she lowers herself slowly. "I'm not in trouble." *How can I explain this? Oh, the man I was falling for, up and left just when I was beginning to have hope I could actually be in a relationship again, then he asked his super-hot, ex-army buddies to keep me safe. Because he doesn't think he can when I'm in no actual danger at all and can fucking look after myself. So, you know, this is now my normal, when I have no idea when, or if, he is ever coming back... Shit.*

My eyes sting with unshed tears.

"Then why are they all here?" She looks really confused and I can't blame her.

"Owen left."

"I know. What does that have to do with you?"

Taking in a shaky breath, I start to explain everything. "Owen and I had a thing."

"I guessed you were sleeping together, but I thought it was nothing serious."

"It was nothing to start with. The night you got shot, he lied to me. Said he would take me to the ball, then cancelled on me, saying he wasn't going to make it. Only for me to find him there when I arrived."

Millie placed her hand over mine, giving it a gentle squeeze. "That's got to sting after what Andy did. Is that why you renounced men that night?"

I smile a little, remembering that moment. "Yep, that's also why I got shit-faced and was not there when everything else happened. Because he took care of me. Carried me to his room and left me to sleep it off."

"I'm happy you weren't there, Charlie. I can't even begin to imagine what would have happened if you were there too. You would have gotten yourself involved. I know you and your kick ass ways, you could have been hurt," she takes a breath, "but that's a different conversation. Carry on." God, this woman is amazing. After everything, she still puts others first. She's not wrong. I would have done anything I could.

"After you got shot, he called me, had me picked up, and brought me to the hospital. He wrapped me in his arms, held me, comforted me..." I swallow the lump that's rising in my throat. "After that, well, he... he, we spent a lot of time together, talked, had the most amazing sex of my life." God, I miss the sex. "I thought... I don't know, but whatever it was, was not meant to be. After a while, he started to change, I only saw him at night. He would sneak in, he would ask me all the questions, avoided anything I asked him. Then he went, left. Gone, not to be seen or heard of since."

"Oh, Charlie, why didn't you say something to me sooner? He's been gone for what? A week?"

"It will be three weeks tomorrow." Her face says it all. "He gave me hope, Millie. After what Andy did, the shit he put me through, he gave me the hope that I could do it again."

"Shit, Charlie." Millie's arms wrap around me, and I feel myself crack for the first time since he left. I can feel this pain, this anger. A deep disappointment in myself for ever believing I could find love.

"I know it sounds ridiculous. We only knew each other for six weeks."

She elbows me in the ribs. "Not that ridiculous. Jack and I were a few weeks." She smirks at me.

But Jack never left you, Millie, I think. He stayed and did everything within his power to help and protect you.

"Did he say why he was leaving?"

Shaking my head, I hold the necklace in my hand and show Millie. "He gave me this, made me promise never to take it off. No matter what." My voice breaks at the last few words.

"No matter what? What does that mean?" That's a question I have asked myself too many times over the past few weeks. I still don't know. I just shrug, not knowing what to say.

"So why are his friends acting like they are your security team?"

Good question.

"Owen asked them to look after me while he was gone. Told them he needed to sort his head out. He blames himself for what happened to you, Millie. Something to do with his past. They won't tell me the details. But I think it's bad."

I don't tell her that he left to keep me safe. It makes no sense to me, so I doubt it will make sense to Millie.

"I knew I should have talked to him sooner. Jack set up meetings with him, but he kept rescheduling them. Except the one on the day he left. Jack and I don't hold him responsible for what ass-face did."

"I can think of worse words for that man." We both chuckle. "Well, that's the whole story."

"How are you with all this?"

"I'm dealing with it. I've started training again, to get the aggression out." Millie's eyes light up, big, bright, and beautiful.

"I loved watching you train before. Can I again? Can you train me?" she asks with a devilish grin.

"Are you serious?" I think my mouth is actually hanging open.

"Deadly. I may have to wait a few months before I do anything physical though, but I can watch to start with. I'll work on Jack. Don't say anything to him yet."

"Yes. I would love that so much. Can you do tomorrow? I'll pick you up."

“Deal.”

Chapter Sixteen

Scuttering

Charlie

Three months later.

AVxtail/9: Some information that might be of interest to you. Meet tonight, midnight. Pin attached.

xxSass29: Thanks.

Walking toward an old building on the outskirts of town in the dead of night, in hindsight, is probably not one of my best ideas. I'm prepared. I have a weapon—a can of pepper spray—tucked into the back of my jeans, plus the skills I've learned during my time in the MMA world.

I should be, okay? Shouldn't I?

It does nothing to stop my heart from racing, no matter how many times I reassure myself.

Fuck. If the guys find out I'm here, they will never let me leave my apartment again. Ever. This is the very definition of putting myself at risk. Something I promised I would never do. I lied obviously.

I've spent the last few months tracking a couple that used to live in one of the apartments opposite a house fire victim. The fire itself was ruled as an accident by the fire department, but I've noticed a signature between three accidental fires so far. It's only small, but I have a feeling it's something. All the victims have a link to the organisation to some degree. Either through where they worked or an affiliation to someone who does.

They never see it coming.

The couple had a camera overlooking the road out front. I need to see what was on that footage. They moved within a day of the fire, left their place to be sold by an estate agent and have not been seen since. I found them with some help on the dark web, from a friend of mine. If you can call people on the dark web friends. They always seem to have the information I need.

Shitting hell, it's dark in here. Creepy as fuck too. Standing just inside the door, I let my eyes adjust to the dark. After a minute, I can make out the room—empty, dirty with lots of broken furniture, but void of any life.

Fuck.

I don't know whether to be relieved or pissed off that there is no one here. But my dark web friend's not let me down yet. If it's a he, that is.

Trying to slow my breathing down, I place my hand over my heart and feel it racing. When my phone pings in my pocket with a notification, I let out a small screech, stumbling at the sound. I curse myself internally for not silencing it before I came out.

> **AVxtail/9:** It's on the table. Take it and leave as soon as you can.

What fucking table?

Moving around the space, my feet crunching over the leaves that have collected inside. I walk towards the far end of the room, finding another door that creaks as I open it, crouching low before I take a look inside.

This room seems a little brighter, a streetlight outside illuminating it in an orange glow through the broken window. Sweeping my eyes over the space, I spot the table, and on top is a small envelope leaning against a can of mace.

Whoever AVxtail/9 is they always leave me a gift, and it's always something to protect myself with. I have quite the collection growing at home. I'd like to say I'm smart enough to not have done this before, but I'm not. Since saying yes to Simon, I've had to use this process a little too often. But the evidence I have gathered is so valuable. I've not even shared it with Simon, for fear of information being leaked to the Summers' organisation. For now, it's just my personal collection... until the time comes.

The floorboards creak as I step closer and the scuttering of tiny feet has me shivering at the thought of mice or worse, rats being in here with me.

I run for the envelope, deciding to see what's inside when I get back home. There's a thrill about doing this, that I love. Don't get me wrong, it also scares the shit out of me every time. I know what I'm doing is dangerous, but it's all for the right reasons.

Heading outside quickly and running to my car, I make the drive home.

When I get back, my phone pings with another notification. This time it's from Leon.

Big T: Where have you been?

Me: Why are you awake at this hour?

Big T: Don't avoid the question. Where have you been?

Yep, I'm going to bring out the sympathy card, if he asks me any more questions.

Watching as the dots appear and disappear, I know he wants to rip me a new one, but doesn't want to piss me off.

Then my phone rings. *Shit, I hate having to lie to him.* Taking a nervous breath, I answer.

"Good morning, Leon."

"I guess I should say happy birthday." It's past 2 am. I guess that makes today my birthday.

"Thank you."

"Why can't you sleep? What's up?"

Lie, Charlie. Lie like you have never before.

"Oh you know, Owen, life, flowers, work, lists, jobs, the same old things running through my mind like a carousel on speed the moment I close my eyes." He laughs, but he sounds tired.

"How did you know I was awake and up anyway? I thought we had sorted out this bodyguard shit," I joke, and he grumbles at the same time. He's been caught out. "I knew you were still checking up on me, Leon," I add, huffing.

"I wasn't checking on you. When I finish work, I do a drive by and see if everything is okay."

"You check up on me." It's a statement.

"Yes, fine, I check up on you. Is that so bad? I don't do it every night, just every time I leave a job or the office. I want to make sure you're okay. Okay?"

"Fine, are you going to bed or do you want a coffee? I assume you are close by."

"You're inviting me around for a *coffee?* In the middle of the night. I'm not some hussy you can call and get your kink on with, you know." This is a side of Leon I never knew. He's funny. Like really funny.

"Don't make me puke." The thought of sleeping with Big T makes me want to vomit. Yes, he's hot, kind, considerate, and toned as fuck. I think his muscles have muscles. He just reminds me of my brothers too much. "I'm off to bed if you are not coming round. I've got a call with Annie in the morning. We're doing a video chat with coffee and a cake before she has to head into work."

"I'm not going to be your plaything. Get some sleep and I'll see you for your birthday surprise."

Laughing wickedly, he hangs up, but I immediately call him back, shouting when he answers, "I don't like surprises, Leon, you know this. Last time I almost knocked you out when you surprised me in the shop. I don't want to do that again."

"That's why I'm telling you now, so you're prepared. Just don't aim whatever is in your hand at my face this time."

We're both laughing now. The look on his face when he walked into the storage room last week was priceless. I'd got my earphones in listening to a podcast. I was so lost in what I was doing that when I turned around, all I saw was someone next to me. Instinct kicked in and I threw a huge glass vase at his head. The moment it left my hands, I realised it was him. He tried to duck, while I grabbed for the vase and we ended up on the floor, Leon with a bruised cheek and me apologising profusely. Layla, my new assistant in the shop, walked in a few minutes later. I'm sure she thinks there is something between Leon and I. Especially from the compromising position we'd got ourselves into. She quickly left the room and avoided me for the rest of the day.

"Night, Big T. I'll be prepared for whatever you're planning to surprise me with."

"You need to think of a better nickname for me. That's shit. I need something that says manly. Big Teddy does not do my street cred any good."

Ending the call before he really does come round, I pick up my bag and head through the back of the shop. Reaching the kitchen in my apartment, I place the envelope down on the table, making myself a quick drink.

While my tea cools, I tear the envelope open, taking out a file.

The couple in question have been hiding in France for the past year and a half. All the paperwork I need is in place as well as the agreement form from them to use the video footage attached as evidence in the trial. And signed statements. *Shit, my contact is good.* They always know what I need.

Uploading the file to my laptop from the pen drive, I click on the video. I watch as the man whose house it was enters the front door. Two men appear out of nowhere and follow him inside.

A few minutes pass and nothing happens until I see a fight breaks out through the window of the living room between three men. One, I'm assuming the victim, goes down and they drag him away further into the house. A minute later, they leave and place a small metal object in the ground. *Shit, that's the flower.* The signature I've been seeing in other fires. They walk away just as the flames start to rise inside the house. Within seconds, the place is engulfed.

I clearly see the faces of the two men who just killed a man. I don't know the reason he was killed; I doubt I ever will, but this is huge. Identifying the men will have to wait for another night. It'll take hours to sort through all the faces I have on my laptop. And I need some sleep.

Chapter Seventeen

Surprise

Charlie

"Happy Birthday!"

"What the actual fuck?" I scream, waking up to the sound of Leon's voice booming through my bedroom. Peaking over the covers, I only have my underwear on, and Leon is standing in my room, holding a bunch of balloons and a coffee.

"Charlie, I warned you I would surprise you." He mocks, whipping the covers from the bed, and I feel the cold air hit me. Screeching, I scramble for them where they now lie on my floor. I watch Leon's face turn the brightest shade of red and he spins around so quickly, his huge body bumps into my dresser, knocking off my stack of books. He tries to catch them, his arms everywhere.

"Why the hell are you naked?"

"I'm allowed to be naked in my own bed, and I have underwear on." I'm laughing hard. "Plus, why the fuck are you in my bedroom?"

"For the life of me, I'm never living this down."

"Why, what have you done?"

"There are more people in the living room." For goodness' sake. Why, out of all the friends to make after Owen left, was I paired with this one?

"Leon! You have got to be shitting me!"

"Nope, Sorry. We wanted to really surprise you," he admits, now facing the wall.

Grabbing my shirt from my chair, I pull it on, then drag myself back to bed. Pulling the covers over my legs. "I'm covered. You can turn around now."

He spins around with his hand over his eyes. "You're an idiot," I tell him, as he lowers his hand down slowly.

"I know," he says, his laugh is so deep it rumbles around the room. "Here." He hands me a huge takeout coffee cup. "I brought you a coffee from Bruno's and we have a breakfast spread being set up in your kitchen, courtesy of Millie and Annie. We all conspired against you."

Walking out of my bedroom ten minutes later, I can't help but smile when everyone greets me and wishes me a happy birthday.

Millie's holding her phone up while Annie waves at me from the screen, laughing her head off. Jack's not here, but Cole and Ethan stand on either side of Millie. I'm sure they have had their orders about making sure Millie rests. She recovered and is doing well, but Jack's still being cautious about her every move.

Sitting around my dining table, I watch as everyone digs in and eats the assortment of pastries, cakes and fruit all courtesy of The Manor's restaurant. I'm doing my best to catch up with Annie. I've propped my phone up against the jam jar, so she can see me and the table.

"Tell me some happy news," I ask, as she sips her coffee. "I want to know what you've been up to." Our calls have been getting less and less lately, the distance and our schedules just don't seem to meet up for us to get together for anything other than a quick text, or a meme. This is the first time I have seen her face for over a month.

"Nothing to tell. Work sucks. I have no personal life, but I am seeing some-one."

Snickering at her, I reply, "so, you do have a personal life?"

"I guess I do?" She shrugs.

"What's he like? Do I know him?

"I don't think so. We met through… work."

He must be new if I don't know him, but then again, the building I used to work in was huge. There was no way I could know everyone who worked there.

"Tell me more."

"Oh, you know. The strong silent type, muscles on muscles, fantastic in bed, which is where I like to keep him tied up." Most of the table turns to look at me and my phone. Annie's never been the type of person to be shy about her sexual experiences. "On that note, and on that great visual of my man handcuffed to the bed, naked, his big… cock on display…" *Yeah, she said it.* "I'm going to go. Have a great birthday, Charlie."

"Ok, speak soon, ye—" She's gone before I get the last word out.

"I guess we should tell you about the other plans we have for you today. I know you're working all day. We thought we would chill at Mike's tonight. They have the gin festival on, with street food and stalls," Leons says, shoving more food onto his already full plate.

"You organised all this?" I ask him.

"Yeah, with help. Mike was doing it all anyway. We just tagged it as your birthday," he declares, wrapping his arm around my shoulder, bringing me in for a bear hug and kissing the top of my head. "Plus, I like to see you smile." My heart warms at the lengths he's gone to.

"I think Leon has a soft spot for you, Charlie," Cole jokes.

"I do," Leon admits. "She's like a little sister to me. You know, annoying, judgmental, needy, bossy."

Jabbing him in the ribs, he doubles over, laughing.

"For starters, Leon, you're the needy one. I'm the same age as you, so it's more of a twin thing. You're the one who annoyed me this morning by waking me up on my birthday." Taking a lung full, I add, "And as for judgmental, you asked for my opinion on that woman you were seeing so I gave you my honest answer. She was awful. You're better off without her." For that, he takes the last of my bacon, shoving it in his mouth.

"Yeah, she was pretty bad. You can do way better," Cole and Ethan agree.

Even with the shock of being woken up, it's turning into one of the best birthday mornings I've had in a long time.

Chapter Eighteen
Double Life

Charlie

Three & bit months later.

I can't help but feel that this is all just some kind of parallel universe I'm living in. Nothing feels real.

My double life.

One where I feel secure and kind of safe, but so utterly lost without him. Without his gravelly voice giving me a sense of deep belonging. His rough touch that would allow me to be wrapped in a blissful reality where it was just the two of us.

Loneliness in a world where I have so many people around me who care so deeply for me, yet it's not enough.

Raking my eyes over the images spread out across my table, files open with the bone-chilling things Mr Summers has been inflicting on anyone who dares to go against him. So much violence written.

This is my second life.

Sneaking around, visiting people and places to help myself and Simon build a solid case against him.

A second life no one knows anything about. I'm not sure if that's a good thing or not anymore. I've shielded myself from the emotion and devastation this case could cause me. I'm in denial, I have to be, otherwise I'd never leave my home.

The things these people do don't scare me; they terrify me. Call me stubborn, stupid, or determined. I won't let them win. I can't. I won't stop until I find what I need.

They don't know about me and that's the biggest advantage we have.

I left Layla downstairs, looking after the shop a few hours ago. I told her I needed to get the apartment tidy before my parent's arrival later.

It's so cold outside, but it's even more chilling in here with the new information I found. Another death I've been able to link to the Summers' organisation. Another fire. That poor man did nothing wrong. He found out something about where he worked, tried to leave, but the night he went home, his family home was burnt to the ground. An accident, they called it, but there's a distinct and recognisable pattern to the way it all happened. Someone wants justice, decides to turn to the police. The fire happens. It's not the only way they kill them off, but this seems to be their preferred choice. Then the flowers are left behind. I don't know why it's not been picked up before, or discovered by the police. Maybe they have people on the force who are on their books.

One that's been done before, a signature, a warning, for those that dare to try and do the right thing. A scorched metal flower, its stem piercing the ground. Its bloom facing the cold night sky. Left in front of five properties I've seen so far. He never went to the police. He didn't make it that far. They never gave him a chance. The only saving grace for him was his family was not there.

The sound of thudding feet brings me back to what I was doing, and realisation. *Shit,* I have all my files open and Leon is about to walk through the door. I know it's him; his footsteps are loud.

Scrambling quickly to my feet, I push everything into the box, running to my bedroom with it in my arms and placing it under my bed.

Mentally checking myself, I walk into the living room, hating that I'm keeping this secret, when they have been nothing but open and honest towards me about what they are doing to try to find Owen. They have trackers on all of his accounts, cars, trucks, and properties, but they keep reminding me he was called the ghost for a reason. If he doesn't want to be found, he won't be. It doesn't matter how hard they try, how far they search.

I shouldn't care, but I do. I just need to know he's okay and not struggling somewhere on his own.

"What time are your parents coming?" Leon asks as he walks in. I'm internally groaning at that question, as he steps into view, after helping himself to a choc-ice out of the freezer, before sitting on the sofa, like he lives here. I love my parents, but when they do anything, visit, travel, dinners, party, they do it big, and very, very messy.

I like things to be tidy.

I'm excited to see them. It's been months since they were back in the country. I also know how exhausted I will be when they leave. "A few hours," I tell him, flopping onto the sofa next to him, resting my head on his shoulder. "It's only a short stop before they fly out to New York to continue their early retirement plans." Leon's eating what's left of his choc-ice. I swear all he does is eat.

"I'm looking forward to meeting the people that brought you into the world." I raise my eyebrows at him. I video called them and told them everything.

They were great about it all, understanding, loving, a little annoyed I never told them sooner. They told me they would have supported me through the divorce. They just wanted to make sure I was happy.

I am.

Ish, sort of.

I miss Owen. The ache in my heart never really leaves.

"I need to ask them if they knew what they were getting themselves into when they had you…" He laughs at his own joke.

"Funny. Why are you at my place again? I thought you had a job to do? Or at least a home to go to?"

As well as my parents coming over, Millie's coming after her showroom/workshop closes. Her design business, 'Millican' which she started when she left the hospital has been doing great. It's their wedding in just over a month. We have a few last-minute things to do before we fly out to Ibiza in three weeks' time.

"I need to be back in the office at four. Ethan's due back from assignment and we need to debrief before Cole heads out to take his place for the next round." After the night at the pub six months ago, when Cole kept complaining about Miss Byron, they started to switch up who went on babysitting duty with her. Coles upgraded the name to bitch-watch. The hate he has for Miss Byron is so strong. I cringe sometimes at the way he talks about her. It's not like him to be so hurtful to someone.

"Help me tidy before they arrive?" I ask, attempting to pull him off the sofa. Leon just looks around, confused. "There's nothing to tidy, the place looks great."

"Fine. Have you said anything to Layla? Every time you walk in, she stops talking. I just don't understand why."

"I've never said a word to her." He frowns, looking as puzzled as I do.

"Maybe it's a man thing," I add, shrugging, while moving the books on the coffee table to the other side. Leons laughs at me, leaning forward on the sofa.

"I'll try and talk to her. See if I can make her feel more comfortable around me."

"Thank you. I'd appreciate it since I can't seem to get rid of you, and I want to keep her." For that comment, he eyes me, smiles, then he moves the books I just adjusted back to their original spot just to piss me off.

My parents arrive at the shop door with bags full of food. Mum hugs me and heads straight for the stairs, arms fully loaded with bags,

"Boo, you have a great eye for this stuff," Dad says, taking in the huge, vibrant mural behind the counter.

"A local artist did it. It's beautiful, isn't it?"

"Ah, you always were great at seeing everyone else's potential," he says, hugging me from the side.

"What's mum brought with her today?" It's kind of a family joke. Wherever she turns up, she always brings food.

"Enough food to feed an army, as usual." I laugh, knowing I will have enough food for a month by the time they leave. It's just what my mum does.

"Great, saves me cooking. Millie's coming around later to go over details for her wedding next month." Dad nods as we reach the top of the stairs.

"How is she? Is she okay? Tell me more about this new man of hers. What's he like?"

"He's one of the best, dad. Exactly what she needs in her life." I love that they care for her just as much as I do.

"Good. After what she's been through, she needs a decent man by her side." I couldn't agree more. Reaching the top of the stairs, Mum's standing there, bags still in her hands, not moving a muscle. I think she's found Leon.

"Who is that *fine* beast of a man in your kitchen? Gosh, he makes the whole area look tiny." Laughing to myself, I move past her to where Leon is rummaging through my fridge again.

"Mum, Dad, this is Leon." He pops his head from the fridge, standing to his full height. Mum's face flushes and my dad just shakes his head at her.

"Mr and Mrs Hudson, it's so nice to meet you." Mum's face deepens to a red-ish-pink. She loves the smutty books just as much as I do, and Leon could be on one of the covers. "Charlies told me so much about you." He extends his hand out for my dad, who shakes it firmly, before he takes the bags from my mum's hands, placing them on the countertop and peaking in to see if there's anything to eat. Moving with him, she swats his hands away, and he chuckles.

"I'd like to say the same, but our dear daughter has yet to mention she has a new man in her life," Dad says flatly, and I freeze at his words. "This is the first we have heard anything about you, son?"

Son?

"No, Dad."

Leon's eyes say it all. Shit. I should have thought about what they would think.

"My apologies, sir. Your daughter and I are just friends. She's with one of my best friends actually. Has been for a while."

My mouth is literally hanging open. *What the actual fuck did he just say?*

Is it possible for your heart to beat faster and sink to your stomach at the same time? Because that's exactly what mine just did. Why did he even... think that, let alone say it. To my fucking parents? We haven't spoken about what Owen is to me, or *was* to me, but this is... unexpected. Shockingly so. It still hurts too much.

"Past tense, *Leon*. I was. Not anymore."

Leon's eyes sweep over me when my words come out a little firmer than they should. My parents exchange a look between them and get to unpacking the bags, spreading the contents all over the kitchen.

"What happened, Boo?" Dad asks, placing a very large chicken down on the counter.

"It's a long story, Dad. One I don't want to talk about. Can you give me a minute, please?" I don't want to lose my shit in front of them.

Sweeping my gaze to Leon, I give him the worst glare I can, then walk back down to the shop, wiping away a stray tear when it falls down my cheek.

"Sorry, my bad." Leon chases after me, pulling me into a hug when he reaches me. More tears threaten. I don't know how to process what he said.

"What was that?" I whisper shout.

"It just came out. Sorry."

Seriously?

"Why would you say, or even think, that I'm still with Owen, Leon?" It makes absolutely no sense. "He's been gone for over six months." I hate that my tears are falling now and Leon is witnessing them.

"I think of you and Owen as a couple, always have... the letter he left me, asked me to look after you. In my eyes, you are his. I know how fucked up that sounds. I really do. But he has never, in all the years I have known him, got the feels for a woman."

"Feels? What does that mean?" I think I already know, but hearing it from someone so close to him... too real.

"Do I really have to spell it out for you?" His words aren't angry, they're caring, in his big gruff way. "I thought you knew already, Charlie. He's god damn crazy about you, he..." My hand covers his mouth. I can't hear it. I'll break if I do.

"How can he?" My anger and frustration, pouring out. "For us to be a couple, you need to actually be together. For him to have the feels..." That sounds ridiculous when I say it. "He has to want to be here, not take off in the middle of the night, never to be seen again. Unless you know something I don't, Leon? Have you found him?"

My head's spinning. Granted, I've not been with anyone since he left. When we go out, having them with me is like the biggest cock block you could get. But it's not through lack of trying...

"Wait a goddamn shitting minute..." Pulling my hand away from his mouth, I shove him. "Is that why I've not been able to get a date when we go out? Because you and the boys think I'm still with Owen. You think I'm his?" His silence tells me everything.

This is fucked up.

"Leon. Shitting hell." Anger, embarrassment and an almost uncontrollable need to kill Leon sweeps through me. "I'm so angry with you right now." Pulling in a big breath, I steady myself, leaning against the wall, calming my breathing. Now is not the time. "You will get back up those stairs, speak with my parents and try not to give any more information away about my relationship status, or lack thereof because of you," I huff out, stabbing my finger into his chest, which hurts me more than it does him.

Six months and not one word from Owen. Not even his closest friends know where he is. I still want him. That's the most shameful part of it all. I'd wait for him. I am his, even if it's not the same for him.

I need to remind myself that even if he comes back, it will be for his friends and his business, not for me. If I couldn't get him to stay before. What are the chances of him coming back for me now? If he really wanted me, then why would he stay away for so long?

After that realisation, I figured I needed to find another outlet for when I think of him. My training's doubled, but I needed more of a distraction.

I started buying things, things that made me happy. Expensive shoes, cute outfits, gifts for those around me, buying huge stocks of Millie's positive affirmation print designs to keep in the shop and sell for her. I'm now the owner of a speciality gin collection with matching multi coloured gin glasses. Light up ice cubes. And a monthly subscription to a gourmet pudding club for two because, who does one for single people?

I eat both.

Huffing out a breath, I snap at Leon, "Go back up. I'll be there in a minute." He disappears without a word.

Am I going to pretend that my life is normal? *Yes.*

Is my life anywhere near normal? *No, absolutely fucking not...*

Two things... three things actually. One, work is amazing. I love every second of it. It keeps me busy in the day. Keeps my mind occupied. *Apart from the impulse buys every time I think of Owen.* It's when I'm in bed at night that my thoughts and dreams drift to him. I can still feel his touch now.

Two, I can't get over him. *Maybe one and two are the same thing.* I desperately want to be over him, but I just can't do it. I still wear the necklace he gave me, even after all this time. *No matter what.*

Three, I'm a little scared for my safety right now.

Taking a seat behind the counter, I think about all the things I have uncovered while I've been working for Simon. We named the leak as Josh, one of their associate solicitors, yesterday. He was the only person it could be. He has full access to all the documents, some even before they reach Simon, Annie or myself. I've started a separate investigation into this to dig deeper into how he could be getting the information to Mr Summers.

It's so risky. If someone finds out it's me getting this information for Simon, they could come after me. I know what that would mean. I've seen the evidence of what they do to people like me. People who are trying to do the right thing. A shiver passes through my body, leaving goosebumps in its wake. It's a chilling thought.

So, yes, I'm pretending my life is normal. Whatever that is.

Making my way back upstairs, Leon has Mum and Dad both laughing about something I've missed. Mum makes so much food, it takes over the table and kitchen counters. It looks like an all you can eat buffet in here right now. Mum's even piling it into my freezer and fridge. Dad's helping himself and Leon's guilty gaze meets mine in an apology, while he towers food on his plate.

Sitting in the middle of all the food is one of the worst gifts I will ever have the privilege of owning. I let out a burst of laughter, lighting my mood. I don't know how they do it. This one tops them all so far. A pair of earrings, big enough to be a centrepiece on the table. Hanging from one very large gold hoop is a very large bright orange velvet hedgehog holding a cup of tea in a green mug (yes, a cup of tea). The other hoop has an equally big, bright pink velvet fox, holding a biscuit. I have never laughed so much in my life. As silly as it is, I know they get me these things to get a smile from me. And it works every time. I may have to hang these up in the shop just to show them off.

My phone beeps in my pocket, pulling it out, it's a message from Millie asking me why I've locked the door.

I give her the ever-changing code to get in the back. After a few minutes, she's at the door, walking very slowly.

"I dislike you very much right now, Charlotte Hudson." She's full naming me again, so I know I'm in trouble. "My legs are dying after yesterday's training session. No, my whole body is in pain. How do you do this every other day? I barely made it up your stairs. I can barely sit on the loo."

"I did warn you. You also asked me not to go easy on you."

"Why would you put yourself through that?" Leon says after swallowing what looks like a whole chicken breast. "Me and the guys will never train with Charlie. She's brutal—skilled as fuck—but a machine."

"Now you tell me, Leon. Thank you very much," Millie says. "I should have known really. I've seen you do this for years, but never really thought about how much it would hurt." I hug her close, feeling lucky to have them all around me

"Bill, Susie, I've not seen you in forever," Millie cries as she embraces them like they are her long-lost parents. Mum and Dad both hug her tight, before dragging her to sit down on the sofa and laughing as she attempts to sit down on her sore legs. She'll be feeling them for days.

My apartment is a mess, but it feels full of love. We're swept away in last minute wedding plans, Mum's never-ending photos of their travels, and questions about how Leon got to be the size he is. I fear dad may start taking it personally if she carries on.

Chapter Nineteen

Hero Complex

Owen

This place is my best kept secret. No one knows about it, not even Leon and my brothers. It's like my own personal safe house. It's isolated. You can't see it from the air. It's hidden by the surrounding woods. Wild and untamed. It's self-sufficient, solar-powered for all the energy I need. I bring most of the basic food with me. Shop when I need more. It even has a small spring that provides fresh water. It was exactly what I thought I needed; Isolated, quiet, peaceful, no-one around for at least fifteen miles in any direction.

I've spent most of my time building the new veranda for the place, thinking this would help me calm my mind. Turns out I needed more, so I've started seeing a therapist online. Working with wood has brought me calm many times before this, only this time it didn't work. The harder I tried, the more I poured myself into it, it still couldn't calm the tormented thoughts that kept coming. The flashbacks at the sound of a loud noise, the fear that gripped my chest.

I can't stop thinking about her, Charlie. It's taken all my willpower to not set my phone up and contact her, or open my laptop to see what she's doing from the security system I installed so I could check in on everything else. Fuck, who am I kidding? I gave in about a month in, and I've been checking in, in my own way.

Have I made a mistake coming here to the lodge? Yes, I'm not sure being on my own is good for me. But at least I got the veranda built.

I've relived it all over and over, retold the memories of what happened during those four days in our unit. The pain and loss of each and every friend who died during our last mission.

I've hit an all-time fucking low. Coming here was one of the worst things I could have done. I can't see a way to fix what's happening to me.

Their names and their faces haunt me. The memories of our time in the unit. How each of them died in our arms. Guilt, that's what it comes down to. Guilt that four of us walked away that day, while the others were flown home to be buried and mourned by their families.

Guilt that it was my responsibility to keep them safe, and I didn't. It was my job as CO. Guilt that I missed a vital part of information, a breach in our team, that led to six of my men losing their lives.

I know I made the right decision to step away from Charlie, but I did it for all the wrong reasons.

All I've done is isolate myself from the people who care about me. I can't think straight.

I've been in therapy for months. I'm on the verge of firing his ass too, just like I did the first guy after two weeks. He only made it worse. Now I can't get them out of my head, and we haven't even touched on Millie's case yet.

This new guy. Fuck, I don't know.

"Owen, you need to listen to what I'm saying. Have you been writing in your journal?" Fucking journaling, not a chance.

"No, and I won't be. I've already told you that. That shit doesn't work."

"Your PTSD is triggered by a number of things, especially in your line of work." He writes something in his notebook about me.

"What are you saying?" My eyes meet his in a warning. We've been doing this remotely over a secure channel on my laptop. My hands clamp together and I can only guess what's coming next.

"Do you think it's responsible to keep working in the security field?" He has to be shitting me. My teeth grind together in frustration. Why can't he see what I need?

"What?" No, he fucking didn't just tell me to get another career, in his backwards way. Stepping away from it, all I've done is think about my friends, the assignments. I miss it, even if the flashbacks still come. I do understand what he's trying to get at, not that I'll give him the fucking satisfaction of letting him know. I just need to get a handle on it. I need something different.

"Is there any other option available within your company that could offer you a more permanent, relaxed role?" He's serious.

"A more relaxed fucking role?" Yes, he did. He absolutely did just tell me to step back from the business I love and the people who support me the most. I miss it all, but to give it up completely and watch my brothers do all the assignments and jobs without me? No. Not going to happen.

"Owen, we have been doing this for months, with no real change in sight."

"You're right. There's been no change in how I feel." If anything, it's stayed the same. I'm just alone now.

"Stepping away from the people I love has made me worse." When I left, I couldn't get it out of my head that it wasn't my fault. I needed an escape. I wanted to be better for Charlie and my brothers. Distorted beliefs, that's what I've come to understand makes me blame myself more than necessary. That's what this dude said anyway. "But if I remove myself from them permanently..." My chest tightens at the thought. Never doing what I love, never being part of my team, never seeing her again. *Fuck that.*

"This time alone has been good and bad for you. You have made some progress in your understanding of your condition," he admits.

I have a better understanding of my PTSD. Millie's shooting was the final trigger. The sound of the gun going off caused my flashbacks to start. The only thing I'm lacking now is a way to get it under control. The distorted beliefs I had and not being able to protect Charlie consumed me. I knew there was no actual risk to her life, but just couldn't process it.

In my mind, I wasn't good enough at what I did, and if any risk came up, well all I could see was Charlie getting hurt on my watch. So I left to keep her safe.

The fire I feel in my veins when I think of what I did, leaving her, still pisses me off. I hate being away from her, my friends, my brothers. I just hope she can forgive me. Or even just understand why I had to do it. Granted, I could have handled things better. Hindsight is a powerful thing, I suppose.

I thought being on my own at the lodge would be ideal, time to clear my head. I thought it would give all the resolve I needed to get my head back in line. To get the negative thoughts turned around and back on track.

I thought I needed to get over this fear of losing everyone I loved. The fear and anxiety I hold close to my chest so that I can protect what's mine, or as Charlie put it, my hero complex.

How fucking right she was.

"No, stepping away has never been a possibility in the long term, and never will be. I love what I do, but I need to develop a way to deal with it, so I can live with it, not push it all away. I know what I need."

"Owen..."

"No, fuck you, doc. I will never stop doing what I love. I will find a way to deal with this." There's an idea forming I think may work.

"Owen..."

I'm letting it all out, I can't hold back. "It's not a negative to have a hero complex, but I do need to understand what is and is not within my control. And you keep telling me to start again, a fresh sheet. That's not helping me."

"That's not..."

"To late, doc. You're fired." Shutting the lid on the laptop I lean my head back on the sofa. This conversation has flicked a switch. I'm not leaving my life behind to start a new one. I've already abandoned the people I care about. I don't want to make it permanent. I said I would be back, and I meant it.

This solitude, the calm and peace, I want none of it unless she's by my side.

Swiping my hands over my face, I know I have a lot to deal with. I can't be there for her yet, but I will. I'll make it up to her when I'm ready.

Walking upstairs, my heart racing with excitement of what I'm about to do, this is the best I have felt in a long time. I need to pack my bag with the essentials I'll need for the journey. I'll leave tonight.

I need to face my demons head on.

There was no way in hell I wanted to cut my family off, my brothers and especially Charlie. *Fuck.* I want to be better for her, for them. My therapist's words ring true to a point. I have to admit. This time away has been both good for me and the worst idea I have ever had.

I jumped in feet first. Facing my issues head on, in a way I thought was right. My head was fucked up. I did what I thought was the right thing to do. I've been here for six months. It's just not worked out for me like I thought it would. I need to try something else. A therapy that will see me facing my PTSD while surrounded by the people who I know will be able to see it from my point of view. And help in only the way they can.

There's only one way to deal with what is going on in my head, and that's to work in the field again. Under the special division. Tracking Dom, our special ops team leader, and his team is going to be a little harder when you have limited access to the system we use to find info on people. I only have a vague location to go from.

I've been MIA, but I have been with my friends and Charlie, every step of the way. In everything. They just have no idea.

Chapter Twenty

Exposure

Owen

A few weeks later.

I walked up to Dom in the middle of a busy market in Goa and planted myself in the seat next to him. His look of shock only lasted a few seconds before he put me to work. I knew it was wrong because of the state I was in, but within minutes I was using my ability to ghost to their advantage and got their case cleared ahead of schedule. It felt good, really fucking good, to be part of it all again. I got lucky I wasn't triggered.

I need to be honest with them now.

"Zan, can I have a word?" I ask as we sit at the bar after getting back to the hotel and his eyes squint in question.

"Yeah, how important is this?" he asks, turning to face me.

"Very," I state.

"Sure," placing his order, he turns back to me, "let me finish up and I'll meet you in my room." Handing me his key card, I make my way up to his room. I hope he'll agree to this. I couldn't have done this sort of therapy with my old therapist. There was no way I could trust him for this. I'm anxious about asking Zan to do therapy with me. He has the experience of being a counsellor and being in the army. He also has my respect and trust. It's risky given we're on missions, but it's what I need to be able to function.

Zan's room in the hotel is simple—a bedroom with a small seating area. Pouring myself a whisky from his minibar to settle my nerves, I walk out of the doors leading out onto the balcony. Looking over the busy street below, taking a sip of my drink, I wonder what Charlies doing. Fuck, I miss her so much.

The door clicks behind me, and I hear footsteps approach. "Let me guess, you need help with something?" he says, coming to stand next to me, his eyes trained on my face. "Everyone on your team is looking for you, O." That's a fucking loaded question, one I know I have to be honest about.

"Yeah, it's a big ask... I have PTSD," I state.

"Fuck, Dom just let you..." He sucks in a breath. "Why should I keep you here?"

"I'd like your help with exposure therapy. I'm here to gain control of it. I don't want to shy away anymore."

His face falls, the reality of my situation sinking in. I don't like the look on his face, a cross between a scowl and shock.

"Holy shit," he says, gripping the railing. "How bad?"

"Bad enough. I have flashbacks." Hanging my head in shame.

"You can stop that right now. This is nothing to be ashamed of, O." My head pops back up at his words.

"What sets you off?" Zan asks.

"Gunfire," I answer honestly. "Loud noises." I hate this already.

"What else is going on?" he asks, eyes scrutinising me.

"I have an overwhelming feeling of not been good enough, not doing enough, and that I won't be able to save anyone around me." That hurt, like a tear in my chest. I feel exposed.

"Jesus fucking Christ. So bad yeah?" he quips. "We just put you straight on a job. That's shit we needed to know about before sending you out there." He's pissed. I get it. I fucked up. I should have never done it.

"Fuck, I know, I know, I just... wanted to be part of something again. But I have a plan. That's why I'm here." I feel like I'm fucking up already. I have to remind myself I'm not. I am good at what I do. I've just proved that I am capable by doing that job.

"Fine, I'm telling Dom everything he needs to know." All I can do is nod. I'm in their hands.

"Yeah, you're kind of my last hope," I say, grimacing as I let the words out.

"No pressure then," he adds with a slight shake of his head.

"How much do you know?" I inquire. They have to know something. I co-own the business they work for.

"We know you freaked out after Jack's woman got shot. But not much more. You've been MIA for six months. Why make an appearance now?"

"I tried therapy. They wanted me to give up this life. Step away permanently." Disbelief crosses his features.

"What did you do? Tell them to get fucked and fire their ass?"

A burst of laughter escapes me. "Er...yeah, exactly that," I admit, still chuckling.

"It's what I'd say if anyone asked me to give this life up." He shrugs when I glance back at him.

"I want to get rid of this shit. I want to be able to control my reactions to situations and noise."

"Fuck, do you realise just how hard that's going to be?"

I've considered it. I've been doing my research. "Yeah, I do," I admit, a headache settling in my temples. I want my life back. I want the business we've built, but most of all, I want Charlie.

"Sit down. I'll need another beer before we start. I'll work out a plan for you, but I'm warning you now, it's going to be uncomfortable. I'm going to need you to be one-hundred per cent honest with me at all times. If *I* feel you can't handle a situation, you're out, no questions asked, you leave. And we reconvene later and discuss."

"I'm in your hands, Zan."

"Good. Order some room service. We'll be here a while." I may be his boss, but right now I'm willing to do anything to get this under control.

A few hours later, Zan's put a plan together: Daily noise exposure therapy, followed by talking therapy and fact-based exposure therapy, where we review the two situations that brought me here.

"It's going to be intense. Are you up for it?" Zan asks.

"Yeah, I am. I'm all in."

"Where are you standing?" Zan asks softly, sitting on the comfy chairs in his hotel room. He's encouraging me to see the scene for myself, and not rush the process. I've had a tendency to flick to the worst parts, and not see the information in front of me. This time I'm going to process it all. I don't need to speak. He's asking me to get me there in my mind, to see it all. Visualising Millie's shooting. I'm stood in the ballroom, Leon by my side, watching Jack make his speech.

"What do you see around you?" Zan asks, making me think of the day in all the detail I can. The crowd, plants, faces I don't know. "What do you hear?" The faint music, Jack's voice filling the room as he hands out awards to his staff. My heart rate picks up when I see Millie move behind us through the crowd towards the door. My throat feels tight, my hands clammy as I flex my fingers. "Tell me what's just happened?" He sees the change in me.

"Millie's just walked away... She's—"

"Pause. Take a moment." I breathe in on the count of four and exhale for six. After a few rounds, my heart rate slows, and I relax my hands. "Keep looking around. Is there anything that looks out of place, anything that shouldn't be there?"

A shake of my head gives him my answer. Everything looks normal. My heart rate slows further.

"Carry on, go slow, look around" I do. The room is still full. Jack calls for Dan to move on to the stage, then looks confused when he doesn't. I only take my eyes off Jack for a split second when my phone rings in my pocket. Lifting it to my ear, I can hear it like it was yesterday. 'RED.' Dan's voice fills my ears. Reaching for Leon, I repeat the word, pushing through the crowd of guests. My heart is in my throat, only looking to Jack when we are almost out, telling him Glen's here.

"Pause again," Zan instructs before I can slip into the chaos that unfolds next. I'm in my head, about to push through the door.

"What were your thoughts right there?"

Without opening my eyes, I tell him, "I wanted the building secure."

"What did you do to resolve that?"

"I hit the alert button and sent Leon around the front of the building."

"Was there anything else you could have done in that moment?"

"No" shit, my shoulders ease a little, "No, there wasn't." Slightly taken aback by my own words, my chest feels a little lighter.

"Good, move on."

Playing out the scene in my mind, I open the door running out to find Millie in front of Dan. They exchange words. Dan tries to grab for her. I pull him back, trying to grab for Millie as I do, but she's too far away. She exchanges herself for Em, catching her as Glen shoves Em away. She runs to Dan, safe. I take a step closer to Millie when Glen wraps his hand around her throat, pulling her back.

"Pause, what's happening? I can see a change in you. You're tense, breathing escalated."

"He's just grabbed Millie."

"How did you make the others safe?"

"I stopped Dan from stepping in, held him back. I should have grabbed Millie."

"Did you assess the threat in the room when you entered?"

"Yes." I frown, even with my eyes closed, a little offended

"What was the outcome?" he asks.

"High risk, unknown weapons, volatile suspect, emotions running high, unpredictable."

"What is the correct action to take in that situation?" Fuck, he's good. I'm starting to see this whole thing the way everyone else tells me they saw it.

"Keep assessing. Clear anyone you can. Make the suspect focus on me and not the victim."

"Is that what you did?"

"Yes, until Jack came in."

"What happened when Jack came in?"

"He was running straight for her. At that point Glen had already stabbed Millie, his gun was drawn. I had to fight Jack to keep him safe. It was the best of a bad situation."

"Best of a bad situation," he repeats before asking *that* question. "Was there anything else you could have done?"

"No, I knew Leon had done what I asked. I trust him. I kept Em, Dan and Jack as safe as I could until I knew I had backup."

"When was that?" he prompts.

"When we kicked the door down, I saw Leon take Glen down. I ran in their direction, ready to help, but he was... feral." I admit, "Unpredictable even. Jack ran to Millie. They were out of the way."

"Was there anything else you could have done at this point?" This question pisses me off, because I know the answer. It's the same every time.

"Yes, get the gun out of his reach."

"Was that possible?"

Pausing before I answer, then letting out a groan, I can see exactly what he's done. "No," I say firmly, annoyed I've not been able to see this sooner.

"Good, we'll leave it there for today. When I open my eyes, I can see the fucking smirk on his face.

"How do you see the event now?"

"Differently, in a good way." I'm a little confused. It's taken my brain a while to catch up to the reality and honest truth of what happened.

"What you did was good, O. How do you think your progress is coming on?" he asks,

"I can see that the choices I made on the day and before were the right ones, that I don't have control over someone else's actions." I breathe out the pent up tension at saying those words out loud.

"We still have a way to go, but this is fucking great."

Bang – the gun goes off; I flinch and nothing else. I feel an uncomfortable buzz in my chest, but that's okay. I can move past that. I relax, mentally patting myself on the back for getting through another round of gunfire. Ten shots per round. This time, no ear defenders.

Grey, our intel, and explosives guy, wonders over, looking smug as fuck. "I knew this would work. Nothing like it. Did it myself a few years back. Start small and work your way up the big stuff." I never thought I would get this far. "Time to go bigger" I just look at him. "Don't get your knickers in a twist. I've cleared it with Zan." Sighing with relief, Grey can get a little overexcited when it comes to making a noise. He wanted to do this using explosives, that was very quickly vetoed by everyone.

Looking down, I remember the words Harley makes me recite every time I walk into talking therapy. 'Know you are safe. Having anxiety is not bad. That feeling you have is designed to protect you. It's uncomfortable, and you can do uncomfortable things.' And we start again, this time bigger, louder and a lot more fun.

Understanding what happened to me and my team in the unit all those years ago was one of the hardest things I have ever done. I know now it was out of my control. I did everything I could have. This team, have been the best therapy I could have ever had. I've lived life again, camped in the wild and untamed lands, ate by the fire, slept in cars and worked on doing what I do best to help the team around me. I've done it all, this time on my terms, in my way, dealing with the trauma that each case would bring. Therapy after each one for the first few months helped me process my actions. I stopped blaming myself for the things I couldn't control. I guess living and working in this life has given Zander a better insight to help those around him.

They all knew I'd been MIA; they knew what happened to Millie, Jacks now wife. We talked. They all went through what they would have done in my place and it was nothing different to what I did. It was strange really. Leon had said all those words before, but I just couldn't acknowledge them. I needed the space my lodge offered. I needed to do this journey on my own. Figure it out my way.

I'm not saying I'm cured. It will always be there, but I understand how to deal with all of it now. If I ever need help, I have Zan on speed dial.

Chapter Twenty-One
Simple

Owen

Six months after joining the team.

"Dom, I've got eyes on the asset. Move in." Crouching down, perched on the thick forest floor, covered in darkness, I see the man we have come to get. He was taken from his place of work over a week ago. His family were sent a video, demanding they pay a ransom of a million pounds or he'll die. It's not a huge amount of money in the grand scheme of what he's worth, which leads us to believe this was more of an initiation test than a political target. When Dom received the call to recover, we tracked him down to this shithole four days ago.

He's injured, his face bruised, a deep laceration in his stomach, bleeding through his shirt. Tied to the post, hanging with his hands above his head. Our job's simple. Get in, extract the asset and get out. Simple, just the way I like things right now.

Eyeing my surrounding, I signal Harley to move closer. The darkness is our friend right now; the forest covered with thick vegetation. It took us three days to travel to this location, thirty-two hours of that was on foot. The guy we need to recover hasn't moved since we laid eyes on him. We won't know the full extent of his injuries until we land back at base. Our extraction is in thirty minutes. We need to move.

Our guy is surrounded by five armed guards. From the intel Grey received, and the background check we did, three of these men are ex-military, with skills similar to ours. Similar. We're better. The other two are nobodies from our records, low-rank foot soldiers. They don't know shit. Getting to this point in their compound, I know we have this. They're amateurs, sloppy, leaving an easy trail for us to find.

We did our research into this group. Small time, wanting to get into the big stuff. What they lack is any sort of respect for the bosses above them. They made a few mistakes while grabbing this guy. Shouting their mouths off, giving it the big I am. Let's just say we don't need to make any fatal moves today. These guys won't last another week in this world.

We move slowly, keeping to the shadows. Silent. Unseen. Only a few feet away now, then it's all go.

Planned to the last detail, everyone knows what needs to be done, to get him out and us back safely.

Harley signals to go in three and we move to the entrance of the makeshift tent where our guy is being held. We want to get him back to his wife and family as soon as we can.

We've surrounded them on all sides. Dom and Zan heading to the back of the tent, myself and Harley sweeping the sides. Grey set up to cover us with his sniper skills on the way out.

Harley strikes first, giving an elbow to the guy's gut. When he folds, she throws another to the side of his head and he goes down hard, hitting the floor unconscious. Out like a light. Smiling, she loves every second of this. Dom lucked out when they met. He's definitely punching above his weight.

I ghost up behind the other guy just as he turns to see his friend on the floor. A swift, effective strike on the side of the neck and he goes down like a sack of bricks. Never even saw us coming.

Fuck, I love this.

Moving the soldiers out of sight, Dom and Zander move in to take care of the other three, while myself and Harley move in to extract the asset.

Unhooking him, and laying him out on the floor, Harley and I make quick work of getting him ready to move. Wrapping any open wounds, binding him to what looks like a human-sized backpack. It allows two people to carry someone out without using their hands, keeping the injured party contained and safe.

Glancing out, I can't see what happening, but I can hear Dom and Zander swearing and the undeniable sound of punches being thrown. I focus on Harley and what we need to get done.

She nods for me to go as she attaches a small set of wheels to the bottom of the pack. They'll help distribute the weight, equal parts pulling and carrying. I help her get his unconscious body on her back. We'll swap when we move out, but this gives her a head start on us. She's got this under control. She'll be safe with Grey watching over her.

Stepping out, I creep into the shadows and watch as Dom handles one of men. He's big, but so is Dom. Zander, on the other hand, needs a little help as he has two on him. I step into sight, and Zan's sharp nod is one of appreciation. Pulling the bigger fucker off him, aiming for his face, I land the first blow to the side of his head. The second to his side. My arm tightens around his neck as I move backwards, giving Zan room to move.

My chokehold on this dude is tight, but he's fighting it. His arms come up to grab my head, his legs kicking gain some momentum. It works and I'm pulled forward. We land on the ground in a cloud of dust and debris. My heart pounds as adrenalin sets in, fists and boots flying.

Rolling in the dirt, he lands a punch to my ribs. Repaying the favour to his face, my knuckles smash into his nose. I get a good few in before my boot meets his stomach, my fist knocking him out cold. Only then do I notice Zan and Dom watching me fight from the side. Covered in sweat, bruises already turning their skin a reddening shade, smirking at me.

"Laugh all you like, arsehole," I joke, taking a moment to catch my breath. "You'll be in the shit when Harley gets hold of you. She's currently running through the thick of this hell-hole with a one-hundred-and-eighty-pound guy attached to her back." His smirk disappears as he turns to run in her direction, cursing me and himself on the way out. Zan and I both run after him, trying and failing to hide our laughter.

Our extraction went well. We came under fire a few miles out but managed to get out without any more trouble. Flying back in the helicopter to the special unit's base we share with the military, we hand over the asset to the medics and give the coordinates to the others and local forces to handle any clean ups.

Everything we do is above board. *Sort of.*

My instinct is to go back to my tent and be alone, but I don't. I sit at the outside table grabbing a beer, settling in, and watching the night sky. My thoughts drift to Charlie. Like they always do. The night always reminds me of her, of us. The dark's like a blanket. It holds me together. She holds me together. Her almost-violet eyes haunt my dreams in the best possible way. I just need to see them again.

Leaning back in the chair, I let the flames of the fire warm my skin as I think of everything I did wrong. Everything I need to make right. I know my brothers will forgive me eventually. But Charlie. I don't know what I will do if she doesn't want anything to do with me. I need her forgiveness the most. My angel. Checking my phone again, it's become a habit. One I never want to kick. Knowing she's safe at home settles my soul.

I know I should respect her decision if she wants nothing to do with me. I should walk away and let her live her life. A life without me. I groan and Zan raises an eyebrow at me, but doesn't say anything.

Every time I think of Charlie, the fire in me burns brighter. Thinking of her with someone else makes me feel possessive. An instinct that makes me want to haul her over my shoulder and lock her up, keeping her as mine and only mine. I don't want another man touching her. *Fuck, it could have already happened.* I'll be lucky if she lets me be an acquaintance at this point. I've been gone too long,

"I think you enjoyed that fight back there. There was a smile on your face the whole fucking time." Dom slaps me on the shoulder and sits beside me. His face is a rainbow of colours with bruises. I'm sure mine looks the same right now too.

"I did. I've loved every second of this, Dom. It's just what I needed."

Taking a sip of his beer, he frowns at me before Harley appears and sits on his lap, planting a kiss to his bruised cheek.

"I ache all over," she says, "pulling that," she points over to the medic tent, "for a mile and half." The expression on her face says she enjoyed it, but Dom's face is pissed off and proud all rolled into one. I guess having a woman like Harley by your side can give you very conflicting thoughts. She's strong, capable, and so freaking independent. It's a fucking miracle Dom managed to get her to marry him. He wants to keep her safe, protected and out of harm's way. Harley, on the other hand, wants nothing of the sort. She wants all the action, all the adventure, and all the love Dom is wholeheartedly giving. *Fucking beautiful.*

That's a real relationship right there.

"That's it then. We have a small job next. Should only take us a day. I've emailed the files to you all already. We leave in the morning." Harley whispers something in his ear and he shifts in his seat, his fingers tightening around her hip.

"How about we head out for a little respite for a week after this last one? It's been a while. We could all do with some R&R."

We all visibly relax at the thought of being able to sleep in, relax, and recover. The last few months have been brutal, even if it has set my mind straight on a few things.

Looking at my phone again, I switch the track and trace program back to receive notifications so I can see what's happening at home. I always check in, but nothing really changes.

"Who you checking on, O? That lady of yours?" Zan smirks from behind his beer. "You seem to check it a lot, but not do anything about it." My feelings for Charlie are no secret.

"If that was my Harley, and she wasn't by my side, I'd be tracking her too," Dom announces.

Harley swats him on the shoulder, but then admits, "I'd be tracking you too, baby."

"You need to take the next step. You need to face them," Dom suggests.

"He's right, O, you've done so well with your exposure therapy. I don't think you even flinched when we were fired at back there." A swell of pride fills my chest at his words.

"He's right, bullets were flying, and you did what you needed to do. I'm proud man," Grey adds. "You can't avoid the next step. It's time."

"What she said," Zan says, nodding along, agreeing with him.

"I know…" Dom and Zan place their bottles down at the same time, both leaning forwards, watching intently.

"It's not going to be easy, but the guys will always have your back," Dom reassures me.

"We have your back," Zan says. Harley just looks at me, knowing full well she doesn't need to say it. I know they do. My shoulders sag a little at what I need to do, but knowing the guys will support me is a good feeling to keep with me.

"Charlie, however, may need a little more work than just an apology," Harley adds, and fuck, don't I know it. I'm expecting the fight of my life.

I knew this was coming. I can't keep doing this. I like giving the orders; I like being the boss. I may still come out for the odd trip down memory lane, but I want my life back. This has healed the old wounds, but I have to face the new ones I have created back home.

"Time to make that call then…" It only takes a few minutes for my phone to fill with notifications, messages, missed calls and updates from everyone back home. After switching the track and trace off, I'm only interested in the ones from Charlie. There aren't many. Mainly missed calls dotted through the time I have been absent.

She's not hounded me, not some like others would. She knows her worth. She's given me what I needed, even when I didn't say what I was doing. She's given me the space to heal.

There's one voicemail from her from only last night. Standing up, I say my goodnights and move to the tent I share with Zan. Sitting on the camp bed, I put my phone to my ear.

"Hey, um, I just wanted to say something… everyone seems to be moving on with their lives, and I… I feel stuck. My heart hurts when I think of you and everything we could have been. I waited, Owen. I waited for you.

"I hate that you left to keep me safe. It means you never got to know me if you think I need to be looked after. I can look after myself pretty well. Just ask Leon, Cole and Ethan. They have seen what I'm capable of. She gives a small, amused chuckle. The undertone in her voice is so sad. My head dips into my hand, while I listen to her sweet voice, making my heart ache to be closer to her.

"I'm fed up of being sad over you. Millie's having a baby. Em and Dan have Daisy, Annie's in love, every one of my friends seems to be happy… I want to be happy, but it just reminds me that I'm not even close to that kind of love in my life. I want to feel something other than the loss, the missing piece of my heart. I tried not to love you, Owen. I tried so hard." She's crying now and my stomach's in knots. *"I need to be over you. I'm going to try.*

"I'm done, Owen. I can't do this anymore. I can't wait for something that was never really there to start with.

"I tried, Owen. I kept my promise to you, no matter what. But I'm not sure I can be yours anymore. It's too hard when you're not by my side." Charlie's voice breaks and she hangs up.

It guts me. I feel sick. I left it too long.

Chapter Twenty-Two

Imploding

Charlie

I've been lying still like this in my bed for what feels like forever. I feel like death. I can't open my eyes. If I move, I think I may be sick. No. I will be sick. My eyeballs hurt, like the cord connecting them to my head has been disconnected or is hanging on by a thread. Gritty, like there is sand in there, and that's even before I work up the courage to open them. My brain is also joining in on this fun little episode. It hurts like hell. Like it's been squeezed by an iron fist, while someone with a sledgehammer is pounding into it.

I need to piece together what happened for me to be in this state. It's been a while. I know alcohol was involved. I just don't remember why I let myself get into this horrible mess.

Backtrack, that's what I need to do. I need to remember. Do I remember getting home? Thinking hurts my head. No. Where was I last night? What day was it yesterday? Oh...

Friday.

Millie and Jack's.

Waiting.

Babies.

My imploding life.

Yep, that's what happened. My life imploded. It was watching everyone else move on, being happy, together, in love, while I can't move from where I am. Figuratively and literally as of this moment.

I imploded. It all comes rushing back to me. I'm so happy for Millie and Jack, married, kids, a beautiful life. I wanted that for them. I sat and watched as they talked babies with Em and Dan, played with beautiful Daisy, and went forward with their plans, with their lives. While I'm stuck. Frozen and I can't get past it, not it, *him*.

I still can't lift my head off of my pillow as the tears start to fall. I'm sprawled out on my huge crumpled bed, alone, like always. I wake up and still feel for him, every time. And every time he's not there, my heart plummets. He's not by my side. Not standing next to me, through the huge life events that have been happening around me over the past year. I can see everyone moving on around me in a blur of activity, while I just can't get there. Stood still. I can't move.

I thought I was doing okay. I suppose I've had a few buffers with me during the previous Friday night dinners. I've managed on rare occasions to drag either Leon, Cole or Ethan with me to these things, but last night, they had to work. As bad as it sounds, I've also avoided a few of the Fridays, making excuses that I have other plans, or work to catch up on. I know Millie sees through the excuses, but she's gracious enough not to pull me up on it.

Last night I was the only single person in the room, and look what happened. I got shitfaced. I don't know how I got home, or at what point my memory stopped working. It's not a great way to deal with my feelings, but at that moment, numbing the pain was better than unloading on Millie and Jack's news about expecting their first baby together.

Groaning, I try to move again; I think I'm still in my clothes from last night. I can't be sure, but I feel uncomfortable, and freaking hot.

I don't want to open my eyes. If I do, reality will kick in, and I'll be forced to get up. I feel like I've been in a train crash. My body hurts and my head wants to detonate into a million tiny fragments. Just like the state of my life.

I need to pee and it's getting painful now. I feel my phone at my fingertips, sighing heavily. I've had a bad habit of late. I order stupid stuff when I think of Owen. Being as it's in bed with me and not on charge on the bedside table, I guess I did something stupid just to add to my humiliation.

My last drunk purchase was a set of garden flamingos, three of them, each one over a metre tall, and as pink as pink can be. I remember buying them, thinking they were the best purchase in the world. Then, receiving them the next day, Layla, who is normally so quiet, couldn't stop laughing, refusing to let me send them back. She has proudly placed them in the shop along with the hedgehog and fox earrings my parents bought me last time they came to visit.

Thank fuck Layla is opening up the shop today. It's my day off officially, but I... I still need the distractions.

Since *he* left twelve months ago; Leon, Cole and Ethan have become like my new brothers—making me miss my actual brothers I've not seen for way too long now. Owen's friends watch out for me, taking me out, and we've had fun. I could have used them last night. Leon would have stopped me drinking so much and cheered me up. Even if they all still see me as with Owen.

Twelve months and I still feel the same as I did the day he left. How crappy is that. It's like I've lost a piece of me. I still wear the necklace every day, no matter what. Just like he asked me to. The engraving I feel under my fingers reminds me of him, his flames, and how he called me Angel.

"That's it..." I say with a gravelly voice, encouraging myself. I need to get up and sort myself out. I can't keep thinking like this. I've got some things I need to get done today, as well as some information I need to send over to Simon.

Last week, I hit the jackpot. I found another video, one that could put Mr Summers away for a long time, one that had been floating around the dark web. I dug deep, deeper than I ever managed to before, and I found the source. Tracing it back to a stabbing that happened three years ago, I asked Simon to pull the records for me so I can crossmatch a few of the finer details. This is it though. We have him. Mr Summers, his partial face is on this video. Knife in hand, while he… stabs someone and kills them in cold blood. We should be able to do a face match using the police program, just to show we have a match as it's only a partial face. I need to know how the case is going and if Simon's informed anyone yet.

It's been a while since we were able to move forward after the last witness went missing and was found dead a few weeks later. It was messy. This is why Simon's kept my involvement a secret so far, but if this goes well, I'll need to be a little more involved, and he will need to inform the courts I helped.

Peeling my eyes open, I dare to look at my phone, then put it down again. *Fuck that.* I need food and coffee before I start the dreaded phone dive to see if I bought anything stupid or called anyone last night.

"Millie. I don't know what to do. How could I? It's tomorrow! I can't leave."

Millie's not said a word, well I've not let her. I'm in a total flipping flap, verbally spewing my thoughts out to my best friend, panicking.

What have I done? Millie's at work, but I rang her as soon as I looked at my emails on my phone and saw the timer I apparently set last night. Counting down, continually alerting me, and reminding me of the extremely bad decisions I make when I'm drunk.

"Slow down. I have no idea what you are talking about. Start from the beginning." I can hear the amusement in her voice. "What did you order this time?" she asks.

"I ordered a goddamn holiday, Millie, and not just any holiday, nooo… I booked myself a five-star luxury holiday in Greece for a whole shitting week." I sound almost hysterical. "And that's not the worst part. I am meant to leave tomorrow! Oh, and it's just for one. Me. All on my own. Just me. No one else.

Me." I can't handle a holiday on my own. I don't want to be alone with my own thoughts for a week. I'll break, I'll crumble, and I won't be able to put myself back together.

"What's wrong with having a holiday? I think you need one. The last time you went away was my wedding, and you only stayed a few days. When was the last time you travelled?" Pacing the length of my apartment, I sit and then stand again, heading into my room to look at my wardrobe and then sinking down on the bed.

Covering my eyes with my arm to block out the sun that is streaming through the window, I say, "But on my own? And tomorrow? What about the shop?" There's so much to organise when you go on holiday. That's why everyone books in advance. Normally.

"You have Layla to help with the shop. Ivy," the woman who hires the workshop "is basically a permanent fixture in the shop now. I'll pitch in. I'm sure Leon will help when he can. I think he has a crush on Layla. It's cute."

"I'm not sure you can crush on someone when you've barely spoken to them. Anyway, not the point, I can't just up and leave everything—" Before I can make any more excuses, she interrupts me.

"Yes, you can. I know why you got drunk last night. You need this." I thought I hid it all so well. I guess not.

"Not even I know why I got drunk last night." It's a big fat lie, and she knows it. Standing back up from my bed that's yet to be made, I walk back out into the living room.

"Yes, you do. I told you that I was pregnant, and you were surrounded by couples and kids. I know you, remember." She does, she really does. "Think of it as a fresh start. Time to have a fling without your new crew crowding you." She has a point. "And move on." Hanging my head, I slump onto the sofa.

"I'm happy for you and Jack, Millie. You know I am." I don't want her to think I'm not happy for them. With everything they have been through, they deserve the best type of happiness.

"I know you are, really, I do. But you're not happy. I know there was something between you and Owen, but you can't keep living like this. He's not here." That was brutal, but they say that about the truth, don't they? It fucking hurts.

"Thanks, Millie." My voice is laced with sarcasm.

"You know I only say it out of love, Charlie. You need to do something other than the shop and hanging around with Leon and his crew."

I hold the necklace he gave me. It's become a habit. Maybe it is time to change things up a little.

"Fuck... I go on holiday tomorrow," I say and Millie squeals down the phone.

"Then we need a shopping trip, right? I'm heading to Bruno's to get us some strong coffee and cake. I'll come and get you in an hour. Be ready."

"Make sure yours is decaf. You're carrying a tiny Millie or Jack in that belly," I add.

"What? Oh crap, well, that's not fair!" She moans and hangs up.

I have a holiday to get ready for.

Chapter Twenty-Three

Blaming Others

Charlie

"What the hell is all this mess?" Looking over to what should be my nice tidy apartment, it now looks like a bomb has hit it, a mess bomb; clothes, shoes, cases, lotions, bikinis, bags, you name it. If you can use it on holiday, then I bought it today, as Leon points out so nicely.

"What's going on?" Caution laces his deep voice. This is far from what it normally looks like. I'm organised and tidy. This is far, far from normal.

"What do you think this is?" I say with as much sarcasm as possible. "Because you all had to work last night, I got drunk, really freaking drunk." My stomach rolls at the thought of it. "Like I don't remember what happened... that kind of drunk. Because you and your crew of boys had to go to work." His brows raise at me in amusement, but I think there's a hint of relief in his eyes, not knowing what I was about to say and taking in the mess of my apartment.

"My crew of boys?" He swallows, concern lacing his face for a split second. Dickhead.

"Yes, your crew of *boys*, and guess what drunk Charlie did?" Pointing an accusing finger at myself, I continue. "She booked herself a freaking five-star holiday to Greece that leaves tomorrow morning. That's what this mess is, Leon. Your fault, that's what this is. And to top it off, I'm going alone, all by myself. Alone." There's a flash of something serious across his face before he looks at me with his brows drawn tight.

"How is this my fault? Why did you get so drunk? It was a Friday night at Millie and Jack's house. What happened?" He looks from me to the mess again.

"Doesn't matter..." I clench my fist to my side, keeping my reasons inside. I don't really want to get into it again. The shopping trip with Millie was bad enough. I've decided that's it. I'm fed up with being sad over Owen. "You have a way of stopping me doing stupid things when I'm drunk, or more so stopping me from getting drunk." Placing a few of the things I bought today in the case that's on my living room floor, I attempt to pack for the third time.

Leon starts picking up the clothes and folding them into a nice pile on the table. This is why Leon is a big teddy bear. He's kind, he knows my mind won't rest until the place is tidy. He knows me.

It's a shame I'm not attracted to him. I mean, he is gorgeous in his own way. Tall, well over six foot five, short dark hair with a beard that's longer than the hair on his head. It's the way he's built though; stocky just doesn't cover the broadness of this man. His arms and thighs alone are wider than me, but it works. He's solid, all muscle. All in proportion. Well, I've not seen *all of him*, so I'm only guessing. Whoever gets this man will be one lucky person.

"I did more than one stupid thing last night, and I can't remember either of them. I just have the proof I did it on my phone." Glancing at the offending item on the table, the feeling comes back to me like a brick in water, sinking.

"What was the other stupid thing you did?" He knows before I say it. It happens more than it should, but I can't bring myself to delete his number. Just in case.

"I called him. I have no idea what I said for three minutes and fifteen seconds, but I called him. Again." Okay, well maybe I have an idea. Not the actual words, but just a feeling I get in my chest when I think about making that call.

It's a mixture of everything—defiance, energy, shame, loss, and sadness, but I think it's mainly regret. That takes it all to the next level. I'll never know what we could have had.

"Oh." The sympathy in his voice annoys me a little. That's why this reset will be good for me. Moving to the sofa, Leon pulls me down next to him. His protective and caring tree trunk arm resting on my shoulders.

"You booked a holiday? By yourself?" pausing, he continues his hug. "I think it will be good for you." I know he's going to be concerned. He's been a constant presence since Owen walked away from me.

"This is still all your fault," I tease while he rolls his eyes. I like being able to blame others. It's easier than admitting my weaknesses and faults.

"What time do you leave? Do you want me to come with you? I could re-arrange some things at work?" I know he would. I can see the thoughts running through his head. I've not really been out of their sight in the last twelve months. I can see he's unsure of me being alone in a different country.

"That's sweet, but I think I need to do this on my own. Millie called it a reset. I think I need this. He's forgotten about me Leon, it's time I did the same."

His expression is tormented, but I know that he's pissed off with Owen, not me. I'm a grown-ass woman, but I can look after myself. With a disgruntled sigh, he squeezes me again.

"If you're sure. Just message me while you're away. I want all the details of where you're staying, flights, transport, room number, and anything else you think I may need... so I know you're safe." I know this friendship was forced upon him, but his smile lets me know he really cares. I know the others do too.

"I'll do one better and send you little videos... so you know I'm safe." I snuggle him a little harder before I move off the sofa. I still have a tonne to do before I leave.

"I'll let the others know. Do you need a lift to the airport?" he asks, standing with me as his phone rings in his pocket, but he ignores it.

"No, I'm driving. The return flight is at an odd hour and parking was cheap."

"Message me when you leave, when you arrive at the airport, when you board and when you land, then when you get to the hotel... then I want updates every day, twice a day, if not more." He looks like he's mentally checking that will be enough to satisfy him.

"Anything else you want to demand of me?" I say in defeat.

"No, I think that's it." His phone starts to ring again. This time at least taking it out of his pocket, he nods at me, then heads for the door.

"See you in a week then." He smiles at me, a light frown creasing his brow.

"See you in a week, Leon. Don't miss me too much," I reply, blowing him a kiss.

Watching him leave, I head to the window and open it fully to get some air in the place before I close it up for a week. I see Leon look to answer his phone. I'm not normally nosey, it's only because he swears and it catches my attention, that I listen in, hiding so he can't see me.

"You bastard." Leon sounds angry, but there's an element of relief in his tone. *Who is he talking to?* He's normally so calm, level-headed.

"Twelve months, you fucking dick-faced-arsehole, twelve fucking months." He glances up at my window, but he can't see me from this angle. My chest tightens. I know exactly who he's talking to. My excitement ebbs away the more I listen. I don't know what to do.

"You're the biggest fucking idiot on the planet. Do you know that?"

He called Leon... not me.

Chapter Twenty-Four
Over it

Charlie

I can't believe I'm on my way. Sitting at the airport waiting for my flight, I've got my case checked in, a book in one hand and a glass of fizz in the other. I've even switched off the shop security notifications from the app. I don't want to see who's coming and going while I'm away. It was getting to the point of irritating anyway. Even with my silent phone, I just can't seem to concentrate on my book or relax. I keep thinking back to last night.

I'm glad I'm not there. I don't need or want to deal with that. I can't help overthinking it all through, I mean, why did Owen call Leon and not me? I know it's a stupid thought to have, irrational even. Leon and Owen have been friends for a very long time, been through so much together. Of course, he would call Leon first... I expected him to come back for them, but I wanted that call. It's selfish of me, but I wanted him to tell me he was coming back. I wanted to be the first to know. I wanted Owen to come back to me, for me, to be with me. I wanted to be the one he reached out to. However stupid that was.

What does that tell you, Charlie? The annoying voice in my head chimes in. I should listen, but I want to wallow in this feeling, at least until I get on the plane.

I've waited twelve months for him. That phone call, and now... it just confirms what I have been thinking. My stomach sinks even further. I've been forgotten. Clutching my necklace in my hand, it still feels wrong to take it off. It's become a part of me, even if I'm a thing of his past. This is mine. *That's okay.* It hurts like a bitch, but that's okay. I'll deal with it like I have done for the last twelve months. I don't know if I will be able to cope seeing him around again when I get back. How can I have him back in my life and not be a part of his? I guess I'll figure it out, eventually.

I know I'm supposed to be relaxing. I'm trying, sitting in the executive lounge, on a sofa that massages you, with my eyes closed. I look like I'm relaxing to anyone who looks at me, but my foot is jiggling like crazy with nervous, angry and frustrated (yes sexually, that too) energy I have running through me.

I am treating this as my reset, but I've brought my laptop in my backpack with the work I've been doing for Simon with me to keep me busy. It was the last thing on my mind as I was packing, but when I knew it was Owen on the phone, I shoved my laptop and pen drive in my bag, knowing I would need the distraction, when the thoughts start to creep in.

Speaking of distractions, picking up my phone, I call Simon's mobile. I need to let him know I'm going away. It goes to answerphone. I know I'm not supposed to but I try his office, and again it's left unanswered. I'll try again when I'm away.

Simon still hasn't told anyone I'm working for him, so I can't send him a message or an email to let him know. We've been careful with our communication, only using personal lines, and using special apps on my phone, making sure it's all secure before we talk.

I haven't told anyone I'm working for him on this either. I know Leon would be upset. It's been killing me keeping this from them. I know they would even help, but if Leon, Cole and Ethan got involved, it would put them at risk and that's something I just can't do, not after how they have become some of my closest friends over the last year.

The case against Mr Summers is not only high profile, but sensitive and dangerous for anyone involved.

Hopefully, by the time I get back, they will have Mr Summers in custody, and I'll be able to talk more freely about it all.

The only thing I don't understand still is how Josh is getting the information out. I can't find anything on how he could be doing it. It makes no sense.

My mind is drawn to the announcement over the speaker system telling me that my flight is now boarding. Grabbing my stuff, I send a quick message to Leon to tell him, then head off towards the gate to try and forget about Owen and the threat I have put myself under.

I want to get out of my head. I've been struggling for so long to try and forget about Owen. I've not given myself a chance to enjoy what I have and do the things I should be doing.

Like taking a holiday, relaxing and soaking up some sun. My life for the last twelve months has been work, train, research and repeat. I need to break the mould a little. This will be good. I'm trying to convince myself I will have a fabulous holiday. Simon will call when he needs me. With that thought in mind, I order some more fizz from the flight attendant, thanking her when she brings it over. First class is the only way to fly. I settle back and think of nothing but enjoying my first proper holiday in years.

Chapter Twenty-Five

Stronger

Owen

One-hundred and fifty-three days. That's how long I spent hidden away from my fucking life,. Away from my friends, my work, my angel. Left with my thoughts about how I had fucked up on every scale. No matter how hard I tried, I still couldn't get Charlie out of my head. She encompasses my every waking thought. *Was she okay? Was she doing well? Has she met someone else? She best not have fucking met someone. Why did I walk away from her? Had I made the right decision? Was she happy without me?* I was driving myself crazy.

Look where that got me.

I know deep down I made the right decision. Being part of this special ops team, it's made me realise what I want, what I need and where I need to be to get it.

It will be a year tomorrow since I left. She is still always on my mind. Deep in my soul, I know she's mine. No matter what happens, she's it for me. I know I made the best decision to keep away; me being away from her will keep her safe.

I was not in a great place. That would have affected us in the end. I needed to get help.

I also know I fucked up leaving, contradictory I know, I fucked up by letting my head and my own issues ruin something good. The message Charlie left me yesterday gutted me.

I fucked up. I really fucking fucked up.

Picking up the phone and placing it to my ear, it rings out. I'm determined to get this over with. And on the fourth time, Leon finally picks up.

"You bastard." It's so good to hear his voice. I don't say a word, knowing full well he needs to rant at me for a while.

"Twelve months, you fucking dick-faced-arsehole, twelve fucking months." His voice lowers to a sort of shouting whisper, like he's hiding. *Is she with him?*

"You're the biggest idiot on the planet. Do you know that?" I laugh a little, but it's full of remorse for what I've missed.

"Yeah, I know," I state.

"God, it's good to hear your voice, man. Does this mean you're coming home? Please say you're coming home. I need a fucking holiday."

"I'll be back in a week, one more job, then I'm back after the R&R."

"What do you mean 'job'? What have you been doing?" I tell him everything, and he never mentions Charlie once.

"Did you keep your promise? Did you look after her for me?" I ask eventually. I need to know.

"I'm not dignifying that with an answer, you idiot. You fucked up big style. That woman..." He laughs like it's a private joke. My stomach sinks. I deserve the shit he's giving. Out of all my brothers, Leon is the one I should have turned to. I can only imagine the hurt when I didn't. "Does not need looking after." There's a hint of something I should have known. Something big I missed out on.

"What does that mean? I asked you to watch out for her? Did you? If I find out you never helped her when she needed it, I'll fucking…" My voice raising at the mere thought of her not having any support.

"You'll fucking what, Owen? What you need to understand is that you should have stayed and seen for yourself." He lets out a frustrated breath. "She's fucking amazing, man. You've been gone too long. Me and the boys have been good to her. Don't you worry."

What the actual fuck? I know he's my best friend, but is he saying he's… they are, they have…What?

"What?" It's all I can say and it's forced through gritted teeth. The camp bed I'm gripping creaks under the pressure of my fist strangling the metal frame like I want to take its last breath.

"We have spent the last twelve months getting to know each other, O."

I can't speak. I don't know what to say. I knew it was always a possibility she would meet someone else, but my best friend? Leon's rumble of laughter starts slow, like he just can't contain it anymore, then it burst into his full barrel laugh. I'm confused for a second, my heart rate still soaring at the thought of him and Charlie… together. I want to punch something. The air in this tent is thick with tension, tension I'm creating, and it's all my fault.

"Hook line and god damn sinker, O," he lets out between his deep rumbles of glee at my expense.

"Fucker. I really thought you had…" My chest heaves with relief, flexing my hands out of the tight fist I had.

"Nah, man. I mean, she's hot, like really hot, and wickedly fit, but she's not for me."

"Right, I just need a minute. So, you're not? Cole and Ethan?" I hold back the question I need to know. I'm being an arse and I know it. These men, my brothers, are good men. There was every possibility she could have fallen for them in my absence, given I asked them to stay close and watch over her for me.

"Nope. Glad to see your feelings for Charlie are still strong." He has no fucking idea.

"Stronger than ever. I'm coming back, Leon. I'll be back in a week. I have a few things I need to finish up, then I'm coming to get my girl. Whatever it takes."

After I reached out to Leon yesterday, I called Cole and Ethan, getting the same shit from them too. I almost called Charlie. I want her to know I'm coming, but I want to look into her eyes when I tell her all the things I need to say. I want to see her reaction, feel her, know that she's mine. Breathe her in. If she'll let me.

Packing up the last few bits I need, I don't leave anything behind. I'm not coming back out here.

I'll see her in a week.

What's a week?

Seven days, one-hundred-sixty-eight hours, and way too fucking many minutes to count. It's too long, but I can't and won't let Dom and his team down now.

I'm counting down the hours until I see her again.

We're just about to head out. The guys are waiting for me in the truck. Excited to get this one done and out of the way. A quick one, no more than twenty-four hours and I'll be drinking a beer, and diving into the sea, before I leave earlier than planned, and head home. It's been a long few months of back-to-back jobs, with hardly any rest in between. It's what we were all trained for, but it still takes its toll on us, and right now we all look a little tired.

Thirty minutes until we need to be at the first destination. I think, now more than ever, I want more of a life than I've been leading, and I want it all with Charlie. One last job before I head home. To my angel.

Chapter Twenty-Six
Mixology

Charlie

This is absolute freaking heaven. I've been lying on this sunbed by the ocean, with its pure white sands, for approximately four hours, I think. I stopped wearing my watch, so time is relative here. I only have my phone, and I only use that to make sure Leon and Millie don't come looking for me.

"Miss Charlie?" Pealing one eye open, I sit up to find Adon, the waiter, at the end of the sun bed holding a cocktail.

"This was sent from the man over there, in the red shorts." The tall glass is on a tray, filled with a drink vibrant in colour, an umbrella, and fruit sticking out of the top. "I made it myself, Miss Charlie. You do not have to take it and I will happily tell Mr Hughs to leave you alone."

"Adon, thank you. What is the drink?"

He looks really uncomfortable for a second, then murmurs, "sex on the beach." I don't think I've seen a Greek man blush before, but he is, his eyes cast down while he waits for me to speak. Adon is short for Adonis. You would think if anything would make him blush, it would be his own name.

"Adon, I'm not drinking it, but thank Mr Hughs for me. I'll stick to my water today. I have a work call later and I would like to keep a clear head for it." It's not true, although I have been checking in with Layla at the shop. She just tells me everything is fine and attaches a picture of her favourite flower of the day.

"As you wish, Miss Charlie. I'll bring you some water over shortly." Adon walks away.

Rolling over onto my stomach, and watching closely from behind my sunglasses, Adon hands the cocktail over to Mr Hughs. The words that come from the other man look rushed, although I can't hear them. Mr Hughs has a frown deeply set on his forehead, his lips pressed together in a thin tense line. He jerks the glass from Adons hands and empties the contents onto the sand, almost smashing it when he puts it back on the tray. I flinch as the tray almost topples out of Adons hand, but he takes hold of it and calmly walks away, bowing his head slightly as he passes my sunbed, muttering, "Wise choice, Miss," for only me to hear.

Maybe Mr Hughs doesn't get turned down much by the opposite sex. His whole demeanour seems to have shifted towards frustration. Odd. But I'm not interested.

Closing my eyes, I lean my head on the soft cushions. I just can't seem to fully relax.

Turning over, I decide that's enough beach for today. It's way too hot, and I feel like I'm now being watched. Subtly, but still watched. I don't like the small shiver that runs up my spine, it's making me uncomfortable. I want to get moving and there is a new trail I want to try this afternoon; I know some of the others guests will be doing it to. I want to catch them before they head out. I'm all for being independent, but I don't want to do a walk on my own. I'm not that stupid.

Walking back into the hotel after the trail and saying goodbye to the other guests, I'm hot, sticky, and somehow very dusty, and in desperate need of a shower. Sophia, the receptionist, spots me from the reception desk and heads over with a glass of cold water. Perfect. *I love this place.*

"Mr and Mrs Lincoln have requested a table with you tonight for the big BBQ. Would you like to accept?"

"That would be wonderful. Thank you, Sophia. What time?" I ask drinking the water down in one.

"The area is reserved from eight, but you are welcome to join them on their terrace for cocktails before dinner." Taking the glass from my hand, she smiles, waiting for my answer.

"Sophia, if I start the evening with Hank and Bridget's cocktails, I won't make it to dinner. I'll be there at eight. Can you let them know, or shall I see if I can find them?"

"I will inform them for you, Miss Charlie." No matter how many times I've asked them to call me Charlie, they won't drop the Miss. I guess it's better than being called Miss Hudson all the time.

Sophia and Adon have taken it upon themselves to check in on me almost every few hours. They say it's part of the service, but I think it's because I'm by myself. It's kind of them.

I'm not sure I want to leave, not with what's waiting for me back home. Walking back to my suite, I need to get clean and maybe take a nap before I start tonight's festivities.

I've created a bit of a routine here for the last six days, breakfast and coffee at the suite looking over the vast, glittering blue sea, followed by a lazy swim in my pool before I get bored of my own company and gather my things to spend most of the day at the beach. Volleying between picking a water sport to try and just sitting soaking up the sun and reading my books.

As well as a Sophia and Adon checking in on me, Hank and Bridget have been keeping entertained most evenings. They're here on their second honeymoon. I have tried to give them space to enjoy themselves, but Bridget told me they have only been on holidays with their family for the past thirty years and they miss the noise and chaos of having them around.

I want to be them. They are my life goals right there.

Thirty years of marriage and only just going on your second honeymoon. They must have a great life. Flying anywhere they want on their private family jet. Each night, they relive the stories and adventures from across the world. Along with the family dynamics I'm not sure I should know.

Every night, drinks arrive on my table during dinner, not just any drink, cocktails, dreamt up by masters of the art... I'm not sure that's the right word for it, but Rico the bar's head mixologist has their full attention all night, putting his skills to the test and by the end of the evening we are laughing, joking, enjoying the company, hot nights and wishing I could ignore the reality of what I have to face when I get home in a few days' time

Switching on the outdoor shower, I strip down to nothing, and I rinse the evidence of my hike from me. Taking a shower outdoors is exhilarating. No one can see me, but it still sends a thrill up my spine when I step out naked, the heat on my skin drying me in seconds.

"You have been very secretive about yourself, Charlie. Tell me more?" Bridget asks her greying hair in an elegant loose twist, sitting next to me at the table, two cocktails in her hands. Her polka dot dress matching her shoes perfectly.

"There is not much to tell." She hands me one of the lime green concoctions she's had the barman produce—the man is a genius and loves to make us something different every night. I take a sip and almost cough at how strong the rum in this one. "I own a flower shop, but I'm new to the area really. I've only been there a year. Moved down to be with my best friend. My friends are amazing, unfortunately I don't see much of my family, but we keep in touch as much as we can." I've had at least three cocktails now, as well as the wine that went with dinner, and my words are flowing more freely than I'd like.

Bridget has a way about her that makes you tell her anything. It's disarming. Her head tilts to the side and I know she's ready to ask the dreaded question: *'What about your love life?'* I don't want her to ask, but there is no way I can avoid it when it comes. I'm surprised she's taken this long to ask, to be honest. The first night we met, she asked who I was here with. When I told her I was by myself, she looked shocked but also oddly respectful. I have no doubt I'll spill the beans about Owen.

Instead, she says, "There is a man over there who can't seem to take his eyes off of you. Have you been introduced?" Definitely not what I was expecting to come from her ruby-red lips. Is she trying to set me up?

I'm not sure how I feel about that? I place my glass down, taking a break from my rising alcohol levels. Given all the conversations I've had with Leon and the guys about giving me space to date, I thought I would love it when I got the chance.

I guess not. I feel a little panicked, like I'd be cheating.

Fucking hell, this is pathetic.

I don't know why, but I get a small bubble of something in my chest... hope. Maybe if I force myself, I'll get there eventually. Have the holiday fling Millie kept going on about. Glancing over my shoulder towards the back of the restaurant, my stomach knots. *Why?* I come eye to eye with the guy from the beach. Mr Hughs. He doesn't look away when he catches me looking, he just frowns again. That's an odd reaction if you're trying to get someone's attention. I frown back at him, before turning back to see Bridget looking as baffled as I am.

"What an odd man?"

My thoughts exactly. My fingers trace the pattern on the tablecloth. "He's not stopped staring at you all night. I thought he wanted to get to know you better, if you get my drift." She winks, and I can't help but laugh at her.

"We met earlier today at the beach." She leans closer as if she's expecting a good story.

"Oh, how did that go?" Her elbows are propped up on the table, ready to hear the details.

I tell all while I hold my necklace tight.

"Men are such arseholes sometimes. They think a drink will buy them anything." Tapping her chin with her fingers in a slow rhythm, she adds, "Is he here alone?"

"I don't know, but even Adon whispered it was a wise choice to turn the drink down." She raises a perfectly manicured eyebrow.

"Well, perhaps it's best that we don't engage him in our conversations then." When I look up from Bridget, I notice him walking away, his phone pressed against his ear, giving me daggers, obviously not happy about something.

"I only have one more day left, and I'm going to enjoy it," I add, lifting my drink and taking another sip of the overpowering cocktail. I don't see Mr Hughs for the rest of the night, something I'm more than happy about, the vibes he was giving off worried me. I do check over my shoulder when I make my way back to my suite that night, just in case.

Chapter Twenty-Seven

Jump

Owen

I feel utterly fucking battered. Mentally, I'm fine, but physically, I feel like I've been run down by a train. *Twice*. I have more bruises on my left side than I care to think about. They run the length of my body after I crashed through a second-floor window to escape the explosion. I landed in a fucking brittle bush, luckily, so no broken bones. It could have been so much worse.

We were only meant to be on that job for twenty-four hours, but if there were ever an example of when shit goes wrong, it really goes wrong, then that was the last four days.

We could have never predicted what happened. It was brutal. Zan fractured his left arm after following me out the window and landing on the dirt beside me. I'm just glad he didn't land on me; that fuckers heavy. We've been comparing bruises since we landed.

Harley was lucky. She was just outside of the blast reach when it went off. Dom managed to get them both under cover before Grey detonated the explosives that sent the run-down office up in flames, then crumbling in our wake.

Dudes got issues, but he's one of the best. Dom's already had words about his timings on the flight over.

It should have been simple—in and out—but the guy we thought had been taken, well, it turns out he was behind the whole fucking thing. Him and his friends wanting some easy money. Expecting his wife to pay out, a way he could get money without breaking the prenup she had written up before they were married. These kinds of people deserve to rot in hell. They were even planning to fake the guy's death once the money landed. All so he could go about fucking whoever he wanted.

What's wrong with people?

As we got closer to the old warehouse, the intel we originally got changed. A local had spoken out to one of Grey's informants. Grey went and did his thing, mingling with anyone who would tell him the local gossip, while we hung back, out of sight, and waited for more information.

Gathering the info we needed before we went in to that situation, held us back by a whole fucking day. Any delay would be unacceptable, but with the sort of information that was coming back to us, about parties, drugs, and women, instead of what should have been a hostage situation, contradicting what we initially had, there was no rescue, no risk to his life, he'd set the whole thing up. We turned our mission into recon to gather evidence against him. Going in with the wrong intel can cost you a life. Plans change, we adapt and move. It's what we are good at.

We waited.

Apparently, the stupid fuckers thought they were on the home stretch, and got a little loose-lipped over some strong homebrew a few nights before we arrived, in the local bar, all Grey had to do was sit and listen, people love to tell a story, the locals told each other what was happening, and Grey likes to listen.

What should have been a simple extraction turned into a fight between three parties. Us, the husband and his friends, and a local gang thinking they were owed the money simply because the husband had implicated it was them who had kidnapped him. Idiots. They'd been partying hard when we walked in. The smell of stale booze, stealing the air. There were four women in nothing but their underwear, sprawled out on the old chairs and desks, enjoying the aftermath of the party the night before. In the run-down offices building. The place shut down eight years ago, abandoned, almost derelict, and stinking to high heaven.

Taking one look at us, as we entered the building, guns drawn, not even a shake in my hands, they realised we had one agenda and they scrambled.

Guns ready, we moved forward, scanning the area for life, and risk. Dom and Zan first, Me and Grey flanking behind, heading to where we knew they were held up at the back of the offices.

These guys fought dirty. When we entered the room, they came at us from all angles, fighting with whatever they had to hand. Unable to realise that it was already over, they were never going to get any money from this. We were in the way of them getting what they wanted.

The fight lasted longer than it should have. After taking down the four biggest guys, we managed to secure the rest of the room. Leaving us with six pissed off dudes, tied up and ready to roll. Dom held them, while Grey set to destroy everything when we left.

With Zan by my side, we moved throughout the building to gather anything we could to get this guy sent down. Images, phones, papers, receipts, all of it, evidence of what was going on. Harley kept watch, frequently checking in, ensuring we could get what we needed in the time we had.

When she radioed in that we had incoming unknowns, we had to act fast. Downstairs, Dom and Grey cleared the men out and into the van that was waiting on the other side of the building. Grey set the timer for the explosives while Dom ran back to get Harley.

That's when we heard the first explosive go off. The whole second floor shook from the blast.

The gang arrived a minute later, the ones that had been implicated by the idiots now bound and hooded in the van. They wanted what was said to be theirs. Money. Listening intently as they entered the building, we both stood still, catching what was being said, not wanting them to know we were there. The instant they discovered there was and never would be any money, not for anyone involved, the firing began. They started ripping the place apart, the sound of bullets hitting any and every surface, glass shattering, wood splintering the thud of them hitting walls.

Looking to one another, shoving our bags on our backs, we ran down the hall only to be confronted by gunfire coming from the stairs, followed by voices screaming to search the place.

Scanning the hall, we both knew it was going to be a dramatic exit. Dom called east window from the radio, tracking us from his phone, sending us running full pelt towards the floor-length window at the end of the hall. Using my shoulder, I braced, smashing against the glass, feeling it shatter around me, the wind as I fell, then hitting the bush a few second later with a crash, only moving when I saw Zander, coming down after me.

Within seconds Grey appeared in the van, a cloud of dust trailing behind him. Collecting Dom and Harley on our way out, we were off, extraction and recon complete.

The only thing we had left to do was hand everything over to the local enforcements. Including the low lifes we picked up and the evidence we collected.

Telling his wife how her husband had betrayed her, and only wanted her money, was heartbreaking. Watching her place her hand over her stomach was worse than I could have ever predicted. Being pregnant with that man's kid is lot to bear when he's destroyed her. I hated walking away, but it's not our place to stay and fix things. We did our job. She has the support system we now offer, something I asked Zan to put into place during our time together, for when things don't go to plan. I just hope she takes the offer of help.

Stepping out of the pool I've been relaxing in for the last hour, the hot sun warms me instantly, water droplets evaporating as they trail over my skin. I love the feeling of the baking heat on my back. I put those memories into a small box to the back of my mind. I don't need to replay what happened. We did well, considering the circumstances we were handed.

We got here this morning three days later than expected. But we are here. Dom and Harley have not come out of their villa yet, claiming they needed to sleep for a week before they did anything else. I'm sure we'll see them for dinner later. I've been alone at the poolside for about an hour, and although it's heaven, I can't help but think it would be so much better if Charlie was by my side.

Placing my sunglasses over my eyes, I lean back on the sun lounger. As much as I want to get back to her right now, I need this break to get straight what I'm going to say without all the complications of having to work alongside it all.

"You need to come down to the beach, man." Zan lands on the sun lounger beside me, soaking wet and covered in sand. "There's this chick down there having a surfing lesson. Not that she needs them, she's fucking brilliant, and the body on her is just divine." He sounds like a puppy in heat.

"Why are you here then and not down there trying to get laid?"

"I think she's taken. I watched the blonde bombshell for a bit on the board. Man, she was good. The way her body moved with the board was fucking amazing." I watch him move his hands like he's smoothing over her curves. "I think the instructor gave up and just rode the waves with her in the end. After a few minutes, I got a feeling I was being watched." Shrugging, he carries on, "When I turned around, there was this guy giving me the evil eye like he knew what was going in my head. He was less than happy I was checking her out, so I headed back. Must have been her other half. Shame. If she was mine, I would have been out there with her, not watching from the sides."

"At least you had the sense to step away this time." Turning my head to look at him, he flips me the bird, then lies back on the lounger. Last time Zan got involved with someone, she neglected to tell him she was still married. Things got ugly. Zan stepped in when her other half started calling her some nasty names. But she just smiled and went back to him, leaving Zan with a black eye and a bruised ego.

"I'll see if I can find her later and show you. She's fucking beautiful, man. Even if she is taken, I can still appreciate a rocking bod and surf skills."

Just thinking about Charlie in a bikini makes me realise I need to head back sooner. I don't want to wait any longer.

Sitting up, I say, "Zan, I'm heading back before the week's over."

"We've only just got here. You can't go yet. Grey's already ditched us for the staff here, trying to find the hidden gems when it comes to local bars and places to visit. Don't leave me as the third wheel in their relationship." I laugh, knowing how hot and heavy Dom and Harley can get in public.

"You're a dick, plus you know they love you like a son," I tease as he is the youngest of us all. "You'll be fine."

"Prick. Fine, Mum and Dad can watch out for me."

"Don't let them hear you call them that. You'll be dunked in that pool and held under."

"No way. They love me too much." He smirks, his bright white teeth shining at me.

"We'll see. When they finally come up for air, I'll fill them in on our little chat."

"Funny. Don't you fucking dare." Dom hates being referred to as the dad of the group.

Pulling out my phone, I switch it back on after almost a week of radio silence. Listening to the notifications come in, I swipe away all the not so important ones. There are a few missed calls from Leon. I'll call him back in a day or so when I finalise my flights. There's none from Charlie. I expected as much after her last call. Fuck, that was hard to listen to. I've played it a few times since. It's not easy hearing her voice and the sadness in her words. Words that are on constant repeat in my mind.

'I waited, Owen, I waited for you.'

She waited for me and I never came. She was still mine, after all this time. And I fucked it up royally. I left it too long. Leaning back again, I close my eyes.

'You never got to know me; they have seen what I'm capable of.'

I can't even express how gutted this makes me. She was right. I was too absorbed in my own mess to really get to know her. I left before I knew how we could be together. Maybe she could have helped me though this in a different way.

'I tried not to love you, Owen. I tried so hard.' This broke me. She loved me, and I missed out on Charlie whispering those sweet words to me. Now she's trying to get over me; a relationship that was never really there to start with.

'I kept my promise to you, no matter what. But I'm not sure I can be yours anymore.' Even if she's not mine, I'll always be hers. I made my own silent promise to Charlie as I placed the necklace around her neck. No *matter what, I will always be yours, heart and soul. There is no one else for me.*

I'm coming home to beg, plead, and do anything I can to get her to be with me, to allow me to be part of her life.

Chapter Twenty-Eight
Noise

Charlie

"Make the most of your last day, sweetie. We'll be sad to see you go, and cocktails tonight won't be the same without you." I'm not sure Bridget even takes a breath. "We have your details and we *will* be visiting. I want to see the flower shop and meet everyone you have spoken so fondly about this week."

"Bridget, let the girl speak, or at least let her enjoy her last breakfast here in peace." Hank's been apologising since they sat at my table a while ago. He's not said any words as such. That's a little impossible when Bridget gets talking, but he's saying it with his eyes. Smiling, I appreciate what he's trying to do.

"Oh tosh. Charlie doesn't mind us joining her. Do you, my dear?" There's no question, or room to even answer, because she just carries on. Eating the rest of my melon. I just listen. I'll miss them both. I hope they do come and visit me when I'm home. "We have two more weeks here on the island, then we'll fly to the UK. We'll come and see you before we head back out on our annual birthday holiday with the family." I'm not sure they ever see their house in New York with the amount of travelling they do.

What a life.

"I think I'm a little jealous of your lifestyle, Bridget," I announce when I can finally get a word in. Hank laughs, and says, "She can speak. Who would have ever thought it was possible to get a word in when my Bridget starts talking. I don't think it's ever been done before."

"Hank, my dear, dear husband. If I never spoke, our world be silent and I know you hate silence as much as I do." There's a sweet look that passes between them. My heart dips. I envy the relationship they have. The closeness, the familiarity and complete openness they have with each other. Maybe that's where I'm going wrong. I need to be open and honest.

"She's not wrong, Charlie. I do hate the silence, and I love that she fills it with her constant chatter." Hank's hand covers Bridget's with an affectionate squeeze.

Now I feel like I'm invading on an intimate moment. "On that note, now you are getting all..." waving at how close they have become in the few short seconds, "I'm off to the beach. Will I see you down there today?" Sliding my sunglasses on to my head, to hold my hair back, and picking up my bag, I slide my chair back, ready to leave them to it.

"Not today, dear. We're off shopping in the old town. Should be back for one more cocktail before you leave this evening," Bridget says as she drinks the last of her tomato juice.

"Sounds like a great plan. I'll see you both later. Have fun." Slipping my bag onto my shoulder, I leave them to bicker about buying useless things for the family. It makes me smile, as it's like looking into a part of my parents' lives, and what they might talk about before they buy me the random, funny shit from their own travels. I'll never let them know just how much I secretly enjoy them.

Snapping a quick picture of the cobbled walkway that leads down to the beach with bright blue skies, and a turquoise sea in the background, I open the group chat I created a few days after I arrived, when I got fed up of sending the same things to both Millie and Leon.

Attaching the photo, I write a quick message: *Last day in paradise. I'm going to miss this place.* I don't wait for their replies, I just slide the phone into my bag, ready to read later when I'm settled on the sun lounger soaking up the hot sun.

Walking towards the steps that lead down to the beach, I wonder how has this week gone by so fast. It only feels like yesterday when I arrived. Why didn't I do this sooner? I won't wait as long next time. I've already been deciding where I'll go next. Maybe Italy.

Walking down toward the beach, I can already see that Mr Hughs is down there. Hesitating for a moment, the sun beats down hot against my skin. Can I deal with his eyes on me today? Chewing the inside of my cheek, I think about the last few days since turning his drink away. He really makes my skin crawl. He's a good-looking guy, but there's just something I don't like about him.

I'm not going to let him spoil my last day. I'm going to enjoy every moment, Mr Creepy or not. I can cope with him for a few more hours. *Can't I?*

I slide out my flip flops, my feet hitting the hot sand, savouring the feeling.

I only have a few hours until my island tour. I'm going on one of the hotel's touring boats. I can't wait. It's a perfect way to end the day before I head back for dinner and then home. I still have no idea how I'm going to handle things when I get back. I'm assuming *he's* back now.

I know the way I've been living my life the past year will change. The new friends I have in Leon, Cole and Ethan will probably dissipate when Owen settles back into life in our small town. I have to keep reminding myself they were his friends first. They were asked to do a favour for a friend. I guess they can file that one away now with the rest of the closed cases they have.

Walking across the sands, towards the day beds, I almost feel at a loss for what's to come.

My case and backpack, and travel outfit, are waiting for me back in the suite ready to collect and change into just before I leave. I've not done any work. I've not needed the intervention from my thoughts.

And just like that, Owen pops into my head and my heart sinks for the first time in a week. A whole week since I really thought about him. Like gave my entire body over to my thoughts of him. I hate how he's still in everything I do, every action I take. There are these moments, brief, floating, fleeting thoughts when I think, what's he doing? Would he have liked this place? What meal would he have chosen? Would he have liked the cocktails? Would he have liked the sea or the pool better? My subconscious asks the questions without me realising, like he's still ingrained in every part of me; part of my muscle memory, even after a year of silence.

I wonder when they will stop, when I'll eventually break this cycle of Owen.

When I find the man who's taking me on the tour a couple of hours later, he's waiting on the boat just off the shore, waving at me. He jumps into the water like a skilled diver and when he comes up for air, I get to appreciate the good looks of this man as he emerges from the sea, a little like the scene from bond, but even better. Dark hair, dark skin glistening as the water droplets cascade down his beautiful body.

I don't feel anything looking at him. I should, but I don't.

Zero tingles, zip feeling, zilch anything.

"Miss Charlie?" he questions. Nodding, I walk a little closer, my feet skimming the water's edge. "I'm Larson. I am very sorry for this, Miss Charlie," His thick Greek accent comes through as he speaks. "The boat is not working. There's a problem with the engine. It will not be going anywhere today." He tilts his head to the side as an apology.

"Oh, well, that's a shame. I was really looking forward to that. It would have been the perfect way to end my holiday," I tell him, disappointment sinking in.

"It will be a good reason for you to come back then," he teases. "I have another suggestion, if you would be interested?" The cheeky glint in his eyes has me very interested.

Striding out the water, out of breath, that was the most fun I have had in a long time. I walk to collect my things from the small locker. I know I'll pay for it tomorrow; my body already aches, but it was *so* worth it. I think Larson thought we would have an easy afternoon when he asked me to surf with him. The waves aren't big around here, but there's enough to keep you up and propelled forward. We ended up in competition with each other to see how long we could stay on. We were out there for hours. I've never felt so free and exhilarated.

The rush from standing on the board, and not falling in was better than sex, kind of, not really. But it was good. I think we even had an audience at one point, a few holidaymakers watching from the beach.

My body now has that sun-kissed, sandy glow about it. The look you can only get from being in the sea for hours on end. I love it. My shoulders sag a little when I realise it's almost time for me to head home. I want to take in the sights before I make a move to get ready. And I know just the place for it.

Taking a seat in the small café, just above the pool area, I order a large water and bowl of fruit to pick at before dinner. I can see everything from here: the pool, the beach, the buildings. It's a discreet, beautiful corner to people watch.

A group near the pool really captures my attention—the way they joke and mess around with each other, laughing, and having fun. I wonder what's brought them here, four men and one woman, an unlikely group to come on holiday together. It's fun to watch their dynamics. I find myself smiling as they splash and tease each other. Grown adults acting like kids, being free.

The woman sits on the edge of a sunbed and says something to one of the guys, stroking his arm tenderly.

Within a second, the air leaves my body as the tattooed flame covered body rises from the lounger. My eyes well with tears, and I can't stop them from falling. I can't swallow past the lump rising in my throat.

He's not facing me, but I would know him anywhere. I think my heart stops when he sweeps his arms around the stunning brunette and jumps into the pool with her.

I'm grateful for the solitude that this position allows me to have. My hands begin to shake, the water I ordered spilling slightly when I try to drink it.

Owen...

I can't catch my breath. It's held in my chest, unable to escape. He's here. With friends on holiday. On holiday with a woman.

The logical part of my brain is trying to tell me there are three other men with them, but I can't unsee the way he held her as he jumped into the pool. The way she wrapped herself around him.

I've been forgotten.

I'm... not enough. I wasn't enough for him. I feel lost as a heaviness settles in my heart..

I'm not sure how long I sit and watch them. I can't seem to look away. Something seems to settle in me. The calm after the storm, the buzz of my emotion flutters down to a stillness I've not felt in a long time.

He's happy. What more could I want for him?

My phone vibrates with a couple of new messages. A welcome distraction. I lift it off the table and try to focus on the words.

Big T: *How is your last day?*

I don't know how to answer that right now, so I don't. Scrolling to the next one.

It's a baby grow, covered with monochrome rainbows. I can't process that either.

Attached is a picture of matching t-shirts and shorts for Em, Dan, and baby Daisy.

Each message I read weighs down the heaviness that feel, reminding me that I came on this holiday alone, the feeling of emptiness creeping in as my friends get excited about the next chapters in their lives while I'm on my own. Still.

Pressing the palm of my hand to my chest, I can feel my heart beating. It's a sad, steady beat, slightly bashed and broken, but still going. My cheeks are wet from the tears I'm still shedding for the loss of what could have been.

That's enough now, I think. If I can't have him, at least I know now that he's happy and safe. Taking everything I have, I slowly take one last look at Owen Archie Stone.

That's it now. Time to head home. Moving from my seat at the small table, my drink forgotten, I wipe my cheeks and open my video app to record a quick video for Leon and Millie so they know I'm alive and heading home.

I'm so lost in my thoughts I don't see the man standing just off the entrance to the café.

"Miss Hudson, I think it's time we had a chat, don't you?"

Shit!

Chapter Twenty-Nine

Fun times

Owen

Dom and Harley finally make an appearance after spending most of the day in their apartment. I didn't want to know what they were doing inside that room, but I have a feeling it's pretty much what they have been doing on that sun lounger since coming out. Only this version is mildly less explicit. *Mildly.*

Looking over at them, I know it's a mistake as soon as the words leave my lips. "Not everyone wants to see what happens between Mum and Dad in the bedroom." The others look at me like I've lost my marbles.

Harley gives me the evil eye, while Dom shoots me a look to say, I think you have a death wish.

Zan and Grey are already in the pool, and like the big kids they are, burst out laughing, quickly ending the building tension when they start a water fight.

After a few minutes, Harley gets up from where she was lying and comes to sit beside me. I know she going to do something, I just have no idea what.

I tense up immediately, Dom smirking in my peripheral like the bastard he is. Harley leans in, her body casting a shadow over me. I've known this woman a long time. She is like a sister, a distant one, but still. Stroking my arm like it was Dom's, she leans closer.

"I'd bet you would love to know what happens in our bedroom, wouldn't you, O? The way he touches me." Her voice is low and sultry, but it has the opposite effect on me, a chill running down my spine while my balls shrivel up and hide. "Maybe even watch?" I freeze, the blood draining from my face.

Leaning in further, she whispers in my ear, "You fucking broody geek." She jabs the sensitive spot on my ribs. In a flash, I pick her up and jump in the pool with her.

Dom follows. It's funny how protective he is over Harley, even when she is as big a badass as the rest of us. I hold on to her, as we all play around in the water, splashing like the big kids we seem to have become since we landed on this island.

Dom can't help himself. After our water fight, he sweeps her from my arms, and they continue what they started on the lounger before I interrupted.

"Have you spoken to Leon about when you're going back?" Zan asks as we sit on the side of the pool, our feet in the warm water.

"I've booked the next flight back in a few days. He's left me a bunch of messages, but I've not read them yet. I'll call him tomorrow. Let him know."

"Good, you need to get back to real life. You can't hang around with us forever. Having the big boss around has been cramping our style," he mocks, slapping me on the back. He's right, I can't, and I don't want to. I need to get my grumpy arse back home and back to Charlie.

"You need to do the same. You're not getting any younger," I add, squeezing his shoulder.

"Fuck you." Zan shoves me so hard, I end up back in the pool. When my head breaches the water, after an ungraceful fall, he grins, and adds, "I'm three years younger than you, arsehole. You're the old man of the group." Technically Dom's the oldest. We both know it. It's just not worth the shit he'll give us for pointing it out. He's ten years older than Harley. Not that it bothers her, but he's always had a stick up his arse about it.

Sharing a look, we get back to swimming and catching the last few rays of sun before it sets over the turquoise sea. No matter where I am in the world, I never tire of seeing the sun rise and set.

Grey comes over carrying a tray of beers and snacks.

"Did you guys hear that scuffle a while ago?"

"No, nor me," he confirms. His excitement is palpable. He loves this stuff. Thrives on gossip.

"What's this about? What's happened?" Zan asks, knowing full well there's a story about to come our way.

"There's a rumour going around some of the guests and staff" He looks so proud of himself, having found a golden nugget of info on his first day here.

"We've been here less than a day and you have the staff in your pocket already?" Zan butts in. Grey's grin just gets bigger; he knows he's good.

"What do you mean, less than a day? It took me less than an hour. These people have some great stories. Anyway... this rumour, that noise I asked you about was a fight, a table been thrown, or someone been thrown onto a table, supposedly. I'm not sure, the details are not clear yet. But there has been a bit of trouble up at the café, just above us." He points to where you can see the small balcony, but not much else. "And we never noticed." We all sit up a little straighter as he recalls what he's heard.

"There was some sort of fight between a guy and a woman, most likely a domestic, but she's not been seen since. That was a few hours ago." Dom moves a little closer at that comment.

"Have you asked the staff, or is this just what other guests have told you?" I can tell he's interested. We all are. A woman going missing is no small thing. We can help if needed.

"Guests mainly. The staff didn't tell me. I overheard. You know I like to listen."

"We know you love to gossip, but if they can't find her, then they should at least be contacting the local police." You can see all the scenarios running through their minds as I look around at my friends. The what ifs, worst and best-case scenarios.

"Looks like they have it handled." I nod towards the doors of the bar, where three police officers are walking towards one of the apartments. We all sit back a little and watch as they make their way through the winding cobble pathway. They fall back into easy conversation, as Grey fills them in on some of the other titbits of information he's found out about the guests here, but my gaze stays on the police. I know it's none of my business, but I'm tense knowing something's happened and we may be able to help. I sense it in Dom too, although he won't admit it.

"They have a BBQ here tonight on the open deck on the beach. I've booked us all a table," Zan says just as my stomach audibly rumbles. How I'm still hungry after all these snacks and beers I have no idea, but if my body wants food to recover after the last few days, it will get it.

"Let's eat and we can check with the staff later to make sure they have everything they need with what's going on." It's like Dom read my mind. I won't be able to let it go before I know it's settled.

"I'll go and check it out now. See you at the beach in ten." Jumping from the lounger, I nod towards Dom before I head towards reception.

I lean my elbows on the highly polished surface of the reception desk, as one of the staff members wipes her eyes as if she's been crying.

"Hi, are you okay? You look upset." I ask as she straightens like she's trying to compose herself.

"Yes, sir... Mr Stone, sorry, I'm okay. Just a little shook up. But I will be okay."

"Is this about what happened earlier? I heard there was a bit of a domestic between two guests." I'm asking as casually as I can. I want the details, but I know it's not my place.

"It wasn't a domestic, sir, but we have it all in hand. Miss... uh, the guest we thought was missing seems to have just gone home earlier than expected. There is no need for your concern." She keeps looking down, avoiding my eye contact, a sure sign she not telling the truth.

"Well, if you need anything, don't hesitate to ask. We, my friends and I are in the business of finding people." At that, she looks up.

"Oh, um... thank you, but the police have it handled." Something's off. If everything was handled, then why would the police be here still handling it?

"The offer is there if you need it," I add, walking away, slowing my pace a little to scan the area. I can see other members of staff looking a little less professional than they should, more focused on each other's needs than what needs to be done. There is also an older couple off to the side making hushed conversation, speaking into the phone with urgency. It could be something completely unrelated, so I bank it and carry on. I'll check again first thing in the morning.

Walking back down to the beach bar, I get a really uneasy feeling that has me wanting to turn my phone back on. Just to check in, but before I can, Dom finds me and walks with me towards the table we have on the beach.

"Zan tells me you're making an early exit from this little respite?" Dom sits himself across the table from me, handing me a beer as he asks the question. The breeze from the sea is warm, more refreshing than the intense heat of the pool area. I like the beach more than the pool. I'll stay down here tomorrow, go for a long swim.

"Yep, thought it was about time. I need to see where things lie with Charlie and the guys. I know the guys will be fine with it eventually. We've spoken on the phone, but I need to hash it out in person. Leon will want to get me in the ring, kick my arse." Dom laughs, knowing full well what Leon's like.

"Have you figured out what you're going to say to Charlie?"

"Fuck. Charlie's going to be a different matter altogether." He smiles, shaking his head. "In all honesty, yes and no. I know what I want to say, but I have no fucking idea if it will come out right when I finally see her again." If she'll even talk to me. I wouldn't blame her if she didn't.

I grab another beer from the icebox after sinking the last one. I think of the things I want to say to her. There's so much that I have no idea where to start.

"You really have it bad for this woman, don't you?"

No shit.

"You have no idea how much she plagues my every waking moment, Dom." My shoulders slump at the thought. When I close my eyes, she's all I fucking see. The first thought I have in the morning and the last one before I fall asleep. Even in my dreams, she's there reminding me of what we had, how good she fucking felt under my touch, the way she would demand and beg for what she wanted, and I'd give it to her willingly, taking any scrap she would give me, thriving on her violet eyes when they locked on mine, holding me captive and just how much I need to have her back by my side.

"Oh, I have some sort of idea." His gaze falls over Harley, who's busy piling her plate full of meat and salad, swatting Grey's hand away when he tries to steal her steak.

"I guess you do." I never realised before just what it was like to be consumed by someone. I've watched Dom and Harley during my time with the team. I've teased and mocked them. But I get it. If Charlie was here, I'd be possessed by her and everything she did. Hell, I'm possessed now and she's not even here. I'm fucked.

"I can feel the tension coming off of you in waves, mate. You need to learn how to chill the fuck out. The sooner you get her back in your life, the better for all of us."

Chapter Thirty

Cagey

Owen

I slept in. I never sleep in. I guess the food, the rest and the sun are doing good things for me. I wanted to hit the gym this morning, but the thought of being couped up in a room full of noisy machines, other people, and cold air-conditioning, felt suffocating. So here I am, running along the beachfront instead.

It's hot, my muscles burn, but I keep going, the sand beneath my feet, the sun blazing behind me. It would be heaven if not for this feeling, a tension I can't seem to get rid of from the events of yesterday.

I checked in with the staff again this morning, but all they said was I didn't need to worry, the issue had been dealt with, and they didn't need any help. They were still cagey as fuck. Not looking me in the eye, keeping themselves busy while I asked questions. Moving paperwork from one side of the desk to another. Fidgeting, evasive.

I don't like it; they're holding back on something. It could just be they don't want guests knowing what happened, but I'm not your average guest. Although, they don't know that.

My plan has come together the more I run. I'm a ghost and it's time I use those skills to my advantage. I want to find out what they are hiding, and I will. By the time I see the others later, I'll have what I need.

My body is wrecked, my chest heaving from the intensity of the heat, the speed and distance I ran, and I'm still healing from my fall. Shirtless and sweaty, I'm in desperate need of a shower.

I turned my phone back on this morning; I had messages and missed calls from Leon and the unit back home. I've not read them yet. I'll answer them later when I get some answers about this woman. I'm sure Cole can help dig around for some more info if I can't get what I need.

Putting my skills into action, I make my way back up to the main reception, where I find three members of staff, all in white shirts and blue shorts, sat talking to... fucking Grey! Sneaky bastard.

He sees me but makes no move to attract attention to me as I open the door to the office. The police were in here when I came through before my run. I want to know what was of interest to them if everything has been dealt with, like they said it had been.

Silently closing the door behind me, I keep my ear open for any signal Grey might offer me if the staff get nearby. I look through the logs from the day, staffing sheets, notes. Accessing the computer system is easy for someone like me. But I don't see anything of use. Closing it down, I notice the floor plan, on the wall and snap a quick photo, If I'm going to find out what really happened yesterday, I need access to the security cameras they have. Skimming the monitors they have in here, it looks like it's linked to a small hut that's on the other side of the complex. That will be where they store the feeds. I'll have to work quick. Most places only hold footage for twenty-four hours, and we are already encroaching that.

Pulling on the draws in the desk, they don't budge. Finding what I need on top of the desk, a small screwdriver, I jiggle the lock, feeling the first click. Just as I start to slide open the draw, I hear the mumble of voice edging closer. Grey whistles his favourite 'time to leave' song—Ludacris' "Move Bitch, Get Out the Way", giving me my marching orders. Smirking, I take one last look around before I step out of the room, the door clicking shut behind me. A few paces out I come face to face with Grey and a member of staff trailing behind him.

His eyes narrow at me, but the smile on his face says we are both doing the same thing. Looking for more answers. It's built into us.

"Been for a run?" Grey nods at my still soaked skin as the staff come into full view.

"No shit. What you up to?" Grey lives on his own schedule, sleeps the latest, but you can guarantee he will be there in a flash when he's needed.

He playfully punches my arm. "Not been to bed yet, old man." How the fuck he does that I have no idea. I can do it on a job, be up for days on end if I need to. But when the respite comes, I'm sleeping. No matter what.

The words I made her promise me come flooding back, like hitting a wall at full speed in a car. *No matter what*. Swallowing down the regret I have at leaving Charlie, I move around Grey to make my exit.

"I'll see you at lunch. Give me thirty and I'll be with you," I call out as we pass.

"Deal, I need to get changed. I'm still in last night's clothes," he announces, and his hareem of new friends follow along with him.

"Good, you can tell me all about it then."

"Will do, old man." Glancing back, I narrow my eyes at him this time. He moves off with the staff, talking like they have known each other for years. Watching him split off as he heads towards his apartment. I head back to mine via the security room, which is currently locked tight. There should be someone on duty. Where are they?

Back in my suite, I walk to the outdoor shower on my terrace. I've had showers outside many times in my past life in the army. Fuck, most of them had been makeshift, just to get rid of the grime that surrounds the job sometimes, but this is pure unadulterated luxury.

I've opted for a cold shower, Charlie filling every waking thought this morning, even with everything going on. I can't seem to rid my mind of the lucid images I see of her, imagining her here with me, in this shower, her white blond hair wet, sticking to her skin, the water cascading down her perfect tits, her nipples hardening from my touch, as I slide my fingers deep inside her. I can't calm the raging hard on I have when I think of my beautiful angel. Taking my cock in my hand, fuck I miss her touch, I let out a groan, just thinking of her hands on me, fisting myself a little harder, thoughts of my last night alone with Charlie flit through my head like a movie on repeat.

Fuck, the more I think of her, the harder I get. The way her smooth, flawless body would melt to mine, the moans she would make while I fucked her with my fingers, making her come so hard I'd feel her wetness gliding down my hand, burring myself so deep inside her I'd almost explode the second I felt her heat wrap around my cock. Fucking her so hard, I'd lose control, bringing her to a peak all over again. Grunting at the memory, we fit together like nothing I have ever felt before. My hand hits the blue-tiled wall in front of me, gripping myself harder, my breath ragged, as the sparks of my own release come to life. My spine tingles with white hot sparks, flaring to life, as the need to come overtakes me, my breath shaky.

My balls draw up and I can't hold back, fisting myself faster, harder. I come hard over the tiles, Charlie's face etched in my mind.

"Sorry to break the bad news, guys, but I'm going to have to cut this little holiday short. We have a new case." Dom places files in front of us as we push the rest of our empty plates from lunch to one side. No wonder they never joined us. They must have got all this ready.

"I've booked a meeting room down the hall from the office as our command centre. Read up on what we have so far. Meet us there in thirty." with that, he moves towards the meeting room, Harley close on his heels.

I don't open the file. I need to get back home to Charlie.

"Zan, give me the rundown." He opens the file, speed reads the basics, and relays it back to me.

"London law firm has hired us. One of their partners was attacked on the property. His office was ransacked, he was left for dead. Currently in hospital with a very nasty head wound after taking a beating. That was five days ago."

"What's the job? We need to find the guys that did this to him?" My brows pinch together, waiting for the answer.

"No. Job's is to find one of his confidential informants, an ex-employee, apparently she was working for him on the sly, feeding him info on a case they have been working on for..." He stops to look over the document again "Over three years."

"Who's the case against?" I can't deny I'm intrigued.

"The one and only Mr Summers," he says with a whistle. We all know that name. He's bad news, really fucking bad news and the reason we have had to find and recover a few dozen people in the last few years.

"Shit, why are we looking for her?"

"From what I can gather, there was a leak in the company. She found something on Summers that could put him away for a long time." His eyebrow raises.

"Fuck, she's as good as dead if they get their hands on her." Whoever this woman is, she needs more than luck on her side.

We all agree. Grey still has his head in the file, soaking up the information, shaking his head as he reads through the pages. We order one more coffee before we make our way to Dom and Harley in the meeting room.

Taking our seats around the large circular table, Dom's set up a board ready for us to talk through what we have and find the best way to resolve this. "I know you've read the file, but I want to go over everything, get all your opinions. It doesn't matter how small a detail you think it is, I want to know.

"We've been brought in on this case because of our location. It seems she was last seen here on the Island." We all sit up a little straighter. "I have a feeling it was the incident that happened yesterday. We are approximately twenty hours behind her. If she has been taken, it's a possibility she has been kidnapped, but I'm not ruling out anything else until we have confirmation either way."

"We need to move fast if that's the case," Zan adds.

"We will be interviewing the staff, and the police have already told us to take what we need, they believe she's not in the country anymore, and that she went home, her passport and travel case disappeared with her, They assume she took another flight home, but have been unable to trace her. It's in our hands to prove this, and find her."

"I've already spoken to the staff. We got friendly last night." Grey winks. "They don't know how it happened. Yesterday was her last day on the island. Her day was normal, arranged to meet the cocktail couple for a drink before she left, but she never showed up. The police were called after the café incident. They assumed it was the same person, but it's not been confirmed. The footage for the area has been wiped from the system."

"If she just gone home, why wipe the footage? It makes no sense. Someone's covering their tracks." Varied versions of agreement muffle around the room.

"Okay, I need you," Dom points to Grey, "to get that in a statement for me. I should be getting an image of the victim in a few minutes as soon as the police send me what I need.

"We need the images from the surveillance footage they have around the area. See what we can get from that. This is a high-risk case, guys. The law firm she worked for wants her found. She's vital to putting Summers away."

"Who discovered she was missing? Seems odd the firm wants her found. Who requested it?" I ask.

Dom stands and paces the room. "From what I can gather, they didn't know she was missing. The guy that was attacked," he opens the file to find the name, "Mr Simon Holland, had the victim's information buried deep on his laptop. They knew nothing about what she was doing for him. They realised the information had been copied, then wiped from the login notifications on his computer, they checked after he was admitted to hospital. Rang to advise her and never heard back. They thought the worst, hired us to find her." Makes sense if she is important to the case.

"What's her name?"

"The staff called her Miss Charlie."

Huh? It's like she's haunting me. Wait... Simon Holland, why do I know that name?

"What's the law firm called?" I ask, my chest tightening.

"Holland and Brooke. It's in the centre of London. One of the top three firms in the country. Why?" Dom's questions drift away.

"What's the victim's full name?" The restriction around my chest grows tighter. Everything goes a little colder as I bark the question out to no one in particular.

"Owen? Why do you look like you have seen a ghost?" Harley asks, clear interest in her voice. The door behind me opens, and in walks two police officers carrying a small box, no doubt containing the last few items, no longer needed as their investigation is closed. My question is lost in the interruption.

I don't want to ask again; I don't. I can't hear it.

The answers in the file. I don't want to look; I have to be wrong. It can't be *my* Charlie. I know she used to work there. I know she was working on a high profile case when she left and I never thought anything of it. It can't be her. Not my Charlie. *My angel.* She wouldn't be doing that work behind our backs, would she?

It burns, the guilt rising like gas to an open flame. I've not been there. I've not been in touch. How would I know? Did anyone know? My whole body's shaking.

Opening the file, I feel like I'm sinking. The voices in the room start to fade. It's there on the first page, written as plain as day, *Charlotte Hudson,* missing.

The phone calls from Leon, it all makes sense. Why else would he call me so much over the last few days? He knows and was trying to tell me. Pulling my phone out, I bring up the app I've been using to check in with everyone. To check on her.

I can find her. A fluttering sensation spreads across my chest. Determination and hope mixing, pressing my lips together as I wait. The promise I made her keep, no matter what, the necklace, it's been my lifeline to her. I can find her. It was a shit move before I left, but I put a tracker in it. I wanted to make sure she was safe, even from a distance.

I failed at that.

I *will* find her. Opening up the app, I hit her name, and it zooms in on her location, banging on the table. All eyes turn to me, confusion on their faces. I'm ready to run. I will find her.

"She's still here." The words are a whisper. The small dot on the screen says she is still here in this complex. How could I have not known she was right here?

The mumblings in the room stay that way as I try and get my head round what's happening. "That's the chick I saw surfing on the beach. Shit, man." Looking over to where Zan's stood swiping images on the table he's just been handed from Dom. It can't have been. She was so close. Standing up abruptly, I almost take the table out.

"Owen? Talk to me." Harley's concerned voice is serious, like she knows what's happening; it's just another sound I don't hear. I'm drowning. I can't break through the surface. The burning guilt and the sharp ice of fear in my veins burst through mixing together to create a desperation I have never felt before, not even when I was in the army.

A faint sound of metal hitting the table, and I'm drawn back to the room. Everyone is looking at me. The officers have gone, after dropping off what they found. I'm stood staring at my phone. How? When I look across to where the noise came from, my world breaks. Lying in a bag is the engraved necklace I had made for Charlie, its chain broken.

The roar that escapes me is feral.

"Charlie."

Chapter Thirty-One

Urge to Kill

Owen

All hell breaks loose. Everyone's doing something, something I just can't seem to do. I don't have to tell them; they know it's my Charlie.

It's my Charlie...

Focus. I've been in these situations before; I know what to do. People being taken, kidnapped, or on the run. But this is... someone I know, someone I... it's hard to separate what I know I need to do from what I want so desperately need not to be true.

My words from earlier play over and over in my head. Haunting me. _She needs more than luck on her side, if she's not already dead._

"Fuck." Slamming my fists into the table, the urge to kill someone overpowers me. I want to cause some damage. I want to hunt these bastards down. I want to hurt them. _No,_ I will rip them to pieces. I will find her. They will pay for any hair that has been even slightly misplaced on her beautiful head. They will pay. Very. Fucking. Violently.

The scenarios running through my mind on a constant loop cause my lungs to constrict. *What if she has been taken? What if she's hiding? What if she's hurt? Is she running? Where is she? What's happened? What if... fuck, I really can't let my mind go there.* My chest tightens further, making it difficult to breathe.

I'm fucking suffocating.

I'm going to kill anyone who has ever laid a finger on my angel.

Fuck, I need to find her. Where the fuck did you go, Angel?

I want to destroy everything around me. I want to level this place to the ground. I'll do whatever it takes to find any trace of what happened and where she could be.

I will find you, Charlie. I fucking promise. If it's the last thing I do, I'll find you.

My phone vibrates in my hand. I'm surprised it can still move from the death grip I have on it. Sitting down, I hang my head between my knees, trying to calm the tidal wave of agonising rage and loss I feel running through my veins, causing a current of unease to ripple under my skin.

I glance down. Leon's name flashes across the screen. Sliding the bar to answer, I hold it to my ear without speaking. Too angry to say anything. Too terrified to let the words flow.

"Shit, where the fuck have you been?" He's shouting at me. "I've been trying to get hold of you, you absolute prick. Charlie is missing..." There's a tremble in his voice. He's feeling the same fear I am.

"I know," I finally manage. It's more of a grunt than actual words.

"What does that mean? How do you know? Is she with you? Please tell me she's with you." I can't focus. This all hurts too much.

"No."

"O, give me some fucking answers. Her place was broken into three days ago, three men trashed the place, that's why I called you the first time. Charlie was supposed to be on the 11.52 flight back to Bournemouth last night, but she never made it. She never got on the flight, never even checked in. I checked every single flight back to the UK last night and this morning, and nothing. I can't find her. She was messaging us until yesterday morning and we've had no contact since. Fucking nothing, O. We need you home, we need to find her."

"She was here. I didn't know, Leon... I didn't know." The phone is taken from my hand and I'm left trying to figure out how I could have let this happen. I left her to try and keep her safe, then this happens.

Fuck, have I just wasted twelve months? When I could have...

"Tell me everything, Leon," Dom says as he walks past me.

"Yes, it's Dom. I have the team with me." There's a pause. "That's a story for another time."

"We have everything. Owen's taking the lead on this. She's your girl." Dom sits while the others stand, all eyes on me. Clutching the engraved necklace, the metal warming in the palm of my hand, I start at the beginning with what we know.

"She... Charlie used to work for Holland and Brooke, from the records. She left over thirteen months ago, started working as an informant for Simon Brooke, just under twelve months ago." *When I left.* I don't say that bit out loud. This guts me. Would she have worked for him, if I had stayed? I need to be out there looking for her, but I know the details are important. I know we need a plan. I can't fly off the handle if I want to bring her home. We need to do this properly.

"There was a rumour going around that Simon has some information on the case, something we are now led to believe Charlie..." it hurts to say her name, "found for him, linking that fucking bastard, Summers, to something that could put him away for a long time. Only Simon and Charlie have potentially seen this information. It was only a rumour until Simon was attacked, and..." Taking a deep inhale, I continue, "Charlie went missing. Any information regarding the case is currently missing from any of the records at Holland and Brooke. We'll need a team there today to take a look around, see if we can find anything.

"Five days ago, her boss Simon was attacked in his office. This is when we think whoever attacked him obtained the information on the case and that it was Charlie who had sent it to him." Taking a breath, I carry on, my whole body a coiled mess ready to explode. "Magnolias, Charlie's flower shop was broken into three days ago," pausing for a moment, I need to ask a quick question, "Leon? Did you inform Charlie about the break in? She should have been notified from the system that something was wrong?" Watching me with careful eyes, he answers, from video call he's on with Ethan.

"We never told her, we wanted her to enjoy her holiday. It's nothing we couldn't deal with. She turned off the shop notifications when she got to the airport, told me she was getting fed up with her phone going off every time someone walked in the door." Okay. That seems fair.

I continue where I left off. "We assume this is where they found out where she was, on holiday in this very fucking resort. Right under my fucking nose." Leon had to pull Cole from a job he was at and it'll be a few hours before he can make it back.

"According to some of the staff here, she had a problem with one of the male guests but kept her distance after an incident on the beach. Then yesterday afternoon, at the café, something happened. The footage has been deleted from the area where she was attacked, but we're waiting on the footage for the hallway. Charlie hasn't been seen since. She never made it to her flight back to the UK and we are waiting on Cole to find out if she landed anywhere else." Her passport hasn't pinged yet.

We've already decided to stick around and see what else we can find out from here, while Leon and the team do what they can from the UK. If she's still here, I want to be here. Until I have evidence otherwise, I'm not moving. She's been missing almost thirty hours now. Our safe recovery window has already lapsed. We all know it, but I won't give up. None of us will.

"Owen, I have some information that might help us target who could poten-tially be leaking the information in the company," Leon says. "A guy called Josh worked closely on the case with Charlie before she left. He called the shop a few days ago, got agitated when Layla said she was away. He hung up after that."

"It's too much of a coincidence. He has to have a connection to Summers. Why else would he call Charlie after all this time? Was this call before or after they trashed the shop in the break in?"

"Before, and I agree, it's too convenient for this to be nothing. I'll send Ethan to bring him in." That kid's going to hate the day Ethan ever laid eyes on him. His methods of interrogation never fail.

"The law firm has had suspicions about a leak for a while now. A Jessica Holland and Annie Threser have been helping look into it. Ethan, you can speak with them. They are happy to help. Annie is a friend of Charlie's," I add.

"Be cautious. If he is linked to the Summers' organisation, we need to tread carefully. Interrogate him where you find him, don't lead him home."

"I'll ask for a private room." Sick fuckers going to enjoy this.

"Take the jammers, make it secure before you do."

"Understood." Ethan stands to his tall six three frame, looks me in the eye, and adds, "We'll find her, O. She's not just your girl, she's ours too." I know he doesn't mean anything by this, they call have a connection to Charlie. I appreciated what they've done while I've been away.

"What else do we have? The footage from the shop break-in should be with you. We've already identified who they are. We just need to confirm their connections to Summers' organisation."

We watch the footage of the shop getting trashed. After all the hard work she put into it, it's devastating. We confirm the names of the three men as, Michael Gambi, Ezera Ferris, and Ernie Williams. While Michael and Ernie are low-ranking soldiers in the organisation, Ezera, on the other hand, seems to be a big deal. We only have a profile shot of his face on camera, but there is no doubt it's him.

At least now we have a lead. We can find and follow them and we may find Charlie.

The hours are passing by too quickly with not enough action. I hate it, but I know it's necessary to get the information we can before we move, and we still have a few loose ends to cover here first.

Chapter Thirty-Two

Protection

Charlie

What the fuck is happening? I want to scream. I'm in shock. My hands haven't stopped shaking since the moment it all went to shit. *How have I gone from a five-star luxury resort to being so alone and freaked the fuck out?* No, that's not even close to how I feel right now. I'm so fucking scared. I'm alone. I want to speak to someone but I can't... I can't and won't contact anyone. I know it will only bring them trouble. I care too much to do that. I've already given too much away.

I will have to do some shandy, and very unlike me, shit to get out of this. If it wasn't for Hank and Bridget, I don't know what would have happened to me; they got me back to the UK early this morning and on a private jet no less.

I've spent the whole flight with my arms wrapped around myself, shaking, my limbs heavy with the weight of what happened, and what's happening, and how I can get out of this.

We landed at one of the smallest airports I have ever seen. Dark and quiet. I'm on the other side of where I want to be. *Home.* Not that I can go there anyway, it's too risky. My car is still at the Bournemouth airport. I know that's pointless even trying to get that now.

If whoever this is, can find me on a Greek Island, book themselves into the same resort, and follow me around, then they know where my car is. They know the people I care about the most. They more than likely know everything about me.

I've been walking along this stretch of road for hours now. It's muddy and wet. My fingers gripping the straps of my backpack so tightly they ache. When I set off, it was so dark, but also easy to hide. The light of day brings a new worry: I need to keep hidden. This road runs through a patch of beautiful forest, true English countryside. I need to get as far away as possible, try and hide for a while I figure out what to do.

Hank gave me some cash, enough to see me through for a while. If I can hire a room for a few days, I'll be able to charge my laptop and take a look through the files I have. I need to see if the guys who attacked me, back at the resort, are who I think they are. Part of the Summers' organisation.

I'm keeping just inside the tree line as I walk, so I can't really be seen, but also so I don't get lost in the woods, I have a feeling I'm being watched. I'm heading to a little town just on the outskirts of the forest. I'll look for a room there. I should have enough, even just for a few days, somewhere discreet.

The trees are providing only some mild protection from the rain that's hammering down. I'm soaked through and only have one change of clothes with me. I left my luggage, back in the apartment back in Greece, only picking up my backpack. There was no way I would be able to run with a huge suitcase trailing behind me. I took what I needed after I was attacked in the hall.

I made a quick plan as I ran to the apartment. When I opened the door, I took a quick look around to make sure I was alone; I didn't have much time. If they were willing to confront me in the hallway, in a public space, then what's going to stop them from going to the apartment to finish what they started?

I changed as quickly as I could, my travel clothes laid out on the bed waiting for me, slipping my jeans and t-shirt on, both feeling a little snug after a week in a bikini and eating way too much food. I placed the hoodie in my backpack. Checking I had the essentials, passport, purse, and some cash I had. I left all my cards in my case; I don't want anyone to trace me.

My phone, on the other hand, I needed to leave it for Owen. I needed him to see what happened. He may be the only one who can help me. I know he's moved on, but I can ask this one favour of him. Can't I? I don't care if he doesn't come after me. I just needed him to know.

They cornered me, and it caught it all on camera, their faces, what they did, what they said and how I escaped.

"My boss wants you dead. We need the loose ends gone, and you're the last one."

I'm not sure if it's the rain or the words that send a chill down my spine. My trainers are wet through from walking in puddles. I've only got ten more miles before I reach the town. I know that from the signs I keep passing. It'll take me a while, but I can't risk taking public transport, not that there is any chance of that on this road.

Running into Hank and Bridget, when I left my apartment in Greece, Hank took one look at me and knew something was very wrong. I was as calm and composed as I could be, but the growing bruise on my upper arm and cheek kind of gave it away, I guess.

I didn't tell them anything more than I had to, that I had to leave but couldn't get on my intended flight home. They ushered me into a private car. Hank said he would take care of everything else.

And he did. Shit, I owe them so much. They have given me the biggest advantage. I need to use it wisely. They even had a bag of supplies put together for me, food, medical supplies and a change of clothes. How they did this I have no idea, but I'm so freaking grateful. I shoved it all into my backpack, ran as soon as the plane landed, no questions asked.

Stepping out of the tree line for a moment, I watch as a small red car slows at the side of the road. I don't move, too cautious to feel good about anything going in my favour. I don't want to hitch a ride if I can help it, but when the woman sticks her head out the window and calls me over, I go. How stupid this is, I'm about to find out.

"Would you like a lift, love? I'm heading to the next town. You look like you could do with getting dry and see a friendly face, even if you don't know me." She looks kind enough. I hate to use the word, but she looks like a mum, joggers, hair in a messy bun, and a sweatshirt that says, 'bat shit crazy, that's what my kids have made me'. I smile and nod, my body agreeing before my mind can catch up with it.

"Great, get in. I'm Misha."

"Hi. Are you sure? I don't want to put you out." I don't tell her my name. The less she knows the better.

"Look, after what my kids put me through this morning before the school run, dealing with you will be a breeze compared to the torture of having three boys all under ten. Just getting their shoes on is a full gym workout"

I laugh despite my mood. "Thank you," I add before climbing in. The car feels warm, and in my wet cold clothes, it feels like heaven. I want to rest my head back and close my eyes just for a second, but I have to force myself not to. I need to keep vigilant. Misha hands me a huge towel covered in gaming logos from the back seat to wipe myself down.

"Sorry, it's covered in mud, but it's all I have." Shrugging, she pulls away as I buckle in.

"I'm okay with it," I reply, dabbing the rain off my hair and face. We fall into an easy conversation and for the next fifteen minutes, she tells me about her kids and what they did this morning. Not once does she ask anything about me and for that, I'm grateful. It's like she knows I'm going through hell and she's just happy to help me in whatever small way she can.

In the distance, I can see the small town coming into view. It's nothing much, but just what I need to able to think for a few days.

As she slows and stops at the curb, I ask, "I don't suppose you know of any rooms I'd be able to rent?" I know it was risky even asking, but Misha seems like a person I could trust. I don't want anyone I knew, or didn't know for that matter, to know where I am,

"I'm sorry, I don't. I only pass through here on my way to work." Misha opens the window as I step out on the path just outside of a newsagents.

"That's okay. I'll see what I can find. Thank you again for the ride."

I find a place to stay pretty easily. It's horrible, so basic, with only a very questionable mattress laid out on the floor, covered in a sheet that I will not be sleeping on and a small table, accompanied by a chair with only three legs, set in the corner. Unfortunately, the bathroom facilities are... vile, infectious, and downright degrading even, for anyone who has to use them. I'm not sure they have ever been cleaned. It would be better to set it on fire than use it. Even worse, they are shared. A shudder runs through me at the thought of using them.

As much as I want a shower to scrub the day away, I have a feeling I'll come out feeling dirtier than when I went in, so I'll pass and use the public toilets down the road to freshen up.

I plug in my laptop and wait for it to charge. While I'm waiting, I contemplate going into town to grab some food, but there is no way I am leaving any of my things behind. The creeping feeling of being watched hasn't left me. I'm not judging those who are in the other rooms, but I know they'd not be here when I returned. And I need what's on my laptop. Slumping down in the corner, I wait.

I drop my head to my knees, my hand reaching for my necklace, to seek comfort. My breathing stutters, feeling the empty space where it would normally lie on my chest.

A sob escapes me when I realise it's not there. I search frantically around me, but there is no telling where I lost it. *I'm so sorry, Owen.* There's no sign of it. It's lost, just like me.

A deeper cry erupts from my chest. I can't hold it in. I can't stop the tears. I don't want to. This hurts, the necklace was the last piece of him I had. Always close to my heart. Angel and flames combined. Us.

Still in my jeans and t-shirt, I'm soaked through. Standing, I strip them off, my skin clammy from being wet for so long. Pulling the spare clothes from my backpack, I inspect them for the first time. They're a little bigger on me than my own things, but they look comfy. A pair of joggers, and matching hoodie, a bralette and some very tiny silk and lace knickers. Where did she get these from?

Peeling off my wet underwear, I slip on the fancy lace ones, still wondering how Bridget guessed my size.

Owen would love these.

He'd watch me as I undressed, he'd edge closer, like any distance between us was too much. He'd eye me like I was his whole world, the possessive growl that would tear from his lips when I would reveal a new set of underwear to him.

My heart sores at the memory of how he would prowl towards me, the gasp that would echo in the room when he would throw me over his shoulder, hold me up against the wall, or march me into the bedroom, intent on making me his. Claiming me. I miss him so much, the way he would savour every second of our time together, making us both as needy as each other.

My heart sinks. That's not what we have anymore. Getting lost in my memories of us is one of the small pleasures I'll allow myself right now. Anything to take my mind off this shit I've got myself into.

But he left. It makes everything he did irrelevant, pointless even. All that time wasted. And for what? Okay, yes, he needed to get himself better, that I understand. That is the only thing that makes his distance sufferable. The other thing, keeping me safe? *How'd that work out for you, Owen?*

Not so well, right? I walked right into the worst kind of danger; I knew what I was doing when I said yes to working with Simon. I knew the risks, but I don't think I really understood that it could actually happen to me. I don't think anyone could actually see this coming.

Did I do it to bring him back? Did I hope he'd find out and come home?

I'm not prepared to answer myself ...maybe? Subconsciously?

"What have I done?" There's no way I could have known.

Pushing the thoughts aside, I finish getting ready, pulling my hoodie over my head, and placing my wet things on the back of the chair to dry before I can place them back in my bag.

I want to be ready to go if I need to. I know they will find me. It's only a matter of time.

The light on my laptop switches to green, letting me know it can at least be turned on. Sitting back in the corner of the room, I open it up and power it on. Finding the pen drive, I plug it in and start my search to confirm what I think I already know.

Dragging up the files I have on all the members of the organisation that are known to us. I start my search for the two men from Greece. The one from the hallway, and the other that appeared a moment later. Mr Summers has a wide reach of people he pays off. From high court judges to people on the street selling what he has to offer, and the ones in between that keep them in line. The enforcers, the soldiers, the money guys, the movers. I have evidence against them all in varying degrees. Things I have found, and matched up to profiles, dates, missing people and deaths. Documents linking these things, or people together.

The only one I don't have is the accountant to link it all together, but that's been kept a closely guarded secret.

I spend the next few hours looking through the files. Maybe I'm thinking about this all wrong, maybe I'm overthinking it all, maybe there is no official accountant. Maybe Mr Summers is the accountant. It would make sense; other than that one video I found of him killing someone, he's never got himself involved. He's discreet a front man. I don't have a scrap of information on anything about one. But if it was Mr Summers himself. Shit, how could I have missed that?

I spot the man I'm looking for a few minutes later. The way he held himself, the way he kept eyes on me. How could I have been so stupid?

Mr Hughs.

Shit.

His Name is definitely not Mr Hughs, it's Ezera Ferris. A higher-ranking officer in the organisation. One that's not seen often. He has men to do his dirty work. He's more a front man for the legal side of things.

That's what he meant then. I'm a loose end they need tying up. I can only assume they know about the video I have, or at least they know I have been digging around in their business.

Oh shit, what if Simon's in trouble? What if that's how they found out about me?

It would explain why I haven't been able to get hold of him. I tried a couple of times this week but got nothing.

I'm shaking now. I need to put a plan together. I need to end this. I need others to know what I have, so I'm not the only one. What I can't do is give away my location.

It's risky to start with, going out in public, but I can be gone before they can trace me. I can get it done before they find me.

Chapter Thirty-Three
Flying

Owen

Cole's been back at the office comms room in the UK for the last twenty-five minutes. We had to take him off an assignment to bring him back. From what I have heard, he hates being the babysitter for this woman anyway. I'm not asking about it. I will at some point, but I'm still raging on the inside. I can't get over how close Charlie was, and I didn't even know.

How could I have not known? How did I not sense her?

Did she know I was here?

Did she know and avoid me?

Did she think she couldn't reach out when all this went down?

We've been on video call for a while, still in this conference room, where the air's getting thinner, making it harder for me to breathe. I'm checking everything Cole inputs into the system to try and get a trace on Charlie. I'm a wreck.

Zan and Dom have gone to take a look at her suite to see if there was anything she left behind or a note... anything that would help us find her.

"O, I have some footage of the hall in the hotel. Have you seen it?" Cole asks. Fuck, this is it.

"No, bring it up on the screen."

Cole connects the footage to the large screen before he presses play just as Dom and Zan appear, holding a suitcase.

"There was nothing in her suite," Dom announces. "It's already been cleaned for the next guests, but we asked the woman at reception if there was anything left in Charlie's room. She burst out crying saying she wasn't supposed to say anything, that they told her not to," he says, holding his hands up to me, ready to deflect anything I say to him.

"Who told her not to?" I bark, feeling the embers of frustration rise further. "Who's keeping secrets? And why?" Jumping up, I want to get a better look at what they have.

"I've asked Harley to intervene. She's on it." Dom sinks into the chair, lifting the case onto the table. "She did, however, give us this. She told us it was left in her room. She said the police thought nothing of it, and left it with her."

"Why would the police think nothing of it? If it was left in her room, why would they think she went home after the attack?" That's doesn't add up. "This would be a reason to keep searching, not close the case," I add, confused.

"I agree. Someone's lying to us," Dom admits.

"Do you think it's possible the police were paid off so no-one would look for her?" Zan's hit the nail on the head right there.

"Shit, that's the only thing that makes it all make sense. Even if we try and question the officers, they'll deny everything." Harley slips through the door and takes a seat next to Dom, linking their fingers together. Before I can ask what she found out, Cole's voice speaks up over the video call.

"Shall I play the footage from the hall?" I nod, bracing myself. It's time we found out what happened.

We watch Charlie in tiny bikini, and shorts. "Fuck," I say. It's a whisper, but it doesn't go unnoticed by the guys, their attention flicking to me for a split second.

She's walking through the door of the hall, from the café to the indoor area, looking down at her phone.

"It looks like she's recording?" I can't be sure.

"I'll pull up the details after we watch this. See what was on her phone," Cole notes to himself. She's too busy looking at her phone to realise there are two people in the hallway. I can't see their faces. One of them is hanging back, letting the other step towards her. She stops dead, looking up. The first guy, says something to her and then a split second later, his hand wraps around her upper arm a visible tattoo on his hand pulling her, towards a seating area, I know his grip must be tight because she flinches, trying to step back. He pulls her forward and we lose sight of them. We don't see what happens next, but one of their backs hits a table. I can't tell which one, but it's with so much force it sends the small table flying. A moment later, we see an arm fall to the floor. It's all happening off screen and we only get glimpses of what's happening.

Is someone helping Charlie?

A second later, we watch as another hand hits the floor. They don't move, not for a while. Did Charlie knock them out? Then she's running down the hallway, phone still in her hand.

"Fuck, she could be hurt," I say, my voice cracking with fear. What happens next astounds me, leaving me confused.

Both Cole and Leon have stood up, and big smiles on their fucking faces, shouting, "Yes, that's our girl." They actually fist bump each other.

Harley looks on in awe, telling me she knew she'd like this woman. Dom's just looking at me, a smile on his face. Zan and Grey just say, "She's fucking hot."

"What the fuck, guys? Did you not just see what happened? My girl was fucking cornered and goddamn attacked. Someone must have been helping her. We need to find out who." They all exchange a look that I don't understand.

"I think you need to have a little more faith in your woman, Owen." Those words from Dom cut deep.

What am I missing?

Cole and Leon agree with him. I don't get a chance for a comeback.

Cole confirms she was videoing at the time. "There's a tattoo on the hand of the guy that grabbed her arm." I point out, Cole put the image into the system to see if we can identify the owner. My mind wonders back to the message she left me over a week ago now.

"It means you never got to know me if you think I need to be looked after. I can look after myself pretty well…"

"What do you know that I don't?"

"That's not our story to tell, Owen, but what Dom said is right, we all underestimated Charlie. Have some faith in her abilities."

"Okay." I trust these guys with my life, and apparently with the woman I want most in my life. "Okay," I repeat. Now is not the time or the place.

"Harley, what did you find out?" Dom asks. Standing up, she opens the suitcase while reeling off the information the receptionist, Sophia, told her.

"It wasn't the police that told her not to say anything. The suitcase was taken from the room before the police arrived." she explains

"That would explain why they took so little interest. Who took the case?"

"This is where it gets interesting. Damn, I love rich people sometimes."

I'm getting impatient, my finger tapping on the table where I'm sitting.

"Harley," I bark, earning me a look from Dom that forces me to calm down a fraction because I think he might kill me if I speak to Harley like that again.

"Chill your boots, ghost boy. I'm getting to it. A short while after the attack, an older couple took the case and handed it to Sophia. Asked her not to say anything and that they would be flying it back for her when they left."

"Who's the couple?" I ask, leaning forward a fraction.

She looks at Grey, smirking. "The cocktail king and queen. Hank and Bridget Lincoln."

"What? Why would they have her case? They have to know more. Did you speak with them, Grey?" This could be something. They have to know something.

"I'll go and track them down now. See what I can find out." With that, he's off out of the room, the door banging closed behind him.

"O, we have everything, or we will do. We will find her. From the looks of things she ran, she wasn't taken. That's gold. And you know it." Harleys right, but I won't rest or relax until she's by my side, safe and in my arms.

Not even ten minutes later, Grey walks back into the room, followed by who I can only assume are Hank and Bridget Lincoln. They look nervous. I guess we can be a little intimidating.

Grey introduces everyone while pouring them both a glass of water before encouraging them to sit and start.

"So you are Leon and Cole. We have heard so much about you. It's nice to put a face to a name. Charlie talked so highly of the both of you, although she seemed a little pissed off at you, Leon. She never said why." Bridget seems to of overcome any nerves, her husband remaining silent by her side.

"We had a day out in the old town yesterday. It was beautiful, bought so many things for the family. I can't wait to give them out." Hank squeezes her hand slightly, as if to keep her on track. "Right, sorry, Charlie... we have been getting on so well. We've had dinner and drinks every night since she got here. She's brilliant. The whole package." *Don't I know it?*

"Anyway, on our way back to our villa yesterday, Charlie literally ran into us, leaving her room." Taking a deep breath, she looks upset.

"She was hurt. You could see that right away. A red, angry mark on her cheek and what looked like a handprint on her arm." My body tenses as she points to the area on her upper arm where we saw him grab her.

"She was shaken, upset, said she needed to leave, but couldn't get on her flight. She had her backpack, but no case. She was scared, but there was a confidence about her... I don't know, like she was determined." She rolls her lips, biting the bottom one before she continues.

"Hank then took over. He told her to trust us, to go and get in the private car we have and he would take care of the rest." Hank nods to agree with his wife.

"My husband sent her on her way, arranged for the car to take her to the private airport, and take her back to the UK. I then added some supplies to the plane for her, a change of clothes, some first aid supplies, and she was gone. We dealt with the security and customs for when she arrived. Security told us she ran as soon as she got off the plane, but she was okay." Looking to her husband for comfort, he brushes his thumb over the back of her hand. There's a wave of relief that weaves its way into my chest, taking my first breath for what feels like hours. *She's alive. Thank fuck for that.* It's quickly replaced my the claws of anxiety. *She's on the run.*

"So, our Charlie made it back on a private jet?" Leon looks impressed.

"Yes, oh and we gave her some money, but it wasn't a lot. We don't carry around that much cash, especially English currency. It was only a few hundred pounds." She looks almost ashamed that she couldn't give her more. "Is she going to be okay? I'm worried for her."

Hank finally talks. "We did what we thought was right, and we'd do it all again if we had to."

"What happened with the suitcase?" Grey adds, leaning across the table and tapping it. It's the one question they have not answered yet.

"Well, we kind of came to our own conclusions about what happened to Charlie. The marks on her arm and face, the way she was running, vague on the information she was giving, like she wanted to protect us from something, or someone. We walked into her room and took it, hid it in our room while the police were here, then we took it to Sophia after they left. Hidden in plain sight. We planned to take it home to take it back to her on our visit in a few weeks."

"Thank you." I can't say any more. I don't know if I should be relieved or not. She's on the run. She's hiding. And I have no idea where she is. There are people after her that will do anything to silence those who know too much. And Charlie knows too much.

"Leon, can you search her apartment above the shop? If she's been working with Holland and Brooke, she has to have files or access to files in there somewhere. We need to know what she does."

"Sure, we looked when she was broken into, but had no idea about any of this. We'll go, see if we missed anything."

"Thank you. I'll be back as soon as I can. I have a place where we can all meet. I don't want to draw attention to the unit. I'll send the coordinates over."

While Cole takes all the car and plane information from Hank and Bridget, I head out for some air. Before the door can close, Dom, Zan, Grey, and Harley stop me, Zan placing a hand on my shoulder.

"You only mentioned you being on that flight back home." Zan's questioning tone leaves me unable to respond. *Of course I'm getting on that flight. What the fuck is he talking about?*

"We are all going to see this through, Owen. We're going to get your girl back," Harley reassures me. Her endless confidence in what we do spikes my own. It feels like she's guiding me through this, and for that I'm grateful.

"All of us," Dom and Grey add at the same time.

"Guy's, look you don't—" Dom cuts me off with a swift, but light punch to the shoulder.

"Don't make me kick your arse, O. There was never any question in our minds about us being part of this with you and the boys. Besides, it's been far too long since we went back home," he adds, reaching for Harley's hand. My shoulders relax, just a little knowing they will all be by my side, helping me get through this.

"You'd do the same for us if we needed it," Zan adds. I would, there would never be any doubt, I'd be there at the drop of a hat.

Giving a slow nod, I add, "I appreciate it. Go grab your gear." My voice cracks with the weight of gratitude and anxiety I feel. Overwhelmed that Charlies okay, and by their kindness. I take a step forwards and bring each of them in for a slap on the back. Harley mumbles something like 'men' under her breath, then hugs me fiercely. Kissing my cheek before I move away.

"Already done, mate. We'll wait here for you," Dom adds, pulling Harley back to his side.

I hate that's Charlie has a huge head start on us. I'm desperate to make up the distance between us. We still have a five-ish hour flight back to the UK to deal with, and by the time we land, she would have gone for almost forty-eight hours… it's too fucking long. But it will get me one step closer to her.

I'm heading back to the meeting room when I decide to make a de-tour to the security room, it's been locked up since the attack the other day. Cole hacked the system to get the hall footage, but there is a camera at the other end of the hall that should cover the area where Charlie was attacked and I want to know why it's not on their system.

Walking up the cobbled path, I spot a young guy unlocking the small cabin before heading inside.

Deciding on the normal approach, I knock on the door. It creaks when he opens it and I'm shocked to see the guy—who looks in his early twenties—has been beaten pretty bad.

"What happened to your face?"

He recoils at my question.

"Nothing, just a fight with a few friends," he says a little too quickly, his eyes on the door behind me,

"Bullshit, don't lie to me, kid. What happened?" I force him to sit in the chair by the desk surrounded by the screens monitoring the entire resort.

"What's your name?" he asks me.

"Why do you need to know?" He looks down, then straightens and looks me in the eye.

"It's important. I need to know your name. Not your real name. I know that's Owen, but the nickname they gave you in your unit."

"What the hell? Kid, you best start explaining otherwise you're going to have a few extra bruises to go along with the ones you already have." I step forward and he flinches but sits steady.

"Then tell me your name. She said you had to give me that so I would trust you are who you say you are." He's shanking, but give the kid some credit, he's not giving up.

My fingers flex at the thought he may be talking about Charlie. *Did she know I was here? Or that I'd come looking for her?*

"Do you mean Charlie?" He nods in silent agreement. "Ghost, they call me the ghost." It comes out in a rush. I want to know what he knows, and I need it now. The kid sags in relief.

"Tell me what you know..."

"The other day, she came running into the cabin. Do you know... is she okay? She had a huge bruise on her face." He looks genuinely concerned.

"I don't know. That's what we are trying to find out. Please tell me everything." It's forced, but it's softened a fraction. I want him to feel comfortable telling whatever it is.

"Okay... When she ran in, she asked me to download a bit of video from the hall just outside the café. She got me to email it to her phone. She sat there right where you are now and saved it. Turned her phone off, grabbed an envelope from the desk and slid the phone in, with a note."

"What did she do with it? Did she delete the footage from the system afterwards? We can't find it?" I'm willing myself to remain as fucking calm as I can, but I'm radiating so many emotions, I can't get a handle on them.

"No, she told me to leave it there, and that others would come looking for it. She even warned me that it would be better if I told my boss I was sick and head home."

"So, you went home? What happened to you face?" I'm not getting the full story.

"Before she left, she handed me the envelope. Asked me to hold on to it, hide it until the ghost came looking. I hid it in the roof tiles." He points up. I have never moved so fast in my life.

Reaching up, I feel around, and there it is. The paper crinkles underneath the tips of my fingers. When I take it down, it has 'Cerberus' written on it. Not my name, my company's name. That stings.

"After that, she ran towards the front of the building. I watched her on the monitors getting into a flashy car, and she was gone." You can see the weight leave his shoulders, getting it all off his chest.

I guess the information matches up, at least. "If you didn't delete the footage, who did?"

"I was just packing my stuff up to get out when two guys walked right in. They did this to my face. One of them searched the database for the footage and deleted a load of stuff from it, and then they just left. Didn't say a word. I went home and came back just now."

"Thanks, kid." I leave the cabin with the envelope gripped in my hand. I want to tear it open and see what's inside, see what's on the note. However shit this is, this is the first bit of contact we've had. It's scraping the barrel, I know.

Settling into the jet, I tell everyone what I know, and what I have in my hands. Dom takes it off me and places it in an evidence bag, then hands it back to me.

"Just for safe keeping. Cole will deal with it when we get back. Don't open it until then."

I can't do it. It's burning a hole in my hand. I want to know before we take off. *What if she hid something else and left it for me at the complex?*

Opening the bag, all eyes land on me.

Taking the knife from my pocket, it slices open the top of the envelope with ease, an old habit from my army days. I peer inside. There, at the bottom, is

Charlie's phone in its multi-coloured case, alongside a small handwritten note addressed to me. Pulling out the note, I open the folded paper. I can see the writing was rushed. You can just make out the words she's written.

Owen,
I'm so sorry I have to get you involved in whatever this is. I also have no choice but to run. They want me dead, and I need to figure out how to end this.
Watch the videos, confirm who they are, send it to the people who need to know. I'll send you more when I can.
Don't look for me, it will only lead to more people getting hurt. This is not your fight. Just keep the information safe.
I'm so sorry,
Please forgive me for not coming to you.
Charlie xx

Handing the note over to Zan, he reads it and drops his head into his hands then passes it on, each one having a similar reaction, cursing under their breath, and shaking their heads.

I can't take anymore, it's too much. Standing up from my seat, I throw my fist into the first thing I see. The cabinet next to me crumbles, cups and glasses flying everywhere, smashing to the floor. Zan and Dom grab my arms and sit me back down.

"We need to be able to fly home, mate. I can't let you carry on." I know Zan's right, so I sit in the chair formulating a plan to find my angel.

She's on her own, alone. And fuck knows where.

Chapter Thirty-Four

Little & Large

Charlie

This is so risky. I need to be quick. I keep checking over my shoulder expecting to see... someone? I don't know.

My heart was racing the entire time I was in the shop. The woman serving me assured me it would be fast uploading the information. After telling her the storage size I needed, she handed me two options. I went with the one I could afford. It sounds ridiculous doing it this way, but if I tried to email the files over or use a web-based file drop system, someone would be able to track me. Although someone _is_ already tracking me but that's beside the point.

If I emailed the stuff I have over it could be intercepted. I can't risk it getting in the wrong hands, never seeing the light of day again or being wiped from the face of the planet. I thought about posting them old school, but decided it would take too long, so I went with a courier service the shop was offering.

After buying the pen drive, I took the risk and made my way to the park. Checking all around me to see if I recognised anyone. I don't. Sitting cross-legged on the wooden bench, it's open, apart from the wall to my back, allowing me a full view of the park around me.

Putting my laptop on my knees, I get to work. Checking the pen drive status as it loads. The woman in the shop was right. It's going faster than I expected. It still feels like too long. I don't like being out here.

Gazing round the park, I watch as families play together, men and women run and people walk their dogs. It's nice to just sit here for a few moments, even if my heart is racing. My body feels so tired that it's hard to lift my heavy limbs. I didn't sleep much last night. *How could I have, sitting against the wall?*

When my laptop pings to tell me the files have loaded, I start wrapping the pen drives, my own back up file, and the new one, in a bit of paper, to keep them protected on the journey, and slide them into the envelopes I swiped from the security hut back in Greece. It seems writing notes has become a norm for me in my current state. Taking a separate sheet of paper, I write the first one, keeping it simple.

For safe keeping.

Boo x

Writing the address I have known for years, I place the note and the wrapped pen drive in the envelope, happy one is done. The second one is not so easy, however, as it feels a little more overwhelming to write. I don't really know why. It just is.

Owen, Guys,

This is everything I have on them...

I pause. I want to tell them more, I really do. I want to let them know about the plan I have been thinking about, but I don't because I know they will try and stop me. They will all get more involved than they already probably are. I want to protect them this time; they have all had my back for the last year. Even Owen is in his own way. It's my time to step up and watch out for them.

Hold it together, Charlie. Even my internal voice is shaky. I start again. Keeping all of my emotions back and contained.

~~Guys,~~

~~I'm sorry~~

Why am I crying?

~~Owen,~~

Absolutely not. Even writing his name seems too much right now, so I keep it simple.

For Safe Keeping, I'm Sorry.

Charlie xx

I feel like I'm saying goodbye. *Maybe I am.*

Wiping away the tears with the palm of my hand, I place everything in the second envelope and write the next address to Cerberus.

Meeting the Courier at the entrance to the park a few minutes later, she reassures me they would be delivered in just over three hours and I hand over the envelopes with shaky fingers. Watching closely, she climbs onto her motorbike, places the helmet on her head, and speeds away, taking a little bit of my hope with her.

A few minutes after leaving the park, I notice I am being followed by two men.

They're lurking. I had my suspicions, but when they kept looking away whenever I would turn, I knew. I feel sick, but the adrenaline running through my veins keeps me going, my heart beating like crazy against my ribs with every turn I make.

In all honestly, I thought that if you did this for a living, follow people I mean, you would be much better at not being seen. Like Owen, he's a ghost in his business. Not these men. Ones taller than the other, like little and large, one fatter, one thinner. Not that either are fat, just not as fit as they should be if they are out to catch someone.

They even look suspicious, like they really want to hurt someone. Well, that someone would be me, I guess. Everyone seems to walk out the way as they pass, and when they don't see them coming, these poor unsuspecting people are forced out of the way.

Roughly.

I keep trying to lose them, slipping into side streets and coming out further down, but they always seem to find me. I recognise them both from the information I spent last night looking through. Foot soldiers. That's their rank, willing to do anything to move up. I can't remember their names, but they definitely work for the organisation.

I hope Owen got my message. It's not even a fraction of the stuff I have on the Summers' organisation, but just giving them the faces of the two men who attacked me in Greece, along with some very damming words about wanting to kill me, that should be enough to raise charges against the two, or at least hold them with attempted murder.

Attempted murder.

The realisation that people are out to kill me comes in waves. I'm grateful it's flows in and out, because if it stayed with me, I'm not sure I'd be able to move. The fear that would overtake me, would be crippling.

I'm suppressing it all. I have to. There is no time to sit in the moment and deal with what's happening right now.

Shit, shit, shit. It doesn't matter what I do. I can't seem to lose them. I've tried everything other than actually running away. Pressing myself up against an industrial-sized bin at the back of a small shop, I slide behind it in an attempt to hide. My pulse quickens as I try and think of something to get me away from them.

Peaking my head out from behind just a fraction, I watch as the two men get a little closer. *Shit,* I'm gulping down breaths to stay quiet. I'm doing my best to not make a sound. I know they can't hear my heart rate or the blood rushing through my veins, but it's all I hear.

I need to get back to the shithole of a room, hide for a while, then I can disappear.

Maybe not disappear. I have a plan forming in the back of my mind. It's probably not the best.

Risky? Yes.

Dangerous? Most likely.

Should I be thinking of doing it on my own? Absolutely not. There is just no way on this planet that I'm going to involve anyone else. I care too much for that. These men are nasty bastards.

I'm not bringing that to anyone I care about.

I'd also like to actually live my life, you know, not hide and be on the run from an absolute total wanker that just wants to kill me.

So, there's that too.

This is too close, for my liking, there only a few feet in front of me. I need to remember my training. All those years I've had to practice, I can do this.

I really want to close my eyes and pretend that I'm not here. Pretend that I'm not watching as the bigger one with huge dirty, callused hands, grip the back of the bin, and starts to move it slowly to the side. My stomach and heart drop. He's making the gap bigger between me, the bin, and the wall.

Fuck.

They know I'm here, then it clicks; give them what they are not expecting. Be a little crazy.

I shout, watching for their reaction. It's perfect. Each looking as surprised as the other, they jump back slightly as their fight or flight response takes hold.

Grabbing onto the side of the bin for support, my foot connects with the larger one's chest, winding him and, in a front kick, I put everything into with the full force of my heel and weight. When he starts to double over, letting out a grunt, my other foot connects with his dick. Hard. He folds over, trying to cup his hopefully bruised and broken manhood just as my fist smashes him in the side of his face. His head snaps to the side, and he stumbles backwards, cursing like a sailor on leave.

His stumble causes him to jolt the small one as he tries to come for me and unceremoniously they both fall to the side, on top of one another. Giving me enough room to get around them, just.

As I start to run, a hand catches my foot and I fall to the floor with a thud, scraping my hand on the gravel.

Letting out a frustrated grunt, I try to pull away, but the smaller one, his grip firm and determined, around my ankle, yanking me back, his fingers digging into my flesh. I kick out using my free foot, aiming for his face, his face flat against my trainer as blood bursts from his nose, the larger one's too busy making strange noises, and mumbling about me being a bitch. I keep kicking as hard as I can, pained groans leave his swollen lips, trying to pull myself away in the direction of the street, until he lets go.

He let go?

Scrambling to my feet, I run, not stopping to think. My knees and hands throbbing, the grazes on my palms stinging as l clutch my bag harder, swinging it onto my back.

Running as far as I can, I only stop for breath a few streets away, ducking into an alley to hide. Sitting down on the ground, I watch as people pass with no idea I'm here, my chin resting on my knees, my whole bodies aching from the fight, and shaking with fear. They almost had me. I need to make sure they don't follow me back to the room. I can't risk them finding me again. Standing up, the pain in my hands bites as I brush myself down. I take my time going back, never in a straight line, waiting and watching everyone around me.

Hours have passed in fear and hopelessness. Once inside the room, I let out a sigh of relief, locking the door behind me.

I stand silently for a long time, my hand reaching for the necklace that's no longer there. I wait, just to see if I can hear anyone approaching, but it sounds like the house is empty.

I can't hear anything; I think I'm alone.

Slumping to my knees, I wince at the jolt of pain the action brings after how hard I fell on them back in the alley. In fact, my heart jumps slightly, in an unsteady rhythm. How is this what my life has come to, running, hiding, planning on taking down an organisation on my own, and being okay with Owen being with someone else? That comes out of nowhere. *Owen*, okay, not really. I'm not okay with it. I'm really not okay with it, but I do want him to be happy, and he looked happy. That's all that matters, right?

I'll get over him, eventually.

I'm shaking, my whole body is trembling.

Rubbing my hands down my face, I feel the sting from where the gravel has embedded itself into the palm of my hand.

Time to clean up. Taking a bottle of water from my bag, I rinse my hands as best I can. With nowhere for the water to run other than the floor, I let it fall, soaking the already stained carpet. Dabbing them dry with my hoodie, I apply some antibacterial wipes that came in the bag of supplies Hank and Bridget left for me. Each press of the wipe stings like mad. Then I inspect my right knuckles, which are already bruised from hitting that man's face.

Once I'm done, I open my laptop, thankful it's in one piece, and starts without question. I start the process of scanning the files. It's become an obsession almost to see what I'm missing, to see if there is anything that can put them all away, to take down the whole organisation and not just the one man. The sinking feeling that's desperately trying to push its way through and overtake me keeps rising, but I won't let it, not until this is over.

I can't and won't let it have me.

My eyes feel heavy as I focus on the screen. Yesterday I spent all my time looking through the files I have to see if... I don't know, I could magically find an escape route back to my life. All I found was what I already knew. I'm fucked if they find me. It looks like they have found me twice now. I have a good memory for faces after trying to memorise as many as I could over the last twelve hours, just in case I was followed. I guess that worked out today.

Drinking the rest of the water from the bottle, I dig out a protein bar and eat it. That will have to be my main meal for now. I need to get some more food, or I won't have the energy to do this.

I just need to decide what to do next. I have to leave without being seen or followed. I also need to find my way to a place I promised the guys I would never go.

Guilt washes over me. I said I wouldn't go there. The fear in their eyes, when they thought I'd been. *I'm sorry, but I have to do this.*

I guess things change, right?

I must have drifted off, because I'm startled awake by the noise coming from the floor below. Shouting, maybe even fighting. Listening a little harder, I try to make out the words...

"Who the fuck are you?" I hear a woman shout, but she stops abruptly.

"You have no right to just break down the door and come in here," a guy says at the same time. There's a scuffle, I imagine a few punches being thrown, then silence. *Shit.* Heavy footsteps pound up the stairs and the tension in me grows. They can't have found me? How are they doing this?

Then it goes silent again and I hear men whispering. "... This one has to be hers."

I'm on my feet before they can finish the sentence, shoving my things in my bag. There is a thud on my room door. It reverberates around me, making me move faster.

I open the window, sliding up the small single pane. Climbing out onto the rusting, rickety escape steps, closing the window behind me as quietly as I can. It's dark, only the street lights lighting my way down, I'm flying down the metal steps, as soon as I hear the door to my room being kicked in, slipping as my feet try to make traction, gripping the railings as the levels change, twisting and turning. Gasping to try and control my breathing as I run, panic trying to claw its way in.

Reaching the bottom of the stairs, and heading to the main street, through the alley that's dimly lit by a yellowing light, it's deadly dark. Gulping down breaths as silently as I can, I realise I must have been asleep for longer than I thought, my mind's slowly catching up with my body.

Trying my best to keep to the shadows, I need to keep out of sight. Placing my hood over my head, I run as fast as my legs can take me, swinging my backpack onto my shoulders as I go.

Coming to the outskirts of the town, I can't just run anymore. I don't know where I'm going. *Focus.* I have no idea where I am. I need to find a place to hide, where I can... get some sort of direction planned.

Moving along the back of a cute little housing estate that's now cast in shadows, I spot a house in darkness. I head to the back garden, through the side gate, and find a kid's playhouse open. Lucky kid, lucky me. I kind of feel bad for taking this as my hiding place, but hopefully the owners will never find out.

Crouching down, I wedge myself in the small two-story wooden structure, which appears to be fully furnished with every toy kitchen appliance you could buy. Even down to the fake food, stacked in the mini-fridge next to the tiny table and chairs, ready for a tea party. It's cute.

Standing up as best I can, I take a peek at the second level. It's more of a balcony. It makes me want to be a kid again, or at least have one of my own, so I can do this for them. *Ha, stupid thought.*

This is better than the room I just paid for. And won't be going back to.

Trying not to disturb anything, I place my things on the floor, pulling out the map I bought from the shop earlier and sit crossed legged on the floor to plan my route. Having just enough light from the fairy lights to see the paper in front of me, it doesn't take long.

I eat another protein bar and take another long drink of water. Reaching into my bag, I pull out some of the loose change I have and place a few coins in the kitchen for the kid to find whenever they play in here next. It's not much, but it will have to do.

Taking what I have and making sure everything is still as it was when I find it, I close the painted pink door behind me, head towards the gate and start walking.

I won't make the same mistake of being found again, or the mistake of going to a built-up area, not until I need to anyway.

Chapter Thirty-Five
Pride

Owen

Stepping off the plane, into our waiting cars, I realise I'm going to have to pay for the damage I caused to the plane after I read her note.

They want her dead.

I hate that she has been missing all this time. There's so much space between us, we are at almost fifty hours now. It's too much. I'm on the verge of ripping everything apart. It's only my friends keeping me together.

The guys tracked the plane she took to a small airport not far from here. They are trying to get the camera footage to see what direction she ran. _Fucking ran._ I need to see with my own eyes she landed safely. I need to be assured that no one traced her there apart from us.

It's all my fucking fault. I'm angry, really fucking angry with myself for this.

If I had stayed, this would never have happened. I know that she would still be by my side.

I fucked it all up.

I want nothing more than to wrap my arms around her, feel her safe in them. I just have no idea where the fuck she is. It's killing me.

Refocus, come on.

The lodge we're heading to won't be a secret for much longer. I want it that way. I want them to know everything. All that I have been up to in the last year, the therapy, everything that has been said between me, Dom, and the others in the special ops team while I've been with them.

But especially how I feel about Charlie.

Cole told me not to watch the videos on Charlie's phone, but I need to see with my own eyes. To hear her voice, to calm the madness I feel right now. There's so much guilt cursing through me, I can't bear it. I'm trying my best to use it to fuel what I need to do, use the anger to my advantage, to find her and bring her back to me. To make her mine, once and for all.

I hate this feeling of uncertainty, waiting. It's *fucking* useless.

I will use my fists, I will reign down hell-fire to anyone that has laid a finger on what's mine, my angel. They will pay for this.

"ETA five minutes," I announce tightly to the guys as I drive down the dirt road that leads to the lodge. "We'll need to walk for another ten after we park the van," I add, my knuckles white on the steering wheel with stress.

After securing the van, next to Leon's truck and Cole's SUV in the shelter, we grab our packs, extra food, and equipment we picked up when we landed and head off towards the lodge.

"Holy fucking shit balls. What is this place? And how have you managed to keep this a secret from everyone? It's huge." Grey's mouth hangs open.

"We all need a place to unwind, right? Well, this is mine" I'm playing it down. I called it the lodge for a reason. I wanted it to sound insignificant if anyone found out about it. When in reality it's anything but.

With the people we have to deal with in our line of work, I wanted a place where we could all lie low if things ever went south. Set on twenty-five acres, it's built over three floors with a basement that's just as big as the main house.

"Well, shit, Owen..." I've never seen Grey lost for words. "I..." He gives up and just walks ahead of me, obviously eager to see it up close.

When we approach, Leon, Cole and Ethan are already here, standing in front of me on the deck. They look the same, slightly more stressed from the creases around their eyes, the worry lines on their foreheads; a reminder of why we're all here. I knew this was coming—time to face the music.

Their bags hit the floor, feet move, and I find myself receiving a curt nod from Ethan with a slap on the shoulder before vanishing inside. Cole stands right in front of me and actually hugs me, whispering, "Ever disappear again with no word and I'll kill you myself," then he's gone too.

Leon moves beside me. "You look like shit, my friend. Let's find our girl, then we'll talk." I couldn't be more grateful.

Over the next few minutes, we all slip into our roles and get organised. Cole's tracking Charlie from where she landed and getting all the information he can on the Summers' organisation. Sitting next to him, I hand him Charlie's phone. "Give me a minute," he says, attaching it to the system.

Bringing up the new software I've been working on while I've been away on my computer screen. "This is for you," I tell him, gaining his attention

"What is it?"

He knows before I tell him anything. Moving out of the way so Cole can sit in my place, he gets to work.

"This is the shit, O. Fucking facial recognition." It's what we have been missing for a while, but I wanted it to be right. Now we have it, it'll give us the edge when we need to find someone. He doesn't hesitate to put Charlie's image in first. It's a photo I've not seen before and takes my breath away. I'm lost in the way she looks so carefree, sitting crossed legged on top of a table at The Brasserie, glass of wine in hand. "It was her birthday. We took her out, all of us. Millie and Jack joined us. It was a great night. Took this while she wasn't looking," Leon informs me from across the room. "We'll find her, O. She's one of us now." I just nod and carry on with what I need to do, determined to bring her home.

"Ready?" Cole's tense voice fills the room and everyone gathers around the huge screens attached to the walls.

The video of Charlie starts to play. She sounds off, chatting about her day, sad almost. Then the camera suddenly swings down. You can hear them, the guys from the hallway, but I can't see much other than the floor.

"I think it's time we had a little talk, don't you, Miss Hudson?" She turns the camera discreetly towards the voice and we get a flash of his face. Cole captures the image and runs it. We already know who it is though. The soon to be dead guy's hand is around her upper arm. You hear her take in a sharp breath like she's surprised.

I don't want to watch, but I know I have to, despite the anxiety crawling into my chest. The camera tilts, giving us a glimpse as he reaches for her.

"I have nothing to say to you," she curses, trying to pull away. In the background you can just make out another man, standing back watching. Cole grabs that image too. *"I don't need your words, Miss Hudson."* He yanks her forward and the tension in the room rises. Me, Cole, Ethan, and Leon all stand, ready to jump through the screen and help. *"My boss wants you dead. We just need the loose ends gone."* Jutting his chin towards Charlie, he continues, *"You're the last one."*

Fuck.

I want to kill him, tighten my hands around his neck for even laying a finger on what's mine. *If she'll have me back after I left her without a word.*

Fisting my hands so tight at my side, to stop the anger from boiling over, my fingers dig into the palms.

When the camera swings back up, the man that was holding her staggers back. *She hit him?* The other guy moves in. Charlie ducks when his fist comes at her face, then she takes him out. I'm not sure how. I can't see what she did, but he's on the floor.

There's a lot of movement from the camera she still has in her hand. Charlie takes a hit to her face, but doesn't say a word. Us, on the other hand, there are audible fucks and shits flying around the room.

The bigger guy backs her up against something. I think she kicks him and he lets her go. She doesn't even seem phased by what's happening. *Is that what she meant when she told me that I had no idea what she was capable of?* A swell of pride forces some of my anxiety away. She's in control, I fucking love it.

She kicks him again as her elbow makes contact with his face. He loses his balance and crashes into the table. I can't quite tell you what I see next. It's a bit of a blur and then she takes off.

We all sit there silent while Cole brings up the footage from the hotel that Charlie managed to get before it was deleted. A full blow by blow view of what happened. Charlie kicking ass, taking two men down on her own, and coming away with barely a scratch.

It confirms exactly how little I know about my girl. She's badass. And way more capable than I ever even could have imagined.

I don't know if I love it or hate it or both, but fuck, she's... *Mine.* A strong sense of pride washes over me, making me feel better for a fleeting moment.

Who knew an ex-prosecution solicitor turned florist could fight like that? Not me, that's for sure. From the smiles on the faces around me, I'm the only one.

"What the fuck?" I cry, swinging around to face the guys I've known almost my whole life.

"You have no idea, mate. That woman of yours is skilled as fuck," Ethan tells me. The bastard's smiling. Fucking smiling.

"How?"

Leon gestures for me to take a seat next to him.

"The men she grew up with—two brothers currently in a special unit in the Army—decided she needed to be able to look after herself."

"I had no idea" I feel so fucking proud of her right now. The way she handled the whole situation, fighting, the ability to keep calm, the way she got everything she needed, and managed to leave on a fucking *private jet*. "She's incredible."

"She sure is, O. Don't fuck this up or I'll have to fuck you up myself." He means every word.

"Once she's back by my side, I'm never fucking letting go, Leon."

"Good, I'd hate for us to lose our friendship over this." I'm taken aback a little by that. He really does care for her. I think I underestimated just how close two people can get in twelve months. "Grown close, have you, Leon?"

He stands. "She's the sister I never had. Don't fuck with her. She's something special."

"I won't," I promise him. There's no way I'm letting her slip through my fingers. I'm finding her, and finding the fucker that is after her, the fucker that wants her dead. They'll have to get through me first.

Fuck, Charlie, I can't wait to get my hands on you.

Ethan got back from Holland and Brooke just before we arrived back at the lodge, filling us in on what he found out from his visit. Apparently, Josh is a shifty fucker. Cole's on it. Digging deeper into him, already searching his work and personal computer. "Anne Threser and Miss Holland were visibly upset by everything that had happened, but something is still off with the whole situation. I knew Josh was keeping a secret. He was careful with what he said, guarded. I knew I was being monitored, even with the jammer in place. I'm sure of it. I planned to grab him after he finished, haul him back, and have some fun with him, but just before I left, Josh handed me this." He places a pen drive on the desk.

"We've watched it and it's Josh telling us everything he knows. He says he called Charlie to warn her. That they knew she was working for Simon before he was attacked."

"There is no way a case like this one should not have gone to court already, not with all the information they have been compiling against them. The leak is the only thing holding the case back. He also goes on to say he knows he's being framed for the leaks and he can prove it. There have to be at least two people passing information out to Summers, some of the dates don't match up, and his logins were used when he was involved in meetings with no access to the system. Josh doesn't seem like the kind of guy to be involved in something like this. He's too soft, kept asking about Charlie, his body language and face concerned and shocked, but I still don't trust him. He seems more... focused on Charlie for other reasons. I think he's been obsessed for a while, even has a photo of her and him together at a work party," Ethan finishes. Grunting in response, a cold shiver runs down my spine at the thought of him ever touching Charlie. He can only hope that we never meet, otherwise, he'll feel the full force of my fist in his face.

"I've got something on Josh's laptop." Cole shares the files to the large screen. "It looks like little Josh has been doing some research of his own. These are the images that were sent to Charlie, images of her husband..."

"Ex-fucking-husband," I mutter through gritted teeth.

"Ex-fucking-husband," Cole mimics, "having a number of affairs behind her back. This is what eventually led her to divorce her hus... him and leave the firm." I scowl, even though it was nicely corrected.

"Finding that sort of information on someone doesn't come cheap." Ethan's been looking at the connections. "If they wanted her out back then, she must have been close to finding something." *Fuck, Charlie, what have you got yourself into?*

"Josh took the photos himself. These are the original files. From what I can see, he's never sent them anywhere other than to his printer. Looks like he followed the ex, then delivered the information to Charlie's desk."

"Men are arseholes," Harley mutters under her breath. "Present company excluded," she adds when we all turn to look at her.

"His loss, my gain." I don't like what he did to her, but it led her to me. For that, I'm grateful.

"She left the firm a short while after when her divorce was finalised. This has to be something, at least to get her out of the law firm."

"It has to be linked. It's too coincidental for it not to be." Dom's been sitting, silent for the most part, I know he's taking it all in before he gives his thoughts. Leaning forward from his seat, he stands, Harley by his side. As always.

"Okay, we need to know what Charlie and Mr Brooke saw to understand the level of shit she's in."

"Fuck." It's almost inaudible as Cole whips his head from the screen to face us all. "The facial recognition picked something up. It's small, but it gives us her last location. It's time-stamped at nine am yesterday morning…"

Before we even knew she was missing.

Before anyone moves or even breathes a word, I've got my keys in hand and I'm running for the door.

Slipping into the driver's side of the van, the door in the back slides open and Leon and Ethan climb in.

Their silent support is all I need.

I'm getting you back, Angel, and I'm never letting you fucking out of my sight again.

Chapter Thirty-Six

Cat & Mouse

Charlie

It's so dark in the woods. I tried to stick close to a road, but soon discovered they would find me when I heard a car screech to a stop behind me, doors opening and slamming.

I didn't even look, I just ran into the thick woodland.

I ran so fucking hard, my body working overtime on the little nourishment I've given it. Hoping to leave them behind even as my feet sank in the wet mud, pushing myself further.

It's a huge game of cat and mouse. That's what this is, and I'm definitely the mouse in this. The tiny little mouse that keeps getting trapped.

I thought it would be impossible for them to find me. I've made sure I'm isolated and well out of reach from civilisation. No cameras, no anything.

I want to sleep. Fuck, I'm desperate for it. I can't hear them anymore; I don't know how long I've been running for; it could be a few minutes, it could be an hour.

Sitting down, if only for a moment, my back resting on a large tree. I don't care that it's wet. I'm already soaked. I just need a minute to catch my breath. Hugging my knees to my chest, my head falls to the side as I try to see what's around me. Nothing but blackness. The moon's highlighting the way when the trees break, but even that's fleeting when the clouds pass over.

My mind's too busy for sleep in reality, my overactive imagination hearing things, envisioning what's coming for me.

Exhausted, but needing to move, I lift myself from the floor

Come on, Charlie.

After walking for a while, the sun is just starting to rise, warming my skin for the first time since the park yesterday. I spot a caravan at the far end of the field, which looks abandoned. Stepping closer, I have to climb on an old tire, boosting myself to take a look in the dirty, broken window. Empty. Walking through weeds that reach the height of the windows, I make my way to the door, covered in tall grass, paint flaking off the outside, its handle rusted to almost nothing. Pulling it open, it creaks and shrieks in objection, on its broken hinges. The smell of decay and mould hits me as soon as I get it open.

Entering the caravan, it's heady, both relief at finding a place to hide, and the fear and utter sadness that washes over me in one fell swoop. It's cripplingly.

Standing in the middle of the dirt of grime, I cry, really fucking cry, not for any particular reason, but for every reason at the same time. Everything's crashing down on me in this moment. The loss, the fear, the exhaustion, the pain, but most of all, Owen. I want to run into his arms and have him tell me, everything is going to be okay.

Covering my face with my hands, I slump to my knees as a loud, guttural cry leaves my chest, Sobbing harder. I can't breathe, my chest heaving with the heaviness I'm carrying. I want him to be looking for me. I know it's stupidly selfish of me. I just want the security he brought me when he wrapped his arms around me. Because right now I have none.

My tears fall like waves of emotion being released. I'd say it's good for me, but I don't feel any better for it, just a little more drained on my already empty resources.

Would it have been different if I had run to Owen? When that man grabbed my arm, what if I had gone to him instead of running to my room?

Although the actions I took before I left and did what I did, contradict my not wanting him involved. I left him what I could, knowing he would be involved to a small degree, but not in the line of fire like me. I can't do that to him, not when he looked so happy in that moment. I just can't help but wonder 'what if' all over again.

The guys at Cerberus should have got the other envelope by now. That's if it even got delivered. If no-one has anything, then I'm alone. I know what I sent to Xander will be kept quiet. He'll keep it safe and only use it when he needs it. That also means I'm truly alone in this.

Scrubbing my hands over my face, I take my first look at the small sanctuary I have found. It looks like it's been abandoned for years, dirt and grime every-where. The bed is messy and unkept like a ghost of a life that existed once a long time ago.

There's a kettle and cups and bowls are set up on the small table by the broken window taped with a plastic bag, all covered in years of mould and other things I really don't want to know about.

Nice.

Taking a deep breath, I regret it instantly; the smell making my stomach churn. Lifting my hoodie up to cover my nose and mouth, I continue to look around, wondering what life would have looked like when someone had this place.

Taking my bag from my back, I reach for my last snack bar and bit of water. I'll give myself a few minutes before I move on. Resting my head on my knees, I don't dare sleep. I have no doubt they will find me again. I need to be vigilant.

Stay alert. It's just getting a little harder to do it. Lack of sleep will do that to you.

One question remains though. How do they keep finding me? I need to figure it out. I'm missing something obvious. I know I am.

Snapping my head to the side, I hear a man cursing. Listening, standing quickly, I dare a peek outside through the broken window. *Ohmygod*, how are they doing this? I have no time to rest. *Fuck*. I need to leave, run. My mind telling me to go, but my body's having trouble catching up. How have they found me again? I can't do this for much longer. I'm so fucking tired.

They're a little way off yet. Heading my way, coming over the field, about a hundred meters away. If I can get out the window at the back, I'll get out without being seen. I need to be quick. These guys don't give up.

Dropping my bag out of the small window first, and leaping out before they spot me, I'm running again, my legs protesting with every step.

I spot a bus coming to the bus stop just ahead. I run as fast as I can to make it. Pushing myself harder.

I meet the bus just as it pulls to a stop. I'd say it was my lucky day, but I don't feel lucky. I feel exhausted, deep in my bones exhausted.

I don't know where this bus is headed, but I'm going there. Taking my seat as it pulls away, I let out a shaky breath. Relief mixing with anxiety rolling off me in waves.

I know I have what they want and it looks like they won't give up until they have it. Maybe that's why they haven't killed me yet. *Yet!* My stomach caves at the thought. *How has it come to this? Knowing I may not make it out of this alive.* My eyes well with tears, my fear and frustration showing in the only way it can right now.

Setting my bag down beside me, I ignore the looks of the other passengers. I know I look like shit. I'm covered in crap. I more than likely smell like it too. The bruise on my cheek, which I assume is now full deep purple, hurts to touch, but I've yet to look in a mirror to see the full extent of the damage.

I start to search through the contents of my bag. I'm not sure what I'm looking for, but I get everything out, placing it on the seat next to me in a pile.

Could it be as simple as they are tracking me? To be able to find me in the corner of a field that surrounded by trees is either really fucking unlucky for me, or they planted something on me. If I want this ridiculous plan of mine to work, if I want it to succeed, then I need to be able to do this without being detected.

I'm franticly searching for a device I don't recognise. I don't know what a tracker looks like. Is it big, small, fat, thin? I have no idea.

I can't see anything that's not mine. Feeling defeated, I start putting it all back in my bag. I flick through my passport and spot a small slice of silver. I know it's not part of my passport. That has to be it. A tracker?

A rush of relief leaves my body. I want to scream it from the rooftops. This has to be it. My fingers tremble. This is the first sign of good luck I've had.

Holding it between my fingers, I inspect it. Paper thin and smaller than my pinkie fingernail. There is no way to know for sure this is it, but I have a feeling it is.

I need to think quick. If I get off, they can track me. I need to leave the tracker on the bus or give it to someone on here. I don't want to get anyone else involved, but if I attach the tracker to the bus, they'll know I've found it when the bus continues its route. But if I can slide it into someone's bag, I'll have a better chance of getting away.

Looking up at the bus route, on the bus window, I spot a place I recognise. I need to head to Xander's. He's been a permanent fixture in my life since childhood, my brother's best friend. I know I can trust him with anything. And I need to get off the bus now if I want to make it there by tonight.

Standing, I press the button and ask to get off, purposely dropping my bag when the driver breaks. Leaning down, I slip the tracker into the side pocket of the man in the seat behind me's laptop bag, breathing a sigh of relief when my actions go unnoticed. I just hope the shitheads that are following me see they are innocent when they follow them to where ever they're going.

Picking my bag up, I make my way to the front, prepping for a long walk ahead.

It's just getting dark when I walk up the drive. Xander lives in a very remote part of the upper-class community, just south of Winchester. I know he knows I'm here because when I reach the back door he's already waiting, drink in hand, envelope in the other, waiting for an explanation.

"Boo, it's good to see you, but you look like shit." I can't help the smile that spreads across my face.

"Dickhead." He just smirks and hugs me before settling himself down in the soft seating area.

"Go get yourself sorted. You know where your things are."

Chapter Thirty-Seven

Boo

Owen

It was useless. Absolutely-god-damn-fucking pointless. She's not here. We found where Charlie's been staying. It's so fucking dark out there. I can't breathe, my lungs seize with every intake, the fear of what she could be enduring right now.

We searched everywhere, the dark streets, the empty cafés and shops, every secluded alley, and shithole in between. Charlie's last location showed her buying a pen drive in a tech shop. The surrounding cameras showed she wandered to the park, coming out a short time later, where she met up with a bike courier.

After that she was followed by two men, in broad daylight. Cole's tracing their movements back to make sure the biker is okay. These bastards are different to the ones in Greece. They followed her into the alley after she tried to lose them, with no success.

There were no cameras in the alley, so we couldn't see what happened or how she defended herself this time. I can only guess what happened. Those motherfuckers cornered her. *Again.* She fought them by herself. *Again.* A few minutes later, she ran out, clutching her bag. We've traced her every footstep, leading back to a room she rented in an even worse dive than some of the shitholes we searched earlier.

Why isn't she coming to me?

What was in those envelopes?

With every turn, there just seems to be more questions, each leading us on her path, trailing behind her. Too slow, it's all taking too much *god-damn-fucking* time.

My jaw's so fucking tense, I can feel the ache in my teeth. I hate that she's alone in this. Does she even know we're doing everything we can to find her? That I won't stop until she's next to me again. Safe. I won't rest, I can't sleep, it's impossible. I can't even sit down, just knowing my angel's out there somewhere, alone, injured and quite possibly in pain.

Every time I close my eyes I see the image of her smiling face, the photo from her birthday, then it fades. The fear in her eyes haunts me, watching them widen, knowing what's coming. I see the pain she's hiding. Her beautiful face pale, her violet eyes broken.

I know she can fight and she fucking does it well, but fighting takes it out of you. It's why we have a respite. We know we need to rest. She doesn't have that option right now. So, I won't rest until I know she can. No matter how long it takes.

No matter what, Charlie. Your promise to me goes both ways. You kept yours until you had no option to break it. Now it's my turn.

I will find you. I will make you mine and you will never fear anything again, because I'll be by your side. Protecting you from anything that comes our way.

Standing in the middle of this godforsaken room, taking everything in, my shoulders tense further up my neck, straightening momentarily when Ethan walks in. I'm trying my damnedest to keep my head on straight right now. I'm hanging on a ledge and he knows it.

"Leon's talking to the people downstairs to see if they know anything." I just nod. I can't talk, not with her broken image playing through my mind.

"I'm not gaining on her. I need the gap to close, Ethan. I need her by my side."

"She's smart, O. We all know she is. If she's managed to hide from us, she's managed to hide from them." I guess that's something. Unfortunately, it does nothing to settle the unease threading through my every fibre.

"It's not good enough. She can't last like this. If she's hurt..." I pick up the blood-stained wipes, showing them to Ethan. "I don't know what I'll do if—"

"Don't you fucking dare finish that sentence, O." Leon's rough voice cuts me off as he walks into the room, his frown line deeper than I've ever seen them before. He relays the words I need to hear. "She's so fucking strong, O. She may not look it, be she fought each and every one of us in that ring and kicked our fucking arses every time. Her skills are wicked." The awe and respect in Leon's eyes give me what I need to keep my head in the game. It gives me the strength to move. Keep going. If Charlie can, I fucking will.

"She'd also love to get you in the ring, O." Ethan's hint of a grin catches me off guard. That guy never smiles.

"Never fucking happening." They both just look at me, silent communication running between them.

"Don't make the same mistake twice, O. She is more than capable of kicking your arse." I don't know if I could get in the ring with her. I just couldn't intentionally lay a finger on her...mar her perfect skin like that.

Now the image of sparing with her plays out in my mind and it turns me on more than it should...

"These," Ethan holds up the wipes I handed to him, interrupting the lust spiral I was settling into. "Must have been used to clean some small cuts, nothing serious." He's reassuring me, but it does nothing.

"Um, what did they say downstairs?"

Leon steps forward, looking over the room, like he wants to throw up at the state of the place. "They said two guys broke the front door down last night, about eleven. Said they were looking for a tall, blonde woman, had a photo and everything. They gave them nothing, just argued that they couldn't just break in. One of them hit the woman, then the guy, and then they barged up here. Said they left a few minutes later, pissed off, apparently not getting what or who they wanted." *Motherfuckers hit a woman.* Not in any world is that ever okay.

"She was here less than eight hours ago," I state. "Any ideas where she went next?"

Dialling Cole's number from my phone, he answers on the second ring. The noise in the background is loud.

"Cole, what the fuck is going on?" I ask, placing him on speaker.

"We have some unexpected visitors. Sorry, O, um..."

"Who?" Panic starts creeping in at the thought of others knowing the location of the lodge.

"Jack, and Millie. I may have told them what was going on. Jack got the address out of me. He threatened my balls, man. Not Jack's idea, apparently. Millie insisted she needed to be close and help find Charlie. And well, Jack's never going to leave her side now she's up the duff." He makes a gruff noise, like he's just been hit in the stomach.

"Fine." I'll deal with that later. "I need eyes on this location. I need to know her next steps. Do you have anything?" I'm irritated that Cole gave the lodges details out. Even if I do trust Jack. I understand Millie's concern. She'll be safe there. I'll need to reassure Jack it's safe. *Fuck... I've not seen him since...*

"Nothing current yet. She's good at hiding, O." Cole loves the chase. It's what he does best. I'm starting to think that maybe she's too good. *What if she's planning something? Why didn't she come to me in Greece? To us, or Leon at the unit? I don't fucking understand.*

"Cole, how are they finding her?" Ethan asks. I hadn't even considered that. He's typing frantically, the click of each key coming through the phone.

"Right, okay, give me a sec... room was let under a false name, cash, no surprises there. That whole place has nothing legit about it."

"So how did they find her, Cole?" The room is so fucking tense, you could slice it with the knife I have in my pocket. "They found her in the alley, they found her in this shit hole. How, Cole?"

"Damn, they must have a tracker on her. Owen... Shit." Silence fills the room and the noise on the phone goes deadly quiet. We all know what that means. If she has no idea about the tracker, they will continue to find her. She doesn't have long before exhaustion gets the better of her. I'm rooted to the spot, the fear I have overtaking any rational thought I have in that moment. Taking a deep, controlling, yet shaky breath, I can't let them find her first. *So what are you doing to do?*

"Owen?" A sweet voice comes over the phone. Millie? "Owen?" She sounds slightly panicked. "What are you going to do about it?" My mind snaps back, focusing on what she said, asking me the question I just asked myself. What am I going to do? Shaking out my hands, I breathe deep, my control slowly coming back. I know what I'm going to do.

"I'm going to find her, Millie. You can bet your ass that I'll find her and never let her go again." I mean every fucking word.

"Good, now what are you going to do?"

There's rustling down the phone for a few seconds. "For starters, you are never going to talk about my *wife's* ass in any context ever again. Got it?" I'd smile at the sound of Jack's protective words, but I just can't bring myself to do it.

"Good to talk to you, Jack. We're heading back. There's nothing else we can do here."

"See you when you get here, arsehole." I laugh. It's a low noise that even takes me by surprise.

Charlie's just out of reach, but not for much longer.

We walk back into the lodge to find everyone working, talking and getting along like always. The atmosphere is tense, but that's when we work best. The ache in my chest feels tighter, the tension in my shoulders giving me a headache, and my lack of sleep isn't helping matters. It's been almost three days since I closed my eyes, but it's nothing compared to what Charlie must be feeling right now.

Watching the faces of my friends, the people I trust the most in this world, as well as Millie, who's sitting on Jack's lap, while he nuzzles her neck, keeps me grounded. I know they will do anything to find her. When Jack spots me, he taps Millie, and she turns to look at me. Leaping off his lap, she comes over and wraps her arms around me.

"It's good to see you, Owen." When she pulls back, the concern in her eyes is palpable. "She's my best friend, Owen. I need her back just as much as you do. Don't be angry we are here."

"I'm not angry, Millie. I couldn't be angry with you, or Jack, for that matter." Jack appears, eyeing my hands that are still on Millie's back from our hug. Rolling my eyes, I remove them and step back. Jack steps in front of me. I have no idea how this is going to go. We're matched when it comes to our height, only slightly different in our build. His hand comes up and grips the back of my neck, pulling me closer.

"You're an idiot. What happened to Millie was not your fault. I lost a friend when you left." Shaking his head slightly, he lets out a frustrated growl. "You missed so much Owen, our wedding, Dan and Em's wedding, the birth of Daisy, and leaving Charlie... well, you fucked up. If you want her back in your life, you're going to need to fucking beg her for it."

My shoulders let go of some of the tension I've been holding on to since Millie was shot. Hearing Jack confirm what I've been told over and over again by Leon, Zan, and the others. Relief, that's what I feel right now. It's awakened a flicker of hope that I can deal with anything that lies ahead.

"Already got my speech ready, and I didn't miss as much as you think I did." I may have been very absent for the day-to-day events in their lives, but I made sure I saw the big events. I may have travelled to Ibiza the day of their wedding, and tapped into the camera feeds now and again, to see baby Daisy come home.

"What's that meant to mean?" Jack looks confused. All eyes land on me. I had no idea they were all listening into our exchange. I should have known better. Nosy fuckers.

No better time than now to come clean, I guess.

Millie comes to stand by Jack's side, interlacing her fingers with his.

"I made sure I was there for the big events, that's all." I'm trying to play it off as nothing, but I can see it in their faces that this is not nothing to them.

A chorus of 'what's', 'shits', and 'did he just say...' ring out around the room.

"I never missed your wedding, or Dan and Em's. I was there, you just never saw me. I was there the day Em and Dan brought Daisy home. I would never have missed it. She's cute." I shrug it off.

Jack lets out a laugh of disbelief. "The ghost," is all he says before walking off towards the back of the room with Millie. "I should have known. He couldn't really stay away for that long. Just you wait until Charlie finds out."

"I know I owe you all an explanation, but not now, okay? Just not now. Can we just focus on getting her back? I'll talk when I have Charlie next to me."

Needing some space, I notice that Leon and Ethan aren't anywhere to be seen. If I had to guess, they found my stash and their new toys in the basement.

Heading to the kitchen, I grab myself a drink before going to the basement. And there they are, big ass smiles on their faces. I bought in a full range of firearms, weapons and some other not so legal items ready for whatever comes our way.

"What do you think? They'll make a nice addition to our standard issue weapons." I mock coming up behind them, the door closing behind me. We all have a gun, not all the time, just in particular situations like our current one. Even in here it's with me.

"I think you are planning for a zombie apocalypse, and have greatly overestimated what you will need," Leon says, dismantling a new rifle.

"Still love the zombie movies, Leon?"

Agreeing with me, he carries on taking out each gun and knife, examining it and placing it back.

"I have something for you too, Ethan. Follow me."

Pushing open the doors at the back of the room, the lights flicker on automatically, flooding the place with light, showing off the full medical room.

"Fuck." I get the chin lift. Without Ethan's funds, when we first started Cerberus, we would have nothing. We owe him so much.

"What is this place, O?" he asks, while he opens and closes the cupboards filled with every medical supply you could think of and more.

"Our safe haven. If I've missed anything, just order it." Handing him a key, I add, "The explosives are stored outside in the lockup."

"Nice. All I need now is to build an interrogation room and I'm set." He smiles.

"Down the hall to the right," I say over my shoulder, walking back to the door.

"You really have thought of everything." I tried. Taking the last sip of my drink, I almost choke on it when the shriek from the alarm system sounds, assaulting my ears.

Seconds later, the three of us are running for the stairs. "We have visitors," I state. My heart rate picks up as my feet thud up the staircase to get to the surveillance system screens.

"Who the fuck else did you lot tell about this place," I bellow as I switch the cameras to see who has triggered the alarm... Millie looks a little guilty for being here, whereas Jack just shrugs. The others all deny anything.

"I can't see anyone. Where the fuck did they go?" Switching between the cameras, I don't see shit.

"I'm right here. You must be Owen? I'm Xander. It's good to meet you."

Everyone moves like lighting, guns drawn, aimed at the man who bypassed my security and walked into the place like he owns it. My gun's secured at my side. I know my guys have me covered.

He's standing so casually. His build and his assertive demeanour, this guy looks like he means business. He's tall, blond, and built like he trains regularly, dressed in suit trousers, his shirt is open at the collar, giving him an air of relaxed refinement. I get a feeling he's more than capable of some, if not more, of the things we are. He has to be either crazy or so fucking self-assured to walk into a room full of ex-army. That's ballsy, or stupid. I haven't decided which one yet.

I can't see any weapons on him. Leon takes a step forward to check him out anyway. He allows us to search him, no one saying a word. Guns still pointed in his direction.

"Who are you?" Ethan asks.

"I've already told you who I am. My name is Xander and I'm a very close friend of Boos'." Hands in his pockets, he looks around the room, greeting everyone with a nod or a slight lift of the chin, none of which are returned.

"Boo?" It's a simple question, so why is he frowning at me?

Cole coughs, telling me I need to know something. I move closer and he whispers, "Boo is a nickname of Charlie's. Her parents used it when they came to visit. She told us only people she was close to call her that." *Right, another thing I didn't know.* Regret invades my chest, like a snake. I have so much to learn about my angel.

"Interesting that the one who seeks her the most does not know this little detail. I guess that's what you get when you disappear for a year." My hackles go up. I want to hurt him. *How well does he know her?*

"I wouldn't if I were you. Let me give this to Cole. He can check out who I am before we go any further." He asks Cole to run a check on Alexander Boltov, gives him a code, and places two things on the desk. Cole eyes me like he has no idea how he knows his name. Signalling for him to go ahead, Cole gets to work, opening a file and entering the code he gave him.

"He checks out, O. Stand-the-fuck-down." Everyone eases back but me. I trust what Cole says, but it doesn't mean I won't read that file later for myself. Or that I trust this stranger.

"How do you know Charlie?"

He looks frustrated, like I've asked the wrong question. "Boo and I, we go way back." There's a glint in his eyes. He knows he's winding me up, and it's working.

"That's the least of your problems right now, Owen. I saw Boo last night." *Fucking hell*, I almost double over at the sound of his words. It's like a blow to the stomach. She's alive, she's okay. Why the fuck didn't he lead with that?

"Where? Why isn't she with you?" Stepping close, I get in his face. He doesn't even flinch. I can't get any more words out. My heart's in my chest.

"She came to me." There it is again, a fucking punch to the gut.

"What...what do you mean, she came to you?" I say, frustration seeping into my words.

"She came to me. She needed something I had, apparently. I'm not happy about it." I fall into the seat behind me. She has to know we are looking for her. She has to know I'd never let her down. That I'd do anything to find her right now. We're so close.

"Why is she not with you now?" Ethan demands from my side, his jaw as tense as mine.

"She left before I could do anything, Ethan."

"How the fuck do you know my name?" he spits out.

"I know many things, you'll see, but Charlie, that one is... determined. She wants to finish this, whatever this is. She didn't tell me anything, but from what I've seen on the memory stick, she's in some deep shit. That's why I came to you. I care about her."

For the first time since he walked into our place, I can see a softness in his eyes.

"I need to get to her. Tell us everything you know." I'm placing my trust in him right now. I have to. He was the last person to see her. Even if he did just break into my place without being seen.

"She left mine in the early hours this morning before I woke, and after raiding my den." He grits his teeth and I like that she's pissed him off. "Boo decided to take a few things I'm not impressed about. Her favourite gun, ammo, and a load of snacks, she also took my favourite truck before she left." There's a lot to dissect in that, but the only thing that sticks in my mind is that she stayed over at his house.

"What are you up to, Charlie?" I mutter quietly.

He holds up a hand, halting my words when he reaches for his phone and puts it to his ear.

"It's about time you called. She needs you. Are you on your way?" There's nodding as he agrees to whatever the other person is saying.

"Good, yes, okay. I'll do it now." He places the phone on the table next to him. "You're on speaker now."

"We have your location. Our ETA is twenty hours. Faster if we can, but it's not easy." A male voice says.

"Do you have eyes on our girl yet?" a second one adds, his voice stern. *What the fuck? Our girl?*

"Who the fuck are you?" This is getting annoying as fuck. How many other men is she *close* to?

"Her brothers, jackass," Xander laughs, and I immediately feel like shit.

"Shit, Sorry—"

"You should be. Find her Owen. We will be there when we can."

Xander ends the call and places his phone back into his pocket. "Now that's out the way, let's get to work, shall we?" Picking up the two small devices from the desk, he hands one to me and the other to Cole.

"This one," he tells the room, "is all the information Boo had on the Summers' organisation, including the video she found. I have a suspicion she wants to end the whole organisation and not just him." Turning to me, the corner of his mouth lifts slightly he says, "And this one is the location of my favourite truck."

Looking at the small device he handed me, I squeeze it my palm like it's my lifeline to her...

I'm coming, Angel.

Chapter Thirty-Eight
Techy Things

Charlie

I've been watching them all this time, sort of. I'm parked up in the back of Xander's truck. He's going to be more than a little pissed off that I took it, as it's his favourite. I can see why. It has everything a person needs to be comfy while they carry out surveillance. It looks good too. It's been a long-standing thing between us. I annoy him, and he always finds a way to get me back. I guess that's what happens when you grow up with someone. He's like the third brother I never needed but got lumbered with anyway.

I knew the truck had everything I need before I took it. He bragged about it when he got it. It has an array of devices fitted that I'm sure do lots of techy things, but I only need one really. That's the Wi-Fi transmitter thing. It's so small, I hope it won't get seen by anyone using the laptop, while it does what I need it to do when I get inside the club.

I'm perched on the soft black leather seats, the tinted windows hide me from view. The video surveillance around the truck and the monitors he has in the back make it easy to watch what's going on around me, plus I can record it all.

If the prospect of going in there wasn't so goddamn scary, I'd be enjoying myself as this truck is huge. More than enough space for at least three enormous people back here. I'm doing my best to downplay what I'm going to do—stepping foot inside the walls of Praise could be a death wish. It is a death wish, but it's the only way forward. I'm shaking. I know what this could mean for me. I'm not stupid.

My nerves come and go like they have done over the past few days. A humming under my skin I can't get rid of.

I've been here for the last few hours. You'd think a huge building like this, that houses one of the UK's biggest crime organisations, would be in the back streets of some crappy industrial estate, hidden, but it's not.

The club is located on the outskirts of one of the most affluent areas in the UK. I guess money likes money. Legal or not. It's surrounded by other buildings, creating its own little network. I know all these units belong to the Summers' organisation. Not all of them are illegal, some you could even call respectable if you didn't know who owned them. I guess they have to launder their money somewhere, right? Praise sits right in the centre, like the other buildings around it are on guard.

I'm parked alongside a large number of more valuable looking cars, so it blends in.

The main entrance of the building is in full view of the front of the truck. I don't want to walk around and spec things out, so I've brought up the maps system installed in the truck to take a look at the area. I've plotted my route to get into the side entrance, using the door that's been propped open. Too many people come and go from the main entrance and even at this time of the morning, there's also security on the door.

My heart does a nervous flip. I have to do this. I need to otherwise, it will never stop. I will always be on the run, looking over my shoulder. I won't get to live my life. I want a future to look forward to. A second honeymoon, kids to spoil one day. The simple things.

I'm not rash or stupid doing this. That's why I didn't say anything to Xander last night. We didn't chat much; I told him what was on the pen drive, but didn't say anything about what has been going on. He would have made me stay in the house, called my brothers, because I'm sure if anyone can get in touch with them, it's him. With all his top-secret-spy-shit clearance passes. Then he'd deal with it. End of story. I hate it when men do that shit.

I didn't want that to happen, so I snuck out while he was asleep. I did pick up my favourite gun before I left. I've not used it in a while, but it's like riding a bike—you never forget.

My initial plan was to get in and see what else I could find. Something that will crush the whole organisation, not just one man. It is risky having no idea what I was looking for. It could take me hours in there to find something, and that was an uncomfortable feeling that didn't sit well with me.

When I walked into the bathroom at Xander's, I stripped, turned the shower as hot as it would go and sat under the water until my skin burned and turned pink.

I decided that I needed to be the old me, the brutal bitch that used to prosecute criminals for a living. I needed her back. I needed that dedication she used to put into every case. And the smile I wore when I discovered they'd been sentenced.

Something in the back of my mind kept nagging at me, like really nagging me, to the point I abandoned my shower and went to take another look at the stuff I have on my laptop.

And that's when I found it. There's no way to be a hundred per cent sure, but from what I can see, it's worth the risk. If Mr Summers is the accountant, then...*shit*. Who's the boss?

I left Xander's not knowing what he would do with the information I handed to him. I just have this sinking feeling in my gut that he'll help me, and it won't be in any way I would like. I guess time will tell.

An hour later, I've made up my mind and I'm going in. There's been minimal activity for the last thirty minutes, so I'm taking my chance while I can.

Planting myself back in the driver's seat and starting the engine, I move the truck to the other side of the units. There's an alley that separates two of the larger buildings. It opens up towards the end, just after the corner right in front of the loading bay and steel door. Easy access, that's what I'm hoping anyway.

With shaky hands, I open the driver's door, grab my bag, and start walking. Clicking the truck's button to lock it, it makes an alarming loud beep, then tells me that all security is activated. *Nice touch arse-wipe. Shit.*

Any form of cover has now been officially broken. Moving a little faster, I enter the covered alley that's dark even though it's morning. My eyes are everywhere, looking for anything. Pulling my cap further down on my head, I make my way down the narrow walkway.

Turning the first corner, I spot three guys standing around like some kind of security for the building. Most likely to stop people like me getting in. Great.

Time to wing it and see what happens.

"Hi, boys," I say as I stroll past them. It actually comes out way sluttier than I intended, but I have confidence in my conviction. I've got to act like this is all normal.

"Hi," the tallest of the three men says and sticks his hand out to block my way. "What do we have here?" I want to react. I have my gun in its holster hidden by my side. I won't use it unless it's really needed.

I can see a way out that won't result in gunfire, but it will end in his arm being broken. I don't want to fight if I don't have to, so, I wait.

Scanning the walkway, I see if there's anything I can use to my advantage if I need it. I notice a piece of fence that's been snapped off. It may come in handy.

"She looks a little out of place around here, doesn't she? Where are you off to?" he says to the others.

"Work. Where else would I be going?" The others have come to stand by him, crowding me; baldie to the right, beardy to the left, backing me against the fence. There's still space between us, but not much.

"Somehow, I just don't believe you, sweetheart. Why don't we look after you?"

"Well, *boys*," I emphasise the words boys because they have pissed me off. I don't need to be looked after or saved. "It's been fun, but if you could, please just move aside. I'd like to be on my way. Otherwise, my boss will more than likely kill me for being late for my shift." I'm working with what I have.

"Sweetheart, don't you want to play?" that does it. Fucking men, not all men, granted, but these men...

"No, I'm really not in the mood for this shit today. Let me pass." The three of them step back as if they are going to let me through, allowing me to move a little way off the fence, giving me the space I need. I can see it in their expressions, the way they side eye each other; I'm not getting out of here. The taller one moves back more, so I step forward. He sticks in front of the other two, while baldie and beardy make a wall behind him. They're relaxed enough, not expecting the fight they will get.

When the tall one looks away, I brace my step. He doesn't see it coming when my fist connects with his sternum. I hear the crack. I love this move. It's quick and very painful. It's going to hurt like a bitch.

My other fist connects with his face as he falls to his knees, his eyes flicking to me briefly, unsure what just happened.

Baldie throws a punch in my direction. I block him, thrusting his arm away from my face, while I punch him in the face as hard as I can, aiming my right leg to his soft body in an aggressive kick that takes him down. I'm fast, my body reacting to the moves they are throwing at me. They don't get a single hit until I hear a voice that distracts me. I feel it in my side, but I don't move. I carry on, but that voice...

"Charlie?"

I know it well even if I've not heard it for over a year. There is no fucking way that's him, I think as I lay another punch into the one with the beard. But my body seems to remember him well enough that it wants to turn to him. I refuse to let that happen.

Using my knee and all the pent-up anger inside me, I really lay into the man. He gets jab after jab to his side and he goes down first, before I feel strong arms around my waist, lifting me.

"Angel, it's me. Stop fighting me." We hit the floor, me landing on top of him, my back to his front. I wind him slightly. Good.

"Like fuck I will, Owen," I yell. "Get the hell off me."

Owen

"Fuck, Angel, stop. I'm not going to hurt you, and I'm definitely not going to fight you." She just keeps going, fighting even though she knows it's me. It's gut-wrenching. I'm causing this reaction. Would she have been the same with Leon?

Taking another elbow to my ribs, she kicks her legs again. I can't take much more, so I let go. My years of training and experience flew out of my mind the moment I saw her fighting. All I wanted to do was get her away from them. Tears cloud her eyes as she glares angrily at me. *Shit.*

"You already hurt me, Owen. Don't you fucking ever do that to me again. Why are you even here?"

"I came to—" I don't get another word out as Charlie explodes.

"You came to what? Save me? Rescue me?" She's spitting fire at me, her beautiful face flushed from the fight I witnessed first-hand.

Fuck. Is it odd, I'm a little turned on right now?

Yep... No, she's fucking hot when she's angry.

"Well..." Leon laughs from where he's standing by the van. My hand comes to the back of my neck, trying to ease the uncomfortable sensation I have flowing through me. The others keep themselves busy with the guys she's left in the alley.

"Well, what, Owen?" Clad in black from head to toe, she's fucking stunning. I can't help the smile that spreads across my face.

"Are you really smiling at me right now?" Charlie throws her hands up in the air. "Fuck you, Owen."

I want to hold her so much. I want to slam my mouth against hers. I want to possess her, just like she possesses me. I won't. I know she'll cut off my balls if I even attempt to do anything of the sort. I understand why, but it doesn't make these feelings I have for her go away. Fuck, I'm... in deep. It's like the first time I saw her. I can't control it.

"I can't help it, Angel. I've missed you. It's so fucking good to see you."

"Shut up. I had everything under control, Owen. Why did you do that?" She's pointing at the guys who have been left battered and bruised by her and tied up by Dom and Ethan, now sitting against the fence.

She walks off in the direction of the truck, then stops when she realises we are not alone. She pauses, understanding setting in her features.

Stepping beside her, I whisper in her ear, "Um, I wanted to help..." I know it's the wrong thing to say even before I say it.

"You have a lot to learn, Owen."

"Oh, I know I do, Angel. This part of you, I fucking love it. Give me everything." I dare to touch her side, gliding my fingers down the length of her waist. Her eyes flicker closed for a second before she rights herself.

The pointed look she gives me has my insides igniting like they have been dormant for a year, and now want to rage a blazing inferno with her.

She ignores me and walks over to the guys at the van, greeting them all. While she lets Ethan hug her, she doesn't let Leon, to his and my surprise.

"What have I done?" he questions, just as I think the same thing. He looks a little hurt.

"You spoke to him," she says, obviously meaning me. "Before I left to go on holiday, and you kept it from me." Leon frowns, then dips his frame to level with her.

"Okay, that's fair, but I did it for good reason. I wanted you to have a great holiday."

"Yeah, that turned out well for me, didn't it?" She walks away from him. I'm smiling like an idiot. I know I am. I'm pleased it's not just me she's pissed at.

Dom and Grey look on. I can guess what each of them is thinking from their expressions. Dom knows that I have a fireball on my hands and a lot of making up to do to get her back on side. And Grey, he just wants to let everyone know what happened here before we arrive back at the lodge. He's bouncing to reach for his phone.

Taking a quick glance round, knowing it won't be long until we attract some more attention, I say, "let's go before we are seen by anyone else." Making my way to the truck I came in. "Load those arseholes into the van." I add, Dom and Grey move to get the guys while Charlie looks for the truck she left behind.

"Not a chance." Xander takes the keys out of her hand and heads to the truck before she can even make a move towards it. Before he reaches it, she shouts at him, "You brought them into this, didn't you?" he just nods. "I won't forgive you for this, Xander."

He stalls for a moment and replies, "I can live with that, and your extra sass." As he climbs into the driver's side. He winks then mutters, "Did you eat in my truck?"

"Serves you right for saying I looked like shit."

He laughs, then smooths his features. "I'm glad you're safe, Boo." Then he's driving off, back to the lodge, before she can even say another word to him.

"Don't hold it against him. We were already looking for you." my hand falls to the small of her back in an attempt to guide her to my truck.

"Umm." It's the only response I get.

"You're with me, Angel." Pointing to my truck, she hesitates.

"No, I'll go with Leon."

"Sorry, van's a bit full, Charlie," Leon says as he throws the third guy in the back, earning him a glare from her beautiful face.

"We have a lot to talk about, Charlie. Get in the truck." Her shoulders sag a little. She knows we can't avoid this conversation.

"This may not be the right time, but after watching you fight back there, I need to get this off my chest. I'm ready to tell you everything, Angel." Opening the truck door, offering my hand so she can step up, she takes it. The feel of her soft palm in mine almost floors me. Sucking in a breath to steady my own reaction, she does exactly the same thing, her eyes are trained on our connected hands. It's the first time I've held her in over a year and it brings the dying embers of my heart back to life.

"Fine, but let me have my say first," she says. Letting go of my hand, she slides into the black leather seat and lays her head on the headrest, closing her eyes. I watch for a second, her chest rising and falling with each breath she takes. What I wouldn't give to feel her pulse under my rough fingers right now.

Climbing in the truck on the opposite side, we sit in silence for a few minutes, letting the atmosphere build between us until it's ready to explode.

"You left me, Owen." I want to take everything I have done back. I want to start again. My hands grip the steering wheel a little tighter.

"I know, it was a shitty thing to do, I could have done so many things differently." sighing, I carry on, "I left thinking I was doing it to protect you. I was fucked up. I couldn't see a better way to do it. I knew I needed help." I lay it all out for her, the talking therapy, the loss, the guilt, the flashbacks, the pain I felt. I can't look at her. I just need to get it all off my chest. "The guilt I have carried with me all these years, when Millie was shot it... Shit." She's just watching me, her eyes tracing my face. "My... PTSD hit me hard, I spiralled. The guys on the special ops team have helped me so much, they taught me that what I did that day and the days leading up to it was enough. They helped me come to terms with the deaths we had in our unit."

She whispers a curse, but her eyes remain on me.

"Yes, I've been away from you and I've hated every fucking second. You've consumed my thoughts, Charlie. I watched from afar when Millie and Jack got married. I've seen baby Daisy." Her eyes go wide at that bit, but she stays silent, biting her lip instead. "I just couldn't be there *with* any of you. I needed to be better, for all of you."

"Owen, that's... a lot. I don't know what to say. I'm angry at you for the way you handled this, but I can't change what happened." Gulping down the rising emotion, I feel lost. I want us to move forward, get past this.

From the corner of my eye, I can see she's trying her best not to cry anymore, and it guts me that I caused this. The tears she doesn't want to shed over me.

"It was all so I could be a better person for you, Charlie. I want us to have a life together. I knew I couldn't give you that, not when I had that fear hanging over my head."

"I understand, Owen." Her voice is firm. As I start to drive, I think she means it. "I know why you left, I get it. I really do. But what you don't understand is that I would have stood by your side while you went through all of that. Instead, you decided to do it on your own. You left me with no consideration for how I would feel about it. About how I feel about you. Fuck, Owen, you could have gone about this differently. You could have told me you were leaving, but you didn't. You left it to Leon to break the news to me. It hurt, Owen, so badly, you tore me in two and I had no idea if you were okay for a whole fucking year. I had to hope you were okay, I had to hope that you would come back to me... then you rang Leon, not me..." Her voice wobbles,

"When I called Leon that day, I wanted to call you. Fuck, I wanted to hear your voice. I just didn't want our first words in a year to be over the phone. I was days away from seeing you again. I wanted to see your face when I explained all this."

"I thought you'd forgotten about me, Owen. Having no contact will do that to a girl. You've moved on..." tears are gliding down her face.

"I'm sorry." It's all I can offer. It's not enough. It will never be enough. I'm devastated by the shit I've put her through.

"That's the thing, Owen. You're not sorry. Why should you be? You did what you felt was right. There is no reason to be sorry for that." How is she this reasonable? Taking a deep breath, she carries on. "So, when I saw you in Greece, I knew you were okay. I knew you were happy. You have a new girlfriend. She's beautiful, by the way. I knew then that I had lost you. You weren't mine anymore." Her lips tremble slightly as she considers her words. I watch as she closes her eyes. When she opens them again, they are more focused than before. "I'm okay with it, sort of. I'll move on. I don't want you involved in my shit. I can't risk the ones I love getting hurt in this. I've seen too closely what these people will do if they get their hands on you... I won't allow it."

I've had to pull over so I don't crash. I can't think straight. *The ones she loves? Am I still included in that?*

Turning my head, I gather her face in my hands and watch as her lips part slightly from my touch. I bring her as close as I can get without kissing her.

"Let me clear a few things up for you, Angel. Harley is Dom's wife. That's the woman you saw me with at the pool. She's like one of the guys. That's it. Nothing more. You have and will always be mine. No matter what happens between us, you are it for me. So, I will be involved in your shit. I'll make it mine. I will be there next to you every step of the goddamn way. No matter what."

There's a long pause. Only the sound of passing cars and the low hum of the radio float through the air. I think I've lost her. I know I have. It won't stop me from being part of her life.

"Okay." It's a whisper on my thumb as it softly passes her lips.

"Okay?" I'm questioning it because I have no idea what she means.

"Yes, okay. We start again, from scratch, take it slow, dating and seeing each other like a normal relationship."

Well, fuck me sideways. I have no clue what to say. Not in my wildest fantasies did I ever imagine that she would say those words to me.

"Shut that mouth and kiss me, Owen."

There's no hesitation. I take her mouth with mine. Our lips meet in a soft and pensive kiss, her moan matching my own. She tastes so fucking good. Just as I'm starting to deepen the kiss, she pulls away.

"Owen. As much as I would like to continue this, I need food and sleep. Take me home."

"I can't take you home, but I can take you to the lodge." She raises her eyebrows and then shrugs like she trusts me, and this time our fingers are interlaced for the entire ride back.

Chapter Thirty-Nine
Promises

Charlie

My eyes sweep over the place where Owen spent almost six months on his own. It's a little overwhelming, almost sad. He was alone here, trying to fight his demons. I hate it. It kills me that I could have been here with him, helping him get through it all. And I really do understand why he did it. Some things you have to do by yourself. My divorce, I did that on my own because I wanted to, I was also embarrassed, humiliated and didn't want anyone to know. I wholeheartedly understand why he did it. That said, it doesn't mean I have to agree with it, or how he went about doing it. He did it for himself, I admire him for that.

On our way back, Owen got me a burger and fries. I had to hold back a chuckle while I ate, remembering Xander's words, 'extra sass', my dark web code name 'xxSass29' a huge hint to what he's been doing for me in my search to take down this organisation. 'AVxtail/9' is Xander, I have no doubt about it, looking out for me in only a way Xander can. After inhaling the food, I fell asleep, only to be woken when Owen's hand brushed the side of my face. I've missed him so much. It's odd how you can feel so lost in one moment, then feel so complete in the next. I can't stop smiling.

I can already see all eyes are on us from the windows. Spotting Millie and Jack, I give them a small wave.

"Where are you taking me?"

He stops and stands in front of me, his hands grazing my hips. Sucking in the air between us, I can already taste him, his lips so close to mine.

My hand comes to his waist, his warmth permeating his black t-shirt. I hold on, digging my fingers in to get a better grip. Pulling him closer, I want to make sure this is real.

"I'm going to take care of you. Angel." *Kiss.* "You need more food." *Kiss.* "Shower." *Kiss.* "Or bath." *Kiss.* "Rest. I'm at your service." Nothing has changed. The way this man makes my body hum, is... overpowering? Inevitable? Uncontrollable.

I never want to let these feeling go. I've not felt this since before he left.

It's only him.

"Owen, you don't need to do this. I can sort myself out. Just show me where it all is." I'm saying the words, I know I don't really mean them. *Do I want him to take care of me? Huh, I guess I do.*

Kissing me again, this time with so much more passion than should be allowed in an open space, my body wants to do to all the sexy, kinky fuckery things to him. My back arches and I press myself into him, just to feel more of him.

"After watching what you have been through in the last three days, I'm not leaving your side until you are clean, well fed, satisfied, and fast asleep." I have a feeling that even then he would stay with me.

I kiss him again. I feel like he's holding back and right now, I don't want him to. Gripping his dark tussled hair with both hands, I pull him deeper.

What was I thinking, saying I wanted to take it slow?

"It all sounds too good to be true, but I think you may be missing one very small little thing." I glance down at his dick standing to attention, pressing eagerly into my stomach.

"There is nothing small about that, Angel." He grins, grinding his length into me, jumping up I wrap my legs around him. I can't help myself. It's been a long time since anyone has touched me, since he touched me.

"Have you been with anyone else?" I blurt out, frowning at myself. I don't want to know if he has, but I also need to know.

"Angel, there has been no one. Only my hand and the memories of you to keep me company at night." I feel the truth in his words. Bringing my legs back to the ground, steadying myself, my fingers stroke down the side of his cheek, loving the rough stubble under my soft fingers. "Same."

His heavy green eyes meet mine. "I'm sorry, Charlie."

"Don't be sorry... just take care of me." A slow smile spreads across his face, and he steps away from me, gripping my hand and bringing it to his lips, placing a soft kiss on my split knuckles that sends sparks that only Owen can ignite in me, to my heart and core.

We make our way up the small steps, at the back of the lodge, quickly realising I have no idea where I'm going. "Show me the way." He doesn't miss a beat, grabbing me by the waist, hauling me up. I wrap myself around him again, my long legs encompassing his hips. My feet resting on his perfect arse, something else I can't wait to get my hands on.

Scanning his palm on the sensor by the door, Owen takes me up two flights of stairs to a huge bedroom I'm assuming it's his by the way it's decorated—masculine, and fresh. Not surprising at all.

"Owen—" I don't get to say another word as his lips descend on mine like the air I breathe is his only saviour. It's only when I reluctantly pull away, needing air, that I realise we're in the most stunning bathroom I have ever set foot in. Deep green rustic tiles, dark wooden countertops, two sinks, and a huge walk-in shower surrounded by a gold-edged screen. On the other side, just below a huge, very modern-looking sash window, is a beautiful rolltop bath, standing proud.

Placing me gently on the edge of the bath, he starts the water running, using the back of his hand to check the temperature. He adds some oil to the water that smells just like him: warm spices and fresh air.

When he crouches down in front of me, I take him in properly.

His hair is a little longer than I remember. I raise my hand to run my fingers through his silky soft waves, then I glide my fingers over the rough stubble on his chin. It feels nice, scratchy in a good way. Darker circles blemish his olive skin under his eyes and worry lines dominate the corners. I want to take it all away. I want to smooth those lines—the ones I know I have made—I want to take back what I did. I want to do it all without letting him know I was ever in any trouble. But right now, I have him next to me, and that's all I have wanted this past year.

He's still my everything.

When our eyes meet, I'm not sure I can look away. My thoughts just stumble to a stop. The forest of green seems to change from light to dark and somehow, I can feel everything he is trying to tell me.

"Charlie? I know it's been a long time, I want to..." His brows pinch as if he's trying to figure out the words he wants to say.

Leaning forward, I touch my forehead with his. "What do you need, Owen?"

"I need to take care of you. I felt so lost when I knew you were missing. Just having you in my home, in my hands, doesn't seem like enough." His voice wavers. I know the feeling.

"Then take care of me. Do what you need to do," I say before kissing his lips softly.

"Can I undress you?" he asks on a breath. I've never seen this side of him. It's humbling.

"Yes." When his fingers stroke down my arms, my eyes close, savouring the sensation he's creating.

Shit, I've missed the way his hands tail over my body so much. His fingers graze my side, and he lifts my top over my head, throwing it to the other side of the room. Looking back up to me, our eyes meet again as he places a soft kiss on every bruise he can see, healing me in ways only Owen can.

Untying the laces on my trainers, he slips them off with my socks. Skimming his fingers back up my legs, he slips off my joggers. They also fly across the room and I can't help but let out a small laugh when they hit the sink and stay there.

Owen takes off my sports bra and adds it to the pile. His hands work their way down my arms, making me gasp as a shiver runs through me. Taking my hands he pulls me to stand. Turning me to face the bath, he places a kiss in between my shoulder blades but doesn't make a move to touch me anywhere else. I don't know if I'm disappointed or relieved.

He comes to stand between me and the bathtub, the flowing water forgotten, replacing my view of the woods with his delicious body. I realise he's taken off his jeans and t-shirt, standing in just his boxers and it's the best sight I have seen in a long time. One I want to see over and over again. Sitting himself on the edge of the bath, his hands find my hips and draw me between his open legs.

With a shaky hand, I trace the flames of his tattoo that lick their way up his broad chest. I let out a gasp when he places a hot kiss on my lower stomach, kneeling slightly, he lowers his head and kisses the apex of my thighs over my knickers. His eyes looking up at me.

I want more of him, my skin feverish for all the things we have missed out on in the last year. His touch is so gentle, my nipples harden from the shivers he's creating over my body. Digging my teeth into my lower lip to stifle the whimper that's trying to force its way out. He backs away slightly, reaching behind him to stop the hot water that's close to overflowing.

Standing, he holds my hand, helping me in. Before I can lower myself, he steps in behind me, guiding us both down, my back against his warm chest. Water breaking over the side, spilling to the floor. I sigh as the warmth of the water sinks into my skin.

We stay like this for a while, his fingers touching me lazily. My head rolls to the side, my own hand trailing the length of his legs I'm so willingly wrapped between. I can feel his hardness growing against my back.

Water droplets cool against my skin as he moves his hand up and over my collarbone.

"I need to touch you, Angel." His words are a deep rumble in my ear. I feel the need pouring off him. I don't say anything, taking his hand and placing it over my breast. He sucks in a breath at the same time I do.

It's only the smallest of touches, but it sets me alight. Lightning races down to my core, setting off fireworks in its trail. I arch my back and his legs sweep underneath mine, opening me for him, holding me in place.

"Touch me," I tell him. I need him more than anything right now. He doesn't hang around. His other hand comes between my legs and strokes my already aching centre. My hips move of their own accord, rocking to get the friction I need.

"Greedy, aren't you, Angel?" His fingers slide against my clit, slowly circling, sending delicious shivers over my body. Pinching my nipple between his rough fingers, I let out a moan I can't hold back any longer.

"Fuck... that sound. I can't tell you how much I've missed that noise." Pressing my clit harder, he gains speed. I'm a mess, whimpering. "Louder," he commands, and I love the tone he's using. I'm practically panting, my hands gripping the side of the tub for dear life as his fingers find my entrance and slide in deep.

"Fuck," I cry.

"That's it, louder. I want everyone to know that you're mine." His fingers push deeper, not moving, while his thumb continues its attack on my clit.

"More," I demand. The water mimics our movements, its heat a caress on my skin.

"More what, Angel? Tell me what you need."

I don't even know if I can form words at this point, my body answering for me as I start to ride his hand.

"Fuck, deeper…" His hand leaves my breast after one last squeeze of my nipple, moving down my stomach, holding me in place. Kissing the side of my neck just where I like it, that's all it takes, I'm lost in a sea of feelings, the warmth of the water, the heat of being back in Owen's strong arms, the burning desire I have in my chest, the tightening of the abdomen, as his fingers work their magic, his intoxicating scent washing over me with every inhale. Sensations envelop my entire body in a heady mix I never want to miss out on again.

Pressing my stomach harder, grinding into me, his groans are my sweet release. He doesn't stop, drawing every last bit of my orgasm out of me, coaxing me to give him more. My body shakes with the force of it and a scream erupts from my soul before I start falling back to reality.

Before I have any chance of recovery, Owen's lifting me out of the tub, holding me to him, bridal style.

"Charlie… I need to…" Lowering his head to mine, I kiss him with everything I have.

"I need you too," I tell him between kisses. There's nothing after that, no words.

Laying me gently on the bed, burying himself deep within me in one fluid motion, gripping his shoulders, holding him to me. "Ohh," I rasp at the sudden intrusion his thick cock filling me so tightly. He's so big, stretching me. He feels so good, perfect, so fucking perfect. My breaths are taken from me as he captures my lips in a mouth-watering kiss. The sting I felt a moment ago lost as it turns to pleasure. The need we have for each other, for what we have missed, for what we want, and so much more.

His movements are slow, loving, and tender. I've never felt anything more for someone as I do him. This man that wants to rescue me when I don't need to be rescued.

When he speeds up his thrusts driven by his own need, I grip on to his broad shoulders as he takes me higher with him. His muscles ripple beneath my fingers with each lustful movement. My legs wrap tightly around his waist, keeping him as close as I can.

"Harder."

Grunting at my command, he drives in harder, deeper, making me ache, the beginnings of my next orgasm igniting. His hand comes up to my throat, his thumb finding his treasured pulse point, a sensation I've missed so fucking much my breath hitches.

"Fuck, that's it," I pant.

"Promise me you will always run to me." The emotion behind his words floors me. His voice trembles as he says each one. They spark tears to roll down my cheek.

"I'll promise… if you promise me one thing in return?" My words are breathy, barely above a whisper, but I know he hears me as his beautiful green eyes lock with mine.

"Anything," he growls.

"Never hide your thoughts from me."

His hot breath whispers over my skin. "Never again, Angel."

"No matter what," I repeat the words he said over a year ago. My body still in his grip, his weight baring down on me. He's so deep I'll feel him for days. Just how I like it.

He fucks into me one last time. My walls contract and I let out a cry of pleasure as we come together.

Chapter Forty

Fuck My Life

Owen

I've left Charlie in bed. I hated leaving her wrapped in the thick quilt. I wanted to be the one wrapped around her, but I need to talk to the guys about what's going to happen next. What we have and how we can take this prick down for good.

The kitchen is quiet when I walk in. Cole's making a round of drinks, so I add my mug to the line-up.

"Where is everyone?"

Smiling at me, he sets my cup under the machine and slides in my favourite coffee pod, pressing the button to start before he turns to me.

"After we all watched you drag Charlie upstairs, Millie and Jack went to rest in one of the rooms, so did Dom and Harley." Handing me my now full cup of coffee, he adds, "Xander left. He said he's got plans for this organisation and to keep him updated on what we plan to do."

Lifting the cup, I groan at the fist sip, hot and bitter on my tongue. I place another cup in the queue for Charlie.

"Leon and Zan have been scoping out the property from the satellite system and getting the floor plans, that are all currently laid out on the dining table, sorting out entry and exit points, and a plan of action. Ethan's playing with his new toys downstairs." I presume he means the men from the van. "He's been there a while. I've been watching on the live feed. Fuck, he enjoys this shit."

"That he does. Has he got anything from them?" Shaking his head, he pops another cup under the machine as it whirrs to life.

"No, basic information, not privy to anything higher up. We'll deliver them to the station when he's done."

"Shame, we could use some good intel right about now."

"Speaking of intel, Grey found out about the explosives lock up. He's determined to set something on fire. I'm sure that man has a problem."

"He'll openly admit it." I laugh.

"How is she?" I forgot how close they have all become with Charlie in my absence.

"Fuck, man, she's so… I don't even know. Strong? In every sense of the word, she's knackered, beat up, but it doesn't seem to bother her. She seemed more worried about protecting everyone else. She's still pissed off with me." His brows pinch together in an attempt to hide his amusement. I can't blame him.

"She is strong. I'm surprised you don't have a black eye. I thought she would have kicked your ass by now." I don't tell him what she did when I ripped her away from those guys in the alley. He'll only laugh harder.

"I would have let her if she wanted to. I talked to her on the way home. Told her everything. That I was sorry, and fuck… do you know what she said?" Shaking his head, he frowns slightly. "She said, I don't need to be sorry, that she understands. Fuck. Cole… she's everything. I told her that I'd do anything to have her back in my life, that she's it for me."

I can see the shock on his face. I'm not normally this open, especially about personal matters.

"She just said, okay." His mouth is fully open now, gaping actually. "I know. I was expecting a fight. I was prepared to beg, grovel, and wait as long as it took. She wants it all as much as I do. No fights, no arguments, just lots and lots of—"

"I don't want to hear whatever was going come out of your mouth. She's like a sister to me."

An hour later, the sun is just starting to set outside. We have a plan, but it's not the best. I've made sure it only involves the guys from Cerberus. I don't want anyone else getting any deeper in this if we can help it.

"We just go in there and see what we can find?" Ethan looks at me and I nod. "Is that the best we can really come up with? It's total shit and we all know it."

"It's the only way we have if we want this to end. If we want Charlie to be safe again," Leon adds.

"Are you all really planning on doing this without me?" Turning around, Charlie is leaning against the wall, watching us. She's not happy.

"That's not what we are doing. You can be involved, but we can't let you get anywhere near there. It's too risky. I wouldn't be able to live with myself if anything else happened to you."

"Right." She's pissed off but calm. I have a feeling it's a lethal combination in Charlie. "So when you said you would be by my side, what you really meant is that I can sit at home and wait for you like a good girlfriend?" *She called herself my girlfriend.* I know that's really not what I should take from what she just said, and I should really hide the smile that's trying to take over my face, but I can't help it.

"Are you fucking smirking at me?"

"I'm not smirking, Angel. It's just you called yourself my girlfriend and you are so much more than that, but I fucking liked it anyway."

When she steps forward, the last thing I was expecting was for her to kiss me. It's brief and leaves me wanting more, but I know what's she silently saying: thank you for being honest with her.

"I will never do as I'm told, nor will I stay at home, or wherever we are, and wait for you to come back to me. It's never going to happen." She's calm and the fire in her eyes right now says she's not backing down. "You have a lot to learn about me, Owen. Now, what I will do, however, is share with you why I was there this morning, and what my plan was, before you lot came in and dragged me away."

Turning around, she sits on my lap, and all eyes now land on my beautiful *girlfriend*. No. that's not going to work, she's so much more. I think only wife will do. Yeah, that's feels fucking right. *Charlie Stone.* Fuck yeah, that sounds good. "Your plan is shit and you know it is. Let me show you what I have."

Over the next thirty minutes, Charlie shows us what she suspects to be the books, the holy grail of information on the comings and goings of the Summers' organisation. Everything we had right under our nose, in almost every image we have of Mr Summers, it's with him, a fucking laptop. An old as fuck laptop, that has no form of Wi-Fi connection. Cole tried and failed to hack it.

"I also have a feeling that if Mr Summers is the accountant. We're missing who's really in charge."

"At this point, we only have one option to find out..." Dom offers

"We need to get that laptop," Charlie says, still sitting in my lap. Fuck, I love that she's here. And not just that she's sat on me, but here with my brothers, as an equal to every single person in this room.

"That's what I was sort of planning to do. In fact, I was planning to use the Wi-Fi device that was in Xander's truck and plant it on the laptop. I could hack it and get what we need."

"You weren't wrong when you said I had a lot to learn about you. Hacking, really?" I ask.

Kissing my cheek, she simply says, "Never underestimate me again, Owen Archie Stone."

"Never again, Angel." I whisper my promise.

Everyone else forgotten, Charlie's lips graze mine. Gripping the back of her neck, I press her lips to mine, taking it deeper, pressing myself into her. My dick strains against my zipper, ready and waiting to make her mine again. Charlie hums into my mouth and I growl in approval, until some rude fucker decides to cough, breaking our moment together.

I pull back, watching as her eyes flutter open. The haze she has right now... I want to keep her just like that: flushed, sexy, and wanting more.

"If you love birds are finished, we'd like to carry on," Cole announces.

Turning slowly to face him, I reply, "One day, this will happen to you. Revenge is sweet."

"Not happening. I'll leave that for you two." He smirks.

"Sorry, carry on." Charlie gestures to Cole and tries to stand up, but I don't let her move.

"If you stand up, everyone will be able to see just what you do to me."

For added effect, I press myself into her, and she laughs the sweetest sound I have ever heard. Wriggling her beautiful ass over my dick to spur me on.

"Is that better for you?"

"Perfect," I add, planting a kiss on her neck just where I know she loves it.

"No fucking way, absolutely not, not happening. I'll fucking lock you away before I let you set foot back in that place, Charlie." I know I'm being a dickhead, an absolute fucking moron, but how can I do this to her?

"I'm not asking you, Owen. I'm telling you, this is the best way."

"No," I yell.

"I need you to listen, and fucking listen carefully. I want to do this... No, I am doing this. Whether you agree or not, I'm going in there and causing the distraction while you guys do your thing and get the laptop.

"Angel, I can't let you do this. It's a death wish." I know I'm choosing all the wrong words.

"You are not letting me do anything, Owen. I'm choosing to do this. They know who I am. I will be able to get them away from the office, or we can go with Ethan and Grey's plan and just blow up a section of the building while we try and get the laptop. Either way, I'm coming with you."

"We warned you about Praise last time you mentioned it. We had no idea at the time you knew more than you were letting on. She knows the risks, Owen." Ethan glares at her like he doesn't want this either, but hell if I know what I can do to stop her. She mouths 'sorry' at him and she gets the chin lift in return.

"Angel, I..." My voice betrays me when I try and say what's on my mind. "I... Don't know how to do this." She comes over to where I've been pacing behind the table.

"Shit, baby, I can't and won't stand by and let you all finish what I started without me. I love you... all too much for that to happen." Charlie admits.

I know I'm going to give in. I can't seem to say no to this woman.

"I know you're trying to protect me, but you need to understand that I don't need your help. I need to trust that you will be there for me. I want... I need you by my side, to stand with me. No matter what."

Fuck my life.

"Okay, Angel, I'm with you, by your side, no matter what."

I've never heard a sound like it. She shrieks. Even with the dread that sits in my chest, it makes me smile that I've made her happy.

"Yes, dream team, baby!" she yells. I just hold her close, not knowing what dangers tomorrow will hold.

Walking into our room, I get undressed and sit on the edge of the bed, in just my boxers, waiting for Charlie. I have a little surprise for her. But I need to get my story out first. It's been on my mind, and I want a clear head going into tomorrow. Giving her this final bit of me, it will help me lay my demons to rest, so I, we, can move forward.

"Now this is a sight I could get used to, you waiting on the bed for me." Closing the door behind her, she comes to straddle my legs. I smile, kissing her softly.

"Angel, I feel like we skipped a whole section on us. Even coming back, we dived right in." I tell her, pulling back slightly to see her beautiful face.

"I feel a 'but' coming on." Tilting her head to the side, her brows pulling together in question.

"There's no but, when it comes to us, I want to tell you about my PTSD." Letting out a breath, as Charlie sinks down next to me, her eyes roaming my face.

"Owen, you don't need to tell me anything if you don't want to." Stroking her knee with the tips of my fingers, I want to comfort her, like she's doing to me right now.

"I want to, Angel." Bringing my hand to her cheek, I place a small kiss on her lips. Taking a steady breath in, I start at the beginning.

"Our last mission in the army went wrong, unbeknown to us, we had a traitor in our team, a man called Eli Mendez." I can still see his face, the regret, fear, and pain in his words, as he told us the truth. "Myself, Leon, Ethan, and Cole were the only ones out of our unit to come out alive. There were ten of us that went in that day. Four days later, only the four of us came out." I remember them all. My face falls at the memory. "We'd been assigned to actively take out some nasty fuckers, who had taken a village in the north of the country." Sensing the shake in my voice, she places her soft warm hands in mine, knowing it's going to be hard for me to do this.

"I'm here." She reassures me, grounding me and urging me to carry on.

"When we arrived, we were ambushed, sitting ducks, and on our own. We lost two men that first day, horrifically in a shootout, followed by four the next. We tried our best to save them. Eli was shot on the first day. He admitted everything." His betrayal cut deep. We all felt it. Four days of hell, no sleep, no rest, constantly under fire and being torched out of your hiding place. On the last day, it all went quiet. We managed to escape during the night, but we had to leave them behind.

"I felt like I had let everyone down. As their CO, they were mine to look out for, mine to keep safe, and mine to ensure they made it home to the people they loved. I failed at it all."

Charlie sighs. I watch as her mouth opens, ready to say something. I jump in before she can. "I still feel the weight of what happened, but I understand now, there was nothing I could have done to prevent it." talking helps.

"Shit, Owen, I can't tell you how much I appreciate you telling me this, opening up to me." My gaze has been on our joined hands. A teardrop lands on my knuckles, my eyes shooting to hers, where I see her cheeks coated with tears.

"Don't cry, Angel, I can't stand it," I say, kissing away the tears.

"I'm sorry, I just... that must have been so hard for you."

"Not as hard as it used to be. I'm good now. I can see things a lot clearer than I used to. As much as it killed me to be away from you and the guys, I needed it. I regret how I did it, but I know I needed to do it." Kissing her again. She holds my hand tight.

Grabbing the box I left beside me, I place it in her hands. Looking up, she looks right at me, her eyes filled with tears.

"This is for you, Angel."

"What is it?" Her voice trembles as she runs her fingers over the blue velvet box.

"Open it and find out." Hesitating for a moment, she spins the box in her hand. "Open the box, Angel."

Biting her lip she flips the lid on the box. I watch as her eyes fill with tears, then shoot to meet mine when she realises what it is, her chest heaving as she gulps down a breath.

"My necklace." tears slip down her cheeks again, only this time I let them fall, this look on her face right now. I know it's a happy one.

"I thought I'd lost it, I thought it was gone forever, I never took it off once, I kept my promise to you." Kissing her, she fumbles to get the necklace out of the box. Moving my hands, I place it around her neck, fastening it into place with ease.

"I know you did, Angel."

"This is new..." she adds, admiring the back of the necklace. Her eyes light up seeing the new inscription.

No Matter What.

"Owen Archie Stone," she stutters. "I tried my hardest not to love you, but you... you made it impossible." This is everything I ever wanted, Charlie in my arms. Everything out in the open.

Holding the necklace in her hand, she pulls me towards her, taking my mouth with hers. I pull away, my breath on her lips. "Are you saying you love me, Charlie Hudson?"

"Yes, Owen, I'm saying, I have always been and I will always be yours, mind, body and soul."

"Fuck, I love you with everything I have, Angel. I'm fucking yours for as long as you will have me." Clutching her closer, breathing in everything that she is, taking her mouth with mine, swallowing the beautiful noise she's making, I kissing her with everything I have.

Never in my life will I get enough of the woman, "Owen, fuck me, then make love to me and never stop."

I don't, and never will.

Chapter Forty-One
Don't Make a Sound

Charlie

I still can't believe I'm sitting in the back of the van, Owen by my side, waiting to head into Praise on a covert mission. I know it's not the right time to be excited, but I am. I honestly thought I would have woken up in handcuffs this morning, attached to the bed, with Owen apologising for doing it and saying that it was for my own good. I guess he's starting to understand me; that I want to do everything I can, and I want him by my side while doing it.

I woke with Owen between my legs this morning. Best wake up call I've had in a long time. After which, he set about strapping a vest to me. It's so thin, but it's going to stop any bullets that come my way. I had to take a few deep breaths when he said that to me. I know what I'm getting myself into here, but hearing those words felt like an added layer of fear.

On the other hand, I've never been more turned on when he fastened the vest around me or when he drew his fingers up my thighs, when he attached the holster to the inside of my leg. I have no doubt that if we had been alone in that room, he would have fucked me right there and then. That man's addictive, magic fingers, magic tongue, and fuck did he use them all last night. I'm not sure how much rest we actually got, but shit, it was worth every second.

Owen nuzzles into my neck, and whispers, "If you don't stop whatever dirty thoughts are running through your mind right now, I'll have to take you right here." That makes me wriggle a little more in my seat, and I can feel his smile on my neck as he places a kiss against my pulse.

"The way I feel right now, Owen, I'd let you." A growl comes from his lips followed by an almost inaudible, "Fuck."

"My thoughts exactly." I smirk as his eyes meet mine. I love that fire when he looks at me. Shit, I want to jump him and ride him like there is no tomorrow.

"ETA, two minutes," comes over the earpiece we all have.

When we arrive, I step out the back of the van. Myself and Owen are being dropped off a short distance from the entry point.

Zan and Ethan head round the back of the club, aiming to gain entrance to the second floor there. Dom and Harley head up to the rooftop, while Cole's in our ear repeating the details of where everyone is, and Millie, Jack, and Grey stayed at the lodge.

The loading bay seems to be deserted. Cole tells us it's not. I guess we just can't see them. As we make our way silently into the offices, I have Owen's hand on me at all times. It's reassuring, but I know it won't be there long. We all have a job to do. Me included. Cole confirms there are apparently three people in the small office to our left.

I'm the distraction. I've got to look like I'm by myself if I'm found. I hope to fuck I'm not. My heart's going crazy. I'm taking as many deep breaths as I can to try and calm myself down.

I'm to set a small fire in one of the rooms upstairs and get out. I can't be looking around the room looking for them It will give them away, and I can't do that. They need to get the device on the laptop. That's Dom and Harley's job. Owen has the hand-held device to start the download, while Cole does the backup from his computer. I know I won't be alone, but I hate the thought of being separated from Owen. I know he hates it too. We have decided to stay silent over the comms, just in case anyone hears us. It's only for backup if things go wrong.

"Go," Owen whispers. "I won't be far behind you. You won't see me. I'll never let you out of my sights, okay?" Taking my face in his hands, he places a quick but loving kiss on my lips. The tremble in his voice, and the sadness in his eyes, it kills me. "I love you," he says, then he's gone before I can say it back. I'm on my own. I can feel eyes on me. I know they are the ones looking out for me. I guess that's something, right?

Moving forward in a crouch position, keeping my head low, I just keep going. I'm hoping this can be a quick in and out. There's background noise from the club. I can hear people milling around upstairs.

Peeking through the windows of the small office, I can see it's empty. Spotting the stairs to the right, I open the door. My heart pounding, as it squeaks in protest at the movement. I slip in and race to the other side, squatting at the bottom of the stairs.

"There are two men in the room above you, Charlie. You can slip past them. Don't make a sound," Cole's voice fills my head. I don't respond. There's no need. I just tap my ear. This will let him know I heard him loud and clear.

I peer up the steps and I can't see anyone, so I run for it. Out of the corner of my eye I see the two guys in the hall. Turning left, I head for the room where I plan to make the distraction.

Before I step inside, I hear noise coming from downstairs that sounds like a fight. I need to be quick. There are only two exits on this floor. Owen made me memorise them.

I have a good idea what the others should be doing right now. The office with the laptop in is on the other side of this huge building. From the data we pulled and images we've found deeply buried on the internet, it seems like Mr Summers has his office on that side of the building.

I think I'm running on adrenaline right now; my heart feels like it's going to burst out of my chest.

Entering the room, it looks like it's used for storage more than anything else.

I don't feel safe. I can't feel Owen's eyes on me anymore. Looking behind me, I can't see anything, but he said I wouldn't see him. I need to trust him. *I do trust him.*

Taking the backpack from my back that Owen and Grey packed for me this morning, I pull out what I need to get this done—a small electrical device Ethan and Grey made. Lifting a large box filled with papers from the floor, I place the device inside. Grey and Ethan said it would only be a small explosion, enough to get them running in this direction and away from Dom and Harley, but I should be out the building well before that takes place. I need to trigger it when I leave the room. It will give me two minutes before it goes off.

Placing the box on the shelf, I nestle it next to other boxes filled with papers, congratulating myself on a job almost done. I pick up my bag and swing it on my back, scanning the hall before I exit the room. I head down the stairs, pressing the button to start the distraction, and setting the countdown on my smartwatch.

When my foot hits the second step down, I hear voices coming my way and my stomach sinks.

I can't go back but I also can't go down. I'll walk straight into them.

Where's Owen?

Spinning round, I head back up, running the length of the corridor, looking over my shoulder every few seconds to make sure I can't see anyone and that no one spots me.

Twenty-eight seconds left.

The voices are almost at the top of the stairs. Quickly looking around, I open the door to another room, checking to see if anyone is in there before I walk in.

Boom. The noise from the explosion almost deafens me. *Small, my arse. I'm going to kill fucking Grey.* The whole floor shakes.

I dive to the floor, scrambling to hide under a desk for cover. The hall I was in thirty seconds ago is now full of smoke.

If they had no idea we were here, they do now.

"Planted." Cole's voice pops up, making me jump. I can't talk. The people running past will hear me. That means Dom and Harley got it in. Owen should be close to them now.

"Fuck... it's not working." Owen's voice comes over the comms.

My back is flattened to the side of the desk, just listening to them rant while I stay silent. Dom and Harley apparently had to leave. He was hurt in a fight. Zan and Ethan are on the opposite side of the building, planting the last of the listening devices and cameras. Owen can't get close to me... he needs the distance to download the information safely—they can't be in the same room.

Owen's desperately asking for my location. He sounds frantic. I can't talk. There are at least five men out the front of the office I'm in, with the doors wide open. I tap my earpiece, but there's too much noise for them to hear it.

I can get the device to work... I can do it.

The people outside the room all seem to fall away, and the corridor goes silent. Crawling on my hands and knees to the door, I stand and see that they're all too distracted by the fire to take any notice of me. I make my way out, running in the direction of the main office. There's another exit there, so I can sort the device and then leave.

Pressing my earpiece, I whisper, "I'm still inside. I'll do it." Checking behind me, I press myself to the wall. The comms are silent. I was expecting an argument, or at least some very choice words from Owen. If I'm the only one close enough to do this, then I'm going to do it.

It's too quiet. Touching my earpiece, I get nothing. It's not working. A bubble of panic starts to rise. Swallowing it down, I move forward. Pressing down on the handle of the door I need to get through, the latch clicks. Dipping my head to look round, I can see the laptop. There's shit everywhere: broken chairs, glass even the desk has been trashed.

The laptop's sitting open on the large, dark wooden desk in the centre of the room. Reaching for it, I freeze when I see what's on the screen. Surveillance footage showing Owen as Cole runs over. It looks like he's shouting, but there's no sound, so I have no idea what's been said. But I can guess. *They have eyes on us, just like we do them.*

I find the device. It's tiny, and the connection has come loose. Pressing it in firmly with my thumb, I hear the program start.

Turning my attention to the footage on the screen, I watch as Owen tries to run into the building, but the guys hold him back.

"Don't you fucking dare come in after me, Owen," I whisper. Owen appears to get the notification that it's started to work. He points and mouths something at Cole, who runs in the direction of the van.

You can see the questions on his face when the others turn up and I'm not with them. I guess they never got my last message.

I can see the progress bar on the device. It's going to take at least a few minutes to get this uploaded. Harley said they would wait for it to be done to ensure it was successful. Should I do the same?

I decide to wait, even if it's just for thirty more seconds, to make sure we get something. I feel so vulnerable right now. I need to remember where I can go to escape.

A sense of dread creeps in when I realise I can't remember another way out. I'll have to go up to the roof, which is how Dom and Harley got in here. It's written in the rules of every scary movie. Don't go up the stairs, but what else can I do?

"Charlie?"

I turn and find a familiar face staring back at me.

"Annie?"

She looks taken aback for a split second before taking her phone from her pristine black suit trousers. I don't understand... she looks like she does or did every day at the office. Well dressed, hair in a bun, heels as high as she can buy them.

Lifting the phone to her ear, she says, "Honey, we have a special delivery in the office. It seems they left us a parting gift." Looking at me with a forced, mocking grin, her words are cold.

"What? Why are you here?" I can't process seeing her *here*. "Have you been taken? What's going on? Are you..." My thoughts don't match what I'm seeing. It doesn't make sense. She's shaking her head, disdain written all over her face.

"So fucking naïve sometimes, Charlie," she sneers and the disgust on her face pales me. I don't want it to be true. It can't be.

"You?" I choke out. Fear, dread, and shock lace through every morsel of my being. I can't move. I can't... I don't understand.

"Well done. Quick at putting the pieces together, aren't you? Although you were slow with this one." Annie comes to stand in front of me, arms crossed over her chest. This isn't the Annie I know.

"You're the one who was leaking the information to Summers?" She laughs, actually laughs.

"You still don't get it, do you? I guess there's no harm in telling you. You won't make it out alive." I stumble back at the ferocity of her words. "I am Mr Summers." She shrugs like this information is nothing. "Technically, he was my dad. I guess you could say I took over the family business when he met an unfortunate end."

Annie takes off her jacket, laying it on the desk beside me. I see it, something I have seen so many times before, the delicate flower tattoo on the inside of her wrist, the exact flower that matches the metal ones left facing the sky, left in the wake of ashes for each and every person she no longer needed. Catching me looking, she smirks, knowing I have it all figured out.

I have no idea who this woman is. I feel sick.

Our eyes meet and she only looks away when a group of men step into the room. "Honey," she says, not even glancing at them. "I believe you've already met my boyfriend"

My gaze lands on the man who makes himself known, a man who looks so different in a suit. He rests his hand on the small of her back. *Ezera Ferris.*

"You... he's..." The man she's told me so many things about is the man who wanted to kill me in the hotel.

Nothing can prepare you for the reality of a betrayal like this.

When the first blow hits my stomach, she doesn't even flinch. In fact, she turns away in her expensive shoes and walks out the door, leaving me in the hands of her men.

Chapter Forty-Two
With Me

Owen

I've lost her. I don't know where the fuck she is, other than she's still in that building somewhere. By her fucking self, when I promised I could have eyes on her all the time. I knew I couldn't be next to her, but I could keep watch while she did what we planned.

How could I do this to her?

"Cole, where the *fuck* is she?" I bellow from the side of the road, which is supposed to be our meeting point.

Looking back at the building, running my hands through my hair, I know I need to find her. I thought I felt fear when she was missing before, but this, knowing she's so close and I can't locate her, this is fear. My whole body feels it, ice-cold shards piercing my soul.

I watched her go up the stairs. I was right behind her, watching through the window. Those bastards tried to get up after her, but I took them down and tied them up. I was about to follow Charlie up when I heard more voices coming my way, so I had to head in the opposite direction. I couldn't risk them seeing me. Then all hell broke loose.

The explosion went off and people ran in all directions. I slipped out in the chaos and assumed she went out the exit on the other side.

But she's not here...

"I can't track her." Cole sounds panicked. "They must be using a jammer. I can't see shit right now." I've got Charlie's necklace tracker on my phone, but right now it's fucking useless with a jammer in place. There's smoke billowing out the windows from the explosion. It looks like the fire's spreading quicker than we imagined.

Fuck, I should have handcuffed her to the bed and done this without her. Yes, she would've killed me when I got back, maybe not have even spoken to me for a few days, that I can live with; this I can't. I'm fucking losing it. My heart and head are both screaming the same thing:

Run, get her.

Now.

I spot two people staggering towards us. *Only two*, my hope on Charlie being with them crushed. Dom's being carried by Harley. Leon runs over and grabs him, sitting him in the back of the truck. His face is beat up and his leg is badly broken from the angle it seems to be facing.

"We got the device in, but we were disturbed before we could get it running," Harley pants. I know this, I didn't realise how bad they had it. Harley looks around. You can see she's mentally checking we are all here, stopping when she sees we are missing one vital member of our team.

"Where is she, O?" There is a flash of fear in her eyes as she says, "Please don't tell me she's still in there." She turns to face the club. My determination rises. I'm not leaving her, not like this. I'm not waiting.

"Not for much longer," I promise Harley before I turn to run, but hands grab me. Leon, Cole, and Zan all hold me back.

"Get the fuck off me. I need to get to her, Charlie," I scream, fighting to get out of their grip. I don't care who hears me. I need to be with her.

Watching as the fire seems to spread throughout the first floor, this is agony. I'd do anything to switch places with her.

"Wait, look at your phone. She's done it, Charlies done it." Cole says, grabbing my arm, I take out my phone and watch as the files start to upload. Cole leaps in the back of the van to make sure it's all backing up, ready to send on.

"If that's getting through, should be able to locate her," Cole says, while Leon shouts at me to "Wait."

Glass shatters from a window on the first floor, as flames burst through, smoke billowing into the sky. People rush outside, fleeing the club, as others step out from the surrounding buildings to watch what's happening.

"Last location was the northwest corner of the building, first floor," Cole shouts, while I'm running towards the burning building. Hearing the crackle of the comms coming back online.

"O, she's still there. It's his office. I'll keep you updated." He knows there's no stopping me. I'd never forgive him if he did.

I leap at the fire escape stairs that lead to the roof. Drawing my gun, I'm prepared to do anything to get my angel out safely. Her words play on repeat as I climb through the hatch on the roof, landing in a small utility cupboard on the top floor.

"I need you by my side, to stand with me. No matter what."

Chapter Forty-Three

Embers

Charlie

Would this have been any better if they had knocked me out? Maybe? At least that way I would not have seen what was coming.

My end.

I'm refusing to cry, but I can't stop my mind from reeling. This can't be real. She is...*was* one of my closest friends. She was at my fucking wedding, *one of my shitting bridesmaids*, but...she, all along, she was the man, the person, the woman we've been looking for. How is that possible? And who the fuck is the man in all the photos we have?

It's so fucked up!

Gulping in air, I'm finding it almost impossible to breathe.

That's the least of my worries right now. Even in my current position, lying on the cold concrete floor. I can't help but think of all the ways she betrayed me. I don't know what hurts most, the aches in my body, where Annie's men threw me around, and left me bruised, the harsh metal of the chains on my wrists, or the lying or the fact that she could do this to me.

All those years, I'm questioning everything we ever did together. Was any of it real?

The way she ushered her men in, her cold, impassive expression as she ordered them, by any means necessary, to get me here to this dark and unforgiving lower part building.

And they did. I was too stunned to fight back like I should have, too shocked at what was happening. Then there were too many of them. Surrounded. I had no choice as they forced me back, dragging me away. Betrayed again. How stupid can one person get, my sham of a marriage, then my work bestie?

The deep loss of friendship sinks in, crippling me. I'm so fucking stupid. Wincing with every twist and turn, I try to free myself. The invading pains in my stomach and chest, a reminder of what they did to me. The burning of my skin as they gripped my hair and held me down. All so they could get me down here, throwing me down a hatch in the ground. It took my breath away. Now it hurts to breathe. I'll have a boot print, on my chest for sure if I can get out of this.

I can't see a way out of this.

The chains are solid, the weight of them as heavy as my heart right now. There are no flames down here, not yet, anyway. Just the drifts of smoke starting to creep in. I can feel the intense heat from the fire that's raging above my head on the ground floor. My skin's pricking from its intensity, sweat soaking my clothes the longer I'm down here.

I've tried to move, but I can't. Bound in chains and attached to rings bolted to the floor.

My wrists and ankles are raw from the force I've been putting into escaping. Crying and screaming out, I did that too. Didn't work either.

The cool of the floor below me is soothing. My tears fall, but they're drying a little quicker the hotter it gets.

This is where they left me, alone. No escape. I can only move my feet and wrists just a little. It hurts so much.

Blinking as the ash starts to fall around my face, lying on the cool concrete, facing the ceiling that's slowly burning above me. Watching the embers dance and turn to ash around me, I notice how heavy my eyes feel and wonder how easily I could fall asleep. The chains don't want to let me go that far. If the ceiling falls in, it's coming down on me.

I want to get out.

The weight I feel in my chest begs to be let free. I just can't see a way. It's crushing me. Whimpering to myself, pulling on the chains even though it hurts like hell, I can't help but feel panicked, along with a strange sense of calm. My mind wants to fight with everything I have, but my heart knows…it knows there's not much I can do right now.

Conflicted.

I've never wanted to be rescued. I trained so hard to make sure I never needed to have a white knight swoop in and rescue me. I guess I was wrong.

The only knight I can see in my mind wears black and prefers trucks to horses.

I love him so much.

I don't want to die, not like this.

When you think about what your last moments might look like, I never pictured *this*. I don't know what I actually pictured, but it was definitely not watching a building burn around me while I'm stuck in a basement. A basement that was not on the plans when we all huddled around the table and planned this together.

Taking in a deep breath, I need to think, but all I do is cough, the air thick with smoke.

Turning my head to the side to avoid the larger embers that have started to fall, my eyes land on the flames that are sneaking in through the hatch at the top of the stairs, the ones they pushed me down.

Fuck, Owen, I'm so sorry.

I don't know where he is. I don't know where he went. I just want to know he's safe and far away from here. I know he wouldn't leave me if he didn't have to. Something must have happened.

Closing my eyes, I just listen to the sounds around me, unable to move. It's eerie, silent, and deafening all at once.

There's a crackle on the comms still in my ear. I'd forgotten all about it. Should I say something? I need to say something now, just in case they can hear me. Even if I don't get to see them again.

"There's so much smoke…" My words come out rough and throaty. "I'm sorry, I'm so sorry." I sob to myself, the crackle getting louder.

"I'm in the basement if you can hear me. I'm in the basement." They come out as muffled words, cries of desperation. "I can't move. I'm chained to the floor." Another crackle. This time it sounds like *fuck*.

"I'm so sorry, Owen." My voice breaks. "Owen?" Nothing. No crackle, no noise at all. The floor's getting warmer beneath my skin. "I don't think I'm going to make it out."

"Char—" Squeezing my eyes shut, I concentrate on the voice I desperately want to hear.

My words are a whisper, but I need to say them. "I can't see a way out, Owen. I'm… I'm scared. I don't know what to do. I can't move… I'm… Shit." More tears as my voice breaks. I can't help the desperate sadness overtaking me. I need him and he's not here. Goddamn I want him here, but I know if he comes, I'll be pissed off, putting himself in danger for me. I don't want him here. As much as it pains me, I want him away from this.

"Angel, I'm coming for you, just—" The line breaks up, but it's soothing just to hear him.

"Owen, No!…I think this is…I want you to know…" I'm giving up, it's so hot in here, I can hardly breathe, the flames at the door are getting bigger every time I dare to open my eyes.

"Don't you *fucking* dare give up on me, Angel!" He's breathing hard, like he's running. My skin is starting to burn from the heat of the flames above me. "I'm so close. Don't you dare fucking give up on me." Owen's voice is crystal clear this time. I'm trying not to but... I think I need to accept what's happening.

"It's too dangerous, Owen, don't..." Breathing hurts now as thick smoke fills my lungs.

"Angel, please..." The desperation in his voice is palpable. I'm causing it, me being here, on the edge of... something, saying the word is on the tip of my tongue, even in my head is hard, it's too final.

"Owen, I can't see. I can't open my eyes, it hurts, it's so hot..." say it, just get the words out, get him to understand "... I never stopped loving you, I want you to know that." There's a growl and then so much noise coming over the comms, I can't decipher it until his voice comes again.

"Angel, listen to me... I am not letting you have the last say today... you can argue with me about it tomorrow..." Tomorrow. I wonder what that would have looked like... wrapped in his arms, safe and loved. Something settles over me. I relax, tiredness washing over me. My hands fall to my sides, hitting the warming concrete floor with a soft thud of the chains that bind me to this place. Whispering, I add, "I'm sorry, Owen. I'm so fucking sorry." Closing my eyes, I've got nothing left.

In the darkness I hear noise around me, loud, unforgiving, urgent, crashes, footsteps, boots running in my direction. Getting louder.

"Angel! Please, fuck." My eyes flutter open and all I see is him. I feel him over me, his arm wrapping underneath me, his smoke-smudged face, his piercing green eyes search mine.

"Freaking hero complex," I mumble, more to myself than for him, but I watch as a flicker of a smile crosses his beautiful face before he huffs out a laugh.

"I've got you, Angel." *Safe.*

I drift, my eyes flutter closed.

<h1 style="text-align:center">Chapter Forty-Four</h1>

<h2 style="text-align:center">Boom</h2>

Owen

My heart's racing so fast, I feel like it's going to beat out of my chest. I knew where she was before I heard her over the comms.

I made Leon lead me through the fire-lit mess to find her using her necklace, the only beacon of hope I had. My clothes are singed, so are my fingers; my eyes stinging from the smoke.

Fuck, when she started telling me not to come, that it was too dangerous, I ran fucking faster. My heart in my throat, smoke and my constricting fear making it hard to breathe.

I move the table over us, to shield us from what's about to blow through the fucking wall.

Goddamn it, Angel. It kills me, seeing her like this, my strong, feisty woman. On the floor. Trying to give me her last words.

Never again, never-a-fucking-gain.

If those bastards aren't dead already, they will be soon. No one does this to the woman I love, the woman I will spend the rest of my life with. Even if she did just out me for having a hero complex. Fuck, this woman, she has me. Heart and fucking soul, until the end of time. And even then, I'll never let her go. Not again. Sliding the table against the wall, I barricade us in, to protect us as much as possible.

"I've got her," I shout into the comms.

"Roger that, O," a vaguely familiar voice confirms. I can already guess who that is. One of two people I know were on their way.

"We'll need heavy duty cutters. These chains are solid."

"Roger that. Five, count down."

Kneeling next to her, the room filled with heavy smoke, choking back a cough, I hold her, eyes streaming as I try to see her in the darkness surrounding us, resting her head against my chest, wrapping my body around hers. And wait.

"Four…"

Clutching her harder, my fingers sinking into her hair, the flames licking and tormenting us in their intense heat.

"Three…Two…" I place a kiss on the top of her head.

"One."

I close my eyes and brace my body, protecting my angel.

The deafening boom takes over the space, vibrating off the walls as the ground beneath us shakes, the table protecting us from the falling debris. Dust mingles with smoke and flames, surrounding us in a deadly haze. The wall to our left falls, creating a hole, and clean air rushes in from the outside. Looking down, she's unconscious, but safe in my arms.

Her beautiful white blonde hair is covered in ash, just like the rest of her. She looks okay, but I'll know more when I get her to Ethan. He's waiting for us along with is everyone else.

She'll be okay. She has no other option but to be okay.

Two men approach in full tactical gear, followed by Leon. I can't see his face in the mask he's wearing, but I'd know his bulk anywhere. Stepping forward, he kneels, using the cutters to set Charlie free from her restraints. Squeezing her hand, he helps me free her. The other two men rush towards us. I know who they are, even if I've never seen them before in my life.

"Owen, we need to move out. It's going to collapse any minute now," one of them says, sweeping a hand over Charlie's hair. "Boo, you have a lot of explaining to do when you wake up," he adds. Standing beside me, both of them give a worried grin at their sister lying in my arms.

Agreeing with a single nod, I stand, lifting Charlie with me. Rushing through the hole they blew in the wall to get us out, we race to the waiting vehicles, Leon close on my heels. Her brothers check her from the sides.

Climbing in the back of the van, I lie Charlie on the floor, her head in my lap, leaving room for Ethan to do what he does best—making her better. Her brothers settle in the front, starting the engine and tearing away from what was Praise.

Ethan's done his thing. She's going to be okay. Growing bruises all over her stomach and chest, and smoke inhalation. Ethan's given her oxygen and she breathing easier now.

"I want a second honeymoon." Looking down I had no idea she was awake. There's a whisper in her raspy voice.

"A second honeymoon, huh?" She opens her eyes, meeting my gaze with sore, red, but still breathtaking, beautiful eyes. She winces slightly, trying to move.

"Yep." How does she do this to me? Makes me smile in one of the worst situations I have ever been in.

"We kind of have to have a first one to be to be able to get a second one, Angel." I'm teasing. And it feels great.

"You're forgetting the whole marrying me part." My fingers brush over her lips.

"Was that a proposal, Angel?"

"Yeah, I think it might just have been."

Moving down so I'm lying next to her, wrapping her in my arms, I bring my lips to meet her, whispering so only she can hear me. "Yeah, I'll marry you, Angel. I'm yours no matter what."

Chapter Forty-Five
Messages

Charlie

Switching my phone back on for the first times since we got back, after the fire,
I'm bombarded with messages from everyone, most of all Owen. Every message
is from when I was missing.

> **The OG:** I will find you, Charlie. I will make sure you're safe.

> **The OG:** The guy on the beach, I'll find him, I'll make him pay for what he's done to you.

> **The OG:** I will find you, I will make you mine, and you will never fear anything again. Because I'll be by your side. Protecting you from anything that comes our way.

The OG: I'm trying my damnedest to keep my head on straight, but it's so hard when I know you're out there, I coming for you, Angel.

The OG: I will reign down all hell-fire, to whoever has laid a finger on what's mine, they will pay for this Angel.

The OG: I'm getting you back, Angel, and I'm never letting you fucking out of my sight again.

The OG: Fucking hell, Charlie. I'm begging you. Come to me. Please.

The OG: You're hurt, fuck it hurts my chest to know that, Charlie. I hate that you're alone in this. Do you even know we're trying to find you? That I won't stop until you're next to me again. Safe. I won't rest, I won't sleep, it's impossible. I can't even sit down, knowing you're out there somewhere, alone, injured, and quite possibly in pain.

The OG: Umm…you sparing with the boys, I don't like it. You won't be doing that again unless I'm with you.

The OG: I'm in the room you booked. I hate that this is happening to you. You're hurt.

The OG: It's killing me, Angel, I need you by my side.

The OG: When I find you, and it will be soon. I'll get down on my knees and beg for your forgiveness, Angel.

The OG: I'm so sorry Angel.

The OG: I'm coming to find you, and I'll never let you go again.

The OG: You could hate me for the rest of eternity, but I will forever be there for you. I will be by your side. I'll take anything you are willing to give me.

The OG: I'm going to need to know the story behind Boo.

The OG: Who the fuck is Xander and what is he to you?

The OG: You ran to someone else, Angel. You will never know how much that guts me. Did you think I wouldn't help? Or find you? You're all I think about.

The OG: I've found you, Angel. I'm never going to let you go again.

Me: Seriously?

Me: Just messing with you, you know I'm yours, no matter what.

Chapter Forty-Six

Epilogue

Charlie

There's nothing better than sleeping with the man I love every night, and waking up to him between my legs every chance he gets. The man can't seem to get enough, and neither can I. That man does wonderful things to my body.

Ever since that day, Owen's been true to his word. He's open with me, sometimes too much.

We tried to take it slow, but we couldn't do it, not when I proposed in the back of the van. We go on dates, we just live together and sleep with each other every night, day and any chance we get in between.

Xander came out on top that day, used all his connections, pulled a lot of strings. He supplied the police with everything they needed to arrest them all, including information on Annie. I have no idea how he got that, but he did. And I'm grateful it was done before we even made it out to the van. Xander and my brothers caught Annie and the others coming from the building. She went a little nuts, shouting shit about how I'd never make it out alive. That they'd have to watch as I burned along with the building.

I'm not going to lie, it still hurts.

My brothers and Xander didn't take that too well and added a couple of extra charges to the long list she will be convicted of. It's still hard to believe she was such a good friend. I've not seen or spoken to her since, and I think it's for the best.

Turns out she was left in charge when her father was murdered, something she was responsible for, and the organisation was passed down to her. Mr Summers was, in fact, the accountant and front man. A high-ranking officer for her who did her dirty work like the others, but was a little more discreet about how he did things. Until I found that video. And messed up their plans. It's fucked up.

My brothers arrived just after Owen ran into the burning building to get me. They, along with Leon and Ethan, took great pleasure in blowing a hole in the side of Praise to get us out. I think they have since formed a solid bromance.

A few days after we got back, Owen filled me in on what happened to Simon. Luckily, he's going to be okay.

Our Friday nights at Millie and Jack's house have become the bit of normal I needed after all that. I love having everyone together. And so does Millie, with her growing baby bump.

"Why won't you set a date for the wedding?" Owen's pinned me to the sofa to ask again why we haven't set a date. He's been annoyed beyond belief about it for the last few days.

When I asked him to marry me three months ago, I would have married him there and then. Broken rib, cuts and bruises and all, in the back of that van. I don't want fancy, I did that before, and look how well that turned out.

Owen already admitted that he would never, in a million years, get on the mat with me for a sparring session. Of course, I took offence that he was trying to go all hero on me again. The guys laughed and said he was too scared to even step foot on the mat, that he was worried he would lose. We all joked about it, but I want him to be able to train with me, and he keeps refusing.

I've asked him constantly if he would come to class with me when one of the others was unable to make it. I'd love him to step in and train with me.

"You know why I'm not going to set a date yet, baby." And he does. When I asked him a few days ago, I offered him a deal: we'll set a date when he trains with me.

He hated it, told me so, and sulked like a teenager for three days. Today he's asked me the same question three times, and he already knows the answer.

He's got to get over those feelings at some point. Right? He knows I'm good. He's seen me fight with some of the guys. Although the last time he came to watch, he did rush the mat when Ethan and I were into it. He tore me off Ethan, picked me up, and took me to the office, where he showed me just how much he loved what I could do, but also how much I was his and hated anyone else touching me. Fuck, it was hot, so fucking hot the way he made me his against the wall of the office, all sweaty and needy. I loved it so freaking much. My thighs clench at the memory of his hands on me.

"You thinking dirty thoughts, Angel?"

"Yep, want me to tell you?" He's pinned my hands above my head, bringing his mouth down to my neck, his lips kissing the sweet spot there. "The way you fucked me in your office." I'm needy already, lifting my hips to meet his. He grinds into me.

"A date for the wedding, Angel."

"Train with me first."

"Angel." His deep tone makes me shiver. I think Alpha Owen is my favourite.

"Don't Angel me, Owen Archie Stone," I say, placing a kiss on his cheek.

"Fuck, okay."

Oh, my life.

"Okay?" Opening my eyes, I'm met with his annoyed dark green ones.

"*Yes,* Charlotte Hudson, I will join you on the mat tomorrow morning."

"Yes!" I think I squeal at him. I'm so excited. I want to grab my phone and tell everyone.

"Just us, no one else." I'm a little disappointed, but yes, finally I get to train with my man.

I still told everyone. Although Owen banned everyone from coming, I wanted to do this at the gym, with all his friends there for support. Instead, Owen drove us to the lodge, where the gym was set up ready for us.

I don't know what to expect from this. There is so much tension between us, a mixture of nerves and unease.

Facing each other in opposite corners of the mat, we stare for what feels like the longest time. God, he looks good in gym shorts, his flame tattoos on full display for me to devour.

"Ready when you are, Angel."

"Oh, I'm ready Owen Archie Stone."

"You may need to stop looking at me like you want to fuck me if you want to fight."

"Or we could move straight to the good fucking part and I'll take you on this mat just how you like it?"

He knows I like him in control. I also love to give as good as I get. But when his eyes rest on my throat, I imagine how his fingers feel when they slide against my pulse and he knows he has me.

"I want to do both, kick your ass, then you can take me on this mat and do whatever you want to me." I smirk. He lets out a low grumble. It's tormenting him to hold back. I'm not sure doing this alone was a good idea, but I'm glad we are, in a way. I have a strong feeling we won't get much training done. And I'm all for it.

"You look a little flushed. You okay over there?" He asks, licking his lips, a wild grin on his wicked face.

"Hmm, just remembering what your hands feel like on my neck" His eyes darken, and he steps forward. I smirk right back at him.

My heart's beating so fiercely, nerves, desire, and love for this man run so deep inside me. I didn't think we would get here. There was a time I didn't think I would see him again. Not after the fire.

I know I laid down this challenge, and this is my own doing, but I never thought he would be here with me on this mat. I would have given in and married him tomorrow. I just liked to see the conflict on his face. I know he likes it when I fight; I know it turns him on, and I know he hates it at the same time. Other people's hands on me. That's when Alpha Owen comes out to play. But being in this moment has all of my senses on high alert, sparks coming to life, ready to blaze and burn anything in their path. I can feel the tension, his eyes sweeping over me in anticipation for what my first move might be. I can hear the blood racing through my system, I'm ready to take on whatever he is willing to give.

I'll take it all, willingly.

I'm poised and ready. "Game on." He moves towards me. I dodge, sweeping my leg low, catching him off guard. He falls with a low laugh but turns around, taking me with him. We land with a thud, me on top of him. Before he can move, I'm straddling him, my arse on his chest. Grabbing my hips, he pulls me backwards. A sharp sting radiates from my backside.

"Ow, did you just bite me?" Spinning my head round to face him, the smile that spread across his face says it all.

"You put your arse in my face, Angel. Of course I'm going to take a bite." He chuckles. "I think I'm going to like training with you a lot more than I thought I would." He grins, nipping it again as I pin him down with my hands and legs. "I've got a pretty good view too."

Not what I was aiming for with this training, but still a wicked outcome, if you ask me. Is this our new foreplay? I'm game if he is.

"If that's how you want to play it, then game on, Owen Archie Stone." I pin him with my legs, hooking his arms so he can't move. Leaning forward, I brush my hands up his thighs. I know he could overpower me, but we decided it was skill, not force at play today.

I trail my mouth down his abs, holding his legs firmly down with my hands. I can see the outline of his already hard dick through his shorts, so I trail my mouth over the bulge.

"Oh, fuck, Angel." His hands try to move and grab me, but before he can do anything more, I'm up and off him.

"Teasing me? Just remember you started this." Owen stands, his eyes locked on mine.

"Oh, I'm ready" I step forward only slightly when he pounces. Stepping to the side, I duck and move behind him, cupping his dick, before jumping on his back, my arms hooking around his neck. I place a quick kiss and a tiny bite on his ear,

"How about next June?" I ask, just before he reaches over his head, grabbing my arms, and pulling me in one strong and easy move. He slams me down on the mat, coming down with me, pinning my arms to the mat with his legs, just like I did to him. I can't move, just wiggle.

Fuck, this is hot.

"Too far away. Try again." I feel his hot mouth through my tight shorts before he presses his face between my needy legs and nips at my aching lady parts.

My back arches, needing more. "Owen," I whimper.

He lets go. We roll around with each other on the mat, trying to gain the advantage over each other and failing. I'm on fire, just for him.

Breathing heavily, his breath caresses my skin, sending white-hot flames through me, his hand sneaking into my hair as he places kisses on my neck, the spot just where he can feel my pulse with his lips. I'm a goner. It's my weak spot, and he knows it.

"Owen," I murmur, my heart rate spiking as he continues to torment me with his wicked lips and tongue. Each touch and sweep driving me crazy.

I thrust upwards, but he doesn't move, his hips grinding against me, his hardness prominent and unforgiving. Lifting his face from my neck, he meets me eye to eye with a devastating grin. Knowing full well I can't deny him, his mouth comes down on mine in a searing kiss. All the fight goes out of me and I'm lost in him. He devours me, leaving me breathless.

His hand grips my hair, his fingers tangling in my white blonde locks, and loving the slight sting, making me catch my breath. *Fuck,* I crave him like the best drug known to womankind. I will always need more of him. Just like he does me.

Moving my hand to get a better grip, I tug on his dark silky hair. Hair that's become a little more unruly than normal. I love it. He trails his hand down to my sports bra, lighting a fire on my skin with each brush of his fingers. I feel the moment he unzips the front of me.

"October?"

Moaning through the sharp inhale as his mouth clamps down on the hard bud of my nipple, I lift my chest to his lips, needing to bring him closer to me.

"Try again." His tongue flicks the tip of my nipple and I cry out.

"When then?" I'm done suggesting. I need this man like fire needs air to burn. And I burn fucking hot for him.

"Next week," he murmurs into my ear. He can't be serious, can he? There's always so much to plan in a wedding, big or small, you need time to do it. And the dress. I know I said I wanted a small, intimate wedding, but I still want an amazing dress.

"Next week?" I repeat only questioning his sanity a little. His hand slips beneath my shorts and into my knickers, cupping me firmly, giving me a glimpse of the friction I need while his fingers tease my entrance.

"So wet for me, Angel." There's a growl of approval that sends shivers over me, urging the need to go further. I grind myself into his hand. I need the friction, I need what he can give me. I need him. "I have a secret to confess."

I moan in protest when he takes his hand away and shoves my shorts down, making quick work of his own. Fisting in dick in one hand, he positions himself at my entrance, teasing me as he rubs himself through me.

"Confess for me then, Owen, before I take matters into my own hands." Reaching my own hand down towards my clit, I circle it firmly, letting out a whimper before he removes it, sucking my fingers into his hot mouth. He lets out a groan.

"Mine," he growls, and fuck does that do all the good things to me. My insides heat, my breathing accelerates and my eyes flutter shut. "Eyes on me, Angel. I want to watch you come."

Sinking himself deep inside me, my breath catches as he thrusts, bringing me higher with each roll of his hips as he hits the perfect spot to push me closer. His thumb traces the pulse on my neck and I'm coming like a freight train with no end in sight. It's hard and fast, taking him with me as I clench and fall to pieces around him.

Breaking eye contact for the briefest of moments, his lips reach my ear. "It's all booked. All you have to do is get your dress."

"Are you serious?" I ask breathlessly.

"As the day I met you, Angel."

Also By Bekki

About the Author

Bekki Vowles writes romantic suspense filled with tension, emotion, and characters you can't help but root for. Her stories blend twists, danger, and heat with strong, complex leads who fight for the love and healing they deserve. She is the author of The Protected Series, an elite ex-military romance world packed with high stakes and heart.

Bekki lives in a small UK village with her husband, two energetic boys, and her beloved fur baby. When she's not writing, you can usually find her curled up with a spicy romance and a glass of wine.